The Reluctant King

The Star-Crossed Series

Volume Five

Rachel Higginson

The Reluctant King

The Star-Crossed Series

By Rachel Higginson

Editing services provided by Jennifer Nunez.

Printed in paperback December 2012 and available in Kindle and E-book format as of December through Amazon, Create Space, Smashwords and Barnes & Noble.

To Ron, Randy and Robbie,
The best and worst kind of brothers.

Prologue

Amelia
Three years ago

I watched him from across the square. He was incredible, completely restrained aggression and feral energy. His body seemed barely able to contain his electric charisma as he bounced around, constantly fidgeting, constantly chewing on his thumb nail.

And he was gorgeous.

His jet black hair was pulled back to the nape of his neck in messy bun that managed to look both roguishly handsome and devilishly dangerous. He had his tux jacket off, laid over the chair he was placed at and I could see the faint outlines of his tattoos through the thin material of his starched white shirt. They covered his arms, his wrists, the back of his neck. I silently groaned thinking about what the intricate lines would look like covering the ripples of his back or contours of his flat stomach.

Avalon.

A shudder rippled through me at the thought of his name.

We had been introduced earlier today, but that was all, just an introduction.

And he hardly acknowledged my presence, let alone taken the time to acknowledge *me*.

Ugh. This was silly. Ridiculous even. My infatuation with him was bordered on obsessive and I felt like nothing more than a pathetic fan girl.

Double ugh.

I hoped my once-princess-status and relationship with his sister would garner me some kind of attention, some kind of reaction. I was two full years younger than him, so I knew I had my work cut out for me, but I also knew I wasn't ugly.

Of course he was a king now and I was sixteen....

I took a deep breath and rocked back on my treacherously high heels. Maybe that was all this was, an infatuation with royalty. Not that I hadn't been around royalty my entire life, just finally I wasn't related to someone.

But even in my argument with myself, I lost. My crush on Avalon was about so much more than his status in the Kingdom or even his accomplishments before he was King. It was everything about him. What he had done for our people and what he was going to do, his focused goals and dedication to a cause greater than himself. He was inspiring and breathtaking all at the same time. And he was funny and smart and cool.

He was the perfect mixture of hero and bad boy and I was lost to him.... even before I met him.

Of course, I kept all these thoughts to myself. I couldn't share them with anyone. My two closest friends were way too deep into this thing to be of much help. Eden would most likely try to talk me out of it and Seraphina would never let me hear the end of it.

Besides it was only crush.

It was only a crush.

It was *only* a crush.

"Are you ready for the dance?" Seraphina whispered in my ear, surprising me out of the blue.

I sucked in an unsteady breath, not sure if I was. Yesterday it was decided that I should dance the wedding party dance with Avalon. He didn't have a partner because he wasn't a groomsman. He had walked Eden down the aisle in place of her recently murdered father. Eden wanted Roxie to be a part of this dance so Titus offered to be her partner. This left me without one and so Eden volunteered her brother to dance with me.

Perfect.

First I had to find the courage to talk to him.

And then I had to find the charm to make him fall in love with me.

Easy.

Seraphina pushed me gently forward, two hands on my shoulder blades and there he was. The world seemed to fade away beyond Avalon. He walked toward me with savage grace, seeming to devour the space between us with conquering steps. His brilliant green eyes locked on mine and I was helpless in the gravitational pull of his body.

I focused on breathing, on keeping steady breaths so I wouldn't pass out at his feet. I just had to keep it together for this one dance, I reasoned. I just had to be calm, cool and collected for one song and then I could excuse myself to the restroom and throw up everything I'd eaten that day.

Which, granted, wasn't a whole lot. I'd had to squeeze into my bridesmaid dress after all.

Avalon smiled down at me and I was lost.

Dazzled.

His complete attention was focused on me, his perfect smile meant to help me relax, his arms wrapped around my waist and holding my hand, pressing me against him. It was his presence that sucked everything else out of focus and left me dizzy and longing. He made me fall in love with him.

I touched him once. He smiled at me. And I was in love.

I was also in trouble.

I commanded my lips to smile back, but I faltered with nerves. Focused on breathing, all I could smell was him, clean, soap, man. He even smelled amazing!

This was not a fair fight.

He opened his mouth to say something as the music started and I felt myself lean forward on my tip toes, ready to drink in his voice and listen raptly to words that were only meant for me.

But then his gaze shifted and his expression fell. My body went tight right along with his as he dropped his arms from me.

When he finally spoke it was not at all what I was expecting to hear, "Go on and finish without me."

My mouth dropped open and I didn't even get a word out before he was walking past me. His hand swung back and smacked me firmly on the butt. I let out a yelp of surprise as the imprint of his hand stung against my skin.

What the hell?

I was only sixteen, but the concept of love was suddenly very jaded. I didn't get what the whole fuss was about with Eden and Kiran, I found the entire ordeal too easy to fall into and even easier to fall out of. In the end, the only thing love gave me was an early trip to my grave because I was sure I would die of embarrassment.

Chapter One

This was not how I wanted to spend my afternoon. This was not how I wanted to spend any afternoon, but especially this one. It was nice outside after weeks of seemingly endless rain. The Romanian sun was finally shining. The birds were chirping, the leaves were changing colors…. and all that other BS.

I shifted uncomfortably on the hard, gold seat and kicked my heel back against the solid base. Dangit, that hurt. No amount of magic could make a throne comfortable.

None.

They were horrible to sit in. And even worse to try to be hospitable in.

"What do you think, Avalon?" Gabriel asked from across the room. I stifled a laugh at how serious he looked in his priest's outfit. I got it, the whole…. dedicated to the cause thing. I mean, seriously, if anybody got marrying oneself to an endeavor, it was me. But I also knew that Gabriel was a badass fighter, with the temper of an angry bull, so the whole black suit, white collar thing looked drastically out of place.

Despite my rude sense of humor, I glared back at him. He knew I wasn't listening. He knew I *never* listened.

My gaze moved from Gabriel who was sitting stoically with that disappointed look on his face again to Silas, who seemed annoyingly entertained, to Angelica and Talbott who both tried to hint discreetly at how I should respond.

At least I could count on them. But really, they were all traitors. The whole lot of them.

It had been three years since Eden and I destroyed the Monarchy. Three freaking years. And here I sat, ruling from this damn uncomfortable throne, the same one I had promised myself I would melt down into tiny little action figures of myself like an upgrade of G.I. Joes, as if the only thing we actually did was lead a successful political coup.

I wanted a democracy. Hell, I would have even taken a corrupt republic over this. Ok…. maybe I was done with the corruption. But none of it mattered anyway because in their first act as a freed people? Yeah, the *freed* people voted to maintain the Monarchy.

And voted to keep me as King. Well, me and my brother-in-law.

Traitors.

All of them.

Besides, who had ever heard of being co-King? It was so not a precedented historical event.

So a whole lot of good that freaking Resistance thing did me.

Granted, the status of the Kingdom was exceptionally improved and my people actually were free in every sense of the word; marriage was open, nobody was being hunted, tortured or killed on a regular basis and my sister got to marry her prince charming. So all was right in the world.

Except that I wanted a people that believed in themselves enough to govern themselves, and a sister who was actually around once in a while, instead of honeymooning her life away. They had been gone for two years. Two years. What on earth could one couple do for two whole years without wanting to kill each other or die of boredom?

Ok, I knew in theory what they could be doing. But that was something I would never, ever, ever, in a million years think about. She's my sister. So gross.

And what about my freedom? I wanted to be free too! Instead I had to put up with an uncooperative know-it-all board of advisors, the same advisors I wanted to give to the people as their democratic council and was shot down. I had to sit on this god-awful throne for eight hours a day listening to people whine about their problems or even worse I was forced to meet eligible girl after eligible girl.

Ok, but that's all I was doing really…. whining about my problems. So I took a breath, and tried to read Talbott again, he was usually the best at giving me a sign. I figured it was from years of prompting Kiran.

"I…. agree," I announced tentatively and then when Talbott started shaking his head furiously I retracted my statement immediately, "I mean, I disagree." I nodded my head authoritatively and propped one elbow onto the arm of the throne with my fist extended in a symbol of power and confidence.

"You disagree about what?" Gabriel asked, his tone of impatience firmly chastising me.

"Uh….what was the question?" I gave in sheepishly and admitted that I wasn't listening.

"The question was simply what you would like to serve at the homecoming dinner for Kiran and Eden," Gabriel repeated. His narrowed orange eyes flickered like a flame and I knew I was in for one of those, "but this is your destiny" speeches.

"Oh, right," I mumbled. I looked down at the man that originally asked the question and realized for the first time that he was the head chef. If I would have been paying one iota of attention I could have put two and two together. Shoot. "Uh, let's have steak. That's Eden's favorite."

"Steak, sir?" The head chef clarified. I forgot his name. I forgot everyone's name....

"Why? Is that not Ok?" I asked, feeling like he was patronizing me. Or maybe I was just being paranoid. I wasn't good with trusting people anymore. They always had an alternative motive since the crown became a permanent part of my wardrobe, one that usually consisted of me marrying their daughter, or niece, or granddaughter, or goddaughter.... or any female within spitting distance.

"It's just....," he hesitated and I watched the internal battle he waged. After two years of my laid back if not aloof reign, people still treated me as if I was Lucan's tyrant replacement. I encouraged him with a benevolent smile, one that I had practiced in the mirror because apparently it was difficult for me to look benevolent. "Steak is fine, sir." He finished without even attempting an argument. Apparently I needed to get back in front of a mirror. "What should I serve for the vegetarian option?"

I tried not to laugh. "Vegetarian option? Do we have very many vegetarians attending the party?" I was not the best at paying attention, but I was certain in the countless dinners and affairs I'd been forced to host over the past three years I had not once been asked my opinion on a "vegetarian option."

"For Princess Amelia," the chef explained and I ground my teeth at the word "princess." She was only a princess by association to the Kendrick line and no matter how well I get along with my brother in law these days I had been working very hard at disassociating all of us with Monarchial terms. It was nothing personal against Amelia, I didn't even really know the girl.

"Well, I'm sure whatever you come up with will be fine," I nodded to let him know I was finished speaking with him and then tried that benevolent smile again. He scurried from the room.

Yep, I needed to practice that some more.

"Somebody please explain to me why I have to waste my day away making menu plans and talking about vegetarian options?" I demanded when it was finally just my board of advisors and me alone in the throne room.

"You're awfully testy today," Angelica clucked her tongue from her place in between Silas and Gabriel. She was more of a mother figure than an advisor, but when I decided to choose one from each kind I knew there was no Witch I trusted more than her.

"I have a headache," I mumbled, letting my head fall into my fingertips.

"You don't have a headache," she scolded me. She stood up to busy herself with something on the other side of the room and that was how I knew she was worried about me even if I couldn't technically get a physical headache. Her hair had turned a blinding shade of white and I could swear it was from the stress of three years ago. She aged over the yearlong battle with Lucan. She was still stunning for a grandma type, all handsome, gentle beauty, but that year was hard on all of us.

"Trust me, my head hurts," I complained.

"Only because you refuse to use it," Gabriel snapped. I sat up, ready to argue, but he was already on his way to a lecture, there was no stopping him now. "Avalon we get it, you don't want to be King, but right now you don't have a choice. This was the future you wanted for your people; tyranny is dead, they are free, and the magic is whole once again. Granted it's not exactly how we imagined life after Lucan, I understand that, but this is what your people want. And by acting like this.... this... petulant child you are refusing to give them what they want, what they *deserve*. You are as bad as Lucan at this point."

"Don't compare me to him," I growled, standing up from the dead King's throne to distance myself as far from his memory as I could. "We are not comparable."

"What he means is, you're as bad as Lucan *today*," Silas clarified in his thick Jamaican accent and if it was anyone else he was talking about I would have laughed.

"Oh, now I feel better," I rolled my eyes and turned to Angelica for help. I could always count on her.

"Maybe if you got married, things wouldn't seem so difficult," she offered and I realized sharply I couldn't count on any of them today. "Maybe if you had someone to share the burden of the throne, things wouldn't feel so impossible. You wouldn't be so grumpy."

"No, no, I am not having this conversation again!" I sighed. "I already have someone to share the throne with. Actually I have two somebodies to share the throne with, they are just never here! Although, maybe I should follow their example and find someone to marry just so I can go on a two year honeymoon!" I threw myself back into the hard, golden chair and ignored the pain shooting up my back from my childish tantrum.

"Sure, if that's the kind of incentive you need, then by all means marry someone and take your extended honeymoon. You will get no argument from any of us," Gabriel laughed humorlessly.

He knew I would never leave the Kingdom in someone else's hands for that long, not even Eden's, not without a stable government in place to fill my stead. And he also knew I was so far from getting married or even thinking about getting married. I hated it when he called my bluff.

"What do you want from me?" I asked Gabriel, knowing he would tell me whether I wanted to hear it or not.

His orange eyes flashed with gravity and he rubbed his hand over his closely shaved head. "I want you to be the leader you're destined to be. You've done an adequate job so far, but we know what you're doing Avalon and the Kingdom isn't going to dismiss the Monarchy just because you are trying to prove to them they don't need you. They want *you*, and your sister and her husband. So, instead of pouting around and not paying attention, why don't you try taking your role seriously? Why don't you explore all the good that could come out of that?"

I opened my mouth to respond, but then closed it. Gabriel had a point. Who was I kidding? I knew he had a point; I just didn't want to give him the satisfaction of telling him so. Which I also knew was very immature. But they were the ones that demanded I become King at eighteen years old.

Now at twenty-one I was very worried resentment had stunted my growth.

My mental growth.

Talbott's phone beeped, interrupting the pregnant pause and saving me from having to reply verbally. Although by the look Gabriel sent me and the dull suppression of his eye color, I knew he knew I thought he was right.

"That was the front gate," Talbott announced after clicking off his cellphone. "Jericho is here. I told them to have him meet you in the receiving room."

I rolled my eyes at Talbott's formal behavior. I was the one that appointed him head Titan, so I really couldn't complain. But still, the receiving room? I didn't need to meet Jericho in the receiving room. I needed to meet Jericho wherever I damned well pleased and then we both needed to get the hell out of Dodge, or uh, the Citadel in this case.

Gabriel glared at me, sending me one of his "I know exactly what you're thinking right now" looks and I swallowed back the leftovers of a Rebellion I was supposed to be done fighting.

"Thank you Talbott," I replied formally.

I started to leave the room before I made myself turn around and act like the responsible ruler of a nation I knew I was. "You're right Gabriel. I need to stop pouting. The people want a king and I am in no position to argue with them since I killed their last one. Besides, Eden will be back in today and she can share the responsibility. I will do my best to embrace this position and do what I can to better the existence for our people." I finished a little bit dramatically, but overall I thought it was a very diplomatic speech.

"So you'll consider finding a wife?" Angelica piped up.

And I needed to get out of the room. I could try to be diplomatic, but not that diplomatic. I watched right along with the rest of the Kingdom how love turned my sister's world upside down. And not in a good way.... There was absolutely no way in hell I was going to get sucked into the rabbit hole called Love.

It wasn't worth it.

Chapter Two

I walked through the somewhat empty corridors of the old castle trying to suppress my love for the ancient building. The stone walls and worn tapestries should feel cold and distant. The massive size of the building itself should feel overwhelming.

But it didn't.

I reluctantly loved it here.

I was always trying to talk myself out of it. My people were tortured and imprisoned here, some were even killed. A tyrant walked these same halls and brought the magic that ran through my people's blood to near extinction. The walls that surrounded the Citadel had been impenetrable for centuries. I was nearly murdered here. My sister was nearly murdered here. My parents *were* murdered here.

I should definitely hate this place.

And yet…. it had crawled its way into my small, skeptical, unfeeling heart and made a home. This was where my grandfather was originally chosen to be King, where it all started. This was where my people had realized that Lucan couldn't continue to hold them under his thumb and had fought back. And this was where I could feel my parents…. Not because of some creepy reason like their ghosts haunted the grounds. But because this was where they had fallen in love, this was the last place they had really called home before they went on the run. And this was where we had spent the majority of our relationship.

Until they were murdered.

Lucan was so lucky he was already dead.

When Eden had exchanged herself for me, she had not only saved my life, but she had given up the one thing that could never be taken from me. The one thing I could never repay her for.

Time with our parents.

I opened the door to the receiving room before I could have another thought about it. My best friend in the world turned from the window and looked at me incredulously. There was no awe in his expression, no reverence, not even a hint that he'd missed me.

Thank God for Jericho.

"What are you so pissed off about?" I huffed.

"You make people wait for you now?" he rolled his eyes. "You really have turned into a pretentious prick."

I laughed, loud and full, a sound that felt foreign, even to my own ears. "That's what happens when all your friends abandon you! You lose sight of the little people and embrace the douchebag crown you were given."

He cracked his wide grin and walked forward to take my hand. "It's good to see you again, Avalon, even if you are a complete and utter sell out."

I let out another burst of laughter and my lungs definitely felt underused. "Where have you been?"

Jericho's face turned serious, his smile faded and I noticed the lines around his smile and near his eyes. He was by no means old, only in his early twenties, but there were signs of stress since I saw him last. Or maybe I hadn't noticed them before, maybe Angelica wasn't the only one showing signs from that year.

"I needed some time away," he cleared his throat uncomfortably and dropped my hand roughly. "I needed some space from this place, you know?"

Ok, so I *was* the only one that still felt attached to the castle. There was definitely something wrong with that.

I cleared my throat too. "Yeah, I know what you mean." I lied.

We were both silent for a few seconds, turning our attention elsewhere in the room designed to be welcoming and comfortable. I wondered if it was a wasted effort as I looked at the chocolate-leather upholstered couches that had stiff, dark wood bench seats and a matching coffee table on top of a burgundy oriental rug. The walls were still stone and the windows were long and narrow barely letting any natural light in.

"So, where am I staying?" Jericho interrupted the comfortable silence, his eyes meeting mine again.

"You decided to stay?" I asked, trying to disguise the hope I felt with a masculine tone.

"Yeah, I, uh, I don't have anything better to do," Jericho shifted uncomfortably, which in turn made me shift uncomfortably.

I knew he was over my sister. Well…. for the most part. But I knew seeing her again after all this time was not going to be easy for him either. He had loved her; like the real deal loved her and she had chosen someone else. Well, truthfully, he had walked away before she could officially choose Kiran, but he had been hurt pretty bad.

That sucked. Just another reason to avoid the whole love fiasco waiting to happen.

"Oh, I get it," I smirked, needing to ease the heavy tension in the room. "You missed me." I winked at him, knowing it would get under his skin.

"Geez, it's like that gold has seeped right into your brain and made you so damn sure of yourself. It's disgusting really," he joked. God, it was good to have someone around with a sense of humor. "Are you sure they counted those votes right?"

"They better have," I growled, more serious than Jericho was. "I made them recount them by hand five times."

"Why doesn't that surprise me?" Jericho sighed.

I walked to the door and held it open for him to pass through. "Oh, I'm sorry, do you want this job? Because you can have it! I will take this crown off right now and give it to you." I lifted the heavy piece of gold off my head and held it out to him, internally wishing he would actually take it from me and release me from the impossible burden.

"No thank you," he laughed. "But uh, I've been meaning to ask you.... the whole lopsided thing? I mean, that wasn't just a Lucan-fashion-statement? Or are you simply trying to emulate our dearly departed former leader?"

"It's heavy as hell, dude," I slipped the questionable piece of jewelry back onto my head and it fell to the side so that it lay crooked on my long hair. "You try keeping this thing on straight. It's impossible."

"Huh," Jericho mumbled thoughtfully.

We caught up as I walked him to the room he would be staying in during the homecoming festival. We spoke every other week on the phone, but it wasn't the same. Jericho and I had always been like girls with how much we talked to each other. It was kind of annoying. And kind of awesome at the same time. He wasn't technically on salary, but he had been traveling all over the world, checking in on different settlements of Immortals. As much as I hated being King, we were all worried about another rebellion.

For the most part the Kingdom seemed happy. But they had seemed happy with Lucan too. And I had never really gotten over the notion that there were others out there plotting Lucan's downfall. My sister had been kidnapped by a rouge group of Immortals that wanted different leadership but the same kind of oppressive power. Those were the people that kept me stationary and willing to lead. I wasn't prepared to let this people suffer under another dictator.

Jericho was one of the only people I trusted enough to report back the absolute truth and see through everyone else's BS at the same time. And he was unattached and looking for a distraction. He was the perfect candidate.

"Jericho," Talbott called from down the hall. He met us with a huge grin on his face and a handshake extended for Jericho. "It's good to have you back." Talbott's Romanian accent rolled over his words, made even thicker by his excitement.

"Talbott," Jericho replied carefully, taking his hand with extra precaution.

"What?" Talbott laughed, noticing Jericho's skeptical eye.

"People aren't used to it yet," I explained, but by the curious looks both of them gave me I knew I had to use more words. "The happiness Talbott, people aren't used to your smile." I gestured to his olive skinned face where a big ass smile seemed way out of place next to his military haircut and thick neck bred for bodyguard positions like his.

Talbott let out a bark of laughter and I watched Jericho flinch from the sound. I smiled at Jericho's uncomfortable attitude.

"It's weird," Jericho muttered, eying Talbott over again like he had been abducted by aliens. "It's drugs isn't it? You're on drugs. The pressure finally got to you, didn't it?"

"No, not drugs," Talbott grinned wider. "It's Lilly. Lilly finally said yes!"

"That's great, man," I laughed with him too and then turned to explain it to Jericho. "Talbott's been trying to get Lilly to marry him for over a year now, but I think she's been trying to keep her options open. Talbott must have finally worn her down."

"It's not that," Talbott all but growled at me. There was the fun-loving guy everyone would remember. "She's been nervous; she doesn't want to be the first interracial couple to get married because she knows it will get a lot of attention. I don't want the attention either, but we love each other, it's silly to wait any longer."

"Congratulations, Talbott," Jericho replied, a huge grin spread wide across his face too. "That's really exciting, I'm happy for you."

"I'm happy for you too," I offered and I really was.

"Only because this helps promote your life-style philosophy for the Kingdom," Talbott called me out.

I laughed, knowing it was true. "That's only part of the truth," I admitted. "I really am happy for the two of you. I can't wait to throw a big old shindig here just to celebrate this!"

"Oh really?" Talbott narrowed his wise eyes on me.

"And invite the whole Kingdom to celebrate," I all but squealed like a girl, envisioning how great this was going to be to promote relationships between our kind. Even though the people were free, they were still a bit skittish of actually dating someone from a different race than them. This would definitely be a step in the right direction.

"And there we go, there's the truth," Talbott announced triumphantly.

"Well, that and I was worried I was going to have to steal Lilly from you and make her an honest woman myself," I smirked, happy to shut him up.

I was saved from whatever response Talbott could come up with by girls actually squealing.... scratch that, it wasn't squealing, it was screaming, and in the ear-piercing pitch only really excited girls could reach.

"Ah, there's the fiancée now," Talbott murmured all love struck.

I was writhing in pain, worried about the health of my ear drums and he was googly eyed and dreamy looking. Gross.

"I take it that's Eden?" Jericho asked in a low voice.

"I'm thinking yes," I replied, but I knew without a doubt it was her. I could feel her. I had felt her since she entered the country hours ago. Although we had turned off our shared monologue since she was now a married woman and neither one of us wanted to do irreparable damage to our subconscious, I was still forever connected to my twin sister. And I would never complain about that.

Not even in a joke.

"Point me in the direction of my room?" Jericho mumbled after Talbott had taken off in the direction of the still shrill sounds.

"I thought things were alright between the three of you?" I probed a little, wondering what the big deal was. There had been lots of girls between Eden and now, even if he hadn't actually fallen in love with any of them. Who cared, anyway, things seemed incredibly easier for him now.

"They are," he shrugged. "I'm just tired and don't feel like dealing with all that." He gestured toward the sounds and I instantly got it.

"I don't blame you," I nodded, understanding completely. "Up in my wing, you're on the first level. I don't know which room exactly, but nobody else has arrived yet and your things should be there for you. If you get lost, just ask one of the serv- uh, employees," I clarified. The castle used to be run by servants, but one dead king and three hundred monthly paychecks later and I could officially call the palace staff employees.

"Thanks," Jericho smiled. "It's good to see you again, man. It's been too long."

"Agreed," I nodded, trying to avoid the awkward road to feelings-ville. "Now go get your beauty rest, princess, because tonight we celebrate!"

We turned in our opposite directions and I followed the sound of girls chattering. There was silence for a beat and by the time I turned the corner to the main entrance corridor Eden had started screaming again, holding Lilly's pale hand in hers. I narrowed my eyes and realized it was the new engagement ring that had her so excited.

I leaned against the wall and stood back to observe. Talbott stood with his arm protectively around his future bride while she blushed to the color of her curly red hair. Sebastian, who had met up with Eden and Kiran somewhere in Western Europe was shaking Talbott's hand while Kiran kept both hands on Eden's shoulders as he towered over them.

My heart relaxed at the sight of them all standing together. We hadn't been together much since the night Lucan died, not like this. We had mourned the loss of parents and friends and we had celebrated Eden and Kiran's wedding, but we had never been like this together, we had never just been normal.

It wasn't just my heart that relaxed; it was like my whole body sighed at the peaceful nature of our reunion. Eden's black eyes flickered up to mine and we shared an understanding look. It was harder to keep things so separated between us now that we were so close, and I felt her relief and excitement in the same way she felt mine.

"E," I acknowledged her, tilting my chin.

She wasn't having that though. She raced across the carpeted corridor, ripping out of Kiran's hands and flying into my chest. Her arms wrapped around my neck and she hugged me until I could barely breathe.

"I've missed you, sis," I whispered, trying to disguise the sudden surge of emotion in my throat.

"I've missed you so much!" She cried. Actually cried. I could feel her hot tears on my shoulder, soaking through my t-shirt. "It's good to be home," she breathed and detached herself from around my neck. She kept her arm around my waist though and I smiled down at her.

"Home," I echoed. Maybe I wasn't the only one that had grown attached to the Citadel.

Everyone had joined us by now and I took Kiran's outstretched hand when he offered it to me and shook it firmly. I hoped he wasn't going to hug me and cry too.

"Those things are a pain in the arse to wear, am I right?" Kiran gestured at the crown on my head and I rolled my eyes in response.

"I was accused of wearing it crooked as a fashion statement," I grunted and then tried to push it back into the center position on my head.

"Ah," Kiran nodded understandingly. "Nobody's head is shaped quite right for that."

Sebastian stuck his hand out next and I took it. "Where's the girlfriend?" I asked, wondering if Seraphina had finally gotten under his skin enough to scare him back into bachelorhood. For some reason I had a hard time picturing Sebastian actually settling down, let alone with the likes of Seraphina who was as high maintenance as they came.

"She's with my sister," he explained, expelling the notion that all of my people were free. Apparently some of them stayed imprisoned by choice. "They'll be along shortly, but Mimi wanted to visit some of the villages nearby."

"Ah," I offered noncommittally, I didn't really know how to respond to that. I had forgotten that people called Sebastian's sister Mimi, but in all honesty I couldn't really remember her that well. I had only met her briefly at the wedding, and only because she was one of Eden's bridesmaids. I did remember that she was really young though and had seemed a bit out of place and awkward next to all of the other bridesmaids that had been my age or older.

"It's so good to be with you again, Avalon," Eden gushed, filling the awkward silence. I smiled down at her; she was so adorable with her mass of hair flowing around her and her black eyes sparkling like onyx.

"Honestly, I'm glad you guys are back," I admitted, trying to cover for my emotional reaction to having my only remaining family near me again. "There are probably one hundred decisions left to be made for this damned homecoming dinner you have me throwing for you and if I am asked to pick out a tablecloth color one more time I'm going to assassinate myself."

"Oh no!" Eden gasped. "Are there really a lot of decisions left to be made?" She looked to Talbott and Lilly for the truth. Smart girl.

"You have no idea," Lilly laughed, shaking her head at me. Lilly was probably the only girl in the world I was as comfortable around other than Eden. She was like a sister, especially since Eden had been gone for a while and Lilly had stuck around the castle in order to be close to Talbott. She had taken on the job of kind of running the castle, since I didn't have a wife and Angelica seemed overwhelmed with just advising me. If she wasn't so in love with Talbott I would have proposed to her myself just to get the Kingdom off my back…. and because I knew I could tolerate her for long periods of time. "Getting Avalon to make a decision about anything other than Kingdom policy is like pulling teeth."

Everyone laughed at my expense.

Psht.

"Hey," I put my hands up and backed away. "You guys are home now, why don't you take a crack at it. I'm sure you have a better opinion on which China pattern you want to use," I narrowed my eyes at Eden and Kiran, not even caring about the exasperated look Kiran gave me. He married the girl, China patterns were his responsibility now.

"You're right," Eden sighed. "Besides I haven't made a decision yet as Queen, what better way to initiate myself."

"This way, your Highness," Lilly laughed, and led Eden down the hallway with Kiran, Sebastian and Talbott following closely behind.

Eden turned to give me a small wave and a look that promised she would find me later to catch up. I gave her an encouraging smile and watched the group walk away. Eden had grown up a lot since I saw her last. She had always amazed me with her ability to make quick decisions and take everything in stride; Lord knows she was thrown into this world without much warning. But she had struggled to adjust; nobody knew that more than me. She had fought tooth and nail against this life, but now that she had it.... it suited her. Kiran, royalty, married life.... it all suited her. She was at peace for the first time maybe ever and so disgustingly happy that I couldn't ignore the pang in my gut that envied her.

Was it love that did that to a person? Probably not. It probably felt good just to not have someone constantly trying to kill you. I mean, I felt that sense of relief too, so I was probably just as happy as her....

The big brass doors of the castle entrance opened and the late fall light streamed into the corridor turning my eyes. Long, tanned, perfect legs caught my attention first. The hazy sunlight lit up around those two extraordinary limbs and my eyes followed the flawless line from tiny, delicate ankle to where the hem of her shorts stopped mid-thigh. I snapped my mouth shut.

In my defense, cascading light from the doorway partially blocked her from view until the door had firmly closed behind her. But if I was really honest with myself those legs demanded attention, and her tiny little fashionable shorts put them on display just for me. My eyes finally traveled up an effortlessly sexy figure and to the most startling golden brown eyes I had ever seen.

In our culture, our people had every shade and color of eyes. Angelica's were actually purple. Golden brown should not have been so startling, but the richness and depth to that particular shade of brown displayed underneath thick lashes and on a face so perfectly pretty and delicate was a little disconcerting.

Their owner cleared her throat, waiting for me to acknowledge her. Had she said something? Was I supposed to answer a question? Shoot, I had spaced out again but this time for an entirely different reason.

"I'm sorry, did you say something?" I asked, still in a daze over those mile long legs.

"Have you seen my brother?" she asked, her voice a touch amused and a touch.... irritated? "Seraphina and I changed our minds; we want to borrow his car."

"Your brother?" I clarified, my eyes falling from those startling golden brown eyes to her full lips that were pouted into a frown. "Uh... who's your brother?"

"Sebastian Cartier?" she clarified like I was the biggest idiot on the planet. "He just walked in here, I swear." She had the sweetest English accent that clipped all her consonants precisely.

"Uh, he went that way," I muttered like I was nervous.... like I was not the king I was.

She straightened her shoulders and flicked her eyes over me with an obvious tone of disgust. What had I done to her?

"At least when Lucan was King I didn't have to worry about him ogling me like a caveman," she mumbled walking past me.

Ah, that's what I had done. I consciously hinged my mouth shut and tried not to snap at the way she defended Lucan. She was right.... I was ogling her.

"I apolo-" I started.

"Don't bother," she looked over her shoulder, dismissing me. Dismissing me!

"Mimi," I snapped my fingers, proud of myself for remembering her name.

"Amelia." She corrected me, turning around and walking backwards. Immortal or not, I was always impressed when a girl could balance in high heels and hers looked especially dangerous as she walked away from me. I forced my mind back to her face as my eyes wanted to linger on those legs and the word "dangerous...." "Only people I like get to call me Mimi," her tone was ice, but those golden brown eyes were definitely not cold.

"Then I'll have to convince you that you like me," I returned, feeling proud of myself for very unpracticed witty banter.

"Fat chance of that," she laughed mockingly in her cute British accent and then turned around and walked away.

I shook my head, still not really sure what just happened. That was Mimi? She was definitely not a child. I stared after those legs wondering if maybe I was remembering the wrong person from three years ago....

Chapter Three

"Are you alright, Avalon?" Kiran asked for the third time, well, the third time that I could remember.

"Uh, fine," I mumbled in response. I shook my head a little, making the crown I was wearing jostle obnoxiously against my scalp. I shouldn't have been worried about my hair.... I should have been above all that. But I reached up to smooth out the long strands that got pulled from my low ponytail. I could be such a girl at times, it was annoying. It wasn't even technically a ponytail, it was this messy bun thing a girl at Canesbury taught me years ago. She said it made me look more grown up and less biker-ish and hell if I couldn't remember her name but I've kept that piece advice with me after all these years. Plus, I have to walk out in front of several hundred people in about two minutes and I want to at least appear as though I'm right where I belong.

Not to mention there's a certain pair of legs I can't get out of my head attending the dinner tonight....

"Do you want to skip the whole introductory speech? I can just go right into what I've written," my brother in law offered kindly. We were standing in the foyer of the castle waiting on Eden while the rest of our invited guests gathered in the main square to mingle and wait for our arrival. I was not the only one anxious for Eden and Kiran to come back to the castle and thus their elected roles as co-King and Queen. And even though it's not the entire Kingdom waiting on us, there is still a very healthy showing of Immortals filling the Citadel this weekend.

"Yeah, that would be great actually," I replied. "Uh, just remember to thank everyone for coming.... I like to remind them they have a choice." I smiled, trying to ignore how awkward it was "sharing" this job. Kiran probably knew what he was doing way better than me, but I couldn't stop myself from reminding him of the smaller points I felt were important. "Oh and I was planning on announcing Talbott and Lilly's engagement, but it will probably sound more sincere coming from you."

Kiran let out an amused laugh, "Are you telling me it wouldn't be sincere coming from you?" I watched him bristle in just the smallest of ways, tension stiffening his shoulder blades. I had seen it lots of times before and I had to suppress my own urge to laugh. Kiran was one of my closest friends and not just because of his relationship with my sister. We had formed our own bromance over the time I was imprisoned here before we killed his dad. Even though we didn't always see eye to eye, he was in the very small circle of people I absolutely trusted.

“Talbott seems to think I care more about what their marriage means to the Kingdom by way of example than about them as a couple,” I admitted, shrugging sheepishly.

Because it was partly true.

“Do you know what? I’ll go ahead and congratulate them, it will definitely sound more sincere coming from me,” Kiran agreed, giving me his famous cocky half-smile.

“Good,” I grunted. “I think my speech was going to make him mad anyway.”

“Why is that?” Kiran asked, but his eyes had turned to Eden who was walking across the hall to us.

I smiled at my sister, so happy to have her home. Her hair was pinned up tonight and while Kiran mumbled stuff to her about the way she looked.... stuff I chose to ignore, I admired the bright glow of her navy blue tattoo under her ear lobe. Her magical color used to match mine exactly, the brightest, most brilliant color of blue. But since her marriage, or rather the consummation of her marriage to Kiran, her magic had mixed with his and now both of their magics had turned a rich navy blue. I couldn’t care less about the color that meant Kiran and Eden were forever bonded, but damn it if I wasn’t still jealous over that glow in the dark tattoo.

“Because he was going to confess his undying love to Lilly and beg her to leave Talbott and marry him instead,” Eden laughed at me, her black eyes sparkling from the humor of it.

“It’s a joke,” I shrugged my shoulders at Kiran whose mouth had dropped open from shock. Eden opened her mouth to call me on my crap, so I tried to explain quickly. “Well.... kind of a joke. What? I like Lilly, she doesn’t talk too much, she doesn’t care about the whole King thing and I don’t have to make an effort to get to know her. So even if I’m not serious about asking her to run away and elope with me, I am kind of bummed that Talbott’s taking her completely off the market.” I grinned widely so they really did see the humor in the confession I was not at all serious about.

“But you need a girl to care about the whole King thing,” Talbott interrupted, walking up behind me. Shoot... hope he was not too mad. “It’s the only way you’re going to get a girl.”

“Was that a joke, Talbott?” I laughed. It was a good thing we hadn’t joined the party yet. In front of the people I had to be the responsible, prodigy leader I was born to be. But with this group it was nice to just act my age every once in a while.

“Here is the thing about my brother though,” Eden narrowed her eyes on me, her face turning completely serious. “Even if Lilly was the girl of his dreams, he would never destroy the opportunity for the Kingdom to watch a Shape-Shifter marry a Titan. He wouldn't do it. He's still too dedicated to the cause to let a little thing like love get in the way."

"What?" I put my hands up when Kiran's gave me an admonishing look. "Eden's right, it's a fantastic opportunity for the Kingdom," I grinned widely at Talbott who had protectively sidled Lilly up next to him.

"So there really is no chance for a quiet little ceremony with only our closest friends?" Lilly murmured, her green eyes accusing me of betrayal.

"Not if you want the blessing of the King," I smirked, happy to be able to use that to my advantage.

"You can have my blessing, Lills," Kiran counter-argued.

"And mine," my traitor sister piped up.

"You two have been MIA for too long for your opinion to really count. Besides, Lilly and Talbott really do care about the Kingdom enough to not want our people to go completely extinct. They care just enough to break through the bigoted boundaries and have a big old wedding to celebrate true freedom," I laid the guilt on thick knowing everyone in this circle would cave at my sound logic.

"Well, when you put it like that...." Talbott sighed bitterly, sending Lilly a pathetically apologetic look.

"Alright, then," I clapped my hands together triumphantly. "What are we waiting on? Let's get this party started!" I said it sarcastically, but I couldn't hide the excitement I felt for the evening. I wasn't usually enthusiastic about any kind of palace function, but the prospect of sharing Lilly and Talbott's engagement with the gathered community had put me in a good mood. There was something else too, something that had ignited the blood inside my veins and made me just a little bit nervous for the evening ahead, but I couldn't put my finger on what it was.

"We are waiting on Sebastian and Seraphina, but I suppose we should head on out there. They can catch up later," Kiran replied.

Talbott walked ahead and held open the door for all of us to pass through. We walked down the ancient castle steps that led out into the main square. Two silk, sheer white tent covers ran the length of the square. They looked modern and sleek in front of the antiquated backdrop. I had been asked my opinion on the décor but had deferred to Lilly before Eden came home. And I was glad I did, I could never have come up with something so simple and stunning at the same time.

The gathered crowd paused at our arrival, all stilled and waiting for one of us to say something. I led the way to the head table where I hesitated for a moment at the middle chair. Everyone waited for me to take a seat, but glancing up at my brother in law and sister I decided the best place for me to sit would be to his left and let Kiran have the middle seat. I moved over accordingly and it felt like the rest of the square had been frozen in time. I offered that benevolent smile I hadn't had time to practice again and was met with wide eyes and slack jaws.

Kiran gave me a questioning look, but quickly fixed his features into confidence. I didn't see what the big deal was. We were both technically King. Granted, I was King because I had been voted as King. Don't even let me start on the irony of that one.... And he was King because he had married my sister. But still, we shared the title together.

And now that they were back, we would share the responsibilities together too.

"It's great to be back," Kiran started into his speech while the rest of us sat and got situated.

I tuned out immediately, smiling when people laughed and seemingly listening attentively when Kiran was not trying to be funny. But I heard nothing. It wasn't a conscious effort to ignore his speech, but more like three years of practice at these things. Or hell, maybe three years of practice at tuning out life in general.

Ugh. I was bored. So, so, so bored. And the reality of just how bored I was with this whole King-job didn't really hit me until everyone had come home. My closest friends had been off exploring the world, traveling, dealing with real conflict and falling in love. And I had stayed behind to rule over a complacent people and their non-existent problems.

I threw parties and made pretentious speeches.

They dealt with real life conflict.

I observed life.

They lived it.

I was once at the forefront of an exciting adventure, and even if it was the difference between life and death at least through it all I had felt alive. And now the apathetic, uninterested version of myself felt anything but.

The crowd broke into polite laughter at something Kiran said and I joined in with a laugh I reserved especially for these functions. But then those legs appeared at the entrance to the square and the fake laugh died in my throat. I let my gaze linger on her exposed limbs, enjoying the style of her short black dress. I swallowed back the acute rush of lust I had never experienced so strongly in my life and let my gaze float over her figure and to her face.

She was staring at me, accusing me silently of the offense I was guilty of. Again. Her golden brown eyes simmered with disgust and a faint creep of heat made its way from the back of my neck to my cheeks. I was embarrassed that I couldn't keep my eyes in polite check whenever she was around, but not embarrassed enough to pull my gaze from hers. And even with the heated anger forcing her eyes to mine, she didn't break contact until a standing ovation from the crowd interrupted our direct line of sight to each other.

I cleared my throat, trying to find some equilibrium and stood with the rest of the crowd. I turned my head the same direction everyone else's heads were craned and nodded with proud approval over Talbott and Lilly. Kiran turned back to me, offering an extra wide smile and clapping enthusiastically. His eyebrows rose as if asking for my approval and I nodded like I had listened with rapt attention to every single word he said.

"I don't think your cousin likes me," I elbowed Kiran, nodding in the direction of Amelia. Our conversation was disguised under the raucous applause for Talbott and Lilly.

"Oh, he's just a little sore that his royalty status was taken away from him," Kiran answered, misinterpreting who I was talking about.

I snorted a response, not really expecting that. I had taken away the royalty status from the entire Kendrick bloodline, Kiran was a fluke because he was married to my sister. Bianca and Jean Cartier had seemed more than happy to let their titles go and had been very supportive of every change I had made so far. If Sebastian was upset about losing his prince title, is that what Amelia was upset about too? Did she just miss being a princess?

When I had seen her earlier today I thought she was visiting villages out of charity. But she was going with Seraphina, so maybe they were just sightseeing. Maybe she was more spoiled than I had given her credit for. My eyes floated over her again as she looked at Lilly and Talbott with seemingly real affection and happiness. She didn't appear stuck up, but wasn't that how she had been raised? Privilege and prejudice all under the guise of well-intended benevolence.

Just like Lucan.

Chapter Four

I swallowed my irritation and outrage and turned my attention back to Kiran who was closed out his speech. I might have to break our no-connection rule with Eden if I was asked specific questions about this speech later. She would understand. And I would make sure I did it only when she and Kiran were in my direct line of sight. Wouldn't want to make things weird between us. Plus she used to fish for information all the time in my head. I half wondered if zoning out ran in our family.

Kiran offered a few more closing remarks and then bid everyone to enjoy their meal. He was greeted with another standing ovation of applause, but this time it was directed at him and Eden. Eden rose half out of her seat and nodded sweetly to the crowd, her cheeks heating with shy embarrassment. Kiran waved away the applause as well and sat down to his meal. Waiters appeared with covered plates and set them before the guests. Our table was served last by my specific request.

When the tables had turned to their plates and the soft murmur of voices and the clinking of silverware against porcelain floated through the cool autumn evening, Seraphina, Sebastian and Amelia made their way to the end of our table. The three of them sat down on the opposite end of where I was. Eden leaned forward to welcome them, and I leaned forward to offer the same kind of polite greeting, but a hand on my arm turned my attention away.

"Do you still have your headache?" Angelica asked. She was seated next to me, and Silas and Gabriel were down from her. We had the only long table in the square, all of our guests sat around circular tables, able to easily converse. This was a tradition from when Lucan and his bloodline reigned. The king at the head table, and all the peons left to sit in the audience. Next dinner function I would say something, the Kingdom needed to realize we were equals.

"Uh, no, I'm better," I answered realizing I had taken a while to respond. "Sometimes this job is overwhelming in ways I never expected."

"I understand," Angelica patted my arm sweetly. "When you put on the crown, I'm sure you didn't realize how much of your time would be dedicated to public appearance."

"Exactly," I relaxed a little. Angelica knew me well and it was nice to not feel like I needed to explain myself, or apologize for feeling stressed. I was sentimental enough to look at her like a mother-figure or even a grandmother, but I loved her, genuinely. She was my Angelica. She raised me, or really contained me, and still looked out for my best interest. "It will be easier now that Eden's home."

"In some ways, but in others it might be more difficult," she offered gently.

I wanted to ask what she meant, but a quiet commotion at the other end of the table caught my attention. Amelia was speaking with a waiter about the plate in front of her; she gestured down to her plate and then put a tender hand on his arm. He floundered in response, his face flushing red immediately. I watched him apologize, looking more and more flustered, before he took the plate from her and rushed back toward the castle kitchen.

"Is the meal not to your liking, Mimi?" I asked as softly as I could manage while still being heard. Amelia turned her eyes my way, startled by my voice.

I met her golden brown eyes and held her gaze. I watched her expressive face flicker with emotion from surprise to something like fear and back to a steely resolve. She didn't seem willing to break our gaze, but there was something underneath her cool exterior that made me nervous.... like I was about to have my ass handed to me.

"I'm a vegetarian," she explained with controlled patience as if I should have known. "I don't eat meat, in fact, steak is one of the more offensive proteins you could have served me. And it's Amelia."

I held back my laughter at her rude answer. I wasn't at fault for her plate mix up, but I was disturbingly happy that it happened. An excited energy edged into my nervousness and I enjoyed her candid response. She was a fiery one.

I should have apologized.... that would have been the diplomatic thing to do.

"Technically, I didn't serve it to you, my staff did. And I had the kitchen prepare a vegetarian entrée for you. If you would have been on time, they would have known which place to serve it to ahead of time." I offered a cocky smile and watched as her eyes flashed with dangerous heat.

Aware that we had an audience, Amelia swallowed her annoyance and replied with a curt, "You're right. I apologize for the confusion, it's my fault." Her throat worked to swallow and I found my eyes frozen to the pretty lines of her neck and the way she tilted her head trying to keep her composure.

"Still, there are less aggressive meats than a slab of steak," she finished so quietly I almost didn't hear her. I had thought she was struggling because she was embarrassed and apologetic, but it was self-righteous anger that sizzled in the air between us.

"Filet Mignon is Eden's favorite," I smirked from my end of the table, anxious to hear how she would respond to that.

"He's right," Eden interrupted from between us. "I'm sorry Mimi; Avalon was just trying to make me happy."

Before Amelia could reply the waiter returned with a brand new entrée, hidden by a silver dish cover. The waiter set it down with a flourish and lifted the cover dramatically. Amelia wiggled happily, clasping her hands together before turning her gratitude on the happy server.

I swallowed a wave of annoyance that the waiter had been the recipient of her genuine smile before I waved off my emotions as ridiculous. Amelia could smile at whoever she liked, which apparently wasn't me for whatever reason. I shouldn't care what one spoiled kid thought of me.

I didn't care.

I turned back to my meal and attacked my own steak as if it were still alive. It was cooked perfectly, with just the right amount of red and covered in a dark mushroom sauce. The bite practically melted in my mouth. Filet was an excellent choice for dinner tonight. All of the guests would appreciate something so delicious.

Well almost all of them.

I snuck a discreet glance at Amelia, watching her cut and taste a variety of autumn vegetables. She closed her eyes and savored the bite. I wasn't close enough to hear, but I was certain she let out a soft moan.

Every clear, rational, logical thought fled my mind and I found myself in a hazy paralysis waiting for her to take her next bite. Feeling the strength of my gaze on her, Amelia opened her eyes and shot me a loathing glare.

"She doesn't mean anything by it," Kiran offered softly next to me. I heard the undertones of protective, brotherly love in his voice. He thought I would be angry at Amelia.

"I'm not upset," I replied curtly, not sure if that was true. I realized my fork was suspended halfway to my mouth and dipped my head to meet it aggressively.

"Ok, good," Kiran laughed a little in relief. "She isn't staying long anyway, just through the weekend I think. And then she is meeting her mum back in Zurich for a humanitarian summit or something of the like."

"Humanitarian summit?" I asked, curiosity sparking inside of me. My blood heated quickly and I felt alive wondering about the pretty vegetarian at the end of the table. When was the last time something had truly interested me?

"Mmm, yes," Kiran talked around a bite of food. "Since their.... I guess you could say conversion.... Since Aunt Bianca and Amelia lost their titles they turned their money and their efforts toward the poor of humanity. They are very involved in numerous charities all over, and are trying to give away everything they own. Or it seems that way anyway. Jean will never let them become poor, but they're right in that we could all live with a little less, don't you think?"

I made an agreeing sound, but didn't push the conversation further. I felt the same way, and had tasked Eden with spreading our inherited wealth around the world in worthy causes. It was also something I had been trying to impress on the wealthiest of our people, but I had always tried to avoid Bianca and so we had never had the conversation. Even if, in the end, she had seen the necessity for Lucan's death, she was still his sister. I had a hard time facing her, knowing how much I cared for my own sister and how hard it would be for me to lose Eden even if she were an evil tyrant. I had a hard time looking Bianca in the eye knowing I had been very instrumental in Lucan's downfall and had a direct hand in his ultimate death.

Our plates were cleared and people began to move around the outside space. There was a dance floor and the music subtly changed from soft background music to big band, jazz, rat-pack stuff that people could dance to. After the first of countless dinner parties, I had abolished the tired, boring formal dining that took five courses and sucked hours of my life into the meaningless vacuum of polite conversation. But in order to appease the people, which I was always about appeasing the people, I had compromised to three courses. Appetizers were served cocktail party style while everyone mingled, dinner was served sitting down and dessert was set out on elegant tables around the square for people to enjoy at their pleasing.

I felt very diplomatic with that decision, until I realized the most important decision I had made as King thus far was about food....

I got up from the table, knowing I had important hands to shake. Eden and Kiran had already been sucked into the endless polite politics of our culture and so I headed in the opposite direction, hoping for a whole divide and conquer scenario. Ok, mostly I was hoping the majority of people here tonight would want to talk to them and leave me alone.

I walked toward the dance floor, not really with a purpose in mind, just pulled in by the expert skills of the musicians and the gravelly voice of the singer belting out Frank Sinatra. All ages of couples waltzed around the floor, lost in each other and the beauty of the evening.

"Avalon, you must be thrilled to welcome your sister home," an older woman grabbed both of my hands, squeezing them in her soft clasp. I couldn't remember her name, but her accent was American so I felt like I should know her.

"I am," I replied easily, still trying to figure out her name.

"And two of your closest friends, engaged? Things really are falling into place for you," she kept hold of my hands and I tried my best to squash the urge to retract them. It was awkward holding them like this.

"Yes, for me and the Kingdom. Our first cross-racial marriage, I cannot wait to see the ripple effects as the freedom of choice spreads through our people," I preached.

"Of course," her eyes narrowed just the slightest and I wondered if she was one of the older generation that was having trouble embracing our new way of life. "Will it spread to you?" She recovered and I wanted to put my face into my palm. I asked for this.

"One day," I offered noncommittally.

Laughter broke my concentration and I followed the sound to those legs again, standing a little ways away. Amelia stood with her back to me, talking with Jericho. I admired her for a moment, her short skirt showed off her long, tanned legs and her dress was all lace from slim shoulders to curvy waist, revealing a perfectly sculpted back. Her golden brown hair was pulled off her neck and up into something only girls had names for; one long strand of glossy hair had escaped and blew against the nape of her neck in the gentle evening breeze.

It was then that I made my decision.

I had to talk to her.

"If you'll excuse me, I see someone I need to speak with," I apologized and when I saw disappointment in the lady's eyes I improvised. "I know Eden was hoping to speak with you though," I gestured with my arm, escaping her weird handhold.

Excitement and entitlement sparked in her gray eyes and she released me immediately, "Of course, enjoy your evening."

"You too," I mumbled, but I was already on my way across the space separating me from Amelia.

I kept my eyes on her slender back, promising myself it was so I wouldn't accidentally meet some talkative person's eyes and get sucked into another meaningless conversation. She was deep in conversation with Jericho by the time I got closer. They were laughing at something, and she had put a hand on his arm just like she had the waiter. She leaned into him, her laugh rose above all the other sounds like musical bells. At the same time I felt both relieved that I had an excuse to join their conversation and an obnoxious stab of jealousy that Jericho had somehow fallen into her good graces so easily.

I cleared my throat before I got to them, mentally berating myself for caring so much what one girl thought. She was exactly what I wasn't looking for in a girl. Spoiled, rich, a symbol of the old Monarchy, a Kendrick.... a vegetarian. I almost turned away right then, realizing I wasn't looking for a girl at all, and especially not this one.

"Avalon," Jericho called out before I could turn away. "Mimi was just telling me about some of her humanitarian work in India." Jericho turned a bit serious before continuing, "Avalon is always trying to get our people to give back to humanity and get involved in charities. He thinks we could all be doing something more with our money."

"That surprises me," Amelia sobered completely, her golden eyes turning to steel. "I mean with all the poverty surrounding this Citadel."

"I, uh...." I stuttered, not expecting her accusatory response. Usually I was the one trying to convince people to do more.

"Or maybe it's easier to preach philanthropy than practice it?" Her eyes narrowed, her arms crossed and she practically turned her back on Jericho waiting for my response.

I looked to Jericho for help; he was the one that pulled me into this after all. I bet she wasn't accusing Jericho of being a hypocrite... her conversation with him seemed so much nicer.

"Eden's in charge of where our money goes," I explained, knowing that since Eden was one of her closest friends she wouldn't be able to fault me. I tugged at the collar of my white dress shirt, it was open at the collar, and I wasn't wearing a tie, but still it felt suddenly suffocating.

Amelia softened just a little, her shoulders relaxed and she sucked in her bottom lip thoughtfully before she continued, "And is that enough, Avalon? Just giving away money? Or do you think philanthropy involves getting your hands dirty too?"

It wasn't her fault there was still a thirteen year old boy hidden deep inside of me. I flashed a grin at her and stepped in a little bit closer so that I wouldn't be overheard, "I've never been able to keep my hands clean, Amelia."

She flinched when I said her name, and I enjoyed the way her eyes flashed to my lips. She stiffened then, tossing her chin in the air like I had offended her and turned to Jericho.

Jericho's eyes had widened in response to our interaction and I wondered what he thought of Amelia's natural defiance. She slipped her arm around his elbow, pressing her side against Jericho's. I refused to acknowledge any of the emotions that bubbled through my veins like hot lava at the sight of their touching.

"Will you dance with me, Jericho? Just like at Eden's wedding?" Amelia asked coyly.

"Absolutely," Jericho smiled at her and then nodded his chin my way.

"I'll catch up with you later," I offered to Jericho, ignoring the way my hand balled into a fist and wanted to punch Jericho's face for whatever had happened at Eden's wedding. "Amelia, have a wonderful evening." I finished politely and then felt some of my jealousy subside when she flinched for a second time when I said her name.

I wondered if she would be asking me to call her by her nickname sooner than she thought. For some reason I didn't think she liked her own reaction when I used her full name. Which would of course encourage me to use it as often as I could.

Chapter Five

I stood on the terrace, staring out at Kiran's mother's gardens while the sun made an appearance on the horizon. Analisa stayed away from Romania since Kiran's wedding. I heard she was in Paris for a while, with the Cartiers, but eventually even the entire continent of Europe became too much and she fled to South America. I knew Kiran was worried about her emotional state, but she wasn't in physical danger so he was giving her space. Or that's at least what Eden had relayed a while ago. Eden had given up her personal Guard, Jedrec, to look after her.

There had been some encouragement from the castle staff to clean up the maze of gardens that spread out behind the castle and climbed and clawed over the tall Citadel wall, but I couldn't bring myself to do it. Analisa had kept the gardens this way for a reason, her own anarchy in a world of hidden imprisonment. A pang of unsuspecting sadness punched me in the gut. Analisa had been devastated after Lucan died and not just because of her husband's death, or the death of those that fought both for and against us, but because at one point in their long, dramatic history, Analisa and my mother had been very close friends.

The tall greenery and clingy flowers were dying out in preparation for winter. The garden existed in a half-dead, half-alive chaos and it irritated me that I felt connected to that damn garden because of it. I rubbed my hands over my face roughly, trying to snap out of this funk I had fallen into.

I needed a change. I needed to do something.

I wasn't meant to stay still.

"They're looking for you," Kiran interrupted my depressing, self-indulgent thoughts.

"Who?" I asked, not turning to face him.

"Your council," Kiran replied with a bit of amusement in his voice. It used to drive Eden nuts the way Kiran always seemed like he was laughing at her and not nuts in the way that eventually made her fall in love with him. It actually irritated the bejeezus out of her. I was starting to get that.

"Ah," I sighed. "Their demands start early. I don't think anybody went to bed before two last night, including Angelica. Where do they get their energy?" I laughed humorlessly.

Kiran stood silently for a beat, taking in the morning sun over his mother's gardens. "Avalon, why don't you let me take over today? You could use a break, and I could use some diplomacy. It's been a while. And frankly, I've been dying to make meaningless decisions and arbitrate some blown out of proportion century long feud."

I looked over at him out of the corner of my eye to make sure he was serious. "You're a terrible liar," I grunted, although I was three seconds from taking him up on his offer.

"Really, man, it's fine. Take the day off. We'll figure out how to share this thing later," Kiran gestured between us and I sighed in relief.

"Thank you, really Kiran, thank you," I offered sincerely and walked away before he could change his mind.

One day of vacation wasn't that big of a deal, and he owed me anyway after years of honeymooning. I firmly decided today I would not answer one question I didn't absolutely want to answer and there was no way in hell I would be making a decision today. I was just going to relax.... take it easy.... do nothing.

Doing nothing lasted all of four hours before I was completely lost. I wandered semi-aimlessly through the castle corridors in search of Jericho and something, anything to do. Jericho had been relatively silent today. I thought I would see him bright and early this morning since he was both a morning person and a worthless sleeper, but nothing.

I tried to remember when he had left the dinner last night, but my memory was a jumble of stuck up aristocrats all vying for my attention. The last I remembered of Jericho, he was dancing with Amelia.

And as if she were conjured by my own thoughts, I heard her laughter as it floated down the hallway in an excited rush of energy. I followed the sound, not sure what I would say to her, or really what she would say to me. She obviously wasn't impressed by my crown or me for that matter. It seemed she could barely keep from rolling her eyes when I walked into the room.

I had no idea what I did to her to make her dislike me so much, especially since I had never even really met her until she arrived at the castle yesterday. But then maybe that was it. Maybe it was simply the crown that her uncle used to wear.

Or oh, God.... I did have a hand in killing her uncle. Maybe that was it. I knew from years of being in the Resistance, Lucan had favored her and somewhat sheltered her from the rest of the Kingdom. She probably loved her uncle and because she was so close with everyone else involved she couldn't blame them.

She didn't know me.

So what if she blamed me?

Damn it. In fact, the more I thought about it, I was sure that had to be it. She blamed me for the death of Lucan. I debated with myself whether Amelia was the kind of girl worth pursuing.... worth apologizing for the death of her uncle? I could do that.... apologize. Right?

Wrong. Amelia was beautiful and feisty and she didn't really care about the crown, but she also didn't like me. I would never apologize for Lucan's death, especially to someone who blamed me like it was a bad thing. Amelia would just have to go on not liking me.

I could live with that.

I turned the corner, hoping to sneak by her without being seen but she was there, right in front of me. We ran right into each other as she turned the corner at the same time I did from the opposite way, a smile still curving her plump lips. She grabbed my biceps immediately to steady herself, and my hands slipped to her waist to catch her.... not completely on purpose. It was a gut reaction.

"Careful there, Amelia," I cautioned in a low voice. The amusement immediately drained from her face and her lips parted as if she wasn't quite sure what to say or do.

"Excuse me, Avalon," she whispered in a throaty voice, her hands tightening against my bare arms as if she needed to get her bearings. "I was just on my way to.... uh, I needed to get.... um, Jericho is waiting for me." She glanced over her shoulder, but her hands stayed on me.

I cleared my throat, and suddenly felt a little uncomfortable. "Jericho?" I asked, trying to ignore the accusation in my tone. I wasn't even sure who I was accusing and what I was accusing them of.

"I just needed to get a sweater," she explained, finally pulling away and stepping back to put a few feet between us.

"Oh are you two going out for the day?" I inquired, mentally cementing my feet in place so they wouldn't take the step towards her they were dying to take. I ignored the annoying voice of reason in my head that reprimanded me for being nosy.

"Yes, we're going to.... um, yes we are," she stuttered in her soft accent. She put a hand to her neck, clasping it in her slender fingers as if she were protecting herself. "I'm sorry, you just startled me," she breathed out quickly, and shook her head.

"I apologize," I smiled slowly, enjoying how flustered she seemed after running into me. "You shouldn't keep Jericho waiting for much longer."

"Jericho," she mumbled like she was just remembering him. "Right."

I moved out of her way and she walked by me in a flutter of nervous energy. Her magic crackled in the air around her, and I felt it brush against mine tentatively, almost curiously, before she reigned it back in quickly. She glanced over her shoulder one more time halfway down the hall and I offered her another smile. She shook her hair out as if she had to do a double take to make sure I was really there, but didn't offer anything but a blank expression in return.

It was the shorts that made up my mind. As she walked away, my eyes drifted to her long legs and the flawless skin between her shorts and her heeled boots and I made a decision that would probably come back to bite me in the ass.

I turned around and found Jericho waiting patiently by the doors to the outside. I had to play this cool, especially if Jericho was interested in Amelia.

Of course he was interested in her. Any sane guy would be. And she was actually *nice* to Jericho. He didn't stand a chance. I was a terrible friend for even entertaining this idea, but there was something in the hallway just now. Something between us and I needed to chase it down and figure it out.

"Hey man, I've been looking for you," I called out as I approached.

"Oh hey," Jericho returned. "Sorry, Amelia and I walked up to the lake this morning. I forgot what it's like here in autumn."

"Yeah, it's something else," I agreed while trying to figure out how to invite myself into their plans. "So what have you got going on today? I thought we could hang. I've got the day off and I've been wanting to…. uh, test some of the cars out on these mountain roads." I threw out an idea off the top of my head. It was a stupid idea, but I couldn't think of anything else.

"Oh that sounds fun," Jericho started, and I could tell he didn't really know what to think. "But uh, actually Amelia and I were going to go visit Ileana this afternoon, maybe stay for dinner."

"Oh that's cool, I mean, we can do the car thing another time," I knew the guilt I was about to lay was the kind of stuff that would one day send me to hell, but I couldn't stop myself and I didn't really want to anyway. "We'll hang a different time. When are you leaving again? Tomorrow?"

"You should come with us," Jericho offered sincerely. I paused, trying to read through his laid back niceness.

"I wouldn't want to impose," I mumbled, not meaning it at all. But I thought I should give my conscience one last effort.

"No, you won't be. It will be fun. Or maybe it won't be…. are you down there all the time?" Jericho asked, and his concerned face legitimately seemed to be worried I would be bored and not that I would try to take the girl that he was interested in.

"Actually, I haven't been down there in over a year. I probably should go with you," I laughed at the truth of it.

"Alright, Jericho, I'm ready," Amelia announced when she walked into the foyer. She hesitated when our eyes met as if she didn't trust me. I smiled happily in return.

"Mimi, you don't mind if Avalon joins us, do you?" Jericho asked casually, holding open the door for her. He was certain she wouldn't have a problem with it and I almost laughed out loud certain she would have a problem with it.

"Not at all," she lied, brushing by me as if I didn't exist.

"Good," I mumbled under my breath and then found myself smiling when she gave me a sharp glance back. I hadn't meant for her to hear me, but there was something thrilling about the fact that she had, like she was very aware of me.

We walked out the castle doors and down the long stone staircase that led into the square. The sun was shining brightly overhead and warming the cobblestone streets. We were having somewhat of an Indian summer and there was only a hint of colder weather on the breeze.

We had to take motorcycles to get to the gypsy village; they were parked underneath the castle in the garage. Three and a half years ago, when we took down Lucan, Eden had destroyed the prisons underground. She didn't care at the time, but the crumbling of the dungeon caused severe structural damage on the entire Citadel; not to mention the giant crevice that practically swallowed the Earth whole. The first year of my rule I had the entire place restructured and made secure so that the castle itself wouldn't fall into the depths of the Earth's core.

Through all of that, the garage had maintained minimal damage. Lucan had kept an entire fleet of expensive sports cars in top shape. They had to be some of the rarest and most expensive vehicles on the planet, since some of them were original models from all throughout the twentieth century. I supposed they were technically Kiran's inheritance, but I couldn't stop myself from drooling every time I got to take one out.

The motorcycles in the garage were more practical and every day, but they were still some of the better models available.

The three of us picked out helmets to match our head sizes and headed toward the section where the bikes were parked. Jericho picked out his bike and started walking it toward the garage entrance.

"You don't have to ride with him," I jutted my chin in Jericho's direction. "I'm a safer driver." I turned on a little charm, hoping to catch her off guard like in the hallway.

"That's alright, Avalon," she replied and I could swear she was laughing at me. "I don't like safe."

I stared at her with a half open mouth as she picked out her own bike, wheeled it to the entrance, climbed on board and then kicked-started the red Ducati. She turned around and shot me a cocky smile before taking off through the open entrance while I was left staring at her taillights. Jericho picked up his jaw off the floor quicker than I could and took off after her. It took me seven full seconds before I managed to make myself move and in those seven seconds I decided something very important. Jericho and I had the kind of friendship that you didn't risk over a girl.

Except for Amelia.

She was the kind of girl I needed to risk everything for.

Chapter Six

I stayed behind Amelia and Jericho on the trip to the gypsy village. I could handle a motorcycle easily, even without the help of my magic. But so could Amelia and I couldn't help but love the sexy way she took the sharp bends of the mountain roads at a too fast speed, or how she played around with her speeds and bike when she got bored. She got bored a lot. Even though we didn't have a long drive, it was like she could barely tolerate it. She fidgeted and wiggled constantly and more than once I had to tear my eyes from her curvy little figure perched on top of that and back to the road to avoid disaster.

Eventually we turned down the narrow dirt road that led away from the main highway and to the small cluster of huts and shacks that made up Ileana's kingdom. Amory and Ileana had been close over time; he had taken care of her and even sought out her advice. She was known for her gift of prophecy. Although she didn't see everything in the future, she had enough visions that her opinion and guidance were highly favored.

Amory had also exposed Kiran and Sebastian to the village their entire childhood. While I was off with Angelica hiding in various places all throughout the world, they spent their childhoods getting to know my grandfather and experiencing his methods of childrearing.

Amory had done his best with Kiran in hopes of making him a great leader one day, in case all his other efforts with Lucan failed. Amory hated how Kiran turned out before Eden; despite all my grandfather's efforts it seemed as if Kiran would be as awful as his father. Enter my sister, and the story changed.

I supposed it turned out for the better, since even I had grown fond of the spoiled bastard.

He, however, knew Ileana on such a deeper level than me; I hadn't even met her until after Amory was dead. And not until we had secured the throne. Kiran, Eden and I had decided to keep an open, mutually beneficial relationship between our Kingdom and the gypsy village and Ileana genuinely seemed to like me. Granted she loved my sister like Eden was her own daughter, but I knew her affection for me would grow.

It didn't usually take females very long to fall in love with me, but Ileana was a bit unusual. And she had no intentions of marrying me, so that made it a little bit more difficult to flirt my way into her good graces.

But I would wear her down.

Eventually.... Especially since it did not bode well for me that I hadn't been to visit her in over a year. I was going to catch hell for that.

Just as long as there was a decent meal at the end of her long lecture, I could sit through just about anything. I was well trained at spacing out, especially if I was in trouble.

Amelia slowed down and rolled her motorcycle next to a very old, very thick tree. She shook out her lush head of hair and didn't even bother with a glance backwards before she was off into the village, immediately surrounded by a hoard of tiny, naked children. Jericho and I followed suit, stepping off our bikes and leaving our helmets balanced on the backs. I wiped the goofy smile off my face and straightened my spine, ready for Ileana's attack. She was a wiry old thing.

Whack.

Ok, maybe not that ready.

"Ow!" I hollered in response, rubbing the back of my tender head. Magic filled in the painful spot with a soothing burst of electricity. Still, my pride was hurt. How the hell did she always sneak up on me?

"You've been away much too long," Ileana chastised me in her Romanian-accented, craggily old lady voice that was filled with so much mischief it sounded like a child pretending to be an old person. "I have many things to tell you, but you stay away!"

"I apologize," I offered quickly, taking a slow step backwards and trying to turn around before she could-

Whack.

This time it was my shin and she darted away while I clutched at my ankle and hopped around on one foot.

"Not good enough!" She barked.

What did she keep hitting me with? A cane? A freaking branch? It hurt like hell!

"Seriously, I'm very sorry!" I cried desperately, still hopping in place while my eyes darted around paranoid. I couldn't feel Ileana's magical current and therefore couldn't anticipate where the next attack would come from. And nobody was apparently going to help me. Jericho was clutching at his sides while he laughed hysterically at my expense and I heard the children in an excited frenzy wherever Amelia was.

"What is your excuse?" she asked from a bit of a distance.

"I don't have one," I mumbled truthfully.

"At least no lies," she stepped in front of me with no weapon in sight. She could easily be mistaken for a beggar rather than a gypsy queen. Her clothes were mismatched rags layered on top of each other, her golden nose ring was large and tarnished, her thick white hair was partially hidden beneath a dirty red bandana and her bangles and oversized golden earrings clanked noisily with every movement. Why hadn't I heard them while she was attacking me? "You've been gone for too long. Amory was never gone this long. Kiran was never gone this long. You," she pointed a gnarled finger at me. "You are gone much too long."

"I know that. I said I was sorry," I apologized again, feeling like a complete bastard. "It won't happen again."

"It will happen again," she snapped back, but her eyes softened and her tone became careful.

That wasn't an accusation. That was the future. She had seen something.

"What have you seen?" I cut straight to the point. Jericho gave me a questioning look but I waved him off. He wandered further into the village in search of Amelia, but some of the children had pulled her into their hut. I shook my head, realizing I hadn't been intentionally watching where she was going, but I knew exactly where she was all the same.

"Do you know that most of your Kingdom doesn't think it can be done," Ileana mused, sparkly mischief returning to her voice. "They believe you will be single for centuries yet, ruling from your lonely castle alone. But I know better." She winked at me.

"Do you now?" I laughed, hoping more than anything she wasn't using one of her visions to set me up with someone. "I hope this isn't the prediction you want to discuss."

She laughed at me, actually laughed, like that was the funniest thing she had ever heard. Her mouth opened wide as she cackled with her head thrown back, revealing nearly bare gums and broken teeth. "I would not waste my gift on your unpredictable and fickle good graces. That would be asking for trouble."

"What does that mean?" I asked, trying not to feel wounded.

"It means that we have more important things to discuss, and you better use your time wisely, or I will take up most of it," she answered cryptically and then led the way to a couple of beat up plastic lawn chairs that denoted her place of honor in the small community. I actually preferred her version of a throne to my pretentious, golden monstrosity. Plus, these were way more comfortable and I got to enjoy the outdoors.

I took the seat to her right and stayed quiet, waiting for her to speak. She gestured first to the large bonfire set up in front of us. It wasn't lit yet, but a large pile of freshly cut wood stood piled on top of each other, ready for the cooler evening. Using my magic, I lit the fire for her with a concentrated burst of electricity and settled into my chair while the small flames grew larger, licking the forest wood and sending heavenly scents of fall and smoke into the air.

The children filtered out of their huts now that there was something to warm their naked little bodies. Some of them had been given handmade scarves and sweaters and pants, and some just slipped on wool socks and beat up too big loafers and stood closer to the fire. The older children were layered in mismatched, ill-fitting clothes and went around with arms full of clothes trying to coax the still naked ones into something that would save their important appendages.

I laughed at a particularly stubborn little boy that would physically attack if anyone came near with a pair of pants. The boy liked his freedom. He stuck up his nose and lashed out with a swift kick if anyone got too close. That is until Amelia came out with a baby on her hip and her hair floating around her face in the early evening breeze. She took one look at the little boy, snatched up a pair of tweed pants and holey sweater and marched over to the little guy. He tried to ignore her, keeping his nose lifted in the air and turning his back on her. But with one soft hand on his shoulder and a whisper of something sweet in his ear, he fought a smile and slipped into the clothes she held out to him. Once he was fully clothed she mussed up his hair and gave him a quick kiss on the dirty cheek. He wasn't able to keep the smile off his face any longer and ran off to brag to all his friends about Amelia's kiss.

"She doesn't like you," Ileana laughed smugly when she caught what held my attention. "And not for the reasons you think."

"So then why?" I asked, knowing I didn't need to explain anything to the old woman or even ask her to explain what she thought was going on. Even if it wasn't a vision, the woman saw and knew everything. I chalked it up to her mixture of intuitive humanity and useful magic.

"Ah, but you cannot win her heart unless you find out for yourself," she mused, taking a cup of something hot and steamy from a girl around the age of thirteen. She offered a tin cup to me as well, and I took it, not wanting to offend my hostess. Hot tuaca. Ugh. Hot alcohol was rarely good, but their potent moonshine was downright dangerous. I sniffed at the steaming clear liquid and found exactly what I was expecting: a sweeter version of gasoline.

"I'm not sure if I want to win her heart," I looked across the fire to where she sat on a set of wooden steps with Jericho. She was laughing at something he said and her expression was so soft and so happy that it made my heart ache for something; something I didn't even know was missing.

"Then you are a foolish man," Ileana snapped, sitting up straighter in her seat. She was such a tiny woman, and I towered over her, it had never escaped my attention when she did her best to make herself bigger while hoping to intimidate me. "But, love makes us foolish too I suppose," her tone softened.

"Either way I lose?" I bit back my smile, thankful that this was not the subject of her vision.

"Ah, you should decide that. But not tonight. Tonight you are not a king, you are a man. And you need to remember that. For men and kings have different needs and desires. And you are not one that indulges anything very often." She sipped her tuaca, holding the steaming hot cup in her tiny, gnarled old hands. "You are like your grandfather in that way."

"Not my father?" I clarified, letting her observation fill me with pride.

"No, you're nothing like your father," she grunted with a bark of a laugh. "Your father knew exactly what he wanted and went after it. You are nothing like him."

I felt the fullness of my pride deflate like a punctured balloon, squeaking out in a disappointing rush of emotion. I forced myself to take a drink of the scorching hot cup of liquid fire in my hands to keep myself from reminding her of how I went after the Monarchy, knowing that wasn't what she was exactly talking about.... except I didn't really know what she was talking about.

Amelia stood up from across the fire, and as if she somehow knew my mood had changed she gave me a look of tight concern. I held her gaze, giving nothing away, but finding comfort in those warm, golden brown eyes that were at this moment, brighter than the flames burning the wood in front of me. She didn't look away until a small child tugged at her hand and then she let herself be led to where I knew they would be cooking the meal for the evening.

"Alright, enough reminiscing," I cleared my throat and forced my mind back to business. "What is this vision you've had?" I demanded, only softening my tone for the old lady's benefit slightly.

"You're not safe. Not anymore. Three years of peace, but they've been plotting and it's your head they want next." Ileana stated quickly, her eyes never leaving the fire.

The breath was knocked from my lungs as if someone had dealt me a physical blow. This wasn't a warning, this was the future. I gripped the hot cup in my hands tightly making the poisonous alcohol slosh over the sides of the tin cup onto my jeans.

I knew this though. Instinctively, deep down inside of me I knew something like this was brewing. But having it said out loud by someone else, someone with a special insight, felt like nails being pounded into my premature coffin.

My Kingdom was too new, too fragile for another civil war. They, whoever those heartless, stupid bastards were, would win just because my people were not stable enough to make the right decisions and see through their bullshit. Hell, they had voted for another king. *Voted* for it. When given the chance for ultimate, democratic freedom after thousands of years of oppression, prejudice and tyranny they had voted to be kept under someone else's thumb! This was going to end badly.

"Tell me what you know," I turned to face her, demanding every bit of knowledge she could muster.

Half of my short life had been spent fighting for something I desperately believed in and the beginning training for it. These bastards weren't going to take down everything I had worked my ass off for over the last ten years without a fight.

A damned good fight, I thought as my magic sparked vigorously in my veins, sending a rush of renewed and dormant energy through my body.

Chapter Seven

"Who are they, Ileana?" I asked in a carefully calculated voice. I felt the rage and frustration simmering in my blood, heating to a quick boil and threatening to explode.

Are you Ok? Eden gasped into my consciousness. She felt the panic thicken my blood even though we had been keeping ourselves separated. It would have been the same for me though, if our roles were reversed.

I'm fine. We'll talk when I get back tonight. I forced myself to calm down, to admit to myself there was no immediate danger and I would stop the bastards before anyone was hurt. If I could control the situation, there was nothing to worry about. And I would control the situation.

Avalon, you're scaring me. Eden confessed gently between us.

There's nothing to be scared about. I promised, making myself mean it. *We'll talk later tonight.*

Eden closed the door to our shared mental consciousness again without asking anymore questions. I loved that about my sister. She never asked too many questions, or pried where she didn't feel like she should. Granted, that trait had caused her a lot of trouble in the past, but she knew when to walk away.

Ileana seemed to have waited for me to finish my internal conversation before she spoke again. I chewed my thumbnail viciously while listening to every single word she had to say.

"For several months there have been visions.... visions of your future. Nothing has been clear, and nothing has been specific. But I have seen your struggles, the whispers of plotting and scheming that happen in far off places. I have felt how they hate you and your family and how they want the crown that you wear to be theirs. Their hatred runs deep, thick and poisonous through their blood. They have wanted the throne for a long time, longer than your young years. And they will stop at nothing until it is theirs. Their evil is worse than the one that came before you," she finished in a raspy whisper that sent chills running over my body.

A cold, unforgiving fear settled in my stomach. Worse than Lucan? How was that possible? And who were they?

"You don't know who they are?" I restrained myself to one question, although my tongue burned with the need to interrogate this woman like a suspect.

"They have been nothing more than ghosts in the night," she admitted sadly. "Until last night. Last night there was something more.... substantial.

But you will not find them yet. They think they have bested you, they think they are still invisible."

"No, they think I am blind," I growled. Both hating myself for becoming so apathetic over the past couple years and them for underestimating me.

"They think you are blind," she confirmed.

"And you have nothing more than that? No location? Names? Family ties? Hell, I would even take rough descriptions at this point... Hair color, eye color, race?" I bit out, trying to not let Ileana feel like my anger was directed at her.

"Nothing," she said with finality.

I believed her. I had no choice but to believe her, the same way I had to believe that her visions would somehow make their way into my reality. There were people out there that hated me, hated what I stood for and what I wanted to give my people. They hated Lucan before me and now that I stepped into his place I would be the one to deal with them.

A small, miniscule, tiny part of me wondered if they hated me for good reason. Did they have something better to offer? Was I the one that swooped in, destroyed years of tradition and a way of life and made things worse?

No. I couldn't believe that. Ok, I couldn't let myself believe that. Doubt and insecurity were a result of restless boredom, not grounded in reality. Things were better for the community as a whole, and as soon as they released their grip on the past they would get even better.

"I should get back," I mumbled without making a move to get up.

"Not yet," Ileana demanded in her playful way again. Serious discussion over and she was back to her old mysterious, mischievous ways. "The evening is still young. And we have made you dinner." She gestured toward the hut with a healthy stream of smoke puffing out a patchwork chimney.

I looked longingly toward the delicious Romanian dinner I knew would make up for the now tepid volcanic-ash tasting beverage in my hands.

"It does smell good," I mumbled noncommittally.

The young but married gypsy women started bringing out platters and pots of stew and setting them up on a long, rickety table in between two of the huts. Men descended on the table of food from every direction without being called, it was like they could hear the sound of cast iron pots being set down on rotting wood from miles away.

I smiled as Amelia walked out of the hut being shooed by one of the older women. She held an extra-large pot in her towel-covered hands to keep from being burned. She laughed at whatever the old lady was saying and her bright smile had my lips turning up at her infectious personality. She set the pot down and then fussed around a few of the other entrees before stepping back and out of the men's way.

As soon as her hands were free and her feet at a safe distance from the mob of men swarming around the food, both of her hands were immediately clasped by two of the young children that had attached themselves to her shadow. She knelt down to their level, muddying her knees in the soft, leaf-covered ground and said happy things to them that made them laugh out loud. I shifted uncomfortably as another painful punch of longing ripped through my heart. I wasn't even sure what I was longing for, I just knew I needed that charming smile directed at me.

"I suppose you should get back to your castle, though?" Ileana brought me back with her voice as serious as ever. "They probably have dinner waiting for you there."

"Right," I agreed, my eyes drifting back to Amelia as she stood up and brushed the dirt and leaves from her bare skin.

"Of course then you'll have to go back to being King," Ileana said apologetically, but I knew better than to believe this gypsy queen was capable of sympathy. But manipulating me to get her way? She was more than capable of that. "And more importantly, she won't be there."

I didn't have to guess who she meant and before I gave my feet permission to move they were already walking towards Amelia without any intention of slowing down. I forced myself to hesitate and stop a foot away from her. I had no idea what my feet thought would be accomplished by running into her, but since my appendages were acting on their own accord tonight, I couldn't really trust my hands to stay at my sides either.

"It smells delicious, Amelia" I commented, drawing Amelia's attention to me.

She turned her head from overseeing the table of food and looked over me with barely concealed annoyance. "Thank you."

She turned back to the buffet line.

"Are you going to get something to eat?" I asked and when she didn't answer, I pressed my luck. "I could get you a plate if you would like? So you don't have to fight the crowd?"

She turned back to me, the infectious smile she wore for everyone else was long gone. "That's alright Avalon, I can take care of myself."

"I never thought you couldn't," I defended softly. My hand reached for her elbow and I found myself leading her to the back of the line before I could stop myself. She bristled under my touch, but let me lead her without making a scene. I placed her in front of me and stood behind her as close as I thought I could get away with without pissing her off more.

"Have you seen Jericho?" She asked in a clipped tone, her English accent making every word she said sound important.

"Not in a while," I answered, thankful for any kind of conversation even if it had to do with Jericho. "I think he might still be out hunting." I remembered the teenage boys dragging him along with them with several old rifles in their hands.

"Oh," Amelia answered simply turning back around to face forward.

"Doesn't it bother you?" I pressed my luck some more.

She waited a beat, audibly sighing in frustration. She straightened her stiff shoulders before turning around, her delicate faced pinched in irritation and her pouty lips that made such a great smile pressed into an adorable frown.

"Does what bother me?" She asked on a sigh.

"Jericho hunting? You are a vegetarian," I reminded her playfully. The line moved behind her and I instinctively moved forward with it, but she didn't. She stood her ground, not expecting me to step so close. She looked up at me, her mouth falling open just barely.

"I know I'm a vegetarian," she tried to snap, but her voice came out breathy and unsure and impossibly sexy. I stared intently into those golden brown eyes, desperate to keep my hands to myself and my thoughts from getting away from me.

We stood there staring at each other for a few more moments, the attraction between us snapping and popping in our separated magic. I knew she couldn't feel my magic like I could feel hers because she didn't have any Titan in her. She was half Witch, half Medium just like every other Kendrick before her. She could feel how her magic was affected by mine and she could feel the heat with which she wanted me, but how our separate electricity reacted to each other was my little secret; my little secret that had started to intoxicate me and cloud my judgment whenever she was around. She was obviously attracted to me, but didn't like me. That alone should be enough for me to stay away. I didn't have time for a girl, let alone a girl that didn't like me. Still I couldn't move my gaze away from hers or talk myself out of trying to get to know her better.

She took a step back, breaking the spell between us. Her eyes darted around discreetly revealing her level of panic.

"So it doesn't bother you?" I murmured.

"That Jericho went off to hunt? Why should it? Jericho is free to do as he pleases," she replied curtly.

"I'm sure Jericho would agree with you," I agreed. "But I meant for the sake of the animals it doesn't bother you?"

"There is a big difference between the livestock farms from your country and hunting in order to feed a village of hungry children," she replied snidely. People had started to just move around us in order to get at the table of food, so when Amelia stepped over to where the backs of the huts met the Romanian wilderness I followed her. The sun had dipped below the mountainous horizon by now, and this far away from the large fire we were cloaked in darkness.

"Is that your problem with me?" I laughed, trying but not succeeding to make it seem like I wasn't laughing at her. "You don't like that I'm American?"

Her response was an indignant snort that had my smile growing. "Avalon is that why you won't leave me alone? You're upset that I don't like you?"

"That's one of the reasons," I admitted in a husky voice. The sounds of a gypsy trio began to liven the night as the fiddle, violin and accordion drifted through the air melting into a fast tempo, melancholy rhythm that called those who had finished their meal to dance around the fire. The cool breeze moved Amelia's hair off her delicate shoulders and around her face and her eyes shone even through the dark night. I leaned forward with only the promise of her soft lips against mine. Her eyes flicked down to my mouth as I moved slowly towards her, her irresistible lips had a gravitational pull of their own and she made no attempt to move.

"Would you like to hear all the reasons I don't like you, then? Would that help cure your curiosity?" She laughed mockingly, turning her head back to the village and moving her mouth out of my reach.

"Probably not," I admitted truthfully. She snapped her head back to me like she was going to tell me anyway, so I had to interrupt. I actually physically had to or I would lose myself even more to the emptiness of monotony, there was something there, something between us and I was going to be damned if I let her talk me out of it before I figured out what it was. I leaned in, inhaling her as I drew closer to her ear. She smelled like lilacs and vanilla and…. happiness. "Dance with me," I ordered softly into her ear.

She shivered under my breath and I felt it to my core. I slipped my hand around hers before she could decline and led her over to the fire. She followed me, letting me drag her along and then pull her into me once we were in line with the other dancers. She looked up at me with wide eyes that narrowed into defiance, but behind her rebelliousness was something like fear.

Yet she didn't walk away.

And even though I could have easily danced with a hundred girls that would have gladly stayed because they wanted to, I only wanted to dance with her because she stayed when she didn't want to.

I could relate. And the thought made me smile down at her, even while she glared unsurely up at me. Before she could change her mind, I put my hands on her hips and moved her with the complicated steps of the gypsy folk dance. The dance was fast paced and there was not time to really talk, but it also kept our bodies close together, constantly touching. My magic jumped and sizzled inside my veins with her so close, her delicate waist in my hands, the scent of her hair and skin intoxicating me.

She let me move her around, not trying to fight the dance, or my touch or what I was realizing was between us. The music picked up speed and so did our dance steps, soon we were out of breath and laughing with the effort to keep up to the practiced gypsies. I moved faster, more accurately and found myself caught up in the dance.... caught up in Amelia. Soon, it was just us dancing around the fire, just us in the Romanian wilderness, just us in....

The song ended, breaking the trance dancing with her put me into. I stared down at her as her chest heaved with the effort to breathe and her hair was pushed back away from her face. Her eyes held mine for a few moments with nothing in between us but the raw attraction that ignited her blood as hotly as it did mine.

It was at that moment the night ended and it was time to leave. I didn't have time for girls. Even if one had finally managed to grab my attention. And I didn't have the patience for the complexity I knew was love.

"Thank you for the dance, Amelia," I forced a strong polite voice, when she had left me frustratingly breathless and dizzy.

Her eyes narrowed on me, and she waited a second before speaking. "I think you should call me Mimi," she struggled to make herself sound stern. "I think I would like it better if you called me Mimi," she agreed with herself, nodding her head slowly.

"And I think I like calling you Amelia better," I confessed, biting back a grin. Her eyes widened with the sound of her name and I couldn't help it, I really liked how she reacted when I used it.

With that, I turned around half loving how I left her staring after me and half hating how I had to walk away from her. But there were more important things than an infatuation with a spoiled princess and sick curiosity for how she made me feel. Hundreds of girls had been paraded in front of me and not one of them had caught my full attention. Amelia would be no different as soon as I distanced myself from her.

And I *needed* to distance myself from her. I needed to get back to the castle and figure out how to protect my Kingdom from another round of evil set on their destruction.

Chapter Eight

"Ah! Sorry!" I all but shouted on my way out of the throne room when I accidentally walked in on a very private moment between Eden and Kiran.

I shuddered against the image I was pretty sure would never be erased from my memory. I wondered if there was a magical ceremony that could cleanse my brain, like scrub it completely clean. That was going to take years of therapy before I could emotionally move on from that. And they were crazy if they ever thought I was going to sit in one of those thrones again.

I shuddered again.

"Avalon, is everything alright?" Talbott asked while walking briskly towards me. He was in full military mode with his soldier style walk and classic black dress pants and gray polo, the casual uniform of the Titan.

"No!" I whined, knowing I was being a baby, but there was nothing I could do to stop it at this point. "Nothing is alright! I will never be the same after that!"

I shuddered again. Violently.

"After what?" Talbott asked but then seemed to think better of the hallway. "Here, let's go in here and we can wait for Eden and Kiran."

"Uh, maybe we should wait before we-"

"Avalon, I'm sorry about that," Eden peeked past the heavy brass door to the throne room. I looked away afraid of what I would see. And then I looked away in a different direction and then in another direction, basically I needed to look anywhere but at her. "Oh don't be a baby, it's not like we were having sex."

I let out a growl of disgust and slapped my hands over my ears. "Don't ever say that word around me again. Ever!"

I got giggles in response. Giggles.

"Sorry about that, brother," Kiran offered.

"Wait, what actually happened Avalon?" Talbott asked, while putting these very awkward pieces together. "Is this why you called me in to talk? Listen I can solve a lot of problems for you, but I don't think that is one of them." And then he laughed. *Talbott* laughed.

"No, that is not why I called a meeting," I snapped. "And, honestly I'm not sure anyone can help with the emotional damage from that." I gestured in the general direction of Eden and Kiran still not able to make eye contact with them.

"You are a full grown adult now, Avalon. Please tell me a little PDA does not make you this uncomfortable," Eden chastised me. And she was right. A little PDA shouldn't make me uncomfortable. But there was nothing little about that public display of affection happening in the throne room, unless you wanted to call it a little PDB.... public display of banging.

"When it's your sister, it should always make you this uncomfortable," I drawled dryly, another shudder shaking my core.

"Is everything alright?" Gabriel asked. He had approached wearing a stern scowl on his face and flanked by Angelica and Silas.

"No, it's not," I sighed, gesturing toward the throne room. There were other rooms we could have congregated in, but most of them still reminded me of Lucan and I tried to avoid them. The throne room definitely still held his signature style, but when I stood inside his once place of honor wearing the crown he used to oppress my people, I stood with pride and confidence because it was my throne room now and I offered freedom to the people.

"Avalon enough! You can't seriously be this damaged!" Eden interrupted, and I felt more than saw how embarrassed she was.

"I *am* damaged!" I defended myself, but then released her from some of her humiliation. "But this is about something more important than my future therapy sessions."

With that everyone filed into the throne room looking solemn and serious. This was going to be a hard conversation. We had succeeded in bringing both peace and freedom to our people and all of us had fought vigilantly to ensure that our people would enjoy the fruits of our labor for thousands of years to come. Hell, Eden and I had even given up our own personal freedom so that the rest of the Kingdom could feel stable with a King and Queen.

But now all of that was in jeopardy and I couldn't even give them concrete details. The crown, that I had slipped on as soon as I was back from the gypsy village, weighed heavily on my head tonight. And for the first time in three years it wasn't because of my own selfishness or boredom. Tonight was the first night I felt a real, tangible responsibility as King to protect my people.

"Earlier this evening I paid a visit to Ileana," I began when everyone was seated around the room. I stepped back to take my seat on the middle throne before thinking better of it. Halfway into sitting, I frantically stood back up from the contaminated seat.

So. Gross.

"The gypsy queen?" Silas asked, his Caribbean accent thick and his gray eyes fierce. "What did she see?"

"For a while she has been having visions of another rebellion," I paused and waited for that to sink in. When no one asked any immediate questions

I continued, "She could not give me any specific details or even a country or place where these visions originated from, but she could say that whoever is plotting to take over this Kingdom has been at it for a while, and they will not stop until they have the throne," I paraphrased.

Other than Angelica's sharp intake of breath, the room stayed utterly silent for a full minute, each Immortal lost in their own deep well of thoughts. Usually prone to fidgeting I was surprisingly still as I waited for the flood of questions. My arms crossed themselves out of a battle born instinct and I chomped down on my thumbnail so that I could think better, or so I told myself. I hadn't stood in this position in a long time, and even though it seemed I should be rusty when it came to strategically thinking about defense and attacking, I felt sharper and more prepared than ever before.

"What's the meeting all about?" Sebastian asked, entering the room without knocking. He was trailed by Lilly and Seraphina.

"Ileana has predicted another rebellious faction," Gabriel explained, while tugging at his priest's collar. I nearly smiled as I watched him struggle against the traditional religious outfit. He hadn't been back to his parish since he left Peru with Eden years ago and he served no religious purpose in my council. Yet, he continued to identify himself with the Catholic Church, even though his orders had been given centuries ago. And even though he was a born warrior, his very nature was fighting against the binding uniform. "She hasn't seen anything with clarity, but she is certain there is a group of Immortals plotting against Avalon."

"And Eden and Kiran," I reminded them, not wanting to be viewed as the lone royal. "There are no vivid details, just that there is someone out there that would like the throne."

"A disturbance in the force?" Sebastian asked on a laugh. My lips twitched at his reference, but I was more than confident at least half this room had no idea what he was talking about. "So there are a few greedy bastards out there that see Avalon's coup as an invitation to play musical thrones. So what? It's not like we don't have the support of the majority of the Kingdom, plus the army is on our side. How could they possibly overtake us? We are the original Resistance, they can't do what we did."

"Why can't they?" I demanded, needing an answer.

"Because we have goodness and truth and freedom and all that on our side. Now that the people have that, especially freedom, they are not going to want to give it all up," Sebastian reasoned.

Silence fell over us again as we contemplated Sebastian's argument. It should be simple to agree with him, it was the truth. We did have freedom and more on our side. That should be enough for any people to embrace and occupy. But I knew that it wasn't. Our own ancestors had given up freedom in exchange for oppression centuries ago and I couldn't be certain that wouldn't happen again.

Ileana's words came back to haunt me as I contemplated an evil worse than Lucan. A feeling like ice cold water doused my stomach, sending me reeling with a fear I refused to accept. I opened my mouth to share her thoughts with the room, but then closed it quickly again. We had to fight whatever this was with a fierce intensity and unwavering dedication. Filling us with an unproved fear would do nothing but cast doubt on our cause and make us our question every move.

"Thank you for the words of encouragement, cousin," Kiran answered Sebastian regally. "You're right about everything of course. But I am not sure we can treat this threat lightly. This Kingdom has given up their freedom before and even still recently they chose a king over a democracy. We need to get to the bottom of this as quickly as we can."

"Gabriel, Silas, Angelica, do you know of any older generation Immortals that were unhappy with Lucan?" I asked, hoping to ferret out the threat before anything happened. Although, after replaying my conversation with Ileana in my head for the last two hours I was almost positive that they would make the first move according to her vision. And until then we would have to play the waiting game, which went against everything in my nature and caused me physical pain.

"Everyone was unhappy with Lucan," Angelica laughed. "I'm sorry Kiran, dear."

"It's nothing I didn't already know, given his ultimate assassination and all," Kiran waved her off with some dry humor.

"There are those that were more than in favor of a new regime, even if they didn't want to join Amory's Rebellion," Gabriel offered. "But none that were motivated to start their own." He sat pensively for a moment before adding, "Or that I knew of."

"There are thousands of Immortals living all over the world, how will we ever narrow them down to even a list of suspects?" Eden observed a bit desperately and I felt the fear of another war snake through her blood. She loved her people too much to want to see another fight break out. We were lucky in the last battle because it ended so quickly. By the time I came face to face with Lucan, the majority of the Titans had joined a very willing army of Immortals desperate for his death. He died because we all took a piece of his magic; the entire Kingdom stood together and demanded his blood.

That night was the first step in a new era for my people.

I could only hope I wouldn't go down as easily. If there was a fight, people would die. People I loved would die.

"Terletov," Eden mumbled into the silent room and I was positive I was the only one who understood her and it was only because of our twin connection.

"What was that, Love?" Kiran asked, putting a hand on her lower back.

"Terletov," I ground out for her. "I should have thought of him immediately."

"But I thought he died?" Seraphina asked in a small voice.

"He did, I mean, Eden took his magic and Lucan had him and his men killed after the Titan Guard brought him back here," I explained, wondering where Eden's thought train was headed.

"I, um, I didn't take everyone's magic," Eden explained weakly. I felt regret and ice cold fear ignite her magic. Kiran instinctively put his arms around her. "There were a few men that escaped. I let them go.... I couldn't.... I didn't want to be the reason any more Immortals lost their lives. I haven't really thought about the kidnapping since it happened. I mean.... I've really tried not to think about it."

I wanted to put a comforting arm on my sister, knowing the very thought of how vulnerable Terletov had made her feel when he shot her and dragged her from Lucan's imprisonment unnerved her. Hell, it unnerved me. And I realized that I too had tried to put that entire incident behind me.

I should have thought of him immediately.

"But there were probably more Immortals involved than what were with you, Eden," Talbott reasoned rationally. And he was right.

"Were you part of the rescue team?" I asked him, having a hard time remembering.

"No, I wasn't. But I was debriefed later. Lucan sent a team of Titans to see if they could sniff anything else out, but our hands were tied with Eden and you and I don't think they were able to dig very deep. They followed a trail from Latvia through Hungary, but then it went dead. Other Titans had followed Delia and Justice to our neck of the woods and so they left the mission in Hungary and returned here." Talbott spouted out the details slowly as if he was struggling to remember them too.

"Gabriel and I will pick up where they left off," Silas stood abruptly. And with his movement I could feel the magical current of the room snap and pop with anxious, determined energy. I wasn't the only Immortal restless and bored apparently.

"I'll go with you," Sebastian volunteered.

I shot a quick glance to Seraphina, wondering if she would give him her permission but she just rolled her eyes and then avoided looking at him completely.

"Alright, and you'll leave first thing in the morning," I conceded, ignoring the devastating pang of disappointment at being left behind. There was a time when I would have been sent first to investigate and control a situation. Now I was chained to a golden throne I couldn't even sit in until it was doused with some seriously strong disinfectant. "We can stop this before anything gets out of hand. Be diligent and thorough and call for back up at the first sign of trouble. I will assemble a team that will be able to meet you at a moment's notice, but for now let's keep this investigation discreet. We don't need to cause any unnecessary attention and spook these guys."

"Or scare the people," Eden offered in a voice barely above a whisper.

I barely contained a growl of anxious energy. It felt good to plan and delegate again, and for plans more important than political parties.

With those final orders the meeting dispersed. I watched as Talbott walked to Lilly and pulled her into his arms. Kiran whispered soothing words into Eden's ear and even Seraphina walked over to give Sebastian a kiss and a hug goodbye, even if there was a weird, strange tension between the two of them.

I stood awkwardly in the middle while Angelica discussed travel routes with Silas and Gabriel. I stood alone. And for the first time in my life, standing alone felt lonely.

Chapter Nine

I woke with a start, fast and quick. My heart pounded, my ear drums rang and a thick sheen of sweat plastered my hair to my neck. I reached out into the thick folds of blankets on my massive king-size bed and felt around until I was sure I was alone. Until I was sure I was safe.

I didn't scare easily. I wasn't scared ever. No, I couldn't remember a moment in my life when I had felt nothing but fear. Sure, there were those moments when fear was stronger than any other emotion, but always coupled with it was confidence, or determination or anger. This fear stood alone and consumed me.

And seriously, a nightmare?

But it was so real. It was so.... they were gone. The details, the events, the haunting dreamscape that tortured me with chills and boiling blood at the same time; the visions that had me hunting down a sword and a gun and setting out for vengeful retribution. They slipped away, back into the abyss of my subconscious.

And I wished they would stay there.

But mine was the kind of life where nightmares became reality, where I had to suffer against the brutal torture of a tyrant, where I watched and mourned as friends died, where my sister's life was exchanged for mine and my parents and grandfather were murdered in front of me. My life *was* the stuff of nightmares. And three years of peace meant nothing when war was on the horizon.

I drew another stuttering breath and ran my hands through my damp and matted hair. I forced myself to breathe deep and even breaths and my heart to slow its rapid rhythm. Whatever was left behind when I opened my eyes would make itself known soon enough; there was no use worrying over it now.

The sun shone through my long windows and I glanced over at the clock, surprised by how late I slept. Usually I was up before the sun, and I enjoyed the quiet peacefulness of a castle not yet awake, before everyone started demanding my attention and required me to make menial decisions.

I stumbled to the shower, stepped out of my boxers and into the hot water I started magically from across the room. I needed a steamy bathroom before I even crossed the threshold in order to wake up.

After cleaning up, shaving and pulling my hair back and away from my face, I dressed for the day in old jeans and a t-shirt, slipping the crown on my head before I left the room. I remembered Lucan in tailored, designer suits and ties every day he was King. Even Amory adhered to a certain snobbish dress code that exemplified a well-kempt, wealthy and responsible man.

Jeans and a worn red t-shirt hardly screamed leader of the wealthiest nation on Earth, but it was also comfortable and practical, not to mention a reminder of my youth and inexperience for any Immortal that approached me. Not that I was trying to sway their next vote for a Democracy by proving I wasn't up to task for the crown. But.... ok, maybe I was trying to do that a little bit.

Plus, I was King after all. I could wear whatever I wanted.

I found Eden and Kiran in the dining hall, surrounded by all of our friends, minus Silas, Gabriel and Sebastian who left very early this morning. My intention was to see them off and offer some last minute directions, but my subconscious decided to hold me hostage in my own personal version of Nightmare on Elm Street. Besides, they were seasoned veterans at this and knew what they were doing. And if they didn't check in with me in a few hours I would call them and get a status report from them, probably just in time for a "fulfill your destiny" speech from Gabriel.

I stood leaning against the doorjamb for a few beats watching all of the activity at the breakfast table. Usually I spent breakfast alone, so I could collect my thoughts before I faced the throne room and all the duties that I faced on a daily basis. If I could help it, I did my best to avoid even uttering a sentence until I was permanently rooted in the seat I would spend all day in. This morning would be different and I didn't find myself minding.

Eden and Kiran sat together giving each other the googly eyes I had been positive would wear off over at least a year ago. Talbott and Lilly were no better, and as much as it made my stomach clench in disapproval, I was afraid Jericho and Amelia were doing the same thing. Seraphina was the only remaining loner and I realized that if Sebastian sat here she would be mimicking the love struck motions too. The whole thing was like a kick in the shin.

Damn, when did everyone go and get paired up and leave me behind?

Not that I wanted to be paired up.

Especially now, when I would have to leave at a moment's notice and possibly be gone and in dangerous situations for months at a time....

No girl would want to be left behind. Plus, when I finally decided I would let a girl into my world, I would be a freaking fantastic boyfriend and demand that she stay home so she wouldn't get hurt in the crossfire, of some life or death situation.

Also, why was I getting so excited about the prospect of a near-future fight?

There might be something wrong with my brain.

Just a thought.

"How did you sleep last night, E?" I asked as I took my place at Eden's right across from Kiran and directly next to Seraphina.

Seraphina might be high maintenance and I would never envy Sebastian for putting up with all her crazy, but the girl smelled good. I leaned into grab a croissant across the table and inhaled thinking I myself might have a good mixture of crazy in me.

Or maybe I was way lonelier than I gave myself credit for.

"Not well," she admitted, turning her concerned black eyes on me.

"Do you remember anything?" I asked, knowing without a doubt we had the same dream.

"Not a thing," she answered and I nodded so that she knew it was the same for me.

"Uh, this is getting gross," Seraphina cut a disgustingly suggestive glance at me and then at Kiran making Eden burst into laughter.

"There is something so wrong with you, Sera!" Eden threw a piece of bacon making Seraphina squeal and toss it at Amelia.

Amelia deflected with a bagel and then eyed the offensive piece of meat like it was a snake.

"Ugh you know meat grosses me out," she complained in a teasing voice.

"I know you need to get over it and start dating," Seraphina countered and my ears perked up while I took a sip of steaming hot coffee.

"That is so not the meat I was referring to," Amelia laughed and I found myself choking on my coffee.

"You alright there, Avalon?" Seraphina asked, ignoring Amelia's attempts at innocent.

"Just fine," I wheezed. I stared Amelia down, waiting for her to apologize for or shy away from Seraphina's brashness.

"Relax Avalon, it's not your meat I'm interested in," Amelia said coyly from across the table.

This time the coffee went straight through my nose. There was no stopping the near death experience.

"Ugh, so gross," Eden complained. "Siblings, remember? No more talking about Avalon's meat."

"Agreed," Kiran, Talbott and Jericho mumbled in unison.

"Avalon," Lilly spoke up pulling my attention from Amelia's eyes that stared me down with the challenge to break the steel gaze first. "Talbott and I decided on a date. Do you want us to run it by you?"

"I'm sure whatever you've picked out will be fine, Lills, you're in charge of my calendar anyway. Just don't double book me," I answered with a playful wink, losing to Amelia in the staring contest of the century, I gave Lilly my attention.

"We were thinking April, when all the trees are budding," she ventured softly.

Seraphina's loud gasp had me chuckling, girls were so funny. "Oh I love that!" Seraphina squealed. "What do you want your dress to look like?"

Lilly's face lit up for the first time I had ever witnessed while the attention was on her. Instead of blushing tomato red and shying away from the spotlight, she rushed into a detailed description about buttons and lace and all-girl-stuff in general.

"Who are you going to have stand up with you?" Seraphina asked next, no doubt wondering what kind of dress she would get to wear too.

"Um, well, you girls, if you want to," Lilly gave each girl at the table a tentative look as if she was afraid they would say no.

I ate my chocolate croissant and sat back to enjoy the show. Girls talking about girl things were always so entertaining. Not that I understood half of what was being said, but still they got excited over the smallest, most insignificant stuff.

"Of course we will!" Seraphina continued to talk in her high pitched squeal and I started to reconsider my previously feelings of goodwill and entertainment. "Eden will of course be your matron of honor, unless that sounds too dowdy for you, then I would gladly step in as your maid of honor."

"No, that's-" Lilly started, but Seraphina was already moving on to something else.

"Will you have any other girls besides us? What about Talbott? Who are your groomsmen?" Seraphina demanded.

"Uh, well Kiran, Jericho, Sebastian and Avalon," Talbott answered obediently.

"So who will be your fourth girl, Lilly?" Eden asked evenly, drawing the excitement level down a few notches. Thankfully.

"I think I'll ask Sylvia. I mean, do you think she would say yes?" Lilly asked, her blush brightening.

"She would love it if you asked her," Eden gushed and I had to agree. The last time I talked to Syl she was dying to visit but didn't have an excuse to leave the hospital. Now she had an excuse.

"That's perfect Lilly," Seraphina confirmed. "And then Amelia doesn't have to dance with Avalon again."

"Seraphina, don't-" Amelia started giving Seraphina a deathly glare at levels of hatred even I hadn't received yet.

"Again?" I asked casually, but my blood had prickled to life and Seraphina had all of my attention. "Why did you say again?"

"I told you he wouldn't remember," Amelia muttered, her cheeks now stained the sexiest color of red. She looked down intently at her breakfast, clearly afraid to meet my eyes.

"You left her standing in the middle of the dance floor, jackass," Seraphina explained, but it didn't really explain anything.

"Our wedding.... the reception.... the dancing?" Kiran prompted, but if truth be told their wedding was a vague memory in my head. I had been trying to handle being the interim King while Kiran and Eden prepared to get married. At the time we didn't want to associate Kiran at all with the crown since we had just killed his father and felt like that might confuse the Kingdom, so I was pretty much doing it all on my own. I was overwhelmed and euphorically happy that we had beat Lucan and freed our people. At the same time I had just lost my parents, several good friends and was finally given time to actually grieve my grandfather. It was the only time in my life where I could honestly admit that I was a bit of an emotional wreck and all I was trying to do was save face and hold it together for Eden and the Kingdom.

Those were not my best days.

So no, the only memory I had of Amelia was a scared child that was too shy to talk to me. She was half the woman she is now and I certainly didn't remember leaving her on the dance floor, or even why I would have asked her to dance to begin with.

"You didn't ask her, Avalon," Eden took pity on me, feeling my confusion. "You were supposed to dance with her since you were both part of the wedding party. She was your partner, we paired you up for the wedding party dance. We rehearsed the whole thing at the rehearsal the night before. You would have been better prepared if you would have attended."

Unbelievable. Eden was still bitter I ditched the rehearsal after all these years. I hadn't seen the point then and I didn't see it now. Except for maybe the whole dancing with Amelia part of it.

Eden shook her head at me as if she was following my inner thoughts. She sent me a nudge of a memory. The outdoor tents, the dance floor, the song immediately following Eden and Kiran's first dance as a married couple....

Oh ok. I nodded, finally understanding while I put the pieces together.

"Really, we don't have to go over this," Amelia muttered. "It was humiliating enough the first time."

"Dancing with me was humiliating?" I asked, turning my sharp gaze on her. Was this why she seemed not able to stand me? Was it something I did at the wedding?

"Except you didn't dance with me!" She suddenly explained all dramatically. I couldn't stop my smile of amusement as she half raised out of her chair and swung her arm dramatically nearly smacking Jericho in the face.

"I didn't?" I laughed at her.

"No you didn't," Kiran laughed too. "Three seconds into the song you smacked Amelia on the arse, and told her to go ahead and finish without you while you walked out of the tent completely."

"I thought you were walking out on my wedding Avalon! It was really disconcerting and you left poor Amelia in the middle of the dance floor all by herself after you had just spanked her on the ass!" Eden laid my offenses out for me when I still didn't seem to get what the big deal was. "You're lucky you came back, brother, or there would have been serious hell to pay." Eden threatened, narrowing her eyes at me.

I sat stunned for a few moments, trying to replay the day in my head. Realization dawned on me when I pictured Angelica's haunted face and how she practically ran from the reception. I had been so worried about Angelica that I really had left Amelia standing there now that I thought about it. And smacking her, that was just to lighten the mood when I knew leaving my sister's wedding was going to cause a huge stir. I slipped back into the reception but after only after a long while and I didn't remember seeing Amelia for the rest of the night. Hell, I hadn't seen Amelia again until a few days ago.

"It was Angelica," I answered their mocking laughter somberly. The look on her grieving face still disturbed me. "I, uh, she.... she left the reception really upset and I was worried about her. I'm sorry Amelia, I wasn't thinking when I left you there. I was just a bit desperate to get to Angelica. I really am sorry," I offered sincerely, looking up from the table to meet her eyes.

She stared back at me like she wasn't sure what to believe, but with my most pathetic and genuine expression I tried to convince her to forgive me.

"Was it really because of Angelica?" she asked, narrowing her eyes into shrewd slits.

"Yes," I half laughed putting my hands up in surrender. "She had just...." I swallowed before finishing, not wanting to show even my closest friends the weakness of my emotions. "She had just glimpsed Eden as she was waiting to walk into the reception and Eden reminded her of my mother. The ceremony had been very painful for her. It was all so soon after.... after everything, that Angelica needed a minute. She composed herself eventually, but I walked her back to the castle anyway. I'm sorry Amelia.... I had to make sure she was Ok."

"Well, damn," Amelia sighed. "I can't fault you for that. Even if you embarrassed me in front of the entire Kingdom." I smiled my most charming smile at her and she shook her head like she already regretted forgiving me. "You may now address me as Mimi," she waved her hand gallantly.

"Not a chance, Amelia," I answered in a husky voice and then I enjoyed watching her shiver from the sound of her name on my tongue.

Yep, this was definitely better than eating breakfast alone.

Chapter Ten

"Excuse me sir," a castle employee entered through the back door of the dining hall. I looked up instinctively. "There is someone here to see you."

"Is it important?" I asked, already feeling the tentacles of regret snaking around my stomach. My eyes flickered to Amelia without my permission, but as soon as we connected she looked immediately away. "Or can it way until I'm finished with my breakfast?"

"It's alright, Avalon," Kiran answered before the butler could. "I'm finished, I'll go."

"Are you sure?" I confirmed, feeling a little bit weird that Kiran kept stepping in front of me to handle the castle business. Maybe he really had missed all the diplomacy.

"I'm sure, really. Enjoy your breakfast," He stood, dropping his napkin on top of his plate and gave Eden a not-for-public-places kind of kiss and then left.

Eden cleared her throat, a little breathlessly after he was gone and I wanted to gouge my eyes out with my spoon.

"I'm finished too, are you ready Jericho?" Amelia asked in an overly bright voice.

"Just about," he answered thoughtfully and then announced to the rest of the table, "Amelia and I are going to do some sightseeing around Transylvania, maybe head back into Sibiu and climb the tower. Anyone care to join us?"

I narrowed my eyes at my best friend trying to figure out his angle. Why was he inviting other people on his date with Amelia? If I were him, I would have gotten her the hell away from this Citadel and every other male alive, and kept her all to myself.

But I wasn't him, which was obvious by the way Amelia's eyes kept darting to me nervously as if she were afraid I would agree to join them. And I was tempted to, seriously tempted to. More tempted than I had ever been to shirk every single one of my duties. But I couldn't justify even chasing after the idea of Amelia while we faced this unknown threat, let alone Amelia herself. I had to focus on keeping the Kingdom safe.

"I'll go," Seraphina piped up. "I don't really have anything else to do since Sebastian left. But Jericho, just so you know, I'm wearing my pink Louboutins and I don't want to hear anything about it. Do you understand me?" She pointed a perfectly manicured finger at him and I had to wonder for the millionth time how Sebastian handled her.

"What is a Louboutin?" Jericho asked nervously.

"It's a shoe," she replied with a practiced pout. "And it's gorgeous and they're brand new and I'm an Immortal so if I say I can hike in stilettos than I can damn well hike in stilettos. Do you understand me?"

By the argument Seraphina was having with herself I wondered if maybe Sebastian wasn't handling her so well after all.

"I believe you," Jericho agreed sincerely.

"Talbott, Lilly, Eden? Do you have some free time?" Jericho pressed. Apparently he was bound and determined to include us all.

"We have a conference call in an hour with Silas and Gabriel about the threat," Talbott explained making it sound like an apology.

"Lilly? Surely you don't have to be part of the call?" Jericho asked.

"I actually have to meet with the staff and cancel some upcoming engagements Avalon was supposed to host. We don't want to invite whoever these people are straight to the castle doors, so we are going to slow down Avalon and Eden's public appearances for a while," Lilly explained sweetly. And even if she couldn't be my wife, I was so grateful to have her in charge of my household. She thought of everything.

"Alright, Avalon, that leaves you, are *you* in?" Jericho asked; his eyes narrowed at me as if defying me to say no. Why did he want me to go so bad? I thought he would want to keep me away from Amelia. I mean, no offense to him or anything but I was pretty challenging competition in the realm of girls.

"I uh-" I started, really struggling to tell him no, when I would like nothing more than to wander around the touristy cities of Romania trying to persuade Amelia I wasn't such a bad guy after all.

But Amelia cut me off and answered for me, "Jericho, I'm sure he has to be part of the call with Sebastian."

I wanted to prove her wrong and explain that Kiran could handle it, but I knew that was irresponsible. Just the fact that she tempted me to turn my head on my responsibilities was enough to hammer in the point that I needed to stay away.

Jericho seemed to sense my struggle, giving me an understanding nod and changing the subject. "I still can't believe that I was in the same village as you and missed this entire conversation," he mused.

"Well, you can be pretty thick-headed at times," I laughed. "And at the time I was having serious, important, life-altering conversations you were off hunting wild beasts."

"And catching nothing," he laughed in return. "It turns out I have terrible aim." I had to wonder if that was for Amelia's vegetarian-minded benefit.

"Hey, Avalon? Can we go for a walk?" Eden asked sweetly.

"Absolutely," I answered, pushing my empty plate forward. I would never tell Eden no, but some quality time with her actually sounded really nice.

We said goodbye to the table of our friends and left the dining room in search of some privacy. It took a lot of people to keep this castle running and different kinds of butlers and maids busied themselves all around us as we walked the spacious hallways quietly. Eden led me through the empty ball room that felt cavernous without anyone in it. Our footsteps echoed off the polished floor and I had no doubt even a whisper would reverberate against the vaulted ceiling. Eden pushed open the balcony sliding glass doors and stepped out on to the long terrace that wrapped around the stone castle and led down into the gardens.

"I've missed you E," I confessed before she could say anything. "I thought after we beat Lucan that you and I would get some quality time together. I mean, I'm happy for you and Kiran and all of that, but it's been nice having you back."

"It's been nice to be back," She smiled at me. "And I missed you too. I wish I could say that we will get some quality time together now, but we both know you aren't going to be able to sit still while there's something threatening the Kingdom." She shook her head at me, and I saw the strong flicker of anxiety in her black eyes.

"Those days are over," I grunted. "You know I can't go off hunting bad guys and leave the throne open for whoever they are to just step in and take over."

"That's why you have us," she counter-argued. "We're here now, so if you need to go Avalon, then go. You don't have to feel tied so this place, because you're not."

"I know that, I know I'm not stuck here. But if we're going to be honest, in a weird way it's started to feel like home."

Eden paused at my words, turning to look out over the gardens that were being bathed in morning sunlight. "I feel the same way. Which doesn't make sense, I know, especially after everything we've been through here.... But there's just something about this place that makes me comfortable, like everyone we lost isn't so far away, like I can be close to them here."

We fell silent again for a few more moments as I quietly agreed with her. But then a thought occurred to me, "Maybe you want me to go? I mean, do you and Kiran want to stay here? Am I in the way?"

"No!" She was quick to assure me. "Absolutely not! There's more than enough room for all of us here. I just thought you might want to get in on the action is all."

"Oh, because I can leave if you want me to. I mean, Kiran seems more than happy to take over the responsibilities and duties here. So if you guys don't need me…." I didn't want to sound pathetic, but after being flooded with sudden insecurities I couldn't help it.

"Avalon, seriously," Eden rolled her eyes at me, and I couldn't help but love how she didn't give into my whining. "Kiran's only stepping in because it's obvious how much you hate this part of the job. He thinks he's doing it for your benefit. Believe me when I say, he doesn't enjoy it any more than you do. But he grew up in it, so I think it comes naturally to him. Plus he's really good at hiding his real emotions…. unlike us." she laughed.

"Ah," I sighed, relieved. I hadn't really been worried that he was going to push me out of my job; I didn't want the crown anyway. Well, not really. But still, there was that warm flood of relief that argued with my reasoning.

"Do you think it will be as bad as last time?" Eden asked in a quiet voice, referencing whatever was ahead of us.

I wanted to lie to her. I wanted to promise her that it would all be fine and that not only would no one get hurt, but that we would stop the threat before it became anything substantial. But I couldn't lie to Eden. I mean, literally I couldn't. She would know if I tried to even soften the truth. Curse the twin bond.

"I don't know what to expect," I answered honestly. "Ileana…. Ileana didn't have any clear details to give me. But from how she talked about them we have legitimate reasons to be afraid, E. These bastards, whoever they are, are dangerous. They're a real threat."

"I was afraid of that," she admitted on a hoarse whisper.

Identical, lasting fear pumped simultaneously through our blood. "It will be Ok, Eden," I promised, knowing I had made this promise before. But last time, it *did* turn out Ok. Granted we went through hell before I could make that promise come true, but it did come true. And even if we went through hell again, I would make sure it came true again.

"It's not even me that I'm worried about, it's you, Avalon. And Kiran, and Talbott and Lilly and every other single person I love that will put themselves right in the middle of all this fighting just to protect our people," she grumbled like we would do it just to piss her off.

"You know you can't save everyone, Eden. We are all in this to protect the freedom of our people. Just because you and I wear a crown doesn't mean that every other one of our friends doesn't feel the same weight of responsibility. We built this thing together, we shed blood, sweat and tears.... together. And we've mourned together. Yes, we have to risk losing those we love, but at least we don't have to go through this alone."

I watched her rub at her navy blue tattoo under her earlobe, it was a nervous habit of hers and it always reminded me that I didn't have a tattoo that glowed. Not that I was short on tattoos.... But today it reminded me of the army we built together.

"Just promise me you'll be careful," Eden demanded and her serious request made me smile.

"You know I'm invincible, E," I laughed.

"No, I don't know that," she snapped, but the tears in her eyes betrayed what real emotions were surfacing. "And you're not. I mean, you're not completely invincible.... You and me, I mean.... there is a way. Amory died."

And the truth of her quiet words rang loudly in the still air.

"Are you worried about Kiran?" I asked, wondering how she would be able to cope if he got pulled into this too. Which was probably inevitable. He wasn't a stand on the sidelines kind of guy.

"Yes," she whimpered, her chin quivering from the effort not to cry. "I just don't know.... I mean, I know with our combined magic and all, I know what his potential should be.... but nobody has gone through this before. Nobody has had to face this. You'll watch out for him, right?"

"Of course, are you kidding me? Nobody's going to hurt him. I mean seriously, if it's between the two of us, he gets to stay around. He's better at the whole king thing anyway," I laughed humorlessly, mainly because it was more truth than a joke.

"Avalon, that's not funny," Eden pouted. "I couldn't make it if something happened to either of you. I mean, I can't lose any more family."

"I agree. And that includes you," I pointed at her sternly. We weren't usually all about the family affection, but facing this gigantic unknown whatever it was had clearly shaken us all up.

We fell silent for a few minutes, just taking in the view and being in the same spot as each other. It seemed like it had been forever since we were even on the same side of the world. As corny as it was, Eden was my best friend, the other half of me and I had missed just being around her. And now we were suddenly facing this problem and I think we both knew that it would take us apart again.

"Is it worth it, Eden?" I asked, surprising her as much as I surprised myself with the question.

"Is what worth it Avalon?" Eden turned to face me, giving me all of her worried attention.

"Caring about somebody during all of this? I mean, is it worth loving Kiran when you could just as easily lose him all over again? We've lost so much.... part of me really believes that I cannot watch someone else I care about die or I will lose my f-ing mind. Is it worth it to fall in love with someone and then have to worry about them when it feels like we will never really have rest... we will never really have peace? And then what if Kiran dies? I couldn't watch you suffer through that."

"Are you asking for me? Or for you?" she asked, her eyes narrowed in thought.

"Just in general," I mumbled, hoping she didn't try to investigate too much further into why I was asking these questions.

"Would you have rather not known Amory than to have loved him and lost him? Or our parents, even though you only knew them for a short time? Or what about me, Avalon? Will you regret knowing me if something happens to me?" Eden asked her questions gently, but they held a real power over me. She was right.

"No...." I admitted reluctantly.

"And when you fall in love with someone, it's not just your feelings involved. But someone loves you too. They are just as worried and anxious about you. They care about your well-being and what happens to you. They are everything you want to be for them." Eden promised and for the first time in my life that actually sounded good. "Do you want to tell me something?"

I opened my mouth to explain and maybe even ask some advice but Kiran interrupted us from the ballroom doors.

"Eden, Avalon, you need to come see this. This threat? It's not so unidentified anymore."

Chapter Eleven

"What is it, Kiran?" Eden gasped when we caught up to him in the hallway. "What's wrong?"

I felt Eden's blood spark alive with concern, and it set my own into a frenzy of boiling electricity. Kiran walked quickly through the halls, his jaw clenched in anger. I struggled with demanding he just tell me what was going on, reminding myself I could be patient. Kiran looked over his shoulder at me, shaking his head in just the slightest way that let me know he couldn't explain whatever it was in the hallway.

Déjà vu hit me strongly from every direction and for a moment I felt completely disoriented. For a moment I was back almost four years ago, and imprisoned inside this very castle. Kiran and I were going through with our plan to sabotage his wedding to Seraphina. I was scheduled to die in a matter of hours and Kiran was determined to sacrifice himself for me. And then suddenly the castle was abuzz with the knowledge that Eden was on her way. Eden showing up last minute at the castle changed so much. But it was the look in Kiran's eyes that reminded me of that moment. The look that said everything we had hoped and planned for had been hijacked and we would be the ones suffering the consequences.

I swallowed against the impatience and walked through the throne room door that Kiran held open for me. Even though the room was not empty, it was completely silent, eerily so. Talbott and a handful of other Titans stood hovering over two individuals slumped into the chairs I usually reserved for my council. The blood had drained from Talbott's face and he was a mixture of rigid attentiveness and careful concern.

Eden gasped, her hand flew to her mouth to stop the torrent of questions I felt bubbling to the surface in her. I didn't blame her. It wasn't just the way Kiran and Talbott were handling the situation without an explanation but it was the individuals themselves. Because of how they were sitting and how awful they looked, I couldn't be sure if they were men or women, or even how old they were. Their heads had been roughly shaved, revealing nicks and small gouges in their badly beaten scalps. They were gaunt and starved, their faces aged in a way that made you positive they were younger than what they looked. They huddled together as if afraid of even the light in the room. They wore ragged clothing that was ripped, torn and covered in blood. Their faces and exposed skin were marred with marks, bruises, cuts and scabs.

These people hadn't just been beaten. These people had been tortured.

But they were Immortal.

And because they were Immortal, if they had been tortured repeatedly, over and over for days, even weeks, their bodies should have healed. I knew this fact intimately because even though I was without magic while imprisoned and my body didn't heal quickly, I witnessed plenty of other Immortals survive Lucan's wrath and recover from it in a matter of hours.

These Immortals were an enigma. They still held their magic, but it lay dormant in their blood. As soon as I was anywhere close enough to feel their electrical current, it felt off.... something felt really wrong. Something was terribly disturbing about them and it had so much more to do with what was running inside of them than their physical appearance, although that was unsettling enough.

"Eden," Kiran began but had to clear his throat before he continued, "Avalon, this is Henri Moreau and Sophie Clement." Kiran introduced them in his flawless French accent and then paused as they lifted their heads to acknowledge his introduction.

Eden gasped when the full damage done to their faces was revealed and I pushed down the bile that rose quickly in my throat. Looking past the swelling and disfigurement caused by torture I could see the softer lines and tilted eyes of Sophie accentuating her feminine features and distinguishing her from Henri's more angular, masculine face. But in front of us were mere ghosts of Immortality.

Kiran continued, "They claim to have escaped a research facility of sorts where they were held after being kidnapped from their homes in Paris."

"What kind of research facility would treat you like this?" Eden asked through thick emotion and watery eyes.

"The kind that tortures and murders Immortals for the sake of an unexplained research project," Kiran spat, completely disgusted. My mind struggled to catch up, to fit pieces of this puzzle together that I was certain I was missing.

"They say it was run by a man who calls himself Terletov," Talbott explained carefully. I watched his jaw tick as he waited for our reaction. "Dmitri Terletov."

"That's not possible," Eden gasped. "I still have his magic.... I watched the Titan Guard take him away. I *still* have his magic," she repeated desperately.

Kiran pulled her into his arms, holding her tightly to him while we all thought this over.

"It was.... Terletov...." Henri lifted his head to confirm our fears. His voice was a whispered rasp as if it hurt to just breathe in the oxygen it would take to speak. "I met him once.... as a child. I remembered.... him."

I sucked in a short breath, trying not to be disgusted by the sound of the hoarse wheezing sounds that came with his effort to talk. I was not a compassionate person. I never had been even through everything we went through before. But these people demanded compassion and heartache. They were so broken, so.... haunted. Even as the effort to understand fell in large chunks of misinformation and was mostly still holes, I felt instinctively how this evil was worse than before.... how unprepared we were to face anything like this.

"And was he.... did he have magic?" I asked gently.

"Yes," Henri rasped out.

"How is that possible?" I asked more to myself than anyone else.

The doors opened and several servants walked into the room. They gasped in unison at the sight of Henri and Sophie, all pausing, not sure what to do next.

"Henri, Sophie," Kiran began, giving the servants a look that said they better do exactly as he asked. I held my tongue, now was not the time to point out his habitual royal snobbishness. "We are going to take you to your rooms, where you will be well cared for. We will talk more later, when you feel up to it."

The two refugees nodded their agreement and struggled to stand, leaning heavily against each other. Titans were there immediately, slipping surprisingly gentle arms around them to aid in their exit. The flurry of servants followed them out and then the room was silent again.

"Talbott, I want you to post two Titans outside each of their bedrooms. For their safety and ours," Kiran ordered.

Talbott gave quick instructions to the remaining Titans and then they too left to fulfill their orders with purpose glinting powerfully in their eyes.

The door opened again and another man walked through, a man I had only seen reflected in Eden's memories. His magic was powerful and swirled around him like a vortex of power, if you got sucked into it you would fall into the unknown and never resurface. His flawless midnight skin reflected depthless eyes and the silky ivory turban wrapped around his head added to his mystery.

"Thank you for coming," Kiran greeted him and it became obvious he had summoned the mysterious man. "There are two Immortals that need serious care. I am not positive of the extent of their injuries, but they are very severe."

"Take me to them," the man commanded and I suddenly realized who this man was. He was who they called "the Witch." Lucan's use of him was merely rumors and gossip until he oversaw the contract that Eden signed when she gave herself over to Kiran.

I realized then that he lived somewhere in the castle and that over the last two and a half years I had not seen him once. Although I didn't really understand his set of skills, so I didn't know why I would have needed to use him, or what I would have used him for.

"I'll take you," Eden offered. "Maybe we can work together. I'm positive this will be like no healing you've ever experienced before."

"Eden, I don't want you anywhere near that magic," Kiran growled in response to her compassion. "We don't know what's wrong with them, where they've actually come from or if they really are refugees or spies sent by Terletov himself."

"First of all, Terletov is dead," Eden snapped back and I was surprised by her defensiveness. She was always so patient and loving with Kiran these days. Her flaring temper reminded me of the little firecracker she used to be, back when Kiran had to prove he loved her and that she loved him back. But I knew, because I could feel it, how responsible she felt for these Immortal's suffering. She felt responsible for Terletov's fate, whether he was dead or alive and if he was alive she felt like she was the one that released this evil against us. "Second of all, I have the power to heal other people. You can't feel their magic. You can't feel how.... unbearably miserable they are. They *need* my help."

"Eden's right," Talbott agreed. "There is something seriously wrong with their magic. It's not right. Whatever happened to them, happened at a molecular level. It's unnatural."

"The Queen will go with me," the Witch announced in a deeply melodic voice. "But neither one of us will try to heal them until we have diagnosed their injuries."

"Fine," Kiran ground out. "But Eden, speak with me before you try anything. Please," he finished on a whisper.

"Alright," Eden consented, her demeanor softening now that she was getting her way. She turned on her heel to follow the Witch from the room.

"Eden," Kiran called out desperately before she could completely leave the room. When he had her attention again he smirked that annoying smile of his and confessed, "I love you."

Relief and a sense of security washed through Eden so strong that I felt it to my core and practically reacted from it. "I love you too," she smiled back at him. "Now let me leave so you and Avalon and Talbott can figure out how to stop this fake Terletov before this happens to anyone else." And then she let the Witch lead her from the throne room.

The brass doors closed and Talbott, Kiran and I were left alone. For the first time today I noticed how empty this room felt without the rest of my council. Angelica was not here, but that wasn't surprising since Silas and Gabriel were off hunting a lead.

"First things first," I started, not wanting to waste another second. "Terletov? What are the chances he is actually alive?"

He's not alive. Eden broke into my consciousness and I realized she was eavesdropping. I couldn't stop the smile that made Talbott look at me like I was crazy. This felt like old times.

"Tell my wife to mind her own business," Kiran said sternly, although I watched his lips twitch like he was trying not to smile. When I gave him a confused look he explained, "You two always have this far-away look on your faces when you're communicating telepathically."

"And here I thought we were so sneaky," I complained.

"Not at all," Kiran laughed. "Tell her."

Your husband wants you to mind your own business and stop eavesdropping. I conveyed to Eden even though I knew she was already aware of what Kiran had said.

How about you just get better at hiding our conversations? Eden replied with a good bit of snark in her mental tone.

Done. But don't you dare get me in trouble later. And I'm talking about Terletov and you can't stop me. I declared, feeling proud of myself for standing up to Eden.

Fine. She grumbled, but then I felt her attention get pulled away as she entered one of the refugee's rooms with the Witch.

"I don't trust you two," Kiran narrowed his eyes at me.

"Uh, she's with one of them now," I answered honestly, feeling my own attention wanting to be pulled into the room with Eden. I forced myself to get out of her head and focus on Talbott and Kiran. Eden would save the problem, but we were the ones who needed to solve it and it would do nobody any good if I wasn't here one hundred percent.

"Alright," Kiran nodded, satisfied with my answer. "Talbott what are the chances Terletov is not dead?"

Talbott thought it over for a minute. I watched the wheels in his head turn as he thought carefully over whatever he was about to say.

"There is a chance," he finally admitted. He looked at Kiran first and then directly at me, his dark brown eyes a steely cage of anger. "I did not witness his execution, although the Titan Guard was informed that it happened. And he was not among the prisoners that I released the night of the final battle. In fact, there were no actual criminals in the prisons that night; only captured Resistance members."

I thought about that for a minute and wondered if that was strange. I had not thought about the phenomenon that the prisons were empty of criminals completely until just now. Talbott released everyone from underground before Eden went down and destroyed the dungeons. I had to wonder if there were criminals down there, if Talbott would have released them or kept them locked up; but now I realized the decision had been taken from him, I had to wonder if it was by design.

"Hmmm," Kiran mused and my suspicions were confirmed. "If I remember correctly, there were four other men with Terletov from that Latvian farm?" Talbott nodded his affirmation and Kiran finished. "Were you told they were all executed or just Terletov?"

"Just Terletov," Talbott answered.

"But it's possible my father did not have him killed, isn't it?" Kiran pressed, looking for an answer to a question that would only make more questions.

"It is possible, but I don't know why he wouldn't. Terletov was planning a Rebellion of his own, and he had kidnapped Eden right from under your father's nose," Talbott explained, his accent thick and tainted with frustration.

I chomped down on my thumb nail taking in every detail of the conversation and dredging up my own memories of that time.

"Ok, let's assume we are operating with the truth and that these are not spies. That means that either Terletov escaped this Citadel and Lucan either didn't know or didn't want to admit that it happened again.... or it means that Lucan let him go," I deduced, realizing there were at least a hundred other possible scenarios.

"Alright, so going under the assumption that this is actually Terletov.... then that means what?" Kiran continued. "He is after the throne. And he has absolutely no respect for Immortals."

"He only cares about the power," I agreed.

Avalon. Eden interrupted. *This is not their magic.... He took their magic and replaced it with something else and now what's inside of them.... it's fighting to get out. It's killing them.*

I coughed on disgust and revulsion, trying to process Eden's explanation. *How did he do that?*

From what they've explained.... By experiments. Avalon, bring Kiran up here, you need to see this. Eden demanded.

A chill of fear slithered down my spine. I nodded my head toward the door, and turned around to find Eden. Talbott and Kiran had fallen silent when they noticed I was talking to Eden again and followed without question.

The electricity in my blood felt close to boiling over as I prepared myself for the interrogation to come. Nothing made sense yet, except that Ileana had been right. Experiments? Only one minute ago I had been convinced that Lucan was the worst evil this people had ever seen.

But I had been wrong.

Chapter Twelve

The acrid smell of rotting flesh washed over us in unwelcome waves as we entered the guest room where Henri had been placed. I used magic to settle my gag reflexes and moved to the side of the bed where Eden sat holding Henri's hand and whispering soothing things in a quiet voice.

Kiran immediately moved behind Eden to put comforting hands on her shoulders while Talbott hung back against the far wall assessing the situation with his military paranoia. I noticed then how still the room had become. There were no servants running around trying to take care of this man, and even the Witch had disappeared, although I suspected he was with Sophie. I wondered what I missed in the few minutes we had been apart, and then wonder turned to worry when a lone tear slipped out of the corner of Eden's eye.

I cleared my throat, realizing I was about to be very insensitive, but suddenly feeling pressed for time. "Tell us what happened," I ordered as gently as I could. "Were you released or did you escape?"

Henri's eyes were overly large and deathly hallow on his gaunt face, and when he opened his mouth to speak his breath smelled sour and his lungs rattled with the effort to survive, gurgling and rasping deep in his chest. "He.... let us go.... No reason.... to keep us," his sentences were broken and each word was a struggle to put sound to. "We.... are.... dead...."

"But why?" I choked on the words. "Why did he do this to you?"

"Used.... to be.... Shape-Shifters..... Not any.... more," he answered and the sickening truth to his words rang out in the stillness of the room.

"And you're sure it was Terletov?" Kiran asked gently, his voice weak and full of compassion.

Henri gave the slightest nod, affirming our fears. "There were.... more. Not.... all.... Shifters.... No one es-" he trailed off, his eyes fluttering with the determination not to close. "escapes.... He took us to.... Siberia.... to the old.... Titans...." he trailed off, not able to finish his sentence and I realized our time was out.

"What does he want? Why did he do this to you?" I asked quickly, desperately.

Instead of answering my questions verbally, Henri lifted a long, boney finger just barely from where it rested on the bed. He pointed to me, to the center of my chest, before his finger moved slowly, painstakingly slowly upward where the crown I inherited with this job sat lopsided on my head.

My eyes were glued to his finger as it started trembling with the struggle to stay elevated. And when it dropped to the bedspread in defeat I knew this was the end of his interrogation. It was the end of him.

My eyes stayed on his limp hand in what felt like giving him his last bit of dignity. His chest heaved with one more painful, raspy breath and then the magical current both giving him life and fighting to take it disappeared from the room.

The air and magic whooshed from his body in a breathy sound that smelled worse than death. I lifted my gaze from his finger just in time to watch his chest collapse into itself, leaving his body a concave, defeated shell.

Eden let out a shuddering breath before her tears fell in hot streams of grief onto her cheeks. Kiran picked up her hand and then pulled her to him. None of us knew Henri to grieve him the person that he was, or the life that he lived. But his death was unnatural and even more than that it was traumatic, even for me. And I would always feel responsible and mourn what happened to him.

How could this be going on in my Kingdom? Right under my nose and without me knowing *anything* about it?

Before my brain could catch up with the raw, scraping emotion of anger I my crown into my hands and threw it as hard as I could against the stone wall. It hit with a force strong enough to break apart the surface stone and send the piece of gold clattering to the ground unharmed. For some reason the wall being damaged but not the crown infuriated me even more and a guttural growl shook my chest and burned my lungs.

"Avalon," Eden gasped, tearing from her husband's arms to throw hers around me. She shook against me, her tears wetting my t-shirt and her compassion infusing my anger.

I took a shaky breath, trying to calm the naked nerve endings that felt tortured by the boiling magic inside of me. "I apologize," I offered insincerely to the room at large.

"You are all dismissed," Kiran nodded wearily at the rest of the room that scurried past the Witch who stood in the doorway now, a sign that Sophie had passed away too.

I eyed the crown that lay defeated on the ground, wishing it was in my hands so I could throw it again.

"This shouldn't have happened," I growled. "Not while I am King.... Not while I lost nearly everyone I loved to stop this kind of sickness."

"Avalon it's not your fault. I should have been able to heal him, I should have been able to save him," Eden confessed, her tears renewed. I felt the waves of guilt and self-recrimination move through her.

"It's certainly not your fault, Eden," I all but threatened. "Don't start that. You can't blame yourself."

Kiran pulled her to him again when my words sunk in and he leaned down to whisper in her ear, words that I couldn't hear but I felt her relax a little against him.

"It will do no good to blame yourselves," the Witch spoke patiently to us all. "The only thing that will solve this injustice is retribution."

"He's right," Talbott agreed, walking to look out the windows into the courtyard.

Just then Talbott's pocket chirped and he pulled out a ringing phone. Talbott looked at the cell phone screen before answering it and then touched the speaker phone button. Kiran nodded for the Witch to close the door behind him and the mysterious man obeyed.

"Gabriel, tell me you have something," Talbott demanded.

"We have something but it's not much," Gabriel replied in his Spanish accent, his voice sounding far off and obstructed by background noise. "Terletov's farm is deserted. There hasn't been anyone here in years. The buildings are run down and the house has been vandalized. What's strange is that it looks like the house was packed up in a hurry. If Lucan ordered the Titans to clear the house, they would have done a better job; they wouldn't have left anything behind. Whoever cleared out of this house did it fast and took only what they needed. Looters have taken everything that was valuable, and what is left behind is unimportant."

"Are there any leads? Where they might have gone? Or evidence that Terletov is still alive?" I demanded, speaking loud enough so Gabriel could hear me.

"Nothing like that here, this farm was a dead end," Gabriel answered honestly. "But Silas has asked around and it turns out Dmitri had a younger brother, Alexi, who lives in Zurich. We're going to pay him a visit and see what we can find out."

A small, almost miniscule prickle of relief nudged at the back of my neck. They had something; they had a next step, a purpose. We weren't completely at a dead end.

"Gabriel, Talbott is going to debrief you on what just happened here. I will be in touch with you shortly," I announced and then strode out of the room, past the Witch and the cluster of Titans standing in the hallway awaiting orders.

"Avalon, what are you planning to do?" Kiran matched my long strides with his own, his jaw set and his hands clenched into fists at his side.

"I'm going to Siberia," I said without missing a step.

"By yourself?" he ground out, and I didn't have to be magic to feel how badly he wanted to join me.

"No, I'll assemble a team," I said carefully, knowing without a doubt he would not be included on it. I made a promise to Eden and I intended to keep it. Besides, someone had to run this place. "Jericho will be more than happy to go with me and I'm sure I can dig up Xander and Xavier.... maybe even Titus."

He opened his mouth to say something so I quickly moved on, "You and Eden can run things for a while, right?" I threw in my sister's name reminding him of his responsibilities. When he nodded like it was painful to agree with me, I knew I had made my point clear. "Good. Siberia is where the Titans trained for a while, isn't it?"

Now that it was clear Kiran would have to stay behind, I felt more at ease discussing details of the mission with him. I couldn't blame him for wanting to go with me, for wanting to hunt down Terletov and deliver a righteous reckoning, but I wouldn't risk something happening to Kiran. I wouldn't risk making my sister's nightmares come true. She deserved peace of mind and I was bound and determined to give it to her.

"Yes, they used it during and after World War II, while most of this part of the world was occupied with war. They didn't move back to the Romanian Citadel until after the fall of Communism in the eighties," Kiran sighed, clearly unhappy with his resignation to stay behind.

"What happened to the training facility after they moved back here?" I asked before biting down on my thumb nail.

"A small group of Titans was left to maintain the property and look after it, but other than that it was abandoned," Kiran explained.

"Have you checked on the facility or with the Titans who stayed there since we took over?" I asked, careful not to sound like I was accusing him of anything.

"It was one of the first places we stopped on our honeymoon," Kiran explained and I felt another prick of relief. At least we hadn't been completely negligent. "I knew that since they would be hearing of my father's death second hand I should stop in and prove that I was in charge and that they still answered to someone. The property was a bit rundown and the Titans that kept it were all older generation and a bit rundown themselves. But everything looked and felt fine. Everything but their housing was empty and I would have pulled the Titans from that post all together, but they were proud of their work and had built a life there. I didn't see the point."

"Alright, show me where this training facility is on a map. I'll leave tonight," I announced, confident that we were on the right track, even if we were a few steps behind. I would catch us up. That's what I did. This was what I had been born and raised to do. I was finally back in my element, even though it was under the worst circumstances possible. Even through the desperation, I felt to find this son of a bitch and make him pay for his sins, this was familiar territory to me. I could turn my rage and hatred into action and accomplishment.

And even though I couldn't think about what happened to Henri and Sophie without nearly choking on intended wrath, I could feel the relief of finally identifying the threat, of finally being able to put a game plan together and start to act.

The peace and safety of my Kingdom came first.

Always.

This was the destiny that Gabriel was always going on about. I wasn't good at sitting still and governing menial issues. But I was good at this. I was good at fighting.

And Terletov had no idea just how good I was.

Not yet.

Kiran led me toward a planning room I had rarely used for lack of reason. My blood had already ignited into a frenzied boil of anticipation and adrenaline. I started making a mental list of everything I needed to do. I wouldn't waste time, I would leave tonight. Tomorrow morning at the latest. I needed to call the old team back together and have them meet me en route. As long as no one had gone and fallen in love or somehow tied themselves down, I knew they would be just as anxious as me to jump back into the action.

Maybe I should even call Roxie, I didn't need to bet that she was bored out of her mind.

This time around I wouldn't involve those married couples, especially the ones with children. But my single, unattached friends had spent plenty of time in the field and were probably restless with the everyday monotony of life.

As my magic snapped and popped around me in an anxious cloud of readiness, I prepared my mind too. There were plenty of things I wasn't primed for. And I wasn't delusional enough to deny that this wouldn't be hard and I wouldn't be rusty.

But the prospect of leaving this Citadel with a mission on the horizon made me the most alive I had felt in a long time.

Chapter Thirteen

Silence.

Finally.

The day had been spent in all kinds of preparations to leave. With Kiran here, I didn't think it would be a big deal if I just slipped out for a bit to go chase down Terletov and kill the bastard. But apparently it was a very big deal.

Or Angelica was making it one because she didn't want me to go.

And then Talbott jumped in the argument to complicate matters, demanding to know why I didn't want to use the trained Titan Guard when they were at my complete disposal. He didn't take it too well when I explained that the main reason I wasn't taking them was because I honestly hadn't thought about using them.

They had been enslaved by birth, made soldiers because they were born a Titan and not because of any personal desire to serve the Crown. Even though most of them had been soldiers long enough to be completely dedicated and gladly lay down their life for the cause of this crown, I couldn't in good faith ask them to sacrifice their lives for me for any reason.

Plus, and this was splitting hairs, I didn't trust them to perform at their maximum potential in this kind of environment. The rest of the Titans were theoretically trained in covert ops, but had never needed to use their training in real life. I trusted my team over them. Plain and simple

And then there was that.

I had been on a team once. I had trusted men and women with my life and they felt the same toward me. I could have assembled a Titan team that didn't let me do any of the dirty work and reacted to my every order. Or I could assemble the only people in this world I trusted with my life more than myself, other than Eden of course. The same people that knew exactly how I operated a mission, who took orders from me while complaining and questioning my every decision and the same people I missed deeply.

Although I would never admit it to them.

Or maybe I would.

So I had called them all, interrupted their life-after-war lives and asked them to join me in this endeavor for justice. Titus, Xander, Xavier, Jericho and Roxie were more than willing to meet up with me in Moscow before we headed deep into Siberia for this mission.

Despite the ugly circumstances, it was hard not to get anxious for this mission.

Which was why I had come out here to think things through. I didn't want to just get caught up in being back on the field and mess things up. I enjoyed the idea of getting out of the castle, and I realized how important it was for me to find a freaking activity to occupy my time when we were back to peace, but right now I needed to focus and put this guy down. He kidnapped my sister, and now he was experimenting on my people. Words could not accurately describe how much I wanted to end this guy's life.

The full moon shone down on the dying garden around me, as I sat alone in the middle of the overgrown maze. The leaves had started to fall off the chaotic bushes, leaving jagged, sharp branches sticking out into every path and twisting toward the sky in an effort to find freedom. I sat on a stone bench, tucked away in a little alcove and closed my eyes. I thought through the next few days like professional athletes thought through their next match, visualizing every step, every move, every possibility.

I couldn't predict everything. Or anything really....

But I could visualize my own actions, my own reactions to every possible scenario and emotion. If conditions were far worse than I could possibly imagine, I would be ready. If we were headed into a trap, I would be ready. And if this led to a dead end, I would be ready.

This was a ritual I had performed countless times and it helped slow the riotous nerves that were pounding inside my veins and causing my heart to beat desperately trying to break free from the prison of my body. I vaguely wondered if I shouldn't head off into the wilderness and practice some of my old familiar steps and offensive and defensive moves, when another magic approaching made my senses flare to life.

I opened my eyes just in time to catch Amelia trying to turn back the other way without me noticing her. Not a chance.

"Amelia?" I laughed, hoping to make her feel a little bit awkward for trying to avoid me. "What are you doing?"

She paused with her back to me, her shoulders frozen scrunched up around her neck like she had been tip-toeing out of here old-cartoon-style. I heard her take a deep breath and then watched as she relaxed her shoulders while she exhaled. She turned around quickly, her dark hair flipping around with her. She gave me a sheepish grin that proved how embarrassed she was to be caught, but all I saw was how the full moon lit up the air around her, shining on the prettiest features of her face and bathing her in a seductive light.

"I was uh.... I just wanted walk. I mean, take a walk. I wanted to take a walk. I'm leaving in the morning, there is this conference thing in Kenya that I'm meeting my mom at and I needed to walk through the gardens," she cringed when it was clear she wasn't making sense and I bit down on my thumbnail to keep from laughing at how adorable she was all flustered and blushing. "I love these gardens and I hadn't had a chance to walk through them yet. That's what I was doing, just checking on the gardens." She breathed more evenly when her sentences started making sense.

"Would you like some company?" I asked, giving her one of my best hopeful looks, one that I knew for a fact worked on every girl.

"Oh, no, that's fine. You sit. Here. Stay," she cleared her throat and offered me an apologetic smile. "I mean, you're not a dog.... Uh, do whatever you want to do, but you just look like you're busy."

I laughed at her effort to get out of walking with me, and decided I couldn't give up. Her cheeks were the sweetest shade of red and her golden brown eyes were shimmering with nerves. There was no way in hell I was giving this up now.

"I look busy sitting here on this bench all alone?" I pressed, making her squirm uncomfortably, her hands twisted together in front of her.

"Yes, very busy," she confirmed quietly.

"Well, I'm not," I stood up so that I could take a step closer to her. "Busy that is." The air around her was intoxicated with her scent, vanilla and lilacs and beauty. She looked up at me while I towered over her and I had the strongest urge to pull her against me and kiss her senseless. I couldn't kiss her just yet, she needed to be aware that she wanted to kiss me and I wasn't entirely convinced she was ready to admit the strong attraction between us to herself yet. So instead of kissing those perfect red lips, I did the next best thing. I made my intentions as clear as I could, "Would you like to take a walk with me, Amelia?" I dipped my head so that our mouths were only inches apart and heard her audibly gasp as I completely invaded her personal space.

"I, um.... sure," she resigned and I didn't miss the small sound of disappointment in her voice.

Maybe this attraction was only one sided after all.

Damn.

I turned so that we were standing side by side and started walking into the maze of towering bushes. I had to hold several branches out of the way in order to stay side by side with her, but it was a small price to pay. Besides every time there was a branch, it gave me an excuse to brush up against her, our bare arms pressing against each other and her perfect head of hair just barely reaching underneath my chin. Touching Amelia was quickly becoming something of an addiction for me.

"Tell me what's in Kenya, Amelia," I demanded gently, not wanting to give her an option to refuse to answer.

"Mimi," she corrected, softly pleading with me. I nodded my head, but knew there was no way I would call her by a nickname when I loved the sound of her full name hanging in the tension between us. "I'm meeting my mom for a conference on AIDS."

"Ah," I nodded my head, but suddenly I was really against Amelia gallivanting off to the middle of Africa. "Do you think that's a good idea right now?" I tried to question her decision casually, as if I didn't really want to use my power as King to order her to stay home.

Even though I did.

"Why wouldn't it be a good idea?" She asked and then thankfully reason dawned on her. "Oh, because of the whole Terletov thing?"

'Yes," I chuckled at her indifference. "Because of the whole.... Terletov thing."

"Avalon, we'll be fine," she assured me with a roll of her eyes, which actually didn't assure me at all. "It's just Kenya. And we'll only be there for two weeks or so."

"I thought Kiran debriefed the entire castle, did he not make it clear just how dangerous this guy is?" I demanded a little sharply.

"Please," she snorted. "Kiran made it perfectly clear how dangerous Terletov is, but that doesn't mean I can spend my time hiding away until someone finds him," she reasoned obnoxiously. "I have commitments and scheduled engagements that actually means something to other people. My work with humanity is important, Avalon," she finished sincerely.

I looked over at her, and saw the authenticity in her eyes, the depth of her compassion. I couldn't deny her that. I couldn't tell her to stop her work just because I was irrationally and unsubstantially worried about her. Besides it wasn't my place to be worried about her, she had made that abundantly clear.

"At least let me send a few of my Guard with you. It would make me feel so much better," I offered and then knew I had to play a card I not only resented, but knew she would to. "Please, as your King, I need to know that all my people are as safe as they can be. I need you to be responsible."

"Oh, I see. The King is worried about my safety," Amelia nodded patronizingly. "And is this the same King that plans to hunt down Terletov himself?"

"Why yes it is," I nodded, hoping to have made some progress with my side of the debate.

"How is that fair? You rule an entire Kingdom, but you're allowed to put yourself right in the middle of the drama?" I opened my mouth to respond, but Amelia shook her head at me and continued with her rant. "What if something happened to you? How is hunting down bad guys responsible of *you*? I'm just attending a conference. You are putting yourself directly in the line of fire. If anyone needs to be surrounded by a bunch of Titan Guards it's you, not me."

"It might not be fair, but it's the way things are. And because I rule an entire Kingdom, I'm the one that gets to make these decisions," I argued, but when she looked at me like I was the biggest asshole on the planet I decided to explain further, to say out loud words I hadn't even verbalized to Eden yet. "I have to go, Amelia. He's threatening my people and the freedom I worked my ass off to give to these people," I clarified with a passionate but infinitely softer voice. "I have been bombarded over the last eight hours with opinions on how foolish I am for going. Everyone loves to give me their opinion on what a king should do and how a king should act. But what they don't understand is that the crown means nothing to me, less than nothing actually. It is the freedom that my people enjoy for the first time in thousands of years that keeps me where I'm at, that made me give up my own personal freedom so that they feel safe. And I would give it all up, all of this wealth and power; I would sacrifice everything, even my own life if I needed to, just to ensure that they stay free."

"Oh," Amelia looked up at me with wide eyes and I realized that I stopped walking.

And that she stayed.

"Yes, the people need freedom, but they also need you Avalon," she practically whispered and I felt her words burning in my core. She was right. But it was more complicated than that. "You're their King. The first King in our history that has let them live their lives without governing each and every little detail."

"That's not true, they have Eden and Kiran," I countered, searching her eyes for where her argument was coming from. Did she say these things because she actually cared about me? Or was she just compassionate enough to be tapped into the pulse of the Kingdom?

"They're not the same and you know that. Besides they haven't even been around these last few years. Why you? Why does it have to be you that goes?" She demanded.

And because her eyes had turned steely with her demands and her lips had pursed into a frown, because she wasn't going to accept any kind of bullshit answer and because for the first time ever I wanted to be honest with a girl that wasn't my sister, I was, I was completely honest.

"Because I'm afraid to stay," I whispered, scared if I said it too loud even the trees would laugh at me.

"You? You're afraid of something?" Amelia gasped, clearly disbelieving.

I laughed humorlessly, hardly believing I just admitted that out loud. But I was too far into this to stop now. "Yes! I'm terrified of staying here. I'm terrified that I'm going to live forever and at twenty-one years old I'm already bored to death! I don't get to die. I have this whole future laid out for eternity and I'm terrified I am going to have to suffer through it bored and alone.... And I'm even more afraid that I'm addicted to this dangerous lifestyle and what that will mean for me if I really can keep my promise of peace. I *have* to go on this mission. I have to sort through all the bullshit in my head and find myself again. Because I cannot stay here any longer and endure this monotony while other people go and fight my battles."

I finished with a huge breath of relief, exhaling all of the pent up craziness that had been stewing inside me for way to long.

Amelia just looked at me for a long time as if trying to figure out whether I was telling the truth or not. I could have promised her it was the most honest I had been in my entire life, but I decided to let her come to her own conclusions.

"They won't understand that," she answered sadly. "They won't want you to go."

I ignored her and asked my own question.

"What do you want, Amelia?" I looked down at her, silently demanding that her eyes meet mine. I was rewarded with an intense gaze that saw all the way through me. She had come to her own conclusions about me and for the first time since she walked back into my life I began to hope that whatever this was that I felt was not so one-sided.

"Avalon, you should not call me Amelia," she practically begged. My eyes drifted to the sexy lines of her throat as she visibly swallowed.

I took a step closer to her, our bodies nearly touching. "What do you want, Amelia?" my voice dropped to a lower timber that rumbled in the air between us and not completely on purpose, but I was readying myself for a whole new kind of battle and I wanted to be as prepared as I could.

Instead of answering, she turned her head away from me and said, "Is it weird that coming back here is like coming home? I thought it would feel weird after.... everything, but I can't help it. It's like this place knows me better than I know myself."

Her voice was light and meant to be distracting. And after she finished talking she moved like she was going to continue with our walk. But it was those words that made me reach out to her, those words that I had berated myself over countless times in the last three years. It was those words, spoken by her at this perfect moment that made me take her by the arm and pull her back to me.

I placed both of my hands on her arms like I was holding her in place, but my grip was loose so that if she wanted to walk away she could. I stared down at her and watched as her expression turned from surprise to confusion to dark with the same desire I felt heating my blood and spinning my mind.

Her lips parted as if she was going to talk me out of this, but my body was three steps ahead of my mind and I covered her mouth with mine before I could talk myself out of it.

She let out a squeak of surprise as I pressed my lips against the softness of hers. She practically melted into me, her body going limp in my arms, her head tilted up so she could reach me better. I dropped my hands from her arms to her waist and pulled her flush against me. She responded by slipping her arms around my neck and pulling me down to her. Her body fit mine like it was designed for me, like we were two pieces of a puzzle and only when we were together did we make sense.... only then were we complete.

I slid my tongue along her plump bottom lip and she opened her mouth for a deeper kiss. I held back a moan of approval not wanting to scare her, but this was the best kiss of my life. I pulled her closer to me, not satisfied with even a breath of space separating us. She wiggled against me and my head became completely fuzzy with the need for her.

Before this kiss I had felt an undeniable attraction to her, a need to get to know her better and maybe even a hope in what could be between us; but with her pressed against me and my mouth claiming hers, an overwhelming sense of protectiveness and possession unfurled inside of me. It was slow at first, as if just awakening and then it flooded my veins in a rampant attempt to control me. I wanted Amelia to be mine. And even if I didn't completely understand what that meant yet, I knew I didn't want her kissing anyone else like this. These lips were meant for me only, her perfect little body only meant to press so seductively against mine.

Our kiss grew more frenzied with each revelation that passed through my mind. I chased her tongue with mine, hungry to claim her. One of her hands tangled in my hair, the other tight against the back of my neck. She was as desperate as I was, her breathing labored as her chest heaved against my own.

I could easily have let this kiss get carried away.

But this was Amelia.

My Amelia.

And so I slowed the kiss down. Instead of fiercely ravenous, I kissed her gently and carefully. Treating her perfect lips with the reverence they deserved.

She was the first to break away. And somehow I always knew that she would be, because I could have stood their kissing her forever.

"Avalon," she gasped and I smiled at the way my name sounded caressed by her.

"Amelia," I whispered, smiling down at her. I relinquished my hold on her so I could cup her delicate face in my hands. I had so much to confess to her, I just hoped I didn't scare her with my-

"We can't do that ever again," she announced in a rush of words.

"Why not?" I demanded, realizing it wasn't probably the first question I should be asking, but it was definitely the answer I wanted most.

"Because.... because of Jericho," she was nodding her head almost frantically, her hands pulling at my hands to gain more space between us and it took me a while to come to my full senses again.

"Because of Jericho?" I asked, still very confused, my mind struggling against an equal haze of lust and longing.

"Of course because of Jericho," she replied more confidently, taking a full step back from me.

It took everything in me, every single ounce of will power and maturity not to pull her right back to her puzzle piece spot. She belonged next to me, my body told me that, my mind told me that.... even the heart that I thought was dead to things like this told me that.

"We'll just talk to him, explain the situation," I reasoned, still hoping that I wasn't the only one feeling anything between us.

"Uh, that won't do any good. In fact, it will only cause more problems. A lot more problems," she started glancing around nervously and I started to doubt everything. I knew they were hanging out, but I had no idea they were so close. "I need to go," she said firmly as if I were telling her not to.

And at that point I couldn't even argue with her.

Maybe she really did have to go.

I watched her disappear into the darkness of the gardens in a hurry to get away from me and wondered how in the hell I had screwed things up so bad. I knew there would come a time when I would have to face Jericho and explain my side of the story, but right now the only thoughts in my head were mourning the loss of Amelia. And there were plenty of those thoughts. They invaded every thought and blood vessel, I felt her absence so strong it was painful to my bones. And not just the kissing, it was that she wasn't with me anymore, not by my side, not fitted against me.

I needed to figure this out.

And then I needed to ask Jericho what his intentions were. Because if they weren't absolutely certain with this girl, then I was prepared to fight for her as fiercely as I fought for this crown.

Only with Amelia, I knew that once I had her, I would never regret a single day after that.

Chapter Fourteen

"Avalon, seriously, you're doing it again," Jericho kicked me in the shin from across the aisle. "Stop glaring at me. I'm not Terletov."

"Sorry," I mumbled, realizing I *had* been glaring at him. I had been glaring at him since we left the Citadel early this morning. "I'm just ready to get there, you know?"

Which was true. I was more than ready to get off this train with Jericho and meet up with the rest of our team before I did or said something that was absolutely crazy.

"Yeah, I know what you mean," Jericho agreed. "I'm just as anxious to get this son of a bitch. And get back into some action." He gave me a cocky grin, probably expecting me to agree. Which I did, but I was still holding a completely irrational grudge against him so I just nodded.

"Sure," I mumbled and then my mouth threw up verbal diarrhea all over him. "But isn't that hard on Amelia?"

Jericho paused for a good thirty seconds before he answered, "Amelia? Why would it be hard on her?" He gave me the funniest look like he had no idea what I was talking about which pissed me off even more. He should be concerned about leaving her; he should at least hate it as much as I did. No. He should hate it more because he knew what it was like to have her worried about him, to have her think about him. How could he even think about leaving her and those amazing kisses behind? I was glaring again and Jericho was looking at me like he was uncomfortable with where this conversation was going.

Good.

"Yeah, it's got to be hard on her with all of us gone," I stated with a pointed look.

"Uh, sure, I guess," Jericho relaxed a little, probably deciding that I was just out of my mind. Which I was starting to wonder about too. "She's probably worried about Sebastian I guess...."

"You guys are cute though," I grunted, barely listening to his responses.

"We're.... cute? Avalon are you serious?" Jericho laughed incredibly. "What makes us cute?"

I cleared my throat and leveled my eyes with him. I didn't really know what I meant by calling him cute, it wasn't a word I threw around all that often, but I had said it so now I had to defend it. "You know, always going off together, sight-seeing and what not. You're *cute*," I finished, proud of my argument. My temper was slowly rising beneath my skin and I hated that a girl had come between Jericho and me, especially a girl that had clearly made her choice.

But for the life of me I couldn't seem to get over her.

Jericho snorted and then gave me a weirded-out look, "Sure, we're *cute*. What's wrong with you?"

"What's wrong with me? What's wrong with you?" I snapped, looking around the private passenger car of the train that was chugging through Russia. The autumn tainted countryside flashed by our window quickly, and the dark gray sky above threatened rain. "I shouldn't have let you come. Amelia will be heartbroken if something happens to you, and you're just dumb enough to let something happen to you."

"Dumb enough?" Jericho shook his head in disbelief at me, but I couldn't even look at him anymore. I was way too pissed.

And then I opened my mouth, knowing what I said next was going to earn me a punch in the face.

"Jericho, I kissed her." I forced myself to look him in the eye with my confession; although once I stared him down I realized it wasn't so hard after all. I was very much up for this challenge.

"Kissed who?" Jericho practically choked on his confusion.

"Amelia, I kissed her last night. And she kissed me back. And I'm pretty sure she liked it, but to be fair I was the one that initiated it," I declared, trying not to be proud of my actions, especially because it would kill Jericho if I stole his girlfriend and it really couldn't feel good to know his best friend who happened to also be King was after her in the first place, especially considering that she was obviously not all that faithful to him.

"Uh, that's great man." Jericho stammered.

And suddenly I felt really bad for him. Damn it. I had made this into a competition and he had already conceded the victory to me. I was an asshole. Even though I wasn't willing to step away from Amelia, our friendship was still important and I didn't have any right rubbing it in his face.

"Listen, man, I'm sorry," I apologized sincerely. "I should never have kissed your girlfriend. It wasn't right. But honestly, at the time I didn't know you guys were together. I mean, I maybe thought you liked her, but I swear I didn't know you had made it official."

"Wait, what?" If possible Jericho looked even more confused.

"What?" I asked back, feeling his confusion spreading to me.

"Amelia and I aren't together," he stated plainly. "And I could care less if you kissed her. Actually, it's probably a good thing that you kissed her."

"Wait... what?" I echoed his confusion earlier.

"Amelia and I are not a couple," Jericho explained very slowly. "I don't know what made you think that we were, but honestly, Avalon, I don't like her like that. We're friends and all, but I'm not interested in anything more with her."

Well, I felt like an idiot.

"Seriously?" I asked, because it was hard for me to believe that any guy could not fall for her, even if it was just a little bit. "You guys are not together?"

"Nope," Jericho confirmed and I relaxed into my seat feeling a huge sense of relief. "What made you think that we were?"

"*She* made me think that you were," I grumbled, the sense of relief gone, replaced with cold rejection. "She told me she couldn't kiss me because of you!"

"She said we were a couple?" Jericho asked in disbelief.

"No, not exactly, but she said we shouldn't kiss and when I asked why, she said it was because of you. I mean, she just made it seem that.... I don't know dude, that girl is an enigma." I finished, feeling defeated.

Jericho laughed out loud and I couldn't help but feel like he was laughing at me. "I don't know why she told you that, or why she said she didn't want to kiss you. I'm pretty sure that girl has had a huge crush on you for years. That makes no sense to me."

"Wait.... what?" I asked. Again.

"Ok, all I know is that at Eden and Kiran's wedding she was seriously hung up on you," Jericho gave a smug smile as I sat dumbfounded across from him.

"She was into me?" I clarified, trying to remember when we had even talked outside of the smacking her on the ass thing.

"Yes, she liked you. And I was pretty convinced things hadn't changed by all the sexy glances you two have been throwing each other." Jericho's tone was mocking and if there wasn't an aisle between us I probably would have hit him. "But if she didn't want to kiss you, maybe she is over you."

"This makes no sense," I complained. "If she wasn't interested in me, why didn't she just say that? Why did she use you as an excuse?"

"I don't know, maybe she really does like me. But honestly, I only get the feeling of friends between us. I mean, we've hung out some over the past few years and there has been no attraction between us. And I didn't feel anything change in the last couple of days, but I don't know, I'm not really good at reading girls." Jericho finished seriously. "I honestly don't think she's into me though. I really thought there was something between you two, but I expected you just to brush it off or mess it up or something."

He shrugged his shoulder as if this was the most insignificant conversation ever, while my head spun out of control.

If he had seen something between us, then I wasn't the only one. I wasn't delusional. There was something there.

But if Jericho wasn't an actual reason for Amelia to push me away, then what was the reason? And why was she using my best friend to stop me?

And when the hell would I see her again so that I could find out?

"You really like her?" Jericho asked, clearly not convinced.

I took my thumbnail out of my teeth to answer him with as much conviction as I could verbally convey, "Yes, I *really* like her."

"Huh, I never thought I'd see the day," Jericho stared out the window at the scenery that had turned from countryside to city as we moved slowly through Russia's capitol approaching the train station.

"You still might not," I grumbled. "She's pushing me away for a reason, and it might just be because she's the only female on Earth not completely affected by my boyish charm and alarming good looks."

Jericho laughed out loud at me and I couldn't help but relax a little and laugh with him. This was good. Well, not that Amelia apparently had to make up excuses to keep me away, but at least I wasn't fighting my best friend for her. And even better, since she used Jericho and not anybody else I knew for almost certainty there wasn't another douchebag to compete with.

I really just needed to find a reason to be around her again and judge the situation with all my newfound knowledge. It also helped that she had a crush on me before; that had to be good news.

And I would find her.

Just as soon as I took care of Terletov and made it safe for her again.

The train finally slowed to a stop in the old train station we used for its inconspicuousness. Jericho and I gathered our tightly packed backpacks. We were well practiced in packing light and practically for missions with no end date and had the potential to run for weeks, or even months.

In the hallway we joined the masses of passengers exiting the train and pushed our way through the crowd. Outside it smelled like grease, metal and cigarette smoke; it smelled like a mission.... it smelled like heaven. I couldn't stop the big smile plastering my face even though I knew how out of place a smile like this was in Russia.

I felt them before I saw them, their magics all clustered together and waiting impatiently for our arrival. I scanned the crowd, thankful I stood taller than most of the humans scattered across the platform. Jericho stood with me, searching too. We were stilled in a sea of constant movement, and even while everyone bumped and banged into us, I was hardly aware of the human activity while I anxiously searched out the Immortals I hadn't seen in way too long.

My trained eyes found them across the platform. Xander and Titus sat relaxed on a rusted old bench, while Xavier and Roxie talked in easy conversation, their eyes constantly scanning the crowd and station.

Roxie saw us first, her tiny frame nearly eclipsed by the crowd around her. Her face lit up in recognition and a smile that was rarely ever worn spread across her face. I nudged Jericho with my elbow and nodded my head in their direction. He found them too and I felt as his magic jumped with excitement.

We pushed our way across the platform, the greetings and shouts of hello could be heard everywhere in the station, I was positive. So much for inconspicuous…. But at the moment I could care less. I pulled Roxie to me immediately, crushing her into a bear hug. She wiggled a little, not a huge fan of touching, but eventually she gave in and hugged me back. I kept her tucked into me while I greeted the other guys, until Xander tried to bow to me, then I had to let Roxie go so I could punch him in the arm.

"Don't' even start with me," I tried to sound angry, but I laughed instead.

"Listen to this guy!" Xander announced to everyone. "He's already started to use his King powers to boss us around!"

"King powers?" I laughed, glad these guys took my position less serious than even I did.

"What?" Xavier chimed in, jumping on his brother's joke. "That's what I would call them. Hell, I would get all the ladies with my King powers…." He finished provocatively, making very suggestive movements with his body.

"Oh yeah, except Avalon's apparently doing the exact opposite of that with his King powers," Jericho laughed and he was lucky there were several people in between us.

That was echoed by a chorus of taunting from everyone including Roxie.

Psht.

"So what are you doing with your King powers then, Avalon?" Roxie teased.

"I'll tell you what I'm *going* to do with them," I announced, giving them each a more serious, and in my opinion a more mature, look.

"What's that?" Titus asked.

"I'm going to kill this son of a bitch that thinks he can do what we did," I growled and was met with exactly what I wanted: a chorus of agreement.

This was why I chose these people; they were as blood thirsty as I was and willing to sacrifice everything for the safety of our Kingdom.

Chapter Fifteen

I expected something. I expected really anything.... something telling, something.... revealing. I expected to feel magic from miles away, a facility full of rogue Immortals conducting God knows what kind of experiments.

I didn't expect nothing.

I was prepared for it. But to feel nothing felt.... off.

Which is what I felt as we approached the remote facility used for training Titans once upon a time.

We surrounded the place. It was completely isolated in the middle of the Siberian tundra. A camouflaged outpost of buildings built to blend in with their surroundings. We paired off and attacked from every direction, with the mission to meet in the middle. We had been prepared to fight tooth and nail to get there, but when we all met in the center of an empty courtyard completely untouched and without conflict, it was.... a bit disappointing.

Not to mention confusing.

Our breath puffed out in front of us in hazy clouds, the ground frozen and covered in snow even now, at the end of September. The courtyard we stood in was the center of several warehouses and training facilities that now appeared empty.

They *were* empty.

I would have felt something if they weren't.

"One by one? Or each one together?" I asked the group quietly. There were four buildings altogether and we would attack them in pairs if we went separately: Xander and Xavier together, Titus and Jericho and Roxie and me.

"Together," Jericho answered for the group.

I motioned with my fingers which building we would enter first, a dormitory of sorts that had housed the Titans Kiran spoke with only two years ago. Kiran and I went over the layout of this place in details for hours before Jericho and I left this morning.

I walked up to the entrance and searched the area again for some sign of magic, but still there was nothing. I jiggled the handle and found that it was unlocked, so I pushed it completely open and walked through. My body, magic and mind were on high alert and I waited for the ambush I was positive was still coming.

What had once been an open room setting was now blocked off into separate apartments. Dry wall had been filled in to separate the room into six isolated living spaces, although I couldn't imagine the dividing walls really provided that much privacy. I walked to the first room and stuck my head in the first apartment. There was a small, makeshift kitchen with a refrigerator and stove in one corner and a counter space with bar stools that blocked it off as the eating area, a worn couch and old box TV set and then a single bed shoved to the other side of the room. There was no bathroom, but I supposed they still used the communal bathrooms down the hall.

The room was empty, even of clothing or signs that someone had lived here at all and so we moved to the next room, which was also empty. Each room had been cleared out and left deserted without even a runaway sock left behind. The bathrooms were also empty, but seemed to be in enough working order that I could tell people had been here not that long ago.

We exited the dorms through the back door which led us to a shoveled out, concrete path to the next building's back entrance. This room was just as much of a dead end. It was a training facility with an open floor plan. Heavy black mats lay littered across the floor and various weapons' equipment was scattered throughout. Unlike the dorms, this room had not been used recently, and every surface was covered with a thick layer of dust. It was also freezing, ice plastered the inside of the windows and there was not much difference between inside and outside.

I realized then that the dorms had felt much warmer.

Clearly recently lived in.

We exited the training building out of the front exit so we could walk across the courtyard to the cafeteria. This building was a bit of a mixture of the last two, where the kitchen and a few tables had been obviously used and cleaned recently, the majority of the tables set up in the cafeteria were covered in dust, as were the bathrooms and half of the storage facilities behind the stoves.

Finding nothing in the cafeteria we walked over to the last building. Kiran explained this building as another training facility, but whereas the first training facility had been for brute strength, this one would house more of an educational type environment.

Jericho just happened to be in front at the entrance to the last building so he was the first to walk through. His audible gasp had us rushing into the room behind him only to slam into him since he for some reason did not move forward.

I stayed irritated with him for two seconds before I lifted my eyes and looked around.

Holy hell.

"Holy hell," I echoed out loud. "What the hell was going on here?"

We moved silently throughout the open-spaced room that maybe at one time had been a classroom, but more recently had been turned into some kind of testing facility. Tubing and monitors hung from the ceiling over stainless steel medical tables. Standing monitors were located next to each of the twenty stations, along with a prepped instrument table, including all kinds of sharp and serrated knives that I had never seen in a hospital setting before.

On top of all of that the room smelled sterile; clearly scrubbed and bleached to hide any evidence of the death I imagined happening here. I felt it now…. the magic. It was weak and depressing, disintegrating into thin air even as we stood there. And as I walked through the room I realized the feeling came from the medical instruments and tubing. The rest of my team walked silently through the room, not touching anything but taking it all in.

I was the first to touch something, but I was also the only one that could feel the current of magic circulating throughout the room. I reached out to touch the tubing, curiosity getting the better of me. It was clear and thick, bigger than something that a human would attach to an IV or vein, but I wasn't convinced that wasn't what it was used for. I took a breath before letting my fingers graze over the plastic and I was glad I did.

Excruciating pain seared my fingers as the effect of the plastic pierced my skin. I flinched backward, sucking in a sharp breath. I was glad I didn't put my whole hand around the tube, I wasn't positive I would have been able to let go.

"Don't touch anything!" I demanded, fearing for the rest of my team. This was unlike anything I had ever seen before and I after watching Henri die, I wasn't convinced we would heal right from whatever kind of magic this was.

I followed the tubing with my eyes until it ended at a sharp needle point that could be injected into a person's skin. At the other end of the tubing, the one that hung from the ceiling was a glass container that was attached to the ceiling and split down the middle with another pane of glass. It was like absolutely nothing I had seen before, but it was obviously used to either take something out or put something in.

Or both.

And that was disturbing.

"Avalon, Jericho, back here!" Xander called and I recognized that we were the only ones still standing in the operating room. I shuddered when I realized I referred to this place as an "operating room."

I lifted my eyes to Jericho's and acknowledged that we should go, but not before I saw the terrified expression that flashed across his face. I wondered if he saw the same thing in my eyes, so I turned around and mentally prepared myself for whatever Xander had found. I readied myself for the worst thing imaginable so that when it happened, I could be strong for my team.

Behind the last row of metal tables were a windowed wall and a hallway. Behind the window was an observation room with a long conference table. Down the hallway were four more doors that opened away from the observation/conference room.

Xander, Xavier and Titus each stood in the doorway of three of the rooms and Roxie had slunk down to the floor on the outside of the last room, her hands covering her face, her shoulders trembling.

I approached Xander first, pushing in next to him and then immediately pressing a hand over my nose and mouth. The pungent smell of rotting, bitter flesh met me first and when my eyes adjusted through the painful smell I saw the piles of bodies layered on top of each other, pushed into the corner and left for us to find. I couldn't look at their faces, or their upper bodies. I knew what I would find. I knew what I would see. And the last thing I was willing to let haunt my thoughts was dozens of ghostly, death-filled faces and the unnatural concave chests of these victims. So I stared at the feet, counting the pairs and then swallowing back the bile when the number went over twenty.

I forced myself out of the room and into the next one, pushing Xavier out of the way. There were no dead bodies in this room, but by the stunned, horrified look on Xavier's face I had to believe he came to the same conclusions as me. Tables had been set up in this room covered in boxes that were filled with file folders. On each file folder was a name, printed in typed script. The longer I stood in the room, the more my mind fought to understand what I saw.

There were five tables altogether and each table had a label, a plain, white sheet of paper, taped to the edge of the table. They read: Witch, Titan, Shape-Shifter, Medium and Hybrid.

My mind reeled at what Hybrid could mean, not wanting to investigate that further until I finished my sweep of the building. I called Xander and Jericho into this room, demanding that they shut the door to the other for now and then instructed that they start looking through the files to see what they could find out.

Titus stood in a nearly empty room, hovering over a long table with a huge map of the world pinned to the edges of the table. Little metal pins with red tipped ends were stuck all over the map, covering the globe. Some of the pins were clustered together in large clumps and some were spread farther out as if isolated in that particular part of the world. As I stepped closer to the map, I noticed a handful of green tipped pins that distinguished some of the more important parts of the world to Immortals; Peru, Morocco, London and a few others were marked with green.

I chewed at my thumbnail, trying to make sense of the map. Were the red markers for where Immortals lived around the globe? Or were they places that were somehow crossed out and negated? Or tried out and failed? What did the green mean? Were they going to those places next? Or what?

What did it mean?

I let out a sound I almost didn't recognize as my own, a low growl that built into a guttural scream. I turned around filled with a fury I had never felt before, not even for Lucan and I punched my hand through the weak dry wall, wishing it were stronger.... wishing it had put up a fight, because I needed to feel pain. I *needed* to feel like I fought for something, instead of letting these people suffer and die under my ignorant rule.

"Roxie, what's in that room?" I shouted, breaking up our silence with a rough, furious voice.

"Nothing Avalon, it's empty," she called back immediately. "Whatever was in here was cleaned out and taken with them." Her voice was still weak, and I could tell she was crying, but there was more to her emotion than just sadness, there was vengeful intent and I echoed that very sentiment.

"Jericho," I called, pulling my hand from the wall and brushing off the dust and drywall on my flexible snow pants. When he entered the room I didn't hesitate to give him orders. "Get Talbott on the phone now. Fill him in on this.... this.... situation. And then have him send a team of twenty or more Titans to come clean up this disaster. I want those bodies identified, their families notified and I want funerals held for them. I'll pay for it all. Just make sure it happens."

"Xander, Xavier, get in here," I called next and they immediately responded while Jericho dialed Talbott's number and then left the room to talk someplace more private. "Roxie, you too."

When everyone was assembled around the table I pushed the anger, resentment and fear down, deep, deep down into the locked box in my soul that I would sort through later and turned my trained eye to the table.

"Whatever this is," I started in a choked voice and then paused to clear my throat before I continued. "Whatever this is.... has to be stopped. We have to end this. I cannot allow one more Immortal to suffer what's happened here." I paused again to look each person in the eye, making sure they felt the complete weight of the task and responsibility ahead of us.

"Let's dissect this map, find out where they went and what they have planned. We leave in twenty minutes and we better know where to go next, because we cannot afford to pick the wrong place."

I got four solid nods in response before suggestions started being thrown around and hypothesis made.

We were determined.

And we were desperate.

But most of all, we were vetted in this arena. Terletov would not get away with this again.

Chapter Sixteen

Two weeks. Two f-ing weeks. And nothing. We checked out every single one of those green pinpoints, and sent teams of Titans to scour the red pinpointed areas too. And nothing.

No leads, no more incidents, no more anything.

The only thing we had learned was that the dead Immortals were from some of the cities pinpointed, but they were from both the red ones and the green ones. We had also learned that the dead Immortals were all Shape-Shifters that had left the hidden colonies that had survived under Lucan's reign and joined human society.

But those facts didn't require very deep investigation, and because the dead were still from both the red pinpointed cities and the green, it didn't narrow anything down at all. If anything, it made the whole situation even more confusing.

I ran my hands over my face in frustration and then settled into ripping my thumb nail off with my teeth. A grumbled sigh of desperation vibrated my body and I used all of my will power to stop myself from shouting out obscenities. I glanced around the deserted farm anxiously, hoping that bringing everyone back to Terletov's Latvian estate would bring us some answers.

"There's going to be something here," Jericho said from the driver's seat. I glanced over at him and nodded in approval. Jericho was as fiercely determined as I was, and there was something in that.... something in sharing our common goal of retribution.

"Who's meeting us here?" Roxie asked from the backseat. Her foot tapped frantically on the carpeted floor and she kept fidgeting with her hands. We were all feeling the symptoms of two long weeks of constant travel and no results. If we didn't catch a break soon, I knew from experience we were going to start getting really short with each other.

And violent.

And nobody wanted that.

"Uh," I muttered while I pulled out my phone to look at the text Talbott had sent me earlier in the day. "Andre, Christi, Anton and Mitica..... four Titans that participated in Eden's rescue mission three years ago. They also were part of the group that arrested Terletov and escorted him back to the Citadel."

"I've heard of Mitica, I thought he was a huge Lucan supporter?" Roxie questioned, her hands never staying still.

"He was…. is, he still is. Most of these guys have been relieved of their duties, but they agreed to meet us here. I think they understand what's at stake," I explained, but I felt my entire body tense with the realization that these guys were not going to be easy to work with. Luckily I had access to Eden's memories, so I knew her side of the story.

"What did Talbott tell them? Are you announcing all of this to the rest of the Kingdom?" Roxie pressed, and I knew she was just trying to keep her mind off what could be considered a dismal failure so far.

"No, I'm not announcing this, at least not yet. I want this as under wraps as I can keep it. I don't want anyone panicking, or questioning the fragile state of our Kingdom. We need a strong front, otherwise I'm afraid Terletov won't be the only Rebellion we're fighting," I paused, thinking over my words and fearing I sounded like a dictator as I explained. "I'm fine with the Kingdom wanting new leadership if they are unsatisfied with my job, but I refuse to hand it over unless I'm sure that's what the majority of the people want. But as far as these Titans go, we're desperate, and I am hoping these guys can give us some insight into what happened to Terletov after he was arrested. They've been briefed on everything Talbott knows, and from there I hope they can help."

Jericho slowed the car to the stop in front of the overly large cottage that screamed pretentious douchebag. Latvia was not a wealthy country and the estate of Terletov seeped with old money. It was like he had to assert his dominance everywhere. I wouldn't be surprised if inside the house there were giant statues dedicated to the size of his manhood and the whole place smelled like piss from where he felt the need to mark his territory.

Grade-A douche.

We climbed out of the tiny Fiat we picked up in Italy. Titus pulled in next to us, Xander and Xavier practically fell out of their identical compact car. I felt kind of bad for Xavier watching him shake out his feet that had no doubt fallen asleep in the cramped, miniscule back seat. I mean, not bad enough to trade places with him, but bad enough for a sympathetic glance. Titus was the shortest in their group and I wondered how he convinced them to let him drive.

The Titans we were meeting were already here and gathered in a small clump of testosterone near the barn. When Eden was trying to escape, she caused a little bit of structural damage here and there, but the property showed depressing signs of neglect that went beyond Eden's escape. I walked slowly over to the Titans that were inspecting the dilapidated barn as if making sure it was safe to go in, leaving my team to follow behind me. At the sound of my approach, they turned and greeted me.

I had met them all before, but never spent much time with them since all but one of them chose to give up their Titan service. All Titans were given the opportunity to walk away after I took over. I knew they weren't magically going to be loyal to me or happy with how things ended for Lucan, so I diplomatically gave them the choice to leave everything behind and make a new life for themselves. If they stayed they had to pledge a new alliance to me; not a blood oath, but I trusted their word as an identical promise.

Mitica, Anton and Andre had bailed immediately. To be fair, they were older in years and had served with Lucan and with his father. They knew nothing but the Kendrick line and I was some young punk that had messed up their carefully controlled world. Christi Ludu was one of the only ones of his generation to stay, and for the most part I had come to the conclusion he was a good man. I had just assigned him to Brazil, so I didn't interact with him very often.

And that was part of this whole problem. I knew there were disgruntled Lucan supporters throughout the Kingdom. I wasn't naïve. But with Kiran's support and his active role in our new leadership, I hoped it was enough to pacify them. And if it wasn't, I had kept a close enough eye on those I knew were unhappy to know that they didn't hold the means or enough like-minded friends to organize much of a threat.

Until Terletov....

Which unleashed all kinds of questions for me. How many were a part of this? How long have they been organizing this? Are my people being subjected to their sick, twisted and tortuous ways right now.... while I wander around the world lost and losing.... not helping them.... not fighting for them..... not saving them?

"Thank you for coming, gentlemen," I greeted them, swallowing down the bile that thought train had produced. "Have you had a chance to look around?"

"We have," Christi answered politely in his thick Romanian accent. He tried to offer a bow but I waved him off. "There are several interesting pieces of evidence that would suggest Dmitri Terletov was planning something for a long time, but they don't seem to have been touched since our original investigation."

"You know about the basement room, of course," Mitica spoke up and I was a little bit surprised by his genial attitude. Last time we spoke, he was less than respectful. "I'm afraid we are no help down there, our magic does not work. Yours however...." He paused while his colleagues shot him nervous glances. They were still afraid of the King, whether or not my behavior had justified his trepidation or not. It was still Lucan he was afraid of, if only he could see that. "What I mean to say, is that in our reports your sister was able to use her magic down there."

"Is there anything else that you can remember from your time here?" Jericho asked, breaking up the tension the four of them created.

"I thought of something on the way over here," Andre announced, his light purple eyes flashing with steely resolve making them look like iridescent and gunmetal. Most of the Kingdom was very ethnically diverse, and scattered all across the globe, but when our races were divided after Derrick, the Titans were forced to stay within their Roman roots. In the last few hundred years they have all been born and raised in Romania, with the exception of when training was moved to Siberia. They all look similar though; muscled olive skin, dark curly hair and most are born with deep chocolate eyes. There is always the exception though and Andre's violet eyes made him stand out amongst his friends. He continued, "Eden reported that Terletov begged for death after she took his magic, but that she left that for us to deal with. However, Eden wasn't debriefed until much later, after Terletov had been moved to the prison and this farm cleaned up. I was one of the Guards that physically handled Terletov on our way back to the Citadel and never once did he seem like a man who had given up on life. He was tired, his head would droop and his eyes were sunken in after she drained him of magic, but he never asked us for death or even seemed like a man that would prefer to be dead. In fact, he fought weakly against his restraints, he bit Anton on the shoulder when we tried to get him into the van, and when we attempted to move him from the van to the prison he head-butted me after pretending to be passed out."

"Is that how he got away?" Jericho asked quickly. I could feel the hope in his magic, but I refused to let myself have any of it.

The Titans mocked him with a derisive laugh.

"He didn't get away from us," Mitica spat defensively. "So what? He put up a fight, but nothing else. He was a weak human by then, we were the Titan Guard. He didn't stand a chance."

"But he did get away," I reminded them, although I understood their pride. "I agree with you about him being weak though. I've seen Eden's memories, so I know he wasn't capable of it on his own. He must have had help." Everyone nodded along with him and I swore to myself that if they were just humoring me because I was King I would take away all of their retirement funds. "While he was down in the prisons, did any of you notice that he was particularly close to anyone in the Guard? Or how about when he escaped?"

Now they shook their heads like they had no information to offer for my questions.

Which was frustrating.

I could feel their cocky confidence, hell I was practically choking on the chauvinistic arrogance these four guys were radiating and yet losing a guy like Terletov couldn't possibly be their fault! He had to have been a human when he broke out of the Citadel.... *had* to have been. We're still not sure if he has magic or not and if he does how he got it. So who dropped the ball? Had he even made it to the Citadel in the first place?

Ugh... too many unanswered questions.

"Alright, I want the four of you to split up and partner with one of my guys. Take them through exactly what happened that day and what your role was. I'm going to check out this basement holding room," I waited for everyone to acknowledge me before announcing, "We're not leaving here without some kind of answers. You can go. Jericho, you're with me."

Xander, Xavier, Titus and Roxie had to be the ones to make the first move. I was glad to see that Roxie had chosen Christi to work with. I had no doubt the girl could hold her own, but I wanted this to go smoothly and I had a bad feeling any of the other Titans were going to give her a hard time.

Jericho and I walked forward into the barn and started looking around. The old stone barn smelled like dirt and musty hay. Birds flapped unhappily up in the rafters, angry that we disturbed them. The barn was typical and unimpressive. Old farm equipment hung on rusted hooks protruding from the walls and short, stools and benches littered the hay covered earthen ground. The door that Eden blew off the handles still stood propped against the open hole it had ripped through. Nothing and nobody had been here in years.

Jericho stood next to me yawning and when I gave him a questioning look he nodded at the open doorway that led down into the room Eden had woken up in after being shot in the chest.

"I can feel it," Jericho explained his yawn while tipping his head in the direction of the basement room. "It makes me feel tired, but also like I can't move my magic.... like it's slow and useless."

"You don't need to be in here then," I definitely did not like Jericho feeling anything but perfect form. "Send in Christi, I want to know if he can feel my magic when I'm down there."

Jericho nodded and walked off. I stared at the open doorway for six more seconds before deciding there was no use just standing there. I needed to get down. I needed to find something.

I stomped down the wooden staircase, my body and weight shaking the weak structure. The room was dark and even mustier than upstairs and quite a bit cooler, but it was completely empty. I stood on the last stair assessing the room; it wasn't large, but big enough that several people could have been held down here. A slithering feeling of warning prickled my skin and I felt my heartbeat accelerate before I could question why.

Feeling anxious, I stepped off the stair and turned a slow circle in the room. A glint of metal caught my eye from the shadows underneath the staircase. I stepped forward, thinking it was possibly the bullet that had come out of Eden's chest and realized two things at once.

The first was that my magic was slower down here, I could still use it, but I felt sluggish and out of it. The second thing I realized was that there was a man standing in the corner pointing a gun directly at my chest.

The glint of metal.

Held by a man that had no access to his magic down here, but didn't need it since he had a gun instead.

Chapter Seventeen

Even with the handicap of incapacitated magic I knew I needed to move and move fast. Not thinking about anything other than dodging the bullet I knew would be coming my way; I dove out of the bullet's path just as I heard the click of the trigger. The bullet exploded from the gun aimed for my chest and like in slow motion, as if I were in my own horror film, it ripped through my t-shirt digging into my side and slicing through soft flesh. I hadn't Time-Slowed the moment, but I still felt every second of pain as the bullet continued all the way through the hole it was digging and stayed lodged, buried in my side.

I landed in an uncoordinated clump on the hard dirt floor, gripping at my side where blood spilled out over my clothes and hand. I felt the stinging residue of the magic that was in the bullet and my vision blurred in and out of blackness as I tried to hold on to consciousness. The man in the corner walked forward wearing a twisted smirk. He was blonde, with a blonde beard and even in my pathetic state on the floor I wanted to advise him to shave his flesh colored beard, it looked way unnatural.

"I don't think this is coincidence, your Highness," the man muttered, his eyes glinting with excitement. A wave of darkness washed over me and my eyelids fluttered closed. I forced them open, digging my fingers further into the wound, trying desperately to get to the bullet and rip it out of me.

Eden! I shouted into her head, jarring her from whatever it was she was doing, but she was already there, already sending her magic into me. *I need you!*

I couldn't hear anything from outside the room and I had no idea if anyone else had heard the gunshot. Had it been loud? On a silencer? I couldn't remember and now I couldn't focus through my blurry vision to tell if there was a silencer on the weapon or not. My wound burned hot like lava, spreading the torturous feeling through my body like a sickness. Most Immortals would be unconscious by now, most wouldn't have to feel the pain as it moved through every inch of my body, paralyzing my magic and sucking away my breath.

Avalon! Eden screamed, sending as much magic into me as she could, but to no avail, the pain consumed her magic as quickly as it had mine. *Don't close your eyes! Don't let him win, Avalon!* She cried desperately.

Through shadowy vision I watched my attacker lift his gun to my heart, and then seeming to think better of it, to my head, right in between my eyes. Eden's idea came to her as soon as she could calm her panic and forced herself to breathe evenly. I felt the blue smoke move into me, immediately taking away the sharp edge of pain. The smoke had traveled between us before, and Eden had used it to heal countless Immortals by now, but this was the first time she had pressed it into me while we were this far apart. I could feel how the smoke was still anchored to Eden, even as it cleansed out my veins and organs of the evil magic threatening to cover me in darkness.

The blue smoke pushed against the invasive bullet. I felt a bit of it as the bullet moved out of my body, through the tunnel it had burrowed and clinked onto the dirt floor next to me.

Relief.

This all happened in short, breathless seconds and in the last possible moment the smoke finished with my open wound making me capable of moving again. Before my vision cleared completely I rolled out of the way as the gun went off again, echoing thunderously in the small basement room. The bullet hit the dirt floor and ricocheted off while I kicked my legs out with as much force as I could into the knees of my attacker. He grunted and stumbled, his gun swinging wildly in the air.

I kicked my legs out again, only this time to jump myself into standing and flung my fist into the guy's face, connecting perfectly with his jaw. I felt the bones crunch underneath my knuckles, the sound of his jaw breaking was almost as loud as the gun shot. With my left hand I forced a strong burst of my magic into his gut, sending him flying against a dirt wall a cloud of dust poofing out being him. His weak hand dropped the gun to his side as he slid down to the ground in a sitting position. With one more burst of magic sent at his head, I knocked him unconscious and without hesitation picked up the gun that had sputtered a few feet away.

I examined the gun in my hand, ignoring the shaking of my fingers. I had almost been shot.... In the head.... And I tried to reassure myself that I wouldn't have died, no matter what. But the nauseous feeling racking my stomach and the trembling of my hands warned me that I didn't believe that. He was going to shoot me in the head. And by doing so, he would have won.

I growled ferociously out loud and pointed the gun at the son of a bitch that tried to assassinate me. It hurt like hell and I wanted nothing more than to wait for him to wake up and show him what it felt like.

Except then he would slip into a coma and I'd have to wait until Eden could come heal him before I got my answers. I grunted again and kicked at his limp foot.

I wanted a break and I got one. However, he almost got what he wanted too.

"Avalon, what the-" Jericho shouted from the doorway that he shared with Christi. Both looked

into the room with wide eyes and confused expressions.

"This.... this guy was hiding down here, under the staircase. He shot me," I gestured to my blood soaked clothes and waved the gun around. "He's out now, but he definitely works for Terletov. Get me some handcuffs, two sets," I ordered.

Jericho left right away to get the magical handcuffs that would hopefully keep this guy confined while I questioned him. I stood over him, not trusting him even in his unconscious state, until Jericho returned a few minutes later and tossed the cuffs down to me. I kicked his torso forward and then pulled his arms behind his body quickly, snapping the cuffs on him before he could get the chance to wake up. I did the same to his ankles, knowing that without magic those cuffs would be super tight and uncomfortable against his skin, but not caring. The handcuffs suppressed his magic and that was all that mattered.

I picked him up under his arms, since my magic wasn't strong enough to lift him and then I dragged him up the stairs and dumped him on the barn floor at the feet of Jericho and Christi. The others had heard our commotion and filtered in, staring at the bound man unbelievingly.

"What are the chances," I heard Titus mutter, but other than that mostly everyone was silent.

"I'm going back down," I declared, kicking the guy in the side to see if I could wake him up. "Xander, Xavier, don't take your eyes off of him. Call down as soon as he wakes up."

I turned to go back downstairs when Roxie called out, "What are you going to do?"

"He was down there for a reason. I'm guessing, before he even knew we were here. There's something down there and I'm going to find it," I explained. A few from my team and even the old Titans moved as if they were going to help me so I had to hold up my hand to stop them. "Listen, I don't know what's down there, or who's down there. And nobody's magic works down there except mine. If I run into trouble I will holler for you. Otherwise just assume that I'm investigating and that I'll be fine."

I turned away before anyone could object, but not before I saw the disbelieving faces of the old Titans. For a brief moment I wondered if I should offer like grief counseling or trauma counseling or something. I felt like they might be kind of messed up after working for Lucan all those years and carrying out his orders. I decided to shelve the issue and talk about it with Eden later. No Immortal that I knew would be open for something like counseling, but Eden was different and raised in a human world where they saw the value of talking their problems out with an objective listener. She would know what to do.

Back in the basement, I kept my eyes open, half expecting to meet another attacker. I went immediately to under the staircase and paused. The bullets were not large, but they were magic and emitted a magical current just like everything else. When I stopped to search out the tiny little electrical charges I could feel them, I had to concentrate extremely hard and borrow from Eden but I could feel them.

Eden sat hovering in my head, watching as everything unfolded far away from her. I felt her frustration and fear, her concern and anxiety. It was all echoed inside of me and I wished more than ever before she was here with me. She would work off of me, her magic and mine would collaborate to find answers.

We'll meet up after this. She said softly inside our heads. *Find answers here and we'll meet you.*

I don't want you in danger. I answered and it was the truth. Or half of the truth, because only half of me believed it, the other half knew what kick ass fighters we were together.

Then we won't meet where there's danger. She snapped and I smiled. *But we are going to solve this problem together. You're not going to exclude me, I told you that a long time ago. Now figure out what I missed when I was here.*

Demanding little thing, aren't you? I teased, but it felt good.

She started to say something, but I cut her off with a spark of realization. There, in the wall was a handle. There was nothing spectacular about it, just a lift in the wall that was camouflaged well. As an Immortal, I knew we generally ignored everything not magical. It was a huge flaw, but until Eden, most people didn't realize how debilitating it could be.

Except apparently Terletov had figured it out before all of us.

I lifted the handle and pulled on it. An angry scraping sound filled the room as rusted metal grinded against worn hinges to move. The dirt wall was a well-made façade and hidden behind it was a surprisingly large weapons room. When the door opened all the way, a light overhead flickered on filling the room with fluorescent lighting. Nothing inside the room was rusted; instead everything was clean, shiny stainless steel from floor to walls, to ceiling, shelves and the large table that filled the middle of the room. Guns of every kind hung on three of the walls and on the third were floor to ceiling shelves that were filled, stacked completely with bullets to match.

Holy hell.

Holy hell. Eden echoed. *You're going to have to carry this all out yourself.*

I laughed out loud, realizing she was right.

My fingers brushed over the cold metal of the middle table as I took in every weapon, every bullet, every nook and cranny in the space. My magic pulsed dangerously in my blood as my temper heated with it. The wall of ammunition radiated with electricity, because they were clustered together the collective energy vibrated together in a plus of their own.

"Avalon!" Roxie called down the staircase, "He's waking up!"

I turned my back on the room, ignoring the sickening twist in my stomach and the hundreds of ideas that were flipping through my head for what all of that could be used for. The idea that nobody else had the means to take over the Kingdom was naïve and foolish. If there were any other rooms like this anywhere in the world it would be enough to take the Citadel easily.

All it would take to put me down would be a couple well placed bullets to my head and chest and to Eden's. A growl of rage ripped through my chest at the thought. They would *never* touch my sister.

Never again.

At the top of the stairs I blinked against the natural sunlight filling the barn and made my way out to the yard where everyone stood congregating around the handcuffed assassin. I joined them quietly in case the interrogating had already started, my teeth tearing away at my raw thumbnail.

"If there is anyone else, we will find them," Mitica threatened and even through our differences I appreciated his intimidating presence.

The man on the ground laughed mockingly. I could tell he was weakened and disoriented from the grip of the handcuffs against his skin, but the defiance and hatred in his eyes were unmistakable.

Faraway magic nagged at my neck, making the hairs on my forearms rise. I looked around, panicked and desperate. Were they coming for us? How many were there? Did they all carry guns?

"Get him inside," I ordered.

The other Titans had started to feel it too. They looked around with their military trained eyes, all of their bodies tensing with the warning.

A gargled laugh filtered up from the ground. "You can't stop him," the attacker said. "It's too late. He's going to change everything. Your revolution is nothing compared to what he is planning! He will change it all! He will change it all!" He finished, dissolving into deranged laughter. His aggressive eyes were alight with disturbing glee. This man was clearly unhinged.

And then before I could make another clear thought in my head, the sound of a gun rang out through the quiet countryside. I heard my sharp intake of breath and then the slicing sound of metal meeting flesh. The man next to me dropped to the ground, my mind not even able to register who it was before a second gunshot boomed through the air and another bullet hit its mark.

The older Titans had already taken off in the direction of the magic without waiting to find out who was hit, or if more bullets would be coming. I opened my mouth to order my team to take cover when my eyes grazed over the assassin, realizing he was the target.

My hand dropped to my side, while the far away magic disappeared into the Latvian countryside. The assassin, still handcuffed, lay in a pool of his own blood. His eyes were still wide as if laughing at me, but they were dead now, emitting no light, no life. His mouth hung open and there was an indention in the side of his head where the bullet had entered. His magic filtered into the air, away from his dead body.

I forced my eyes to the other man that dropped.

Titus.

My heart pounded in my chest, ready to rip through my body and find vengeance itself. Rushing air, that's all I could hear. My vision blurred into blackness.

Titus.

I dropped to my knees. This. This was not happening.

I reached out for him, but my hands were numb, frozen to my sides.

"He's not dead," Roxie whispered and somehow her small voice carried through the deafening whooshing sound. "He's not dead," she repeated louder.

He wasn't dead.

I took a staggering breath, forcing air back into my lungs, forcing the rage to subside enough so I could see again. I lifted my head as if it weighed a million pounds and saw his wound then. He had turned, at the last second, Titus had turned and the bullet had gone through his neck instead. Inside one side and out the other. Roxie worked furiously fast to stop the bleeding.

"How the hell....?" Xander trailed off, I could hear in the silence how he struggled to piece together what just happened.

"Sniper rifle," I answered with a gravelly voice.

"Sniper rifle?" Roxie gasped. "But how is that possible? How did it kill him?" Xander and Xavier had ripped off their shirts and she was using them to press against the open wounds of Titus's neck. His magic was still in there, still struggling to heal him, but his eyes were rolled back into his head.

I was a strong man.

But I wanted to vomit.

"With the same bullets that incapacitated Eden when she was kidnapped," I explained further. "Only these were made for a sniper. Get him in the car, now. Jericho, open the trunks of all three cars. I'm going to clear out the basement. I'll bring it to the top of the stairs, and Xavier help Jericho load the cars. As soon as we have those weapons we're going to meet Eden."

"Where is Eden?" Roxie asked in a delicate voice. I could hear the thick emotion being barely contained.

Paris. She answered quickly before I could ask her. *We're on our way to Paris for Mimi's birthday. We'll meet you at Gabriel's home outside the city limits. Do you remember where it is?*

Yes.

Ok, see you then. I felt her sniffle.

I love you, E.

I love you too.

"Paris," I rejoined my reality and answered Roxie. "Gabriel's house. Get him loaded. And then Xander, find the rest of the Titans and tell them they're coming with us. They are carrying ammunition for one and I want to go over this with them when Titus is more stable." I snapped out my orders quickly, efficiently. My mind and body screamed against this injustice, but I knew how to hold it together. I knew how to stay the panic and terror and get things done. I would deal with these emotions later.

"He's stopped bleeding," Roxie announced, relief shaking her shoulders as tears streamed down her caramel colored face. "His magic is working again," she finished in a tight whisper.

He still needed Eden.

I turned to sprint to the barn and Jericho matched his steps with mine. "We're lucky the sniper missed you, Avalon."

I stopped in front of the open doorway to the basement. "That bullet was never meant for me. The sniper had one job, and that was to get to the other assassin before he said anything he wasn't supposed to. Titus was simply in the way."

"But how did they know?" Jericho asked as his mind struggled to put all the pieces together.

I paused for one second more. How did they know? My eyes flickered quickly, but efficiently around the barn, looking for cameras, for anything that would give it away. I didn't want another question to add to my never ending list. I needed answers!

There wasn't time now. I needed to get the weapons and ammunition loaded in our cars and get the hell out of here. I needed to get Titus safe.

"Search the body, Jericho. Find out what you can." I started down the stairs, determined to get this done and get out of there. "And then burn it."

Chapter Eighteen

Big breaths. Big deep breaths.
That's all I could focus on during our seemingly endless drive to France. Twenty-five hours of breathing.

And while I focused on breathing, Titus focused on not dying. Well.... not consciously. His ragged, uneven breathing mocked my own the entire way, but if I didn't focus on something I would have lost my mind.

Eden was waiting for us when Jericho pulled into Gabriel's gravel drive. She had been waiting for a while. We had tried several times to transfer the smoke and heal Titus with it, and even though I could produce it, it wouldn't heal for me, it wouldn't do *anything* for me.

To say I was extremely frustrated was the understatement of the year.

"Move!" Eden demanded when Jericho and I tried to move Titus into the house.

I stumbled out of the way while Eden released her healing blue smoke on the backseat of the tiny Fiat. Roxie sat pinned underneath him, cradling his head in her hands.

The world was a blur around me. I knew there were several people watching on, but I couldn't focus on their faces. Xander slammed on his breaks next to our Fiat and he and Xavier jumped from their seats to watch the healing process. Christi Ludu would be on his way too, with the rest of the old Titans and the confiscated ammunition, but I couldn't focus on that until I knew Titus was going to live through this.

My heart hammered in my chest, a rhythm that had not slowed since the incident happened. We hadn't even caught the sniper, he had disappeared into the thick Latvian forest before we could catch up with him. And now Titus's life hung in the balance from a bullet that was made of pure poison for us.

I felt Eden's smoke work on Titus, touching the infected wound, spreading throughout his blood to heal him. I took another deep breath, but this one finally felt fulfilling, I finally felt like the oxygen was actually getting to my lungs.

It was working.

I wanted to believe that Eden's smoke could cure anything. She could cure the King's Curse for God's sake and that was as bad as it got for us.

Except.... was this worse?

The pain wasn't as excruciating and unconsciousness found you a lot faster, but this felt worse for so many more reasons. First, death was a lot quicker with a bullet than it was the Curse. Second and probably most importantly, this was designed by an Immortal. This weapon was created and manufactured to kill other Immortals.

Even when Lucan was King he had only used swords. Terletov was an entirely different kind of monster. Sending snipers to take out his own henchmen so they couldn't give anything away was possibly the worst kind of brutality I had ever seen.

Or possibly not.... I had been through a lot. It was hard to mentally wrap my head around a scale of horrible events. They could all tie the spot for number one for all I cared.

So whether the guns and bullets were number one or not didn't really matter. My whole life was all some messed up shit.

As the smoke worked through Titus's body I stood paralyzed watching. This couldn't happen again. This couldn't happen to anybody.... but the echoes of truth bounced back and forth in my head. Titus wasn't the first casualty and as much as I refused to admit it to myself I knew he wouldn't be the last.

I rubbed at my eyes, forcing myself to focus, forcing myself to breathe easier now that Titus was getting better. I shook my hands out at my sides, knowing there was no nail left to rip off. My thumbs were raw and tender, the nail bitten down to flesh.

A small hand slipped into my nervous, trembling one and I looked down to see Amelia at my side. Her touch had the calming effect I needed and except for my heart completely stalling and then jumpstarting rapidly in my chest, I was able to focus on Titus without drowning in panic.

She wasn't looking at me, her eyes were straight ahead, watching as Titus coughed himself back to consciousness. Her tiny hand felt delicate and fragile in mine. I held onto her like she was my only lifeline, but gently so not to hurt her. She could have pulled away at any time, but I felt myself chanting a prayer that she wouldn't.

Eden finally coaxed Titus into sitting, which was difficult in the tiny back seat of the Italian car. He wasn't as tall as Xavier, Xander or me, but he was bulky and big. His shoulders took up most of the space in the backseat and Roxie had to wiggle out from underneath him to give him more room.

My sister had started to ask him questions about his injury, making sure he was fine. His hand rubbed at the entry and exit wound in his neck distractedly, but he was answering her and seemed to be lucid.

I heard Amelia sigh deeply and then felt her relax next to me. Her ease pulled my attention to her and when I looked down at her I swear she was even more beautiful than when I left her only a few weeks ago. Her long, brown hair was down and wild in the fall wind, her big doe eyes were glued to Titus and she was chewing on her bottom lip as if biting it so fiercely would help heal Titus.

I had a job to do, there were questions that needed answering and I should really check to see if Titus was Ok. I needed to let go of Amelia's hand and join Eden and Kiran who stood hovering behind her.

But then again.... Eden and Kiran were already over there. And Titus seemed to be doing much better.

"You and me need to talk, Amelia," I whispered in a voice that was hoarse from the trauma of the last twenty-five hours and tense with a need for this girl that I couldn't even begin to understand. It ignited my magic, set my blood on fire and there was a hunger deep inside my chest that wanted to consume her in all the best ways.

"Not now, Avalon," she reprimanded me and then tried to pull her soft hand from mine. I turned to face her and grabbed on to it with both of mine, desperate to feel her skin against mine for just a few moments more. "You need to go check on Titus." Her voice was quiet but fierce and if I wouldn't have looked up into her pleading eyes I would have thought that she meant it. But the ravenous look in her gaze made me brave, made me certain.

"And you should probably go say hi to your boyfriend," I taunted, rubbing my thumb gently against the palm of her hand. She shivered.

I took a step closer to her, hiding the smile threatening to ruin my plan.

"My boyfriend?" She squeaked, when my thumb moved from her palm to the inside of her wrist, moving back and forth, barely touching her.

"Jericho, right? I asked him what you guys had going on after you ran away from me," I looked straight into her eyes and was rewarded with a nervous glance in Jericho's direction.

"You did?" she whispered.

"I did," I promised. "And he told me the truth."

Her eyes flickered anxiously in Jericho's direction again. A sense of amusement filled me, and I realized how sick that was, but I couldn't help myself. She had made me suffer since she walked into my life and I was enjoying making her squirm.

"And what did he say?" she pulled her bottom lip in with her teeth and it took every ounce of willpower I had not to take that lip between my own teeth.

"Avalon!" Sebastian called from across the driveway.

I didn't even know he was here.

"What?" I tried not to answer angrily. Amelia looked extremely relieved with her brother's interruption and she pulled her hand from mine as if she had just won some unnamed competition.

I wondered for a second if they shared the kind of connection Eden and I did because that was awfully convenient for her.

"We need you," he shouted back. I turned to give him all of my attention because I could swear he was angry. When our eyes met though, he simply seemed anxious over Titus's condition.

"I'll be right there," I answered back.

"I, uh, I'm going to start dinner," Amelia excused herself quickly and darted back into the house.

I let her go, smiling to myself while I walked over to the Fiat where everyone was still congregated. Christi Ludu had arrived with the other three Titans and Gabriel and Silas had come with Sebastian.

"What were you talking about with my sister?" Sebastian demanded before I even got close to Titus.

"Uh, nothing," I mumbled, wondering if this was going to be an issue. Sebastian and I hadn't ever really spent a lot of time together. We had a friendship, but he wasn't in my innermost circles or anything. I trusted him, but mostly because he came to the Resistance way before even Kiran did. But that was all Eden's influence. He had been a huge help while Eden was imprisoned in the castle, but so had Kiran by that point, so we just had never really gotten to know each other.

"It didn't look like nothing," he accused in his clipped English accent.

"What did it look like?" I asked, feigning innocence.... something I was definitely not good at. He opened his mouth but no words came out and he seemed to stumble over exactly what to accuse me of, so I changed the subject before he could put a thought together. "Hey, where's Seraphina? I thought she never let you too far off your leash?"

Xavier snickered nearby.

Sebastian looked around uncomfortably and shook his head. "Um, I don't know where she is. We're not always together. I haven't actually talked to her weeks, so who knows what she's up to." He tried to sound casual, but I picked out the irritation in his tone loud and clear.

"Oh, you mean *she* hasn't talked to *you* in weeks," I deciphered, much to his chagrin. He shot me a nasty look.

"Don't you have a Kingdom to run, here?" Sebastian shot back.

"Right," I grumbled. I turned back to Titus, but he was well into the recovery stage by now and honestly it looked like Eden and Kiran were dealing with the situation just fine.

I didn't have a Kingdom to run at the moment. I had a supposed-to-be-dead guy to hunt down and make dead again. I met Gabriel's orange, fiery eyes from across the crowd and tilted my head in the direction of his barn. He nodded once and then nudged Silas before stalking off purposely in that direction.

"Xander help get Titus up to one of the bedrooms so he can rest. Xavier work with Christi to figure out what to do with all this ammo. If we can destroy it, do it, if we can't figure out a place where nobody will *ever* find it. Roxie go help Amelia with dinner-"

"Oh, just because I'm a girl, I have to help cook and clean for all the boys?" Roxie spat and I wanted to laugh at all that big attitude coming from such a petite little thing.

"No one said anything about cleaning.... yet," I laughed at her as she flipped me her middle finger and then stomped off toward the house.

"Jericho, Sebastian you're with me," I finished my orders and everyone jumped into action.

I walked over to the barn feeling the pressing down of déjà vu. It had been years since planning had taken place in this barn, but it was as natural as breathing. Gabriel and Silas stood over a dusty metal table with a flat topographical map of the world pinned down.

"My church was broken into last night," Gabriel announced when we had all congregated around our old work station.

"Your church?" Jericho asked, clearly in shock. "How could you possibly tell?"

I held back my laughter. I had been there once.

"The nuns who work there called to tell me," he explained, not amused with Jericho.

"There are nuns that work there?" Jericho whispered in disbelief.

"They said it was by people like me," Gabriel ignored Jericho, running a rough hand over his closely shaved head.

"By which they mean.... Immortals?" Sebastian clarified. I could see the scrutiny on his face and had to fight to repress my laughter. I knew my good humor was a release of adrenaline after the tense last few hours, but I also knew that Gabriel and Silas were also different kind of beings all together. To be fair they had both seen and lived through very dark times. Gabriel had lived at the palace when my parents were there, and suffered through the wrath of Lucan after they fled. And Silas had been a huge part of helping my parents escape. Their world was skewed by a horrific past, but their dedication and loyalty to the future of this Kingdom could not be questioned.

"Yes, of course," Gabriel sighed.

"We think they were after information about my colony," Silas explained.

"So then, to Peru," I announced even though it could have gone unspoken.

"Yes," Gabriel sighed, tugging at his collar. "But...."

"We won't leave for a couple days," I read his thoughts and answered them. "We need a break. We're chasing a lead, not a person with this one and I know that we all need a break. I'll give Titus time to heal and decide if he wants to stay with us or not. In the meantime we're going to keep brainstorming all of this and see if we can't come up with more answers."

Not just for Terletov, I thought selfishly.

I needed answers about Amelia too.

Chapter Nineteen

With a plan in motion, I felt like I could relax, at least for a couple hours. I knew my brain would take over eventually and sooner than my deadline I would be itching to get back on the road again, but for now I needed a break.

A serious break.

Titus was up and moving around, although he did admit he felt a little bit sluggish. I could deal with sluggish. Sluggish was expected after a close call with death. What I could not have handled was a coma.

Or worse.

Damn it, thirty seconds into my break and I already had myself riled up and ready to get back onto the hunt.

"Avalon, everyone's eating, come on in," Amelia called out in her sexy accent from a ways behind me.

A smile replaced the tension in my face and I turned away from Gabriel's freakishly-always-blooming sunflowers to the doorway of the cottage. I wondered for the millionth time how I couldn't have noticed her only three ago. She was gorgeous. Her eyes were narrowed, untrustingly at me and her curvy little hip was propped against the doorframe. Her skirt was short, but those gorgeous legs were covered by thick gray tights, which almost made my curiosity unbearable. And knee high black boots? She was trying to kill me.

"I didn't mean to make you wait, I apologize," I offered, realizing I was always apologizing to her.

"You didn't. Make me wait, I mean," she straightened her posture and fidgeted nervously, her right hand pressing the fingers of her left hand back as far as they could go. "Eden sent me out to find you. She said you would be hungry."

Eden could have easily called me herself, without ever lifting a finger. Huh....

I closed the space between us faster than she was ready for and she bounced back against the stone wall of the small French house. She looked up at me from under thick lashes. Her magic was already intertwined with mine, although I could tell she was trying to hold it back.

Only Titans were capable of feeling other Immortal's magic, unless there was a physical and emotional relationship between the two. Once the magic between two Immortals started to intertwine, they could both feel the separate magic once they started to touch. I couldn't tell by the fearful look in her eyes if she could feel my magic or not. I didn't want to scare her off, she was obviously skittish, but I did want her to feel it between us.

I wanted her to know this was getting deeper between us.

"I'm glad we have a moment to talk," she broke me from my thoughts and I realized I had been staring down at her, trapping her from escaping.

Oops.

"Yeah? About what?" I asked and even I could hear the sexy sound to my voice. This girl did not stand a chance.

"About Jericho," she replied, and I could tell she was forcing herself to stand strong. Her gaze flickered to my lips and I forced myself not to move a muscle, not even give into the cocky smile I was biting back.

"Ok," I nodded my ascent, knowing there was nothing to talk about.

"I didn't mean to give you the impression that Jericho and I were a couple," she started sheepishly.

I couldn't help myself; I leaned in towards her and was rewarded well when her breathing picked up frantically. "You didn't?" I asked casually.

"Uh, uh," she shook her head like she was trying to clear it. I leaned in further. "We're obviously not.... a couple," she clarified and then laughed breathlessly. The cool autumn breeze lifted her hair off her shoulders and she reached up to brush her hair out of her face. I inhaled her perfume; she's all around me and all I could smell was vanilla and lilacs. "What I meant is that I like Jericho. I don't know if he likes me back or anything yet, but I um, I really like him. And I didn't want you to get mixed signals." She cleared her throat, seeming to focus better and straightened her shoulders.

"What are you so scared of, Amelia?" I whispered, dipping my head nearer to hers. She turned to look out at the sunflowers, pulling her lip in with her teeth.

"Scared of? Nothing," she was quick to defend herself and when I chuckled at her, she changed her story. "Well, right now I'm a little frightened that you're going to try to kiss me again."

"Liar," I ground out, so close to her I could feel her heart beating against my chest.

"Liar?" she asked, turning her face back to mine. Her tongue moved slowly across her bottom lip inviting me to prove it to her.

"Mmm..." I agreed, still waiting on her. But when her defiant little chin tilted in my direction I lost all logical thought and intention and captured her mouth with mine.

She let out a moan against my lips and my hands responded to the sound by grabbing her roughly around the waist and pulling her into me. Her answer to that was kissing me deeper; her hands snaked around my neck, holding her body against mine. I pressed her into the wall while our magic threaded together around us. I felt her electricity pulsing wildly inside mine and I consciously covered hers completely with my magic, claiming her as mine.

Eden squeaked inside my head. *Sebastian's looking for you. And he's pissed!*

I grunted out a growl of frustration, giving Amelia one last desperate kiss. Our tongues tangled together, her hands were hot against my neck, twisting almost painfully in my hair. I slipped my hands under the hem of her sweater, pressing against the silky heat of her skin. She felt incredible in my arms, like perfection and excitement.... like I could handle the weight of forever if I had this to look forward to every day.

Because I could tell that this would never get old. No matter how long this infinite life of mine lasted.

This.... Amelia.... was my completion.

I felt Sebastian's magic approach and knew I had to end this. Although, since this girl was so intent on playing games with me, I decided to test out a theory and play my own games. Regretfully I pulled back, separating our lips. She followed me, trying to stall the ending and I let her get one more sexy kiss in, her tongue teasing my bottom lip before it turned into a bite. My breath whooshed out of me as my blood heated fast to a boil with desire.

I could play games too, but with kisses like those I would never be in control.

"Told you," I mumbled against her lips, where they still worked feverishly for me to lose my mind.

"Told me what?" she pulled back, her eyes bright and wild with adrenaline.

"That you were a liar," I laughed. I buried my face in the crook of her neck, taking one big breath of her and then kissed her creamy skin slowly.... gently.

She shuddered in my arms just as Sebastian reached the other side of the door. I pulled away, leaving her to glare after me. She looked adorable with mussed hair and swollen lips. She stayed against the wall like I had physically molded her into it. I gave her a casual smile and then turned away to meet Sebastian right as he pulled on the handle.

"Thanks for letting me know about dinner," I called back to her. "Oh, hey, Sebastian."

"Avalon, everyone's looking for-" he stopped when his eyes found his sister, still pushed against the stone wall. "Mimi, is everything all right?"

"Mmm-hmmm," was her dazed and weak reply. I couldn't have stopped the smug grin that spread across my face if I wanted to.

Sebastian's stare moved from me to his sister and then narrowed in distrust. I scooted by him quickly, not wanting to hang around for probing questions. Amelia wasn't quite ready to admit she had feelings for me for whatever reason but I couldn't deny the sense of satisfaction that came with leaving her all confused and flustered. I smirked to myself, but then dropped it when the kitchen and dining room filled with people seemed to scrutinize my every move. Everything stilled as I moved to get a plate down from the cabinet. I elbowed my way through the small space to get to the stove, deciding we could not all stay here, there just wasn't enough room. I felt every eye follow my every move and I knew it had to do with the shit-eating grin I was wearing, but I couldn't seem to wipe the damn thing off my face.

"What?" I asked out loud.

Nobody answered; they just got back to eating. The sounds of forks and knives scraping plates filled the house and soon low chatter distracted everybody from my awkward entrance. Everybody except Eden, who sat at the table with a knowing smile of her own.

Just enjoy the show. I mumbled inwardly to her. She turned and winked at me. Brat.

I opened my mouth to embarrass her in a lame attempt to at revenge for thinking she knew everything. Even though she had saved me from Sebastian and his overprotective-brotherliness, I still felt the need to even the playing field on which she seemed to have the advantage right now. But before I could say anything, a violently strong wave of nausea smacked me in the face and I reeled from the hit. My mouth watered disgustingly as if I suddenly had way too much saliva and my throat burned like it was preparing for what was coming up.

I had never been sick before, and other than the disgusted feelings that came with watching Immortals destroy their own kind, these feelings were completely new to me. I clutched at my stomach and set my plate down realizing it was the food that was making me feel this way and that I was very abruptly no longer hungry.

Damn.

The last thing I wanted was for Amelia to see me unable to eat her dinner.

The nausea hit me again and I realized it was twice as strong this time. Out of the corner of my eye I watched Eden lean forward and clutch the table. She could feel it too.

Panic was the first emotion I had to sort through as the room spun around me. Eden and I didn't get sick. What the hell was going on?

King's Curse? No. This was miserable, but way to gentle.

Residual from Titus? Possible. But not probable.

My gaze flickered back to Eden who was turning green trying not to throw up all over the table in front of everyone.

"Magic, Eden," I growled through clenched teeth, hating how my mouth just kept watering. The feeling was unpleasant and irritating and I had no desire to find out what throwing up felt like. I had Eden's memories to fill in the blanks for me.

Eden. The sickness was coming from her. It had to be something left over from Titus.

The green color of her skin turned bright red with embarrassment, but she listened. Her magic solved the queasiness and I could stand up again without feeling like I was going to faint or puke. I felt so much better, but a quick glance at Eden revealed that she was still panicking.

"Are you Ok, E?" I asked, rushing over to her. I tried to keep my voice low so I wouldn't embarrass her anymore, but I was worried.

"Avalon, I'm fine," she laughed off. I heard the nervous tones in her voice and wondered if anyone else did.

"Eden, Love, is something wrong?" Kiran was at her side in a second, looking from me to her for an explanation.

"I'm fine, babe, Avalon's overreacting," she shot me a sideways glance that was.... angry. Why was she angry?

"E...." I warned. She stomped discreetly on my foot.

"I don't like peas," she whispered to Kiran, pretending like she didn't want to offend Amelia.

She did like peas. Kiran should know that and realize something was wrong. I wasn't going to say anything, it wasn't my place. But Eden shouldn't be keeping things from any of us.

"You don't? I've seen you eat them before," Kiran commented, his forehead creasing in concern. Good man, Kiran. I was happy he wasn't oblivious. Something like that could have gotten by Eden if the tables were turned, but the rest of us were observant.

"Uh, I don't like canned peas," she adjusted her lie. Only this one could be bought, since the entire dinner had been thrown together from a collection of canned foods. This was a trick any of us in the original Resistance could have done and I had to wonder how a pampered princess like Amelia had been able to pull it off.

"Oh," Kiran relented, not looking convinced.

"You guys worry, way too much!" she sighed and then got up to empty her still mostly full plate.

I stood with Kiran watching her walk away.

"Avalon is she telling me the truth?" Kiran whispered in a hoarse voice.

"I don't know. Does *anybody* like canned peas?" I deflected.

"I guess that's true," Kiran mumbled and then followed Eden upstairs where presumably he was going to get to the bottom of this.

What's going on, Eden? I growled. *Be honest with me, I'll know if you're lying.*

Avalon, it's nothing. It's just left over from healing Titus today. The same kind of stuff used to happen after I healed people with the King's Curse. She explained patiently, but she sounded exhausted. I felt as she gathered stuff for a shower and knew this would be a short conversation. Very short.

Not the exact same. I reminded her.

Well, I didn't heal Titus from the King's Curse, did I? she snapped.

It wasn't like her to get irritable either.

If it happens again, then we'll worry about it. For now, let's just assume it had something to do with Titus, alright? She asked calmly this time.

Ok, fine. I agreed and then left her head completely. She was getting in the shower to avoid me and to avoid Kiran.

Something was going on.

Chapter Twenty

"Is Eden ready yet?" I asked impatiently. She had been taking her sweet time getting ready to leave and she was driving me crazy. Since she had completely blocked our telepathic communication when my nagging had gotten maybe a little extreme, I had to resort to asking her husband, who was equally as unamused with me.

I had two nights in Paris with Amelia. What had turned into an emergency stopover was now a diplomatic visit. It had been decided that Eden, Kiran, Sebastian, Amelia and I would stay at the Cartier's house and do a proper visit while we waited for Titus to get back to full strength.

Everyone else was staying at the cottage and planning out our next step. At first I was maybe a little upset about the living arrangements.... It physically hurt me to walk away from a mission to go endure diplomacy in a stuffy house with stuffy people.

Then Amelia had called me a petulant child, and immediately my attitude changed.

This wasn't going to feel like suffering through monotonous duty, this was going to be a challenge. I had two days to make that girl fall for me.

Well, one and a half and I was losing that half the longer Eden took.

"Avalon if you're so anxious to get into town why don't you take one of your cars and

we'll follow behind when Eden's ready," Kiran offered. I could tell his patience with me was running thin, but I suspected it had more to do with how worried about Eden he was than my whining. "Either Sebastian or Amelia can ride with you. Or go by yourself, Bianca and Jean are expecting you."

"Excellent idea!" I beamed. I should have thought of this thirty minutes ago. Argh.

I walked outside and threw my backpack in the trunk of the Fiat and then went on a mission to hunt down Amelia. The moon was bright overhead, full and huge. It lit up the countryside so luminously I barely had to use any magic to see through the darkness. I knew she wasn't inside the house and so I went on a search for her on the property.

The field of sunflowers lay behind the cottage on rolling hills. I surveyed the area with a mixture of distrust and hope. Girls loved that Gabriel bewitched the flowers to bloom all the time. Even now their large, flowery heads tilted toward the light of the moon. But honestly, they creeped me out. Flowers were supposed to die. Everything had a season, born to this world and then eventually taken from this world. And Gabriel had defied the natural order of things with his bewitchment.

I paused when I saw Amelia's figure standing in front of the stretching field. Her hair whipped around behind her in the breeze. She pulled it over her shoulder, tying it in a ponytail to keep it out of her face. I watched her slender shoulders rise and drop with a long sigh. The nape of her neck was exposed to me and I wondered if she knew what revealing that kind of perfect skin and silhouette could do to a man?

Probably not. She probably had no idea the hold she had over me.

I cleared my throat so I wouldn't scare her when I approached and then sidled up next to her, careful not to touch her. She stared out at the flowers, deep in thought and only acknowledged me with a lift of her eyebrow. Her arms folded around her as if to protect herself from me. And she shivered in the night breeze although I knew she couldn't be cold.

We stood there for a while, watching the night and the unnatural sunflowers.

"These flowers give me the heebs," I admitted, breaking our comfortable silence.

"The heebs?" she asked, her nose crinkling with the question.

"You know, the heebs, like heebie jeebies," I explained.

She laughed out loud, the clear tone of her voice carrying into the wind. It made me smile with her. There was just something so charming and open about her personality, something that made me want to always laugh with her, or smile with her. She was smart and observant, quick and compassionate, shrewd and breath-taking all at once and she wasn't even aware of any of it.

"How very brave of you," she commented, her laughter dying down into an amused smile. She looked down at the flowers and crinkled her nose again. Was this her confused expression? "And why do they give you the.... heebs?"

"Probably because they don't die," I answered honestly. "They're supposed to die. It's like Gabriel froze nature here, like he stifled it, smothered it and not allowed the natural course of life to take place."

"That's awfully ironic," she challenged. "Considering you fought tooth and nail for our people so that we wouldn't have to face the natural course of things."

I pondered that for a long moment, taking in her argument and her delicate profile that never stopped watching the flowers. "That's not true," I started gently, so she would know I wasn't being defensive. "Lucan, excuse me, not even Lucan, it started with Derrick. The Kendrick line was the one that stifled our natural course, froze our people in a way of life that was foreign and unnatural for them. Nobody knows why we were gifted with these abilities and longevity, but we were. Our people were always supposed to be able to live and never die, to have incredible powers, to be separate from the human race. It was our people that changed our nature. Flowers are not meant to live forever, but we are. The chance to die was taken from these flowers, like our chance to live was taken from us."

Amelia was silent for a few minutes, thinking over what I said. When she finally decided to answer I sucked in a breath and held it. "You're right, of course. Life was taken from our people and you are the one that gave it back. And you're right that in some things death is welcome, death is.... needed. But Gabriel offered to these flowers what no other flower on Earth can have and that is a chance to be immortalized. It's not a tragedy, it's a gift. A gift that one day you'll give to your future wife too."

I quickly brought my thumb to my teeth and chomped down. She was right. Very right. But more importantly was she hoping it would be her?

Or was that just wishful thinking on my part.

I nearly choked on the thought, my circulation stuttering inside of me. Marriage? Was I that far gone with Amelia already? I couldn't be. I barely knew her.

I shook my head, trying not to have those kinds of thoughts yet. Mostly because they would freak her out, but also because they were kind of freaking me out by not freaking me out. I found myself ready to think this through, ready to think about her in that role in my life.

I was supposed to be the life-long bachelor, married to the cause. Had I changed? Or had the cause changed?

"I don't like Jericho," Amelia admitted so softly I thought I had imagined it. "I mean, like more than a friend."

I paused for a while, waiting for her to say more and when she didn't I offered, "I know," with as much humility as I could muster.

"But that doesn't mean I like you either," she announced on a sigh.

"I know that too," I did my best to hide my smile, but it was no use. It was like one of those trick geometry questions. Not liking Jericho did not mean she liked me. She liked me completely separate and apart from Jericho.

"Stop smiling," she grumbled, which did nothing but make me smile bigger. Our magics danced around us, hers careful and tentative, mine embarrassingly aggressive. I couldn't help it though, my magic had a mind of its own, a demanding mind of its own. Besides, the hungry clawing I felt to get to know Amelia better, my magic already felt like it did know her better and as the electricity slowly sizzled and popped around us, it almost dared Amelia's magic not to respond.

As if she was acutely aware of the cat and mouse game our magics were playing, she shifted next to me and cleared her throat. Most of me hated that I still made her so uncomfortable and she didn't seem to trust me or herself around me. But there was this small part of me that loved seeing how she reacted to me, how her body responded to my movements, how her magic answered mine. My hand started moving before my mind could remind it that I might not like if she rejected me and I reached out and took her hand in mine.

She didn't reject me. Her spine straightened for the briefest moment before her hand relaxed into mine. She was all smooth, soft skin and slender fingers and my hand completely covered hers, contrasting it with my calluses and masculine strength. We stood there looking over sunflowers that were starting to change my opinion of them. She didn't push me away and deepened the hold, slipping her delicate fingers between mine and stepping closer to me.

When I kissed her, it was hot. *She* was hot.... sexy and irresistible. And there would *never* be another feeling that rivaled her body pressed against mine. But standing in the night air, enjoying a comfortable silence, with her just holding my hand like she was happy to stay there forever.... like she trusted me to let her stay there forever.... was a whole new kind of feeling I had never experienced.

Ever.

My magic swelled the longer we stood there, so that it was a shield around us, covering us both. Her magic didn't stand a chance as mine took hers inside of it, consuming it, melding it to one energy field. She never looked at me, never even acknowledged me standing next to her, save for the easy touch between us. Then she let out a soft sigh, almost quiet enough that I didn't hear her. But I did hear her.

I turned to face her, I needed to know how she felt, if she would give me a chance. But then staring down at her, I couldn't find words to break the moment. And I wasn't even convinced I wanted to. Hell yes I wanted to know if she would give me a chance. But if she was still so set on denying there could be something between us.... at the moment.... I didn't know if I wanted to hear it.

Her face tilted to mine, slowly, tentatively. Her deep brown eyes grew big as our gazes met and the wind was knocked from me in a whoosh of breath. She paralyzed me, there in the dark, in the middle of the country, she immobilized me with that big-eyed stare. In that moment I knew the rejection would be worth it, the chase, the effort, the time I would put in to pursuing her would all be worth it.

She was worth it.

"There you two are," Sebastian huffed from behind us. The spell was broken and embarrassment muddled with fear flushed her face. Amelia immediately dropped my hand and shook hers out like I had burned her.

Great.

Damn it Sebastian.

I turned around and glared at him through the dark. He either couldn't see that well through the night or he was pretending not to notice me. I swallowed back the "king card" not even sure what reminding him of it would accomplish. Amelia had shrunk back into herself again.

Damn it.

"Let's go ahead and go. Titus seems to be fine now and Eden is still managing things in the house. Kiran says they might be here for a while," Sebastian explained. "I don't want mother and father to have to wait for us much longer."

"Alright," Amelia agreed and walked off with her brother without even giving me a glance back.

I had planned on riding back with Amelia, but none of those plans included Sebastian. I started plotting as soon as their bags were loaded and we climbed into the car. I decided to take things especially serious when Amelia climbed into the backseat and Sebastian sat down next to me.

I had no problem with Sebastian. He was a friend, even a good friend at times. But I could more than understand his overprotectiveness for his sister and I really hated feeling empathetic when I had my own agenda.

Hell, it's not like I had been Kiran's biggest fan. In fact, it wasn't until I saw how far he was willing to go to protect Eden, how easily he would have given up his own life to save her that I even granted the guy the time of day. Those were extreme circumstances though. And I would never be willing to put Amelia in those kinds of dangerous situations to prove my feelings for her to her brother. I would protect her from ever having to go through anything like what Eden went through. Sebastian was going to just have to get over this. I had enough of an uphill battle trying to convince Amelia I was a decent guy, I didn't have time to woo Sebastian too.

Or maybe Sebastian had the right idea. Hadn't Amelia said it? Whoever I chose wouldn't just be Queen, she would share the burden of living forever with me. I knew I could be a prick, but more than putting up with me, living forever was a hell of a lot to deal with. It wasn't fair to assume she would want that life even if I did convince her she had feelings for me.

Still, when we pulled up to the Cartier's estate in the middle of Paris, after a silent drive from the country I had firmly resolved to let Amelia go, so I was surprised by the instinct that flooded my senses and took over my will completely.

I pulled up to the drive with the intention of letting the siblings out at the door before I pulled the car around to the back of the house. However, as soon as Sebastian stepped out of the car and became distracted with a Titan that was asking about bags, I slammed the passenger door shut with my magic and took off onto the streets of Paris like I was running from something.

I smirked at the wide-eyed reflection of Amelia in my review mirror and felt the surge of adrenaline for what I had planned.

"What are you doing?" she gasped, clutching at the seat around her.

"I uh, I thought we would.... sightsee," I shrugged my shoulder casually, whipping out my phone to text Sebastian a half-assed explanation so he wouldn't worry.

"Sightsee?" Amelia asked slowly, her eyes still as round and big as ever. "I think you just kidnapped me."

I chuckled. Ok, maybe she was right. Kidnapping was definitely not a smooth way to go about this. And this was in absolute opposition to the argument I had just worked up on the drive here.

But clearly I wasn't thinking with my head right now.

Chapter Twenty- One

Amelia stayed quiet as I drove through the busy Paris streets. I half expected her to jump out of the vehicle at any of the places I had to stop and wait, paused in standstill traffic even this late at night. But she stayed still in her seat. Her magic snapped around her with an irritated edge, but at least she didn't try to escape the car.

Which stupidly gave me hope.

I parallel parked on a side street off the Champs de Elysee, squeezing in between a Mini Cooper and a Smart Car. I shivered at the sight of the Smart Car. So. Ugly. Every male bone in my body rejected the idea of something so weak and powerless.

The car was uncomfortably silent after the engine died and I wasn't exactly sure what to say. Honesty seemed to be the best policy here, but I didn't want to scare her off either.

"Avalon...?" she broke the silence, her tone calculating and questioning. "What are we doing?"

"Sightseeing? I repeated my earlier excuse but it sounded weak out loud and in the open.

"So you said," she mumbled. "You didn't want to ask me first? See if I actually wanted to go with you?"

"Uh...." I stammered. I turned around in my seat so that I could look her in the eye. It took practically all my courage to meet her gaze, but I forced myself to do it. I made this bed, now it was time to lie in it. Hopefully she would keep me company though. "Would you have said yes?" I asked.

"I'm not sure," she mumbled through teeth that were biting at her bottom lip thoughtfully.

"Are you going to get out of the car with me?" I pressed my luck.

I noticed the slight twitch to her lips and confidence grew like wildfire in my veins.

"I'm not sure," she repeated.

I believed that she wasn't sure, but I also believed that she wanted to spend time with me more than she would admit. Swallowing back insecurities that had been nonexistent until Amelia showed up, I reached for her hand that played with a loose string on her kneecap. I picked up her fingers gently in mine, sliding the pads of my fingers against hers. The barely there touch was so intoxicating, my body rushed with heat. Amelia's eyes darkened into depthless pools, her gaze flickering between our hands and my eyes from underneath those thick lashes.

"Please?" I asked through a thick voice.

She nodded her affirmation with the smallest tilt of her chin, her teeth still punishing her bottom lip. I stared at her for a full minute more before talking myself into letting go of her hand.

And when I did pull away, I had to fight feelings of emptiness. Without her hand in mine I felt lessened and incomplete. I swallowed roughly against everything that could mean and settled with taking her hand into mine as soon as she crawled from the back seat and her feet were firmly on the pavement.

She didn't hesitate.

I smiled like an idiot.

Progress.

The breeze was cool the further toward the middle of the night we got, but neither of us noticed as we walked along the Champs hand in hand. Paris was one of those fantastic cities that were always alive no matter how late the night got. We walked through crowds of noisy tourists and past street vendors painting idyllic portraits or peddling delicious smelling food.

The wide street was lined with expensive, designer shops and cafes that flowed onto the sidewalk with tiny tables squashed together. The scents of cigarette smoke and strong coffee drifted around us and I felt like sighing with contentment.

I didn't. But I felt like it.

I hadn't felt this alive in a long time.... possibly ever.

My hand instinctively tightened around Amelia's, afraid she would let go, afraid this moment of perfection would dissolve around me and I would be left struggling to breathe, the emptiness of an endless future looming over me.

"What's the plan, Avalon?" Amelia asked in a smoky voice, pulling me back to the present, back to her. I looked down at her, noticing that she was actually relaxed and at ease with me.

"I don't have one," I admitted. "I just wanted to get you alone." I laughed after the honesty fell out of my mouth before I could stop it or grapple control of my mouth.

"I see," she laughed too. "And now that you have me alone....?"

She was flirting with me? She was flirting with me! I knew no woman could withstand my irresistible charm. Nervousness I didn't even notice coiling my insides tight dissipated as I decided to unleash the full caliber of my charisma.

I paused on the busy sidewalk, pulling her forward with the hand that was held in mine. "Have my wicked way with you, of course," I whispered in a gruff, intense voice.

"Of course," she murmured back, heat flashing in her eyes.

My hand slipped to her waist, and I yanked her forward against me. Pedestrians had to move around us since we stood in the middle of the sidewalk, but my focus was completely narrowed on Amelia. She swallowed, her pretty throat working with the effort.

I bent down to her slowly, giving her plenty of time to pull away. I hoped we were beyond all that, but I couldn't pretend to understand how this girl thought. My lips brushed against hers just barely, her soft lips teasing and torturing my will power. I told myself I would respect her here, in the middle of all of these people, but I felt my resolve tumble out of my control the minute her breath heated the air between us.

I allowed myself one more feather light kiss. My hands tightened on her hips, revealing a desire that I refused my mouth. Her tongue swept out and across my bottom lip sending a shiver, a real, honest to God shiver, down my spine.

I stepped back, putting space between us. I sucked in a deep breath while the world tilted and spun around me. My heart hammered in my chest, beating a rhythm that seemed to include more than my heart.... more than my life.

"Can I take you to one of my favorite restaurants?" Amelia asked in the most beautiful, breathy voice.

I nodded my approval, not trusting my voice to be strong enough to answer. She slipped her hand into mine and pulled me down the street after her. People moved around us, by us, bumping into us or talking loudly near us, but I missed it all. My world shrunk and narrowed to include only one other person, and the realization was surprisingly contenting. There was a grin plastered to my face and I tried to wipe it off, I tried to not do the whole stupid, foolish smile thing, but I couldn't.... She.... Amelia.... was something so incredible, so meaningful, I wondered if I'd ever be able to think straight again.

We were peacefully quiet as Amelia led us through a maze of side streets. Her hand stayed in my mine the entire way, and I was content to follow her. I had wanted this to be my thing, my big show of chivalry or something like that, but she had this way of overpowering every alpha male instinct in me until I was putty in her hands, willing to let her lead me anywhere and do anything she wanted, and at the same time ramping up all of my testosterone until I was a possessive, psychotic Neanderthal and I felt the strongest urge to throw her over my shoulder and declare "Mine!" to everyone we passed.

We finally stopped at a tiny little café with a small outside seating area filled with Parisians enjoying bottles of French wine and smoking in the crisp night air. She led me through the tables and into the dimly lit café where the hostess showed us to a table tucked away in the back of the restaurant.

Amelia chatted in French with the hostess as if they were old friends and before the human girl who seemed to be in her early twenties left us she gave Amelia double air kisses on both of her cheeks. I pulled out the chair for my date, and helped her get settled before I took my own chair across from her.

"Friend of yours?" I asked, admiring how the soft light from a candle in the middle of the table darkened Amelia's eyes but kept her red lips perfectly illuminated. God she was gorgeous.

"She's the daughter of the owner and chef," she explained. I stared at her lips, completely mesmerized with their every movement. "I told you, this is my favorite café, I come here a lot when I'm in town. Her name is Evelia, or I call her Evie and she has a three year old daughter named Claribel who is the most precious thing you've ever seen. Evie's husband was killed in a motorcycle accident when Claribel was only a baby. Evie works for her father in the evening while her mother watches Claribel. She is the most beautiful person, Avalon, but her heart is broken. I wish there was something I could do for her, some way to help her heal from losing the love of her life and the hardship of being a single mother.... I mean there are tangible things I can do for her, but it's like her pain is so much deeper than physical needs. I just hate it for her."

I sat silent for a long time, not sure how to respond to Amelia's compassion. I had never met anyone like her before, someone who put everyone before themselves, who thought about needs and feelings and hardships that would never even cross my mind.

I didn't like to think of myself as a selfish person, I mean I had risked my life for the sake of thousands of people I didn't even really know on like a personal level. I would do anything for the people in my life and I would kill anyone that tried to hurt them. But for the most part, the human population never crossed my mind at that deep of a level, save for the Gypsy village but Ileana refused any and all of my help or money.

Amelia thought about everyone, about everything.

She was a beautiful person. She radiated with light and love and warmth.

She was incredible.

And if she said anything else.... Anything else at all, even if it was about the weather.... I knew I would fall for her.

I would lose myself to her.

"What?" she asked shyly, her cheeks blushing under my open stare.

And that was all it took. I was lost in her.

"I just.... it's nothing, I uh, I've never met anyone like you before," I finished lamely, knowing the intensity of my feelings for her would scare her off if I was honest with her.

"I hope that's a good thing," she laughed self-consciously.

I reached for her hand across the table, hating that we had a table separating us. I smiled at her, or at least widened my smile, because I was pretty sure I hadn't stopped smiling since she agreed to get out of my car and spend time with me.

"It's a very good thing," I promised and then was rewarded with a deeper flush to her cheeks. "Are you hungry?" I asked, hoping to calm her down a little bit, I could feel her jumpy magic as I made her nervous with my interest in her.

"Not really," she admitted and I hoped she was being honest with me. Although we just ate dinner not that long ago and I wasn't really hungry either. "But their cappuccinos are fantastic."

I signaled the waiter over then and gave him our order for two cappuccinos. As soon as he was gone, I refocused my attention on Amelia not even knowing where to start. It could be said that I had never been tongue-tied before in my entire life. But looking down at this beautiful creature across from me, I didn't even know where to start.

"Avalon, seriously, why are you looking at me like that?" Amelia laughed at me. She shook out her hair and averted her gaze.

I laughed with her, a little self-consciously, hoping I wasn't scaring the hell out of her. My only encouragement was that she didn't pull her hand out of mine. "How am I looking at you?"

"I don't know," she fidgeted a little, fixating on the table cloth. "Like.... like you're shocked I'm sitting here with you."

"I *am* shocked I'm sitting with you." I squeezed her hand in mine and gave her a crooked smile I hoped came off as charming. "I keep waiting for you to remember how much I irritate you."

"Irritate me?" she asked, her eyes flashing with confusion. "You don't irritate me. You.... I just.... I don't think I trust you yet."

The waiter came back with two small cups of strong smelling foamy coffee. I watched her closely as he set down our drinks in front of us, letting her words sink in and trying to figure out what to do with them.

As soon as he left she took a sip of her coffee, her eyes darting around the restaurant nervously. She was probably hoping I would let the whole thing drop, but I couldn't.

"I'm trying to decide if I should be thrilled you don't find me obnoxious or worried because you don't trust me," I admitted lightly, hoping she would explain better what exactly there was not to trust me with.

"Ok, maybe I was a little too generous earlier. You're not irritating me tonight," she smiled at me, batting her thick eye lashes innocently.

I chuckled at her sense of humor. "I figured as much, I've been told I'm a very difficult person to get along with."

"Who told you that?" Amelia asked, leaning forward and resting her chin in her free hand.

"Mostly Eden," I admitted. "And Jericho, and Kiran and uh, Talbott.... Lilly says that a lot too I suppose. Actually the list could go on and on," I pouted thinking about my council and my list of friends and old teammates. "But in my defense I don't exactly try to get along with all of those people, or uh, any people."

"That's what I mean," Amelia bubbled animatedly. I gave her a questioning look and so she continued. "What makes me different? Why are you trying with me Avalon? And why now? You've known me for years and until I showed up in Romania you barely noticed my existence."

"Only because this is the first time I have been around you since Eden's wedding," I defended myself and worked at keeping my tone gentle. "I'm fairly certain if you would have been a more permanent fixture in my life I would have been trying for years now."

"I don't understand why," she mumbled, tearing her eyes from mine to stare down at the tablecloth again.

"Do you really not know how amazing you are?" I asked, and felt myself smile again just because I couldn't help it. "You're compassionate and sweet, you're confident and humble, you don't put up with my BS or let me get away with anything. You are this incredible woman and I just can't seem to get enough of you. I want to, no I need to get to know you better. I can't help myself, I can't.... stop myself and I honestly don't want to."

Amelia looked up at me, her face shy and half hidden in the candlelight. She was silent and thoughtful for several moments before she finally responded, "I don't want you to either."

Chapter Twenty-Two

"I have to ask you," Amelia asked seriously after a moment. She withdrew her hand from mine and tucked it under the table away from my reach. I bit back my objection and stilled the nervousness simmering in my chest. "How dangerous is Terletov?"

All at once I let out a breath of relief because this wasn't the question I was expecting and I was happy that she wasn't pulling away from whatever was between us. At the same time though I was wary to go into too much detail with her because I didn't want her to worry.

Terletov was my problem. And it wasn't just Amelia; I didn't want *anyone* to worry. Well, except me. I could worry because I would take care of him.

"He's dangerous," I admitted, even after convincing myself to keep her sheltered from the truth.

The exciting atmosphere of the beginning of a relationship was completely sucked out of the air between us and we were left somber and serious. Even her magic that had been happily flirting with mine retreated.

Damn it.

I had even more of a reason to hate Terletov.

He was apparently in the business of torturing Immortals and ruining my dates.

"More so than my uncle?" she asked, her eyes revealing her depthless concern.

"In some ways, yes," I held her gaze, deciding I very much wanted to pull her into me and comfort her. She was too considerate for this not to affect her. I had ordered for the details of our findings to be kept confidential and knowing what kind of guy Sebastian was I knew she hadn't heard any of the more gory aspects of our trip to Siberia. I planned to keep it that way. Her lips parted so that she could ask more questions and I decided to offer her more information to curb her curiosity. "Lucan was dangerous because the Kingdom followed him without question. I mean.... he was the King. He obviously had unlimited power. He was the ultimate authority and he abused his power and his people. Terletov is dangerous because he wants the same thing. His plan seems to restore Lucan's totalitarian rule only extend his cruel reach to every citizen. Whereas Lucan was bred to believe and act the way he did, Terletov was given options and chose this path completely free of influence. I don't know much about him, but I do know that he, if given the chance, would make what our people went through with Lucan feel like vacation."

"And you've seen evidence?" Amelia asked, her golden eyes lit up with scrutiny. "I'm not trying to offend you Avalon, but your democracy is new and untested. Are you sure he is not just a concerned citizen that doesn't trust you? That he simply believes he would be a better ruler?"

I swallowed back my impatience. I was used to people just going along with whatever I said. It hurt my pride to have Amelia question me. Was this what she meant when she said she didn't trust me? That she actually didn't trust me as King?

That was a slightly frustrating revelation.

"I am positive he is not a concerned citizen," I all but growled and then regretted it immediately. She wasn't in Siberia. She didn't see the carnage or feel the evil. She wasn't with Henri and Sophia when they passed away, rotting shells of what they used to be. "Amelia, trust me when I say that this man is the worst kind of evil. He has no respect for our people, or life in general. His fight isn't to ensure our people have the right kind of freedom, or democracy, he wants to ensure they remain enslaved and imprisoned."

"What are you keeping from me?" Amelia's eyes narrowed as she dared me not to answer.

"Things that would never let someone like you forget their horror," I replied softly.

"Avalon, I can handle the truth," she pressed. She leaned across the table, her fingers finding mine as she gently traced a line from my fingernails to wrist in a clever plea to get me to open up. I smiled at her tactics not minding them one bit.

I looked her intensely in the eyes before I said, "Believe me when I say I am very aware that there is very little you can't handle. You're so strong." I paused and let my words sink in. A flush crept up the base of her throat, quickly moving to her face and darkening her complexion.

God I loved that look on her.

"There is more to this than I am willing to share at the moment, obviously. But it has nothing to do with me not trusting you or assuming you're not ready to hear any of it. I'm still processing it myself and if any of this were to get out to the public I'm afraid of the consequences." Her hand stilled on mine and her face flushed deeper with anger. I chuckled at her defensiveness and continued quickly, "Again, not because I don't trust you, but because this is a very sensitive matter and frankly I don't trust the rest of the world." I gestured around the room, revealing my deep level of paranoia.

She withdrew her hand, but some of the heat faded from her cheeks. "Alright, Avalon, if you don't want to tell me, then I guess I'll have to interrogate my brother."

She was challenging me. Damn it if I didn't want to prove myself to her.

Heads up, a very irritated brother is about to interrupt your plans, A. Eden burst into my thoughts and if I wouldn't have been frustrated with the entire situation and how the date was turning out I would have applauded Eden's timing.

"Speak of the devil," I murmured.

Amelia shot me a questioning look just as her cell phone rang. Her confusion turned to a satisfied smirk when she read the number on her phone and answered.

"Hello, Sebastian," she said happily. She paused to listen to whatever he was saying. I could have used magic to eavesdrop, but I frankly didn't want to hear anything Sebastian had to say at the moment. "It's just coffee.... No, I understand.... Alright, tell them I'll be home soon..... Yes, yes. Alright. See you soon."

She ended her phone call and looked up at me with a decidedly thoughtful expression. "I didn't mean to pressure you tonight, Avalon. I'm just.... I'm just obviously concerned for the Kingdom. I don't want any more fighting or dying or coups-ing. Do you know what I mean? And not knowing, or not being informed I just feel helpless and I hate it. I sat through the entire last ordeal completely out of the loop. I was treated like a child and sheltered from everything. I don't want to be that little girl anymore."

"Nobody knows that more than me, trust me, Amelia," I promised, my voice dropping to a deeply lower register, just thinking about how much of a little girl she isn't. "And I will never treat you like one." I paused and let her blush reappear before commenting reluctantly, "I take it Sebastian asked you to come home?"

She cleared her throat nervously and then nodded, "My parents are anxious to see me."

"Ah. Well, then, we better not keep them waiting." I smiled and discreetly tucked a handful of Euros under my empty cup to pay for the coffee and tip the nearly nonexistent waiter enough to pay his rent for a while. Maybe Amelia's generosity was rubbing off on me.

"Whatever you want," she grumbled adorably.

"Well, I wouldn't say going to meet your parents is exactly what I want," I murmured, not able to hold back my playful smile.

"Did you forget that you're King?" Amelia slipped her arm into mine without being invited as we stood up from the table and a thrill surged inside of me. "You're supposed to be able to do whatever you want."

"Mmm, I'll keep that in mind." It felt like she was flirting with me and insinuating something I wouldn't let myself believe just yet. But still, when she snuggled closer as we walked back to the car I leaned over and pressed a kiss on the top of her head.

Not for any other reason than because I wanted to.

And Amelia had told me I was supposed to do whatever I wanted.

I woke in the place I created, the place I designed for her. I looked around and decided I was pleased but made no effort to move.

This was risky. This was maybe going too far.

But with all that had happened, I had forgotten to tell her happy birthday.

I took a steadying breath and gathered my courage.

And then I called her.

Electricity snapped and crackled in my brain with blinding intensity before she appeared before me. Her golden brown eyes opened immediately, wide-eyed and fearful before they settled on me and relaxed.

"Avalon?" she asked, her voice full of amusement.

I smiled at her, standing to my feet so I could pull her to hers as well. "I forgot to tell you happy birthday."

She let out a soft, nervous laugh and turned in a circle to take this place in. "I've never Dream-Walked before," she whispered.

"I've only ever with Eden and Kiran," I paused thinking about those times. "It was awkward."

She smiled wider and stepped up to me. "No cake?"

"No cake," I smiled down at her.

The white sand beach we stood on was warm beneath our feet, the moon bright and the stars twinkling above. I designed the place with lanterns lining our space on tall poles stuck deep into the sand. There was water that lapped at the shore a little ways away, the sound was like music in the warm night air.

Amelia was wearing a thin tank top and very short shorts as her pajamas and I was only in plaid pajama bottoms. Her hair was a mess, wild and unruly and her face completely bare of makeup.

She was breathtaking.

I held out my hand to her and she looked at it skeptically. "What exactly are your plans to celebrate my birthday?"

"Will you dance with me?" I asked.

"There's no music," she answered but put her hand in mine anyway.

I pulled her to me, slipping my other arm around her waist. Ever since the gypsy village I had been fantasizing about holding her against me again. I nodded to an old school turn table that sat on top of an oak stand. Not very hip looking, but my version of romance. I used magic to move the needle and the familiar squeak scratched the vinyl before the slow, sultry sounds of big band jazz filled the air around us.

The stars twinkled above our heads. The sand glistened beneath our bare feet. Amelia danced close in my arms. Perfection.

"Thank you, Avalon," she tilted her head up to me, her chin resting on my bare chest.

"Happy birthday, Amelia," I murmured down to her before capturing her lips with mine for a short but infinitely sweet kiss.

I didn't know how this rated on her inventory of birthday gifts, but this was going on top of mine as one of the best. I held her until the sun came up, memorizing the feel of her skin against mine, the fragile feel of her tiny hand in mine.

I could have held her forever.

If only the sun didn't need to rise. If only there was this kind of perfection in my life and nothing more.

I released her back to reality just as dawn was breaking. She was quiet but happy with the night and I wondered, in the cold light of day if her feelings for me would change or if this gift had been a bridge to her heart I would be able to travel often.

Breakfast the next morning was a catered affair. Bianca and Jean had given up their servants after Lucan was more or less dethroned, but that didn't mean they were used to functioning without help. I joined everyone for an early meal where we would talk about our plans.

I had been up most of the night reflecting on the next step to hunting Terletov and felt a bit conflicted. Our original plan was to hang around Paris for two days so Titus could recover, but since Eden healed him he had called late last night to say that he was fine. I believed him. And that was important because some guys would have faked feeling one hundred percent to get on with the mission, but I trusted Titus enough to know that he would never put the mission in jeopardy by being anything less than absolutely ready.

So he was ready. And the more space we put in between us and whoever ransacked Gabriel's church the less likely we would be to finding anything out. That should have been enough for me.

Hell, remembering anything that had happened up until now should have been enough for me.

But there was another side to my emotions apparently.... Another side I hadn't even known existed until Amelia showed up and that other side wanted, no, demanded that I stick around for the next day and get to know Amelia as much as possible. In fact this brand new side all but completely revolted at the idea of leaving early.

And now that I sat around a long, formal table, with her on the other side practically begging me to carry her into the other room and ravish her with her sleep mussed hair and form fitting tank top and sweat pants, I realized just how close this new side was to winning the argument.

"Avalon, are you still planning to stay for another day?" Bianca asked as if she could read my thoughts. "Sebastian says that Titus is better."

"He is better," I agreed. "I wanted to give him plenty of time to recover, but if he is as well as he says he is than we will probably leave this morning. I don't want the trail to go dead before we have a chance to chase it." Damn duty and responsibility.

"Where is the trail?" Jean asked in his bored voice that had more to do with how he was raised than his actual emotion behind the tone.

"Peru," Sebastian answered, giving a pointed look to his parents that I didn't quite understand.

"Who will you take with you?" Amelia asked. I met her eyes from across the table and I was rewarded with a small, friendly smile that reassured me I hadn't imagined there really was something between us. Although if we left this morning I had no idea when I would see her again.

"Gabriel, Silas, Sebastian of course," I nodded at Sebastian assuming he was already planning on going, "And then Jericho, Xavier, Xander, Roxie, Titus and the retired Titans if they're up for it. We don't always see eye to eye, but they have an insight into Terletov that I don't."

"Mimi, aren't you in Lima for the next few days for that human trafficking seminar?" Bianca asked casually.

But I was a former member of a resistance and had studied Bianca over the years when running intel. I knew she wasn't as casual as she was pretending.

"I am," Amelia nodded, looking back down at her breakfast.

"You should meet up with Sebastian when you're finished," Bianca stated. "It would be good for you to get some of this experience."

"No!" I practically shouted in unison with Jean, her father and Sebastian her brother.

"It's enough that you go to all of these humanitarian projects in dangerous areas, you don't need to join your brother on these death missions," Jean lectured with uncharacteristic emotion in his thick French accent.

"He's right, Mimi," Kiran agreed.

I was satisfied that so many other people had her best interest in mind, but a little unsettled that Amelia actually seemed put out by it. She wasn't really considering joining us, was she? Besides the fact that the mission was dangerous, from a director's point of view she had absolutely no experience.

"I'm glad you're all in agreement on how I should spend my time," Amelia huffed, pushing her plate forward.

"It is dangerous, Amelia," I reminded her gently. "Look at what just happened to Titus. We were lucky Eden was so close."

"Not you too, Avalon," Amelia groaned. "I am not Lucan's spoiled niece, and I would greatly appreciate it if you all stopped treating me like her." She gave each male at the table a nasty glare in turned.

I shot her a charming smile, believing we had collectively made our point when a violent surge of nausea threatened to bring my breakfast back up. I leaned against the table, resting my face in my hands as I tried to get the sickness under control. My magic could not work strong enough and I had no idea where it was coming from until I caught the feint smell of eggs in the air.

Eggs?

Before I could examine why eggs would make me feel ill, just the thought of them had me reeling again.

"Are you alright?" I heard Kiran ask.

"Ugh, I'm fine, I'm just pretty sure those eggs were spoiled," I mumbled through my hands.

A pause before, "I'm glad to hear that Avalon, but I was actually asking Eden."

I didn't have to see Kiran's face to hear the irritation in his voice. I should have known Eden would be feeling sick if I felt sick. We had gone through the King's Curse and enough battles together to prove that physical pain affected us both. But we weren't really supposed to get sick outside of the King's Curse.

Especially not with something as asinine as food poisoning. And this was two days in a row.

Of nausea.

When we're around food.

Wait a minute.

Eden? I demanded in our heads.

Not now Avalon! She pleaded just as she reigned in control of the sick feelings and her magic. *Please!*

"I'm fine," she smiled brightly at Kiran. "Um, Avalon wasn't feeling well, it must have affected me as well." And then in our heads, *Just let me figure this out first, please.*

Uh, huh. I agreed, in a bit of a daze.

"I, uh, I need to prepare to leave. Thank you for breakfast," I nodded to the Cartiers and then got the hell out of there as fast as I could.

That better not have been morning sickness.

I was going to kill Eden if that was true. Well, first I would probably hug her until it was dangerous for her unborn baby, but then I was going to kill her.

There was probably nothing more emasculating than going through three trimesters of something only women should be blessed with.

On the other hand.... I would probably be awesome at being an uncle.

Chapter Twenty-Three

"You wanker, how dare you keep something like that from me!" Kiran accused as I was packing up the last of my overnight bag in the fancy guest room of the Cartiers.

Kiran and Eden had burst into my room all swirling magic and radiance. She confirmed my suspicions. Or probably her suspicions....

"It's true?" I ignored Kiran who looked decidedly more at ease today. I hadn't realized how disheveled and run down he had been over the last twenty four hours.

Eden nodded shyly, her eyes brimming with tears.

"You're pregnant?" I clarified, knowing she was but needing to hear the words out loud.

"Yes," she whispered, a tear of joy slipping from the corner of her eye.

I crossed the room in three steps and swept her up into a tight hug. "I'm going to be an uncle," I laughed.

"Of course you would only be thinking about yourself," she mumbled. I could tell that she was overwhelmed. Actually, I could feel the hundreds of emotions going through her and it was a bit disconcerting. She was excited and happy, completely thrilled and filled with joy, but at the same time terrified and unsure, she was nervous, anxious, sick.... She was too many things.

I separated our connection, hoping she wouldn't notice. But honestly, there were too many feelings for me. I was happy and that's all I wanted to feel.

"Not true," I defended myself. "I'm so happy for you."

"I know," Eden agreed softly.

"I would like to say though, that next time you feel her morning sickness you clue me in," Kiran lectured. "You have no idea what I've been going through the last few days. I was sure you picked up something weird on your mission and Eden was going to die by default."

I laughed. Loudly. "You would blame me for something like that."

"You're damned right," Kiran nodded enthusiastically. "You're a liability to my happily ever after."

"To be fair, I obviously didn't recognize it as morning sickness until this morning and even then if Eden wouldn't have figured it out on her own I'm not sure I would ever have gotten it. It's not like I really thought I would ever get pregnancy symptoms. I mean.... ever." I reiterated. Suddenly I was panicking. "Oh no, what else do I have to go through?"

Eden laughed at me. "Nothing, I have it figured out. I just didn't understand what was happening before and it kept sneaking up on me. I promise, now that I know I will not let you feel sick anymore."

"Better safe than sorry," I mumbled and I know she felt the disconnect between us, but she only nodded her approval. "So when will you leave for the Citadel?"

"Eden doesn't want to go back to Romania," Kiran replied and I could tell he wasn't happy about her decision.

"Why not? You obviously need medical care," I immediately took Kiran's side. My sister was notorious for her stubborn tendencies.

"I know that, but I am not about to get it from the doctor/notary/weirdo/one of the three wise men," Eden bit out sarcastically, referring to the Witch back at the castle.

I laughed again, her assessment of him was not that far off. "He was not one of the three wise men."

"No, but he did slice my hand open in a blood oath and I am not about to let him near my hoo-ha," she grumbled.

I immediately covered my ears like a child. Some topics would always and forever, as in forever ever, be off limits.

"You can't go to a human doctor, E. Won't they want blood tests and what not? You're not human, remember?" It was a legitimate question. Sometimes she didn't remember.

"There is one human doctor I can go to," Eden said firmly. "We're going back to Omaha, Aunt Syl will take care of me."

I beamed in response. Sylvia would take care of Eden, and it might do her some good to be back in her home town. Plus, Kiran could still run things from the downtown club. She had thought this through.

"That will be good for her," I turned to Kiran who was looking at Eden with all of the love any one man was capable of holding. She was his world, that much was clear.

"I suppose," he relented, his face softening as she returned his gaze.

This was getting gross.

"Eden, I'm so happy for you," I broke whatever weird love connection was happening around me and pulled her into another hug. "You're going to be a fantastic mother."

Kiran cleared his throat suggestively. "What about me? Don't I get a hug and a speech?"

He was joking. Thank God.

"I'll leave the hugging up to my sister, but seriously man, congratulations," I shook his hand feeling even closer to my brother in law.

He wasn't just in charge of taking care of my sister now; he was in charge of raising and protecting my niece or nephew.

"When are you leaving?" Eden asked, nodding at my backpack.

"Half an hour. We're meeting back at the airport. There are too many of us to use Gabriel's small plane," I explained.

Eden shuddered. "That's probably a good plan. He flies a death trap."

"Eden, it's not a death trap because we're-"

"I know, I know…. magic," she waved me off impatiently.

Kiran and I smiled.

"Be safe?" she asked, knowing it was useless to assume I would be.

"Probably not," I admitted, giving her a playful smile. "But I will be thorough and that's the best you can ask of me right?"

"Will you kill him there or bring him back to Romania?" Kiran asked and I liked how he already assumed my victory.

"Probably bring him back to Romania. You know with the whole 'I'm pushing for a Democracy' thing, it's better to give the people the benefit of the doubt rather than murder our citizens on the down low, no matter how scum of the Earth they are."

"I'll meet you there after you wrap this thing up," Kiran offered.

"Sounds good." I paused for a moment and thought things over. I didn't want to admit there was a possibility of failure, but I had to include every option in my plans. "Kiran, just in case though, maybe you should make plans to inform the Kingdom. If we don't catch up with him soon, I'm afraid of what that could mean for innocent people just because they weren't warned. I'll be in touch in a few days and depending on my progress we can go from there, but I want to be prepared, just in case."

"Absolutely," he nodded.

"Give Sylvia my best," I changed the subject and pulled Eden into one last hug. "And take care of the little pot roast."

"Pot roast?" Eden laughed.

"You know, because you're cooking him," I clarified. I mean, that was obvious.

"Him?" Eden asked again.

"Obviously," this time I rolled my eyes. "An heir."

"Obviously," Kiran agreed with an identical eye roll.

"Sure, obviously," Eden laughed at us. "Call when you get there."

"Sure thing, have your own safe travels," I demanded and then they left me alone.

Putting the last of my meager belongings into the suitcase I felt her before I heard her. Her magic infected my room with the feel of her. She was everywhere around me and I stilled myself before I could toss her onto my bed and move our relationship right along in the best ways possible.

I forced myself to take my time zipping my backpack and putting it on before I let my eyes find hers. She stood in the doorway, her long wavy hair tumbling over her shoulders. She was wearing fitted trouser pants and a white blouse that seemed very grown up but in that sexy secretary way.

"Hey," I offered her a small smile.

"Hey yourself," she grunted in her cute little accent. She was irritated.

Shit.

"Uh, come to see me off?" I asked, knowing it would get me into more trouble, but honestly I couldn't help myself.

"Not quite," she shook her head just slightly. "I'm a grown up, Avalon."

Ah, there it was.

"I am well aware, Amelia," I promised, letting myself look her over from head to toe and then back up again. I thought I was being subtle, but by the way her eyes narrowed on me I didn't think she thought I was.

"Then I should be allowed to go on this mission. You're as bad as my brother and my father and even my cousin for goodness sake. I'm not twelve anymore, I don't need anyone fighting my battles or protecting me from the rest of the world." Her stance was very casual as she leaned against the doorframe, propping her hip to the side, but by her tone I could tell it was all an act. She was rigid with irritation and self-righteousness. And while all I wanted to do was kiss her until she relaxed and melted into me, I couldn't help but going on the defense just a little.

She might not be a little girl, but she still needed protection. *My* protection.

"Nobody is treating you like you're twelve," I said firmly so that there was no misinterpreting my meaning or my authority. "But you do need protection, Amelia. Hell, the entire Kingdom needs protection, but not everyone is as lucky as you to have so many capable people willing to give it to them."

"Oh please," she rolled her eyes. Actually rolled her eyes at me! "Lucky? Hardly. I am sheltered, and fussed at, and hidden away from the world while life happens around me. You, and my father and brother have all conspired against me to make sure life will just pass me by while I don't get to enjoy any of it."

Was she kidding me?

"Keeping you out of a mission is not locking you up in a tower," I snapped. "So stop acting like a spoiled princess. Not three weeks ago you were on your way to Africa, and nobody stopped you. You are living life, a very full life, but I think I can speak for all of us when I say that we would all like you to keep living that life. This mission could be a death sentence for anyone of us and I refuse to put you in that kind of danger."

She was silent for a long time, staring me down with her piercing rich, full brown eyes. I stood my ground, a position I had learned from being a leader for the last five years and not because I felt as strong as I appeared. Her gaze was unnerving and really intimidating if I was being honest. But I could not admit that she was getting to me.

Nobody got to me, so it was a little surprising that Amelia had been in my life for such a short time and could already unseat me with one intense glare.

This woman had power.

"Fine," she gave in and I forced myself not to act like an ass in celebration. "I understand your concerns for the mission."

"Thank you," I conceded graciously.

"But I am still on my way to Peru for a Human Trafficking Summit," she explained. "And before you can talk me out of it I will just tell you that there is nothing you can do to stop me. You and all of your forces will be there and my parents have already forced a Guard detail on me with Kiran's help, not to mention I plan to meet up with Analisa and she has her own detail."

"That's very responsible of you," I sounded like her father now and inwardly kicked myself. She rolled her eyes again.

"Anyway, I really don't feel like taking the jet with all of the Titans by myself," her voice softened and her eyes grew big with her petition. I was in trouble before she even asked what she really came here to ask. "So do you mind if I just tag along with you until we get there?"

And then she smiled.

"No, I don't mind," I agreed immediately.

She stepped into the room completely and I took a step toward her without even realizing what I was doing.

"Really? I mean, I think it will be fun. But I don't want to be a distraction," she admitted and her attitude was completely replaced by her flirtatious energy.

"Amelia, I'll be distracted by you whether you're with me or not," I mumbled coming toe to toe with her.

She blushed a deep red. I lifted my hand to play with the end of one of her long waves, rubbing it together in between my fingers. She looked down at her hair in my hand and then up in to my eyes underneath her thick lashes. My heart did this kick start thing where I swear it completely stalled for a moment before it started thundering in my chest.

Something flickered in her eyes, like she was resolved not to be this close to me, but I was wholly set on kissing her. I licked my lips in preparation and heat flooded her gaze, deepening the color of her eyes. I dipped my head down to her, forcing myself to take this slow.

But before I could taste her she had bounced up on her tip toes and gave me a quick kiss on the cheek.

What the hell?

"I need to gather up a few more things," she said in a rush already walking away from me. "I'll meet you downstairs in a few minutes."

Damn it, what just happened?

Women.

Chapter Twenty-Four

Contrary to popular belief, or at least my belief, Amelia did not sit by me on the plane trip over to Lima. She barely even acknowledged me.

Which was weird.

She kind of stayed in her brother's shadow and talked with Titus the whole time. I was not jealous of Titus. I mean, I didn't need to be jealous of Titus. Amelia and I had this amazing connection, she wasn't interested in Titus.

She wasn't.

Titus and Sebastian had this weird bromance thing going on, and Titus had probably been around her a lot, spent a lot of time with her because of Sebastian. She was more than likely just worried about him after everything.

Reassuring myself of this every five minutes did nothing to pacify my rapidly declining mood though and by the time we had suffered through Peruvian customs, gathered our baggage and filed into taxi vans that would take us to our hotel I was beyond irritable.

"What's wrong with you?" Jericho asked from the seat behind me.

We had ordered three separate vans, since we were traveling in such a large group. It wasn't until baggage claim took two hours and we were settled in all of our different vans that I realized our entourage was way too big. Not to mention packed full of alpha males. I should probably split us up in some way, but right now we only had one lead to follow and so we were stuck together for now.

I decided to get everyone settled at the hotel before I made a final decision. And frankly I needed to see Amelia off before I could really focus on the mission at hand. Her Guard hadn't arrived yet and so she would stay close to us until they did. I wasn't sure when her conference or summit or whatever started, but I wasn't letting her out of my sight until there were at least four armed Titans surrounding her at all times.

She was obnoxiously distracting.

"Huh?" Jericho prodded and I realized I hadn't answered his question.

"Nothing," I growled.

"Really? You seem kind of testy," he laughed. "Is there something about the mission I don't know about?"

He was taunting me.

"Nope, same plan as always."

"Oh," Jericho paused to think thoughtfully. "Is everything Ok with Eden?"

"Yep," I let the word pop grumpily. Actually Eden was better than ever, but even that thought couldn't bring me from my dark place.

"Problems from home?" Xander pressed, joining in Jericho's merriment.

"Xander," I growled in warning.

"I think I know what his problem is," Xavier offered studiously from next to me. We were the only four in our van. Gabriel, Silas, and the other Titans occupied another eight passenger van, and Titus and Sebastian had chosen to ride with Roxie and Amelia. We probably could have all fit in two vans, but some of us, like me, needed leg room.

And right now I *really* needed space from Titus.

The seventeen hour commercial flight over here had fried my nerves into sparking electrical shorts that were bound to shock anyone that got too close.

"What is it?" Xander asked in rapt suspense, even going so far as to lean forward with his chin in his hand as if Xavier held the secrets to the universe.

"Titus," Xavier announced seriously.

A feral growl escaped before I could reign in my temper.

"Oh you mean because Avalon's so worried about him and what almost happened?" Jericho held a straight face but he was dying to laugh.

And I was dying to hit something.

"That's right," Xavier announced. "Avalon is *very* concerned with Titus and his recovery."

"I hate you all," I snarled.

That made the van erupt with laughter.

"But if you had to choose, I mean like rate us. Who do you hate the most?" Xander asked through gasps of laughter.

"You," I grumbled.

"That hurts my feelings," Xander sobered a little, clutching at his heart.

Which only made everyone laugh harder.

I even had to crack a smile at their ridiculous behavior. And once the corner of my mouth turned up I felt a lightening of my insides. Jealousy, in all its crushing glory, was a relatively foreign emotion for me. And it did not suit me at all.

There had never been anything to be jealous of before. There had only been one thing in my entire life that warranted enough of an emotional response for me to be jealous of and that was the Kingship. And even then it was more concern for my people than jealousy of what Lucan had and I didn't. And in the end I had wanted it bad enough that I simply took it.

Which was what I decided I would do with Amelia.

I was new to the entire boy-meets-girl thing and honestly had no idea what I was doing. But I knew what I wanted.

Her.

I wanted her.

As the banter around me shifted focus, I stared out at the congested, bumper to bumper Lima traffic. Exhaust piped into the air around me as cars inched their way through the city center. Lima was smoggy and polluted with thick, contaminated air, but even still I felt connected to the city.

Our magic ran deep in Peru, pulsing and beating with the ancient earth. I felt it in this city, as soon as I walked out of the airport. Sky scrapers and buildings rose all around me testifying to the busy life of the city but I felt the ancient undertones of our magic, the pressing electricity that would grow and spread the further out of the city we traveled.

The mountains called out to us and with the cry of our unexplainable, mysterious magic I found clarity.

Amelia.

It all came back to Amelia.

Eventually we pulled into the circular drive of the five star hotel, the last vestige of luxury we would partake in before heading out on the field. The vans came to a stop and we unloaded, flowing into the red-tiled lobby with our large group. I couldn't even imagine what the humans milling around or working behind the desk thought of our multicultural group. Several of our people still wore their sunglasses to hide their unique eye colors. However, there was no disguising Gabriel's orange flames that flickered wildly behind his aviators. Even I had to do a double take at their intensity now that we were in his home country.

We wouldn't be able to get to his home town until tomorrow. From experience I knew he was struggling not to leave our group right now and go check out his parish.

And I couldn't blame him. I wouldn't have followed orders. He was a better man than me.

But I also couldn't risk sending him alone or with only a few men and being attacked.

He looked over at me from across the Mayan-themed lobby and nodded in silent acknowledgement. His gaze was stoic, set in determined resolve. He would wait on me, for that I was grateful. I respected his obedience, even though he felt somewhat like a mentor to me.

The girls checked us in, Roxie speaking in her fluent Spanish and then we were off to our row of rooms on the seventeenth floor. We all had a roommate; I believed that was important, you know to maintain camaraderie and all that. It was my own damn order, but as I watched Amelia slip into her shared room with Roxie I suddenly regretted suggesting to Jericho that we share.

I followed Jericho into our room, and immediately we spread out. Both of us only had a backpack, but somehow our things multiplied as we took over the room and made it ours. Jericho stepped out onto the balcony that overlooked Peru's capitol. The sun was setting over Lima and the lights from the clustered buildings were shining like beacons across the city that rolled out from under our vantage point.

I stood there for a moment in indecision. The view was nice and definitely demanded to be appreciated. And I couldn't damn well appreciate it with Jericho blocking my way.

"Get out," I ordered suddenly very decided with what I was going to do.

Jericho turned from his place on the balcony with a confused look, "What?"

"Get out," I repeated clearly. "Listen, I have some work to do and I need you out. Like now."

"You're seriously going to kick me out?" Jericho walked into the room, his expression complete unbelief.

"Listen, man, I'm sorry, but yeah, I need you out." He grunted an incredulous laugh so I attempted to pacify him. "If it means anything, I'll owe you one."

Granted I hadn't tried very hard.

"It doesn't mean anything!" Jericho half shouted. "You are literally kicking me out of my own hotel room! Where am I supposed to go?"

"I don't know, but it has to be done," I argued solemnly.

"Whatever," Jericho sighed and I could tell he was only a little bit mad at me. "I'll just get my own room. I should have done that in the first place. I should know better than to try and put up with his royal sulkiness."

He grabbed his backpack off the bed he claimed and gathered whatever odds and ends had made their way around the room.

"Thanks man," I said seriously, feeling a little bit like a douchebag.

"It better be worth it, Avalon. Like seriously, you need to lock this down. You're way too moody for this mission. Get the girl, and then get your head on straight." Jericho lectured from halfway out the door.

"That's the plan," I agreed.

"Good." And then he stalked down the hallway.

Once he was gone I couldn't hold myself back any longer. I counted to ten bouncing on my toes and then I rushed out the door and down the hall. I didn't know Amelia's exact room number, so I walked toward her magic just a few doors down.

I stood on the opposite side of the heavy wooden door gathering my nerves. I was determined and focused, but that didn't mean I felt any kind of confidence. And since this was the first time I had ever put myself in this kind of vulnerable position I didn't know if this was how every guy felt when he was pursuing a girl, or if this was Amelia exclusive.

But either way, she had stripped me of the pride and surety I was used to. I was the King of a damned kingdom and yet as I stood at the threshold to her room.... to our future.... I was a stripped down version of myself, all arrogance, all poise buried beneath a mountain of nervous anxiety.

There were other girls in this world, other eligible candidates for Queen. But at the core of honesty was the realization that if Amelia rejected me there would be no one else. Somehow this girl had swept in and captured every part of me. I belonged to her. She *owned* me. And if she didn't want to be with me, there would be no one else. I would spend the rest of my days pining for a compassionate, feisty, spoiled princess.

And it would suck.

Really bad.

I mean, I might never recover.

But that foolish knowledge was better than even pretending another girl would be able to bewitch my attention like Amelia had.

So with a shaky breath I raised my hand and took the plunge. I decided in the quick second it took for her to open the door that I would approach this situation the only way I knew how.

I would lead.

And even if I spent the rest of my life following this girl to the ends of the Earth, which was a real possibility. A possibility I was more than fine with.... I would lead her into this today. Because for whatever reason she was being way too stubborn about what was between us.

She needed to be led.

Amelia opened the door, the look of surprise on her face barely hidden. Her long, wavy hair floated around her as she moved the door in a jerky motion out of the way. Her big brown eyes widened with her shock and her perfect lips pursed as if she was stopping herself from saying what was really on her mind.

"Amelia," I acknowledged in a voice husky from nerves.

"Avalon," she sighed my name and a hot heat flooded my veins. "Do you need Roxie?"

I swallowed a laugh at her words and an underlying current of lust and reminded myself of why I was here. "No," I paused and held her gaze with mine. "I need you."

I let my intentions hang in the air as her lips formed a little O in more surprise. She looked adorably confused and only the movement of Roxie in the background kept me from pushing her against the open hotel room door and kissing her senseless just to prove how much I needed her.

"Come with me," I whispered and held out my hand.

She glanced over her shoulder and when she turned back to respond she was chewing on her bottom lip as if she didn't know what to say.

"Amelia, come with me," I demanded a little firmer.

She nodded her head with a nervous tilt of her chin and put her delicate hand in mine.

I turned away from her to hide my cocky smile and led her back down the hall to my hotel room. I swiped the key card into the lock and then turned the handle and led her inside.

In the solitude of my room I felt her nervous magic spread out from her like a bird getting ready to take flight. She was painfully jumpy and I felt her own anxious emotions reflected in mine. There were so many reasons to fear what I felt for her or the future that lay before us, especially in this moment of uncertainty while Terletov ran wild. But at my very center, at the most elementary part of my soul I didn't want to be uncertain anymore. I wanted, with firm and unquestionable certainty, I wanted to know that this girl was mine.

I wanted, no *needed* to know, that whatever happened after this moment, that Amelia Cartier belonged to me in the same way I already belonged to her.

"Avalon, I-"

Before she could say anything else, something principal and dominant took over me completely. The lock clicked in the door behind us at the same time she said my name and all reason snapped and disintegrated into miniscule pieces inside of me. I took the hand that I still held in mine and pulled her roughly to me.

Whatever she was going to say was lost the moment my lips crashed down to hers. I felt her surprise deep inside her magic as it stuttered in the air around us. I playfully bit at her bottom lip to bring her out of her paralyzed shock. And then I swept my tongue over the exact spot hoping for something, for some kind of response to the desire that was bubbling so quickly inside of me I knew there was no coming back from this. Not ever.

So when she answered with the softest moan and she pressed herself tighter to my chest I lost all ability to think reasonably.

She kissed me back fiercely and without reserve. She opened her mouth to mine and I claimed her in that kiss. I didn't know if she realized what was between us yet, but she would. And the longer I kissed her, the longer our magics wrapped together in the same passion we kissed with, the sooner I knew she would admit it.

I would just have to continue kissing her until she did.

Chapter Twenty-Five

With the same certainty I knew that I was breaking down whatever impossible wall Amelia had built between us, I knew I couldn't push her further than this kiss. But that didn't mean I couldn't make it the hottest, most memorable kiss ever.

If she did decide to still reject me after this, after I laid it all out for her, then at least I would leave her with a very memorable kiss that would not be, *could not be* rivaled among men.

Yes, Avalon St. Andrews god of all kissing.

Her mouth worked against mine in a perfect harmony of tangled tongues and crushing lips. I grabbed her waist with both of my hands, holding her tightly against me. I pushed her backward until she was pressed against the bare hotel room wall. She sighed as her back hit the wall, her hands moved up slowly taking in each inch of me like she was shy but trying to memorize how I felt at the same time and then in a perfect moment of unrestrained want she tangled them in my loose hair. As her hands worked to get a tighter hold of me, she pressed herself into me, melting her body against mine. Our magic was like a frenetic energy field around us, mine swallowing hers up as I drew it into mine.

I couldn't let her be the same after this kiss. I had to change her so that there would always be something missing without me next to her, without my lips against hers.

It was selfish. I could admit that. It was an egotistical, bastard thing to do. But I wanted a chance with her. I was fighting for her in this kiss.

And I was determined to win.

I deepened the kiss with those thoughts on my mind. My arms wrapped around her with a desperate need to feel as much of her against my body as I could, with a need to prove to her how badly I wanted her.... how much I *needed* her.

She reacted to me, moved with me and I had never felt more of a sense of pride in my life. This girl wanted me as much as I wanted her. A completion I didn't know I was missing swelled and spread in my chest as she gave me as much of herself as I gave her in that kiss. She clutched at me like I was a lifeline, like if she let go of me she would collapse on the ground. Like she would be lost without me.

I groaned against her mouth with that thought. I didn't know when it happened but that was me. I was lost without her. Wandering aimlessly. Somehow even though I could acknowledge that she had become everything to me, letting me have her, letting me hold her, the truth and solidity of those feelings cemented that reality to the deepest, most real part of me, to every nerve ending and blood vessel, to every thought and image in my head. To my core.

I slipped my hand from her waist to the back of her thigh. As these thoughts flickered and flashed in my head I couldn't even pretend that the perfection of Amelia kissing me didn't awaken my very male nature. Desire flamed through me, setting my magic to an electrified boil. Our magics snapped and popped around us and when I lifted her leg off the ground she went willingly, wrapping her leg around my waist and then she lifted her other leg as I reached down to grab it.

I kept a tight hold on the back of her thighs while she wrapped her arms around my neck like she wasn't just holding on for balance, but like she was clinging to me for breath.

This wasn't just a kiss that was shattering Amelia's world.

This kiss was shattering mine.

She was shattering me.

There was never a more perfect feeling than Amelia wrapped around me, holding on to me as if her life depended on it. Our lips had not stopped moving against each other, my mouth swallowing her soft sounds, my arms wrapped securely around her, I wasn't sure if I would ever let her go.

I felt myself walking, but didn't remember making the conscious decision to move my feet. Before I knew it though I had walked across the room, Amelia in my arms and laid her down on the bed. I wasn't far behind, I couldn't be far behind, and so I was down with her, daring my lips to move from hers and explore the rest of her skin.

She shivered when I moved to kiss her jawline, down to her neck and back to the place behind her earlobe. She dug her nails into my shoulder as I kissed and tasted as much skin as I could before I felt drunk from her.

I slowed down from the frantic kissing of a desperate man to a man that now had possession of what he most desired. Frantic, desperate longing turned to reverent, absolute worship. She didn't move out from underneath me or stop the kiss when I slowed down and I had to acknowledge that was a real fear for a moment. Her fingers started tracing slow patterns on my shoulder blades and even while I shivered underneath her I could finally admit to myself that my fears were no longer justified. She sighed my name when I moved my kisses to her exposed collar bone and I sunk impossibly deeper into her possession.

We kissed forever, or for only minutes, I couldn't tell. There was no time in that kiss, no way to determine anything outside of the taste of her on my lips and the feel of her underneath me. She trembled and shifted beneath me, she pressed against me and clasped her arms around me like she needed me to survive, and she made the sweetest, softest, sexiest sounds I had ever heard.

I didn't think I would ever stop kissing her, or would ever want to, but as the long lines of light disappeared from the room and we were shrouded in the heavy darkness of night I started to worry about her.

And it wasn't fair.... because I had set out to prove to her that she was mine, but now that I was doing exactly that I suddenly wanted to make sure I was hers. I wanted to confirm that her feelings were as strong as mine and that all this kissing stuff was Ok with her.

And mostly that there would be a lot more of it in my future.

It was kind of annoying, since I could have happily kissed her until the end of time. And now I had to talk about feelings when there was a real possibility she could still reject me.

Damn it.

I slowed the kiss down, detangling my mouth from her and ending it by a simple peck on her perfect lips. I was rewarded with her stretching up to meet my lips for one last lingering kiss.

That meant something right?

I looked down at her, memorizing her face, the beautiful lines of her jaw, the sexy pout to her lips, the depth and wholeness of her eyes. She wasn't going to speak first, I knew that, but at the same time I felt like I had lost the ability to verbalize any kind of coherent thought. I wouldn't survive rejection and even though the last, however long it was, tried to speak up inside my head and remind me she kissed me back, I couldn't get over the fear that she would come to her senses and realize she didn't like me and never would.

"Hey," I finally sighed, smiling down at her.

"Hey," she smiled back. She lifted her fingers and brushed my hair out of my face and my whole being sighed with the movement.

I nuzzled into the crook of her neck, hating the inches of separation between us. She giggled and squirmed as my breath tickled her skin but I just pulled her closer to me so that we were both lying on our sides facing each other. She was cradled in my arms.

This was the most perfect moment of my entire life.

A mixture of the fear that was still crippling me and a deliciously hazy fog from her kisses prevented me from speaking. She had to be the first one to break this second silence. "So you kissed me?" she asked as if she were confused on the details of the last few hours.

"Is that Ok?" I tested taking liberty by kissing the side of her mouth and then her jawline and then her ear. I wanted to remind her that even if her brain told her it wasn't Ok, her body was clearly in agreement.

"Uh, huh," she murmured. She leaned into my lips and then stretched her neck to give me better access. "It's Ok."

"Good," I laughed, my voice raspy and low. "Because I plan on doing a lot more of this."

Her fingers wandered down to my side and slipped beneath my shirt. She made trails of gentle lines up and down my bare skin making me quiver.

Damn it, she made me *quiver*. What girl had that kind of power?

"You do?" she sounded so innocently confused I paused from paying her neck such reverential attention and propped my head up on my hand to stare down into her gorgeous eyes.

"Mmm," I nodded my head slowly, holding her gaze with the intensity of mine. "I don't play games very well Amelia. I conquer things. So we are done with this game. I might not have conquered you yet," I waggled my eyebrows trying to lighten the situation. She slapped me on the arm. "But I do plan on taking this very seriously…. I plan on taking *you* very seriously."

"Avalon, you can't seriously mean you want to date me," Amelia laughed incredulously and tried to wiggle out from underneath my arms.

I wasn't having that. I tightened my hold on her and laid her back on the bed so that I could partly hold her down, but mostly so I could draw her back into kissing me.

"That's exactly what I mean," I whispered.

I kissed the side of her mouth to tease her and I was rewarded when her lips turned into mine immediately, like she couldn't stop herself from kissing me…. like she was as addicted to me as I was to her.

"But you don't date," she said against my lips in a breathy voice that had me pressing closer to her despite her argument.

"I do now," I growled, deepening our kiss. Her mouth opened to mine and I extended the kiss meeting her tongue and swallowing her gentle moan.

"Wait, wait," she panted, out of breath, her fingers pressed gently against my chest.

I obeyed, but dropped my head against her shoulder in a resigned sigh.

"Amelia," I said sternly, lifting my eyes to meet hers. "I haven't dated before because there was no point. There was no girl that could hold my attention for more than five minutes, let alone trap me inside this never ending tornado of emotions and anxiety and…. want."

She raised her eyebrows in surprise, but then lowered them into a scowl. "I'm not just a conquest Avalon. I am not a war you can win."

I laughed at her fierce anger and her scowl turned into a hateful glare. "Believe me when I promise you I have never thought of you that way! If anything, you have waged a war against me and won."

Her expression softened infinitesimally. "What do you mean?" she squeaked.

"Ever since you arrived at the Citadel Amelia, I have not been able to stop thinking about you. My mind is usually a constant whir of activity, but never before has it been because of a woman. And yet my thoughts are consumed with unanswered questions about you.... What are you doing? What are you thinking about? Who are you talking to? What your lips will feel like against mine? Which even my wildest imagination never did them justice by the way.... complete perfection." She blushed beneath me and my confidence grew exponentially. "Do you feel the same way about me? Am I even a blip on your radar? What will happen when I ask you to be my girlfriend? And ever since I found out Eden was pregnant, I can't seem to stop myself from asking questions about what our children will look like."

"Eden's pregnant?" she gasped and then her face blushed to the most beautiful deep red. "Our children? Girlfriend?"

She yelped her questions. I smiled down at her, but inside I was a crumbling ball of anxiety.

"Mmm," I settled on paying more attention to the soft skin of her neck, rather than stay for a minute more under her scrutiny. "I want you to be my girlfriend, Amelia. I want you to consider what that means for you, what forever would look like with me."

"Avalon," she pushed me away so that I was forced to meet her eyes again. "Are you serious? You really like me?"

"Amelia, I more than like you," I admitted. "I will wait until you're ready to hear exactly how I feel about you, but you need to know that I have only ever planned to make this decision once. Forever is a long, endless time. And I want you to be sure before you give me any kind of answer."

Well, that's what I said. I stayed diplomatic about the whole thing. But what I meant was that she needed to say yes so that I didn't completely implode into tiny bits of nothing in a future that didn't exist without her.

She was silent for a while, but she held my eyes tangled in her serious gaze. She was searching for something, something like the truth and I wasn't about to back down to her. She had the truth, I had just laid everything out to her and I would prove it no matter how long it took.

"I have a crush on you," she blurted in her adorable English accent and then covered her mouth quickly with her hand.

"What?" I asked, completely confused.

She laughed then, shaking beneath me in her fit of giggles. A tear ran from the corner of her eye as she dissolved into more laughter. I smiled down at her and caught the stray teardrop on my pointer finger.

"What is so funny?" I demanded but I couldn't help but laugh along with her.

"I have a crush on you," she gasped and then settled her laughter. "I've *had* a crush on you, Avalon for.... for forever. At Eden and Kiran's wedding I fell head over heels for the new King."

"Are you serious?" I demanded, my voice gruffer than I intended. But after all this confusion, after she made me chase her like a madman, she had a crush on me the whole time!

"You were all recklessness and trouble and I was just so young back then," she pouted, reaching her hands up to smooth the lines of my collar. "You didn't even look twice at me. And here I've been pining after a man that didn't even know I existed for years."

"You've liked me this whole time?" I clarified incredulously.

She nodded, biting her bottom lip again as if she were afraid I was mad at her.

"Jericho? Titus?" I asked still grumpy with her for not falling immediately into my arms and declaring her undying love for me from day one.

"Attempts at finding something else.... anything else to protect myself from you," she admitted with a casual shrug of her shoulder.

"What do you mean?" I demanded.

"After Eden's wedding I was crushed. I mean, as crushed as my young heart could imagine. I really thought you would notice me and fall as immediately in love with me as I had you. But you didn't. You didn't even spare two glances my way. So I decided to forget completely about you. You and your cocky attitude and devilishly handsome good looks."

Her flattery pacified my frustration with her stubbornness and I allowed her a small, tiny, miniscule smile. She pinched my cheek in response.

"But I didn't forget about you, I *couldn't* forget about you." She continued. "So I decided to just avoid you at all costs and hope that someone else caught my attention even half as much as you had. But then as soon as I walked into the castle, there you were. And worse you were staring at me like you were a man dying in the desert and I was the first drop of water you had seen in years. And I wanted to run from you and every feeling I felt and was convinced you didn't."

"But, but.... but.... Then I pursued you," I argued, still confused.

"And I was convinced it was just because I had grown up and finally caught your attention. I heard all about the girls that you went through. I didn't think I could take being just one of your conquests," she admitted in the sweetest, most unsure voice ever. "I was protecting myself."

I couldn't think verbally. I didn't want to think verbally. I crushed my lips to hers, taking her mouth in the most passionate kiss I was capable of. My hands slipped beneath her thin t-shirt but stayed planted on the soft skin of her waist. My mouth moved against hers in aggressive possession and I tangled our tongues together like she said, like I was a man dying of thirst and she was the drink of water that would save my life.

I slowed down into soft, gentle, loving.... that's right.... loving kisses, pouring my emotions into her like now I was the water and she was the glass. She responded. I wanted to shout that. *She responded!* She kissed me back with the same emotion plunging into me, drowning me and I would happily give up air and breathe only her until my last, final breath.

"Why were you protecting yourself?" I breathed against her lips.

I didn't want to stop kissing her, but I had to. I had to get to the base of our feelings for each other so we could do this.... live the rest of this together.

"I didn't want to get hurt," she admitted shyly. "My feelings for you were too deep."

"But it didn't work," I tried to make my statement into a question, but my determination made me say it in a way that could make her believe it was true.

"No, it didn't work," she shook her head and held my eyes tangled in her gaze.

"I'm glad it didn't work," I smiled at her, lifting her hand from my shoulder and kissing her knuckles.

"I'm sure you are," she laughed at my arrogance.

"Do you need to think about this.... us?" I forced the words out of my mouth but they felt heavy and vile on my tongue. Her eyebrows pinched together in confusion and I knew I had to explain. I thought these words would be hard for me, that they would come out unsure and anxious, but as I prepared myself to explain I realized this was one of the easiest speeches I would ever make. "Do you remember saying that whoever I asked to be with me would have to live forever too? You made it sound like a burden, like living with me forever was an impossible thing to ask of someone." She opened her mouth to protest, so I silenced her with a quick kiss. "You were right. Asking someone to be with me is a huge request. Not only am I asking you to be Queen, and give up whatever life you are leading now, I'm asking you to take on my magic and live with me.... be with me for potentially ever." I laughed at the irony of my love. "You see, when I say I want to be with you forever, I literally mean.... forever."

Her eyes danced at my joke. She brushed her fingers across my forehead, pushing my hair out of my face. "It is a lot to ask. Do you think I'll get tired of you?" she asked seriously, but the light in her face let me know she was joking.

"I'm serious," I pouted. And then more seriously, "Amelia you can walk away from me as soon as you can't stand me anymore, but I would like to try. I would like you to be with me for as long as you can stand me."

"And how long will you be able to stand me?" she asked. A flash of fear crossed her expression.

I dipped my head closer to her so that I was ready to swoop in and kiss the uncertainty away from her as soon as she would let me. "Always," I whispered.

"Always?"

"Always," I confirmed.

She nodded her head then, her eyes filling with unshed tears. I stared down into her beautiful, perfect face and waited. But then her lips quirked into a small smile and her fear was replaced with unwavering certainty and she nodded again.

"Ok, Avalon," she whispered. "I want to try too." And then her fingers tightened on my collar and she pulled me into the most perfect kiss of my life.

Chapter Twenty-Six

Hours later, after the hottest makeout session of my life, Amelia laid cuddled up in my arms. There was a word floating around in my head that I wanted to share with her, but I was afraid that I would scare her. She had just admitted to "try" this out, not to marry me and definitely not to live by my side for the foreseeable and future forever.

Although technically that's all I had asked of her.

But her, tucked into my side, tracing lazy circles on my bicep with her delicate fingers had cemented into my mind exactly what I wanted and it was a whole hell of a lot more than a trial run.

Not that I wanted much.

I mean, only everything.

Except I talked myself out of asking her for it and offering her my everything in return.

Well, for right now.

I had to prove to her that I was serious and that she wouldn't be just another set up that I would get bored of. Hell, I could *never* get bored of her. I could never give her up. And even the idea of her deciding she wasn't into us was hard to swallow. I couldn't even think it without pulling her closer to me as if my physical proximity to her would keep her from thinking those thoughts.

"You need to throw Lilly and Talbott an engagement party," Amelia announced casually.

"What?" I laughed at her subject change after the thoughts that had been rolling around in my head.

"You do!" she defended her position.

"That's what Eden's for," I explained as if she forgot I had a sister and a co-ruler to do that kind of dirty work.

"Yes, but everyone will expect that because Eden is her best friend," Amelia argued.

"Exactly."

"No, wait. This is everything you want. Talbott and Lilly will change everything for our people, they will break the invisible barrier keeping others from doing the same," Amelia explained gently.

"I know all this," I smiled down at her. She was adorable when she was trying to prove a point.

"Ok, good. Then you should also know that our people don't think of Eden as their Queen. I mean, they do. They know that she's the Queen. But they think of you as the King that makes all of the important decisions and runs things. Eden and Kiran have basically been on vacation for the last several years. You have been behind the wheel of the machine and the people associate you with the actual power of the Kingship." I opened my mouth to argue, but she shushed me by placing one of her irresistible fingers over my lips. "If you really want their marriage to make an impact then you have to be the one to endorse their union. You already let Kiran announce their engagement when it would have been much more profound coming from you. If you want real change then you're going to have to buck up and play benevolent King."

She giggled when I chomped down playfully on the finger that had silenced me. "Are you always this good at diplomacy?" I pounced on top of her, loving that her point made sense. I tickled her sides so that she squirmed and writhed underneath me. It wasn't the easiest thing for me to admit that I was wrong and even more so that someone else could be right.... but somehow the fact that Amelia had her head wrapped around this whole..... Monarchy thing, made me fall for her all the more.

"It's easy to be good when you're so bad at it," she giggled, gasping in between words while I attacked her relentlessly.

She wiggled her arms from underneath me and pulled me down to her mouth with her hands tightly on my collar. It was a move I was very quickly becoming fond of.

"Mmmm," I murmured against her, trailing kisses along her jaw and ear. "You're so unbelievably sexy."

"That reminds me," she declared in a tone that was not so much sexy but attention grabbing. I lifted my head reluctantly from her soft skin to look her in the eyes. "While we're on the subject of diplomacy...."

"We're not on the subject of diplomacy," I argued, dipping my head back to pay her neck some much needed attention while she let out a soft sigh of approval. "We moved on to a new subject."

She laughed and her chest moved against mine. "Have you thought about filling the rest of the Kingdom in on Terletov?"

"Mood killer," I moaned grumpily and plopped back down next to her. I lied though. Even Terletov could not stop me from wanting this girl. I pulled her close to me and thought over her words. "I've thought about it."

"And....?" she started drawing those circles again, but this time they were on my wrist.

I focused.

Ok, I really, really tried to focus, but damn this girl would get me to agree to anything at this point.

"I'm not sure it's such a good idea." I breathed out unsteadily.

"The people need to know, Avalon." Amelia reasoned, but did not stop with the circles. "You can't protect them if they are not protecting themselves and right now they don't even know if there is a threat."

"I don't want to cause hysteria, or plant doubt in our fragile infrastructure." I had a valid point, but it came out not even close to confident.

"Why not give them a chance to strengthen our framework? Give them a chance to trust you completely by you trusting them." Her voice was so sweet, so wise, she was every single thing I needed in a girl....in a wife. And she was going to make me fall completely in love with her, body, mind and soul before I even let her out of my bed. How could I have ever overlooked her? Even as a younger version of herself she had to have been captivating.

"Any more points you want to make before I agree to this plan of yours?" I asked dryly, relenting to her idea.

"Yes, actually," she laughed. "If you don't make a claim for your people, Avalon, Terletov will. Without full disclosure, he is more than welcome to swoop in and take over. He doesn't have to share what he's doing to Immortals to gain their following. He is working against you around the clock. We don't know what he's doing with these.... experiments, but he obviously has a following. And unless you are upfront and honest about what is going on that following could potentially grow and organize until you have no Kingdom left. Your silence could land our people right back under another tyrannical rule and get yourself, along with your friends and family killed."

Her serious words immediately sobered me up. I pulled her against my chest, losing my fingers in her thick hair. I had a long list of people I loved and cared about, but suddenly the one I was most scared of losing was lying in bed with me and she didn't even know the depth of my feelings for her.

"You make very good points," I grumbled pathetically into her hair.

"I know," she agreed smugly.

"Don't go to your conference or summit or whatever," I begged.

She stiffened next to me, surprised by my change of subject. "What?"

"Don't go. Stay with me. It's dangerous and I'm a complete selfish bastard for not sending you away somewhere safer. But I need you with me. I need to know where you are and that you're safe," I paused for a moment and when she didn't respond, I pleaded like an idiot. "Please, Amelia, stay with me. I promise I will protect you."

She cleared her throat as if she didn't know what to say and I waited a full, tense minute, crushing her stiff body to me in fear that she was going to leave me.

Finally, she relaxed into me and breathed out a whoosh of air, "Alright, Avalon, if that's what you want."

"It is," I agreed. I looked down into her face and stared straight into her eyes as if I could see into her heart, as if I could tattoo my words onto her soul. "You're exactly what I want."

She didn't respond. It was like she couldn't respond. I had wanted to relay the intensity of my feelings for her, but I didn't mean to take the words completely out of her mouth.

But then her expression softened and she filled with light, that was the only way I could explain it. Her magic blossomed around me, taking flight in the room and her face lit up with the sweetest, most loving expression I had ever seen.

She was mine.

Finally.

She didn't have to say it; she didn't have to verbalize her feelings. She would soon. And I would soon. Her face, her expression, her body, her magic said it all for me. I didn't need to hear the words. I *felt* them.

She belonged to me in the same way that I belonged to her.

And in that thought there was freedom and hope and joy all at once.

"Ok, now it's time for you to get out," I ordered. I hopped up to my knees and pulled her up by her hands.

"Um, what?" she asked, uncertainty flickering in her eyes like a candle about to be blown out.

"Yep, come on," I was serious. She had to get out of my room. Like now.

"Where are we going?" she asked, seriously confused.

"I'm walking you to your room," I explained, pulling her off the bed and walking backwards with her hands in mine. I had to gently tug her along while her feet kind of stumbled in obedience.

"Oh, I uh, I guess I thought you would want me to stay," she mumbled, giving a longing glance back at the bed.

I smirked. I couldn't help it. "I do want you to stay. I really, more than anything in this world, want you to stay. But that's why you have to leave. I promised I would protect you and if you stay even a minute longer I won't be able to."

"Who are you protecting me from?" Amelia asked, still absolutely confused.

"Me," I growled and then pulled her to me. I kissed her in a way that would erase any doubts that I wasn't still obsessively into her. I also erased any confusion about what I was protecting her from. I held her body against mine, my hands possessively on her back to keep from breaking my promise. My lips moved against hers hungrily, desperately. She gasped against my lips when she realized what I was protecting her from and it made me want her all the more.

When I finally pulled myself from her she was winded and dazed. I smiled down at her and her wide eyes were both surprised and heated into liquid pools of dark brown. She was breathtaking.

"Do you see why it is imperative that I walk you to your room now?" I asked, struggling to catch my own breath.

She nodded as if she was only agreeing because I asked her to and it made me smile. She could still walk away from me at any time, but I was determined to make it the hardest decision she ever made.

I opened the door for her and when she walked through it I smacked her on the butt so that the sound reverberated in the echo-y hallway. She jumped at the contact and gave me a stern look over her shoulder which only made me smile like an idiot and my hand itch to do it again.

We made it to her door where I resigned myself to a reserved kiss on the lips, quick and subtle.

"I will see you tomorrow, Amelia," I looked down at her and realized this was the happiest I had ever been. And she was the reason.

"Goodbye, Avalon," she smiled coyly at me. I think we both realized she held all the power now, but she took it easy on me by opening her hotel room door and walking backwards into the obscure darkness.

"Goodbye, Amelia," I say to a closed door.

I stood there for a few more wistful seconds. Her magic was separated from mine now, and I hated the feeling of loss that came with it. I need her in my arms again, completely wrapped up and tangled together with me and everything that entailed.

"Finally!" Xander called from across the portico that led to the elevators.

"It's about damn time," Jericho agreed.

"You're lucky I didn't make a move first," Xavier called seriously.

Good, I was glad there had been an audience. Now Xavier's threat would go unwarranted. Amelia was officially off the market.

"Goodnight gentlemen," I called over my shoulder as I all but jogged happily to my room.

Stop whatever you have planned. I'm throwing Lilly and Talbott an engagement party. I announced to Eden the minute the door was closed behind me.

I woke her from a deep sleep and she mumbled something in return that sounded like a bunch of strung together curse words.

I laughed at her and tried to explain. *It's important that I put all of my support behind them. The Kingdom will respond to my endorsement more so than yours and Kiran's.*

Whatever, Avalon. She finally got out.

And while I have you here, I want you to invite the Regents to Omaha. We need to hold a meeting about Terletov. It's time to trust our people with trusting us. I finished sternly.

This couldn't have waited until morning? Eden groaned.

Oh, right. Go back to bed. Love you sis. I laughed.

Love you, too. I knew that she was smiling now. *I'm happy for you Avalon. You couldn't have picked a better girl.*

She admitted right before she rolled over and went back to sleep.

And as much as I would have liked to believe Eden's blessing wouldn't have mattered, I couldn't. Because it did matter, her opinion mattered. Which made Amelia all the more amazing, because Eden loved her too.

Hell, it was time to be honest.

I loved her.

I loved Amelia Cartier.

Chapter Twenty-Seven

"Good morning," I smiled down at Amelia the next morning while we loaded into rented vans. This time we were condensing our travel to two vans until we reached Gabriel's home town of Urubamba.

"Good morning," she whispered in a small voice.

We were alone on this side of the van, but only because I had handed out menial tasks to everyone else and followed her from the lobby. I was apparently a stalker as well as her boyfriend.

So that was good....

"Miss me?" I asked, my lips turning up in a smirk. I knew she missed me. It was a bit arrogant, maybe, but I had missed her in the short hours of the night we had left after kissing through half of it. I shouldn't have been so pleased with how empty and lonely my magic felt without hers, but knowing hers felt the same way filled me with some kind of possessive pride. Besides that her magic jumped and clung to mine the moment I met her in the lobby of the hotel, reminding me of the power two Immortals had over each other.

"No," she grumbled and rolled her eyes.

"Not even a little bit?" I teased, stepping closer to her so that her back bumped into the side of the van.

"Mmmm, maybe a little bit," she laughed as I swooped down to kiss hungrily at her neck. She laughed and slapped my arms playfully.

"Just a little bit?" I moved up to her ear, paying special attention to the soft flesh of her ear lobe, biting and kissing it alternately.

"Ok," she breathed heavily, grasping at my shoulders and digging her fingernails in, which only confirmed that I was doing exactly what I should be. "Maybe a little bit more than a little bit."

I stopped then to lift my head and look into her eyes. They were darkened with desire, an emotion I was positive was mirrored in mine, but just as I moved to take her mouth into mine we were interrupted.

"What is going on Mimi?" Sebastian demanded.

Damn it, I should have sent him up to an errand on the roof.

"Nothing," Amelia mumbled, straightening her long sleeved t-shirt and stepping away from me.

"Well, nothing that's your business anyway," I laughed and then shifted uncomfortably when Amelia did not laugh with me.

"I thought you were headed to the human trafficking thing?" Sebastian asked slowly as if he were reminding her.

"I decided not to go," she explained. Her voice was soft and gentle, completely at odds with how firm her magic felt around me.

"Really?" Sebastian narrowed his eyes and shot me a hateful glare. "So you're going home?"

"Not exactly," Amelia clicked her consonants.

"If you're not going to your convention thing and you're not going home, where *are* you going?"

"She's going to stay with us," I blurted out, unable to stand the obviousness hanging between us.

"You're taking my little sister on our mission?" Sebastian's eyes narrowed further and his tone of voice let me know exactly how much he disapproved.

"Yes, I am," I pooled my confidence and answered with a smug smile.

"And this is a good idea to you? You think that taking my little sister on this mission is a good idea?" Sebastian growled.

"Sebastian stop!" Amelia ordered, her patience completely evaporated. "Avalon invited me along, stop being ridiculous."

"Avalon invited you along because he thinks he's going to scare you into dating him," Sebastian's jaw ticked along with his words and he had to lift a hand to rub at a throbbing vein on the side of his neck.

"Enough, Sebastian," I commanded in my King-voice, the same voice I used to interrupt angry disputes I mediated and used to get Gabriel to back off when he started going on about my destiny and what not. When I was satisfied with his silence I explained, "Amelia doesn't need me to trick her into dating me, she went willingly. No scare tactics required. As far as this mission goes, she is not just your little sister; she is a capable, independent woman that is more than qualified to defend herself. And I'm sure she doesn't appreciate your demeaning attitude nor your overbearing commands."

Sebastian gaped at me, not prepared for that speech at all. But in my defense I was starting to see a pattern with the men in Amelia's life all treating her like a child.

She wasn't a child.

I could testify to that.

Easily.

She on the other hand, did not gape at me. She let loose a little surprised laugh and then in front of her brother, the now gathered rest of our group and God Himself pulled me down by my collar and kissed me long and hard. My hands moved immediately to her waist and all thoughts of an audience or spectators was gone as I enjoyed being wrapped in her magic and having her body pressed so willingly to mine.

"Thank you," She whispered against my mouth when she came back to herself and realized we were standing in front of a shocked crowd.

"I'm not sure what I did, but you're welcome," I answered, my brain a bit fuzzy as the blood in my body worked to get back up there.

"Why are you all just standing around here?" I barked when I turned to face everyone else. I wasn't nearly as impatient as I was pretending to be but I did not appreciate the looks of complete disbelief. Was it so hard to believe that I could get a girl to kiss me? "I'm anxious to get up there, let's go." Though I was happy to see Sebastian sufficiently shut up. He glared at me with a little less resigned anger and gave his sister an apologetic smile before turning to find his seat.

Everyone filed into the vans on my command although nobody had too much to say. We were tense and on edge as the buses left the city and started the slow winding journey up into the mountains. Gabriel drove the lead van and Jericho, driving the van I was in, struggled to keep up with him even with his magic completely in the driver's seat.

Peruvian driving was definitely different than any other kind of driving and what Jericho knew and understood. So while Gabriel navigated the sharp turns and tight spaces, weaving in and out of slower, less aggressive drivers, Jericho's expression kept hardening and his vocabulary kept dissolving into worse and worse curse words.

I took Amelia's hand and enjoyed the show.

Several hours later we pulled onto the narrow side street in front of Gabriel's parish. There wasn't much of a church left to begin with, but it was Gabriel's and I understood his protective nature.

Gabriel was my parents' age. He had been a part of the select group of students chosen to study with Lucan in Romania. He witnessed the decline of Lucan's moral compass, the murder of an Immortal and a human for being in love and then what happened after my parents left the Citadel. Even though he kept his past mostly to himself, I knew that it was those events that made him decide to leave the Immortal community and make a life in the human world.

Unfortunately, the human world was *terrified* of him. I mean, you couldn't really blame them with his fiery eyes and no-nonsense way about him. Seriously, I could hardly imagine what a church service would be like under his scrutinizing eye. I felt like he would be able to get people to confess to all kinds of sins and misdeeds just by looking at them and raising an eyebrow.

Still his church had several nuns that were assigned to him by a higher Catholic council. And it was those employees he was most concerned about now.

I kept Amelia close to my side, gripping tightly to her hand. We were the first to follow Gabriel through the church doors where he paused to move his hands reverently in the sign of the cross. I had been here once before, but it was a while ago, before I even met Eden. Amory had brought me here to introduce me to Gabriel and explain his renewed efforts in the Resistance. Even though Gabriel had born a mark of the Resistance from an earlier time he had refused Amory at that time, saying he couldn't leave his parish.

The sanctuary hadn't been in the greatest shape back then.

Now.... it was worse. Much, much worse.

Pews and kneeling benches were upturned and seemed to have been tossed or thrown across the room during the course of some kind of scuffle. The statue of Jesus that stood above the pulpit was knocked over and one of the outstretched arms broken off, making the painted blood that dripped from the crown of thorns seem disconcertingly authentic. The door to the back was blocked by the crumbling structure of the back wall and there was a smell.... a burning flesh kind of smell that sent prickles of heat rising all over my skin.

"Gabriel?" I asked in a low voice, hoping he would have an explanation. "You talked to your nuns?"

"Days ago," Gabriel growled. His orange eyes flashed ultra-bright behind his aviators and he rubbed his hand over his shaved head.

The rest of our entourage filed in behind us and I heard the audible gasp from Roxie. The small sanctuary was quickly filled with our large number of people and I heard one of the older Titans ask what this place was. I remembered then, that because of some weird moment in history when Gabriel saved Lucan's life, Lucan had let Gabriel leave without incident. And in an even weirder uncharacteristic move, Lucan had apparently let him be over all this time.

Well until he joined the Resistance with Eden.

"Gabriel, we must go to the back," Silas commanded sternly in his Jamaican accent. He tilted his head toward the room that was almost completely obscured by debris and gave his friend an encouraging nod.

"Stay with your brother," I whispered to Amelia, hoping whatever was between them before was long gone. "I'll be back in three minutes." And then to everyone else, "Everyone hang here for a minute, Gabriel, Silas,

Jericho and I are going to check out the back." I nodded to Jericho and he immediately followed.

We made our way through the debris, Gabriel shifting everything out of the way with his magic. We filed through the arched doorway and walked past confessionals that had been smashed to pieces and beyond a small kitchen type room. There was a short, narrow hallway with doors on either side. I assumed those were the living quarters and followed Gabriel's lead as he knocked harshly on each door before opening them to investigate the inside.

There were no people here, which was upsetting, but I was at least given hope with the fact that there weren't any dead bodies either. For that I could breathe a sigh of short-lived relief.

"This is my room," Gabriel announced solemnly when we approached the last of the small bedrooms.

He pushed open a heavy wooden door that had been abused and hung limply off its hinges. Inside the dark room was a single bed, a nightstand and a lamp. Gabriel didn't seem as pacified as I had been with the lack of bodies. In fact, he seemed more on edge than ever. He surveyed the room carefully before turning on the bedside lamp and shedding light onto the room.

All of our eyes fell to the same place at once. On the wall, across from the doorway, written in what looked like blood was a note.

A note meant for me.

How long will this Kingdom remain faithful to a King that cannot protect them? Let's find out.

A guttural, feral growl ripped from my lungs and the bed was up, tangled in my magic and thrown against the bloodied wall before I could feel sanity again. And when instead of calm reason, I felt the hopeless depths of frustration my outburst was followed by a string of curse words that couldn't even begin to describe the anger bubbling up inside of me.

Gabriel stumbled back against the cold cement blocked wall and slid to the floor, his caramel colored hands covering his face in despair.

"Who else was here, Gabriel? Were there other Immortals that could have been here? Besides your human nuns?" Jericho asked in a measured tone. I wanted to believe he was in control of his emotions, but one look at his brewing expression and the fury heating his gaze convinced me he was only holding it together long enough to make the next step in our plan.... only long enough until he could channel all of his anger into fighting, until he could find retribution.

"No, there were none. Only humans," Gabriel answered gruffly.

"My people," Silas whispered in terrified realization.

"Your colony has been hidden for centuries," I reasoned, but the thick blanket of fear settled on me, and suddenly I felt like I was suffocating beneath it.

"We have not been careful since Lucan died," Silas's accent was thicker than usual and his voice barely rose above a whisper. "I have not been back to...." he trailed off and I was as afraid of his next words as he was to say them. "I have not been back since your coronation."

"How many days do they have ahead of us?" I demanded of Jericho.

"Four," he answered, fear now mingling with his rage.

"That's enough," Silas growled.

"No, it's not," I reasoned, forcing myself into confidence. "They would still have to hunt. And your people are capable. *More than* capable. What's their contingency plan? Where would you go if.... Where would they have gone if Lucan found you?"

"The city of kings," Silas answered, his gray eyes sparking with determination.

"Get in the vans, we're going to Machu Pichu," I commanded before turning on my heel and leaving the sadness of Gabriel's church behind. There were no dead bodies, there was hope.

When I was alone in the hallway I paused, taking in deep, cleansing breaths.

It was there. Faint, but calling. The magic was there in the distance. Machu Pichu would have answers.

And if not answers, then a fight.

Chapter Twenty-Eight

I pulled Amelia close to me once we were in the van. I wrapped my arms around her waist and I buried my face in her hair. I inhaled her sweet scent, and memorized the feel of her touching me.

Jericho started our van and we were off, flying through the narrow mountain roads with the tall, majestic Andes rising on every side of us. The sun was setting over the mountain peaks, blocking out the sunset completely. Soon we would be shrouded in darkness, perfect for a fight if that's what it came to.

"I shouldn't have convinced you to come," I whispered to Amelia and then placed a kiss on the nape of her neck. I let my lips linger on her skin, relishing the taste of her flesh. "It's too dangerous. I was an idiot."

Amelia shivered underneath me, convincing me I needed to pull her even closer. But she turned in her seat and lifted her hands to my face. Her eyes were golden pools of warmth and affection.

"No, I'm glad I came. I wouldn't be able to.... I would hate not knowing how much danger you were in, or when I would hear from you again." She paused and kissed me sweetly on the lips. "I'm a good fighter Avalon. I'm more than capable to hold my own. You don't have to worry about me."

"That's not possible," My voice was suddenly gruff with emotion. "I trust you, of course I do. But I can't not worry about you." I turned in my seat to face Sebastian. He was staring at me not even trying to disguise his distrustful hatred of me. At this moment, with danger and uncertainty looming before us, I didn't blame him. But I couldn't give him an excuse so I gave him an order instead, "Sebastian, your only job when we get there is to protect Amelia. I don't want her anywhere near me where she could be identified as something I care about. They cannot know she is a weakness, Ok?" She started to protest so I amended my order to cater to her feminist ways, "I'm not saying I don't want you to fight. We need everyone we can. These people are ruthless. Hell, they kill their *own* people to protect their secrets. But Sebastian you are not to let anything happen to Amelia. Do you understand?"

"I do," Sebastian bit out. "I'm not happy you let her come Avalon, but thank you for keeping your distance."

"Why? Why do you have to stay away from me?" Amelia demanded, her cheeks flushed with anger. She looked so sexy with her eyes narrowed on me and her arms folded in defiance I had to stomp down the urge to lay her down on the bench seat and pass the time to Machu Picchu in a more entertaining way…. "I want to be with you! What if something happens to *you*! What then?"

"Amelia," I assured her, taking her neck in my hands and tilting her chin up with my thumbs. My hands looked huge next to the delicate perfection of her slender neck and face. "Nothing will happen to me. I'm King for a reason, remember? But if these men see a connection between us, they will stop at nothing to get to you. They are merciless like that, single minded and destructive. And that would kill me, more than any kind of magic they use against me, losing you would *destroy* me. I will do whatever I need to in order to protect you, but I'm not going to give them a reason to purposefully go after you. It was selfish to bring you, stupid and selfish. But know that I will be watching you the entire time. Nothing will take you from me."

Amelia nodded her response and I felt her tremble beneath my hands. I didn't know if she was choked up from my open speech and admission of how deep my feelings for her ran, or if I had truly scared her. But either way I was thankful the gravity of our situation had sunk in.

"Be safe?" she asked through glassy eyes.

"Mmm, I don't like safe," I whispered, quoting her, before closing into to kiss her.

Darkness. That's all there was in the ancient city of Machu Picchu. Even the empty parking lot was completely shrouded in the black ink of night. The moon was hidden behind cloud cover, the only light appearing in a small window of bone colored stripes. We could all see, our magic keeping the lack of light from being an obstacle. But even so, the stillness of the thin mountain air gave me anticipatory goose bumps.

The magic was strong here, so strong it was nearly choking. The vans had stopped and the clicking and groaning of the engines shutting off were the only sounds in the motionless night. The tiny noises seemed to echo off the mountain sides in the quiet of nothing that surrounded us.

Whatever tourists or human workers had been here during the day were long gone and all that was left was age old stone and the history of kings long buried. And the magic.

There was magic everywhere. Fearful, frightened…. tortured.

And then in other places angry, hateful…. aggressive.

We had converged together. We would meet here and fight. They had the advantage of being here first, but we had the benefit of experience.

And being generally awesome.

Through the darkness my eyes found Silas. He was staring back at me, his gray eyes cutting through the night like a fuzzy television channel. He shook his head once, indicating that his people were not here.

In one regard, that was a good thing. On the other hand, who were the Immortals here then?

If Silas's colony hadn't been found, who's had been?

"On my lead," I commanded my van, knowing the second van would wait for my move anyway. "We'll head into the city. Be ready immediately, we might not make it that far before they attack." I stood up as much as I could in the cramped van and made a move for the door before pausing with one last piece of instruction, "Be careful with the city. Try to avoid any permanent damage, unless it's at the cost of your own safety." And then to Amelia, "Stay with Sebastian."

She nodded with a resolved tilt of her chin. I loved that she was ready for this, that she wasn't afraid of what was outside this door.

And hated it at the same time.

I slid open the rusty door and stepped onto the dirt and gravel parking lot. I cringed without realizing it, until nothing immediately came flying at me. I allowed myself to relax with practiced confident aloofness and signaled for the other van to empty with us.

I walked forward, toward the magic and the ancient ruins. Machu Picchu had a vast and haunting feel to it in the emptiness and dark. It seemed to stretch on forever, sprawling across the mountainside and up to the peak. The night seemed to whisper across the thin air, telling the stories of other kings that had died here, warning me not to become another fallen ruler, cremated by the earth beneath my feet.

I breathed deeply through my nostrils and stilled my thumping heart. I dared a glance behind me; I quickly surveyed my group of skilled warriors until my eyes landed on Amelia. I drank her in, deeply, one last time and then I entered through the tall gates and met the enemy I came to destroy.

My team entered behind me and spread out in a protective half circle. We hadn't all fought together before, but the Titans that tagged along fell into an easy pattern of practiced experience. I refused to let myself look at Amelia, but I felt her magic down from me. It was everything I could do to keep my magic from hers, to stay separated from her just in case they had anyone capable of paying attention.

We stood there, with the parking lot and entrance gates behind us and the layered city before us. Their magic pulsed around us, but there were too many buildings and places to hide for us to pursue them. If they ran we would of course follow, but until then it was safer to wait them out.

I gave Xander a discreet nod allowing him to release the taunting I knew would be coiled tight inside of him. He grinned in reply and cupped his hands around his mouth to project the sound.

"Bad guys! Bad guys!" he called in a playfully mocking tone that had several of us snickering. "Come out, come out wherever you are!"

A muffled cough sounded in the night but was quickly quieted. I nodded again to Xander, giving him a look of approval and at the same time warning everyone to raise their magic and prepare for the battle.

Threat level orange. DEFCON five. Or whatever. It was time to be prepared.

"Look," Xander continued, displaying how very unimpressed he was so far. "We know you're out there and we have places to be, things to do, *Kingdoms* to run. It's time to come out and play."

I couldn't help but smile. The anticipation of battle, the thrill of a fight ran deep in my blood and had awakened my inner warrior, the most real and alive part of my soul. I flexed and clenched my fingers, and bounced on my toes. This wasn't just about my addiction to action; this was about punishing an evil that deserved my wrath.

This was about vengeance for too many needlessly dead Immortals.

Movement from behind nearby stone structures caught my attention and I stilled my body in expectancy for confrontation. Out walked two Immortals, wearing grins of excitement and vibrating with aggressive magic. They were large, well-toned, and I instinctively knew they would be challenging opponents.

I argued that they weren't Titans though and so we had somewhat of a tactical advantage. Still, they weren't the only two. There were more out there and before too much more time passed I knew we would meet the rest of their gang of merry men.

"Ah, if it isn't his royal highness, the great King Avalon," one of the men picked up Xander's taunting tone and used it against us. "Come to arrest us? Turn us into one of your many minions, weeping at your feet? Kissing your ring?"

His friend sneered beside him and gestured to those around me. "Look how willingly he calls them to be slaughtered. He cares nothing for you," the man's tone turned serious and he looked along the line as if meeting each individual in the eye. "He is asking you to give up your lives for a fight he doesn't even understand yet. And you will do it. You will all do it." He ended with a note of pure disgust as if I were the worst kind of evil.

This was a new place for me to stand in. I had never been accused of this kind of cruelty before. I had accused others of this same thing, but never once had I been on the receiving end.

It kind of sucked.

And I hope my people knew me better.

"You are sheep," the first man spat.

A heavy silence hung in the air for only a second before Titus stepped forward to defend me. "We are sheep? We saw one of your men kill another, simply because he was captured. You murder your own brothers to ensure silence, and you accuse our King of being cruel? I will be a sheep; I will gladly follow Avalon even if the course is still uncharted. But I refuse to be disposable for a deranged cause like you are. Give up your futile fight and surrender. Not only will you not win tonight, but you will not succeed at all. Walk away from whatever you have been promised, because I swear to you that you will never get it. You underestimate Avalon, and you underestimate how devoted his people are to him."

I wanted to hug Titus. It was girly and beyond out of control, but in that moment I wanted to hug him.

I decided to fight instead.

"He's right; you're fighting a losing battle. You may still have secrets from us, but they will not matter after we destroy you all. Give up now, come willingly and you will receive something lighter than death. Fight now and you will give us no other option than to stop you." I offered benevolently in my most Kinglike voice. See? I could be benevolent.

No practice necessary.

"Not a chance," the second man growled. "Our cause is worth fighting for."

There was absolute certainty in his voice, complete conviction. And it actually hurt my heart because I had been where he stood. Hell, I was still there. I just knew my cause was the right one, and that I stood on the side of goodness. He was convinced of something evil and cruel. No matter what his greater hope was, murdering innocents was and always would be the worst kind of evil.

"Your cause is killing your own people?" I questioned, disguising the complete disgust in my voice, hoping they would still change their minds. "Hurting? Torturing? Kidnapping? That's not a cause, that's murder. And it's a path straight to the pits of Hell even if you can defeat me. Don't lose your life or your soul believing another man's lies."

"Dimitri Terletov is not a liar," the first man ground out.

"Then where is he so that he can defend himself?" I demanded, hating that he wasn't the one talking to me. These men should know better, they should realize he was sending them to be slaughtered.

"With your sister," the first man laughed before sending a burst of his magic directly towards my head.

I ducked out of the way while my mind reeled and spun with the realization that Eden, at this very moment could be in extreme danger. I turned around, sending my magic spiraling towards my enemies while I willed myself to focus on this fight first.

The first punch was thrown so to speak and the battle began.

Men descended on us from every direction, ready for a fight, ready to end my reign and my bloodline. I fought back immediately, but only half-heartedly as my mind spun with dangerous possibilities for my sister and her unborn child. And at the same time I fought to save my own life, with only the soft promise that I could feel her still alive. We were connected and she wasn't crying out to me. That had to be a good sign. The only option was to finish this fight and then find Eden. Until then, my willingness for mercy had run out and each one of these men would be made to ultimately pay for treason.

Chapter Twenty-Nine

Rocks and ground exploded around me as the two sides of this battle converged into one destructive entity. I sent up a prayer asking for forgiveness as I watched the ancient ruins shatter in the night. I moved forward, meeting the two men that spoke for their absent leader while the rest of my team each connected with another fighter.

I turned so that Amelia would stay in my peripheral, but I had to be honest with myself and admit that I was very proud of how she handled herself. I noticed not only Sebastian but Jericho stay close to her too and this time I could let whatever jealousy remained go and realize he protected her for me.

Well, and maybe for some residual friendship they shared.

But mostly for me.

I held back a smile when I realized she had been right. She was good at this, a natural. She blocked magic and retaliated quickly, never hesitating, never backing down. I watched for half a minute, as long as I could before I had to engage in my own fight.

This was the wrong time to get turned on. But Amelia kicking ass.... damn.

I refocused forward and blocked a strong ray of deadly magic from either side of me as the two men tried to take me from different directions. I leapt at the guy to my left, keeping my body low and angled for his waist. I connected with strong muscle, but I was prepared for the impact unlike him. I wrapped my arms tightly around his thrashing body and sent us flying over a steep incline.

Physical contact was a trick I learned from Eden. Not one of my Immortal ever expected human reactions like physical violence. We were spoiled with our powers, save for the Shape-shifters, of which at least three of my people had turned into some ferocious animal. But Witches and Mediums, even Titans fought with magic and nothing more. So while others came at me with enough electricity to seriously knock me on my ass, I caught them off guard by *literally* knocking them on their ass.

But hell, wrestling down sharp stone steps was painful no matter what species you were. I kept our momentum going, ignoring the cuts, gashes and broken bones that were working hard to heal themselves while we continued to fall. The other guy clung to me in a desperate attempt to get me underneath him. We were falling too fast for logical thoughts to happen naturally, so while he struggled to get his hands into a position to zap me with magic I used my hands that were already wrapped around him and released a powerful surge of energy.

His body immediately went limp and with a few more rolls and bumps we came to a stop at the base of a huge stone structure. I panted against the pain and effort it took to get down here. While my enemy lay unconscious at my feet, I took the free minute I had and quickly absorbed his magic as fast as I could.

My sister and I were the same in that we hated stealing magic from others, but we also recognized the necessity of it in situations like this. Unconscious or not, if I let him keep his magic, he would heal and then be right back after me. I had to take it, to protect myself and everyone else.

By now I was practiced and well equipped to take magic in seconds. I stood over him, leaving him mortal and effectively removing him from this fight. His life-light flickered in and out now that it would take a lot more to heal since he was completely human. I didn't waste time with him but leapt up the hill needing desperately to make sure that Amelia was Ok.

I was delayed by the popping bursts of the other Immortal I had been fighting when his magic found me from a higher vantage point. He stood at the top of the steep hill, sending powerful waves of magic down at me. I jumped out of the way of his electrical rays, healing where he already got me in the process. He was a good shot and several times I leapt through the air, flipping over and ducking to avoid being hit in the head. I darted all across the incline in what felt like a video game scenario.

A bad video game in which I didn't have any extra lives or second chances. And had to move uphill the entire time.

A video game I would play to save my own life.

I needed to fight back, to get in a position I could reverse the advantage. I stepped behind a stone archway that led both up and down on a carved stone staircase. The sounds of battle echoed in the night, stones smashing and crumbling, grunts and cries of pain, the rabid sounds of ferocious animals that were also my teammates. Battle was loud and chaotic, horrifying but familiar at the same time; I recognized the sounds like they were part of my home, part of the deepest parts of me.

I was born for moments like this.

I gathered my breath and prepared for a struggle. I wasn't naïve to the fact that around me it was silent. While the rest of the mountainside was lit up in the efforts and defenses of my friends, around me was still and quiet. The traitorous Immortal was moving toward me.

I was ready.

I felt his magic approach and stepped around the archway separating us. He reared back, surprised with my close proximity. I raised my hands so that they looked like I was trying to pacify him, but really I was readying for an attack.

"It's not too late," I spoke in calm tones, hoping to appeal to whatever logic remained inside of his brainwashed head. "Give up now, before you end up like your unconscious friend down there."

"You don't get it," he growled at me, raising his hands defensively in a mirror image of me. "It *is* too late. It's too late for you, and your family and every other Immortal that believes the lie that they are safe. He is executing his plan as we speak and you don't even understand what you're up against."

He was vomiting a lot of words, but not really saying anything revealing. There were more secrets than I could begin to wrap my head around, but the most disturbing part of the unknown was the conviction this guy spoke with. Whatever he was hiding had him completely convinced, he was a believer. I just didn't understand exactly what he believed.

"But is it too late for you?" I asked in a carefully measured tone. These people were all psychopaths. All of them.

"Yes," he snarled out and then he lunged for me. His magic came at me and I had a millisecond to block it before it hit me in the chest. I leaned back and Time-Slowed simultaneously, moving my shoulder out of the way just in time. And then I released my power over time and shot back with my own electricity, aiming for his feet.

I missed my target when he leapt out of the way, but was quick to aim again when he landed a few feet away. He turned around and shot back at me, our magics meeting in the air between us. The blinding energy crackled in the night air. Sweat poured from my forehead from the effort it took to keep his magic at bay.

I had fought a lot of Immortals in the past, a lot of talented, dangerous Immortals. Somehow he seemed stronger than any one of them. I tried to chalk it up to the fact that I hadn't been in a real fight in a few years, but his magic was extremely intense and more aggressive than mine.

I took a shaky step forward and tried to push against his energy field. I met only resistance. And then he took a step forward and when he pushed against me, I was forced to move back. That step alone made an angry, determined beast inside of me awaken. My arms trembled and I was on the verge of losing my foothold.

It was time to get creative.

I dropped my arms at the same time I dove to the side to avoid the release of his energy. He was expecting opposition, so when my magic disappeared he staggered to the left. I took that advantage and shot out an incredible bolt of electricity at his feet. He flew backwards, crashing into the stone archway. I took his moment of weakness and started to pull his magic into mine. Where most Immortals had to be physically touching to steal anything from another Immortal, I had the advantage of being able to steal magic from a distance. Perks of my bloodline. He resisted of course, shooting at me weakly from the ground. One of his shots of magic hit me in the shoulder and then another in the knee, but I refused to give up. I stumbled forward, willing my magic to heal my beat-up body while I remained in motion.

My magic was stretched a little too thin and stalled in the effort. My shoulder throbbed and my knee gave out so that I had to continue pulling his magic from the ground. He shouted out a vicious growl that echoed loudly in the valley below. He was propped up in a sitting position against the background of rubble and he looked defeated, even before he was.

When his magic was completely absorbed in mine, his head lolled to the side and he didn't seem like he could lift his arms if wanted to. My magic, finally being free to concentrate on only one thing, worked to heal my battle wounds and when my knee felt strong enough, I stood up and walked over to him.

He worked, with a lot of difficulty, to lift his head so that he could look me in the eye. "If it means anything, I wouldn't have told you anything anyway." His words huffed out in clouds of heat opposed to the cool night.

"What?" I asked in confusion.

A twisted, evil smirk lifted the corners of his mouth. He let out a long, resigned sigh that turned slowly into a sinister laugh. I braced myself for something…. anything, like the ground exploding around me or more Immortals dropping down from helicopters. Anything, really.

"I wouldn't have told you anything," he breathed slowly as if I had trouble understanding him…. as if I was the victim and he the winner.

Then it dawned on me. I jumped towards him just as the slice of a bullet whooshed by me. The bullet connected with the guy's face, directly in the middle of his forehead, his skull compacted from the impact. He slumped forward, devoid of all life.

The sniper. The f-ing sniper.

I didn't have time to make sure he was dead, but I was positive he was. I took off running toward the magic that came from up the mountainside. Another bullet cut through the night, right past my ear, missing me just as I had weaved to the right. Dodge and weave, that was the first thing to remember when running into bullet fire.

I would find him, whoever he was. This silencing of all my prisoners thing had to end, and it had to end now. I didn't have to check to know my other victim would be dead too. Terletov cleaned up his messes. But I had to wonder what his end game was if he kept a sniper nearby but only used him for his own guys. Not to mention, I was dying to see what this weapon looked like.

I wasn't moving fast enough and I could feel him begin to move away from me. I decided I had to pick up the pace and since a vehicle was out of the question I pulled on my ancient magic, deep from the well of my innermost being so that I could shift into a puma. My skin prickled and snapped with frenetic energy as it spread over my skin from hair follicle to toenails. Every inch of my body bent and contracted with unimaginable electricity, the magic changed the very molecules of my body into something different, something infinitely more primal but incredibly fast.

The change lasted only seconds but in that short time frame the air was sucked from my lungs and it felt as if I ceased to exist completely before my body morphed into an entirely different species. I went from standing upright as a man to bent over and pounding against the ground on all fours as an animal.

The sensation was a little disconcerting to be honest.

But having practiced this move before, I took it all in stride and pursued my prey. My paws dug into the soft earth of the mountain side and my deadly claws kept traction with each step so that I could launch myself forward with incredible speed. My sleek coat made fighting against the whipping wind easy. My athletic front and hind legs stretched as far forward as they could go, working to bring me to my goal before he escaped. A growl of epic proportions ripped through my narrow lungs and I became as much of the animal as my brain would allow in order to hunt this enemy down.

He was still a ways away, but by tracking his magic I felt him pick up his things and move further from me. Whoever he was, he was shy. Apparently he didn't want me to introduce myself, which bothered the hell out of me.

Although I couldn't blame him. I had a whole lot more than a handshake and swapping war stories in mind for our initial introduction. Like a face-punch and a broken nose.

Or maybe I would keep this animal form and rip out his throat with these killer teeth.

And then much worse things.

I took the solitude of my chase to check in with my sister. I wanted to believe she was fine, that I would have felt something or she would have said something to me if she wasn't and so far the communication between us had been silent.

Eden. I called in the calmest tone I could manage, while simultaneously pursuing a sniper I planned on murdering, or at the very least imprisoning and trying not to panic about what could possibly be a horrible fate for her.

Avalon, is everything Ok? Are you *Ok*? She gasped in a terrified inner voice. *Are you a.... are you a panther?*

I took a deep breath in and then let it out slowly while I examined her surroundings. While my shifted form leapt over rocks and low to the ground structures, and my cat eyes stayed trained on where I knew the sniper had taken off, my mind assessed Sylvia's living room. Kiran sat next to Eden, they both enjoyed a relaxed, laid back evening in Omaha.

Nothing was wrong.

Eden was safe.

Eden, seriously? I'm a puma. And I'm fine. I admitted when the haze of red rage had receded from my vision. *We found some trouble near Silas' colony but we are taking care of it. Are you Ok? I need to know, Eden, is there Guard with you? The guy.... the guy I just fought said that you were in trouble. Is everything Ok there*?

I focused on the pursuit for a minute while she relayed everything I said to Kiran and then I watched as he stood to speak with his head Guard. Eden's heart fluttered inside her chest, she was nervous, I could feel it from here. But for now she was safe.

We're fine. Eden reassured me.

You're fine. I breathed.

I slowed my running pace to a prowl when the magic I chased sped up and disappeared completely somewhere in the obscurity of the mountains. He must have gotten in some kind of vehicle, because suddenly he was just gone.

Just like that.

A deep roar rumbled in my chest and I immediately shifted back to my human form. I needed to yell curse words and kick things and assert my male dominance and frustration. I couldn't do that while I was walking on all fours.

As easily as I transformed into the jungle cat, I transformed right back to standing and became myself again. I panted heavily, sucking in breath that had been taken for me in the seconds it took to shift. I ran my hand through my wild hair, pulling it out of my face and manhandling it into a knot on my neck.

"Damn it," I growled out, still channeling the puma. I was frustrated and tired of feeling like I was losing.

Finish there and then call me, we'll figure this out. Eden instructed. I felt her pull her knees to a chest and rock back and forth on one of Sylvia's couches like a little girl.

I will. Don't worry about this, E. It's probably bad for the baby. I got this, I'll call you later. I ordered, and part of me instinctively tensed up realizing how much Eden needed to be protected right now with the baby growing inside of her. At the same time that same part relaxed just saying the word "baby." How cool was this baby going to be? It was like the future of this Kingdom.

Alright. She sighed. I love you, *Avalon.*

Love you too, sis. I replied back.

Communication was cut off abruptly when I heard Amelia scream in the distance. Her powerful shriek reached me even from my vantage point. Panic turned my blood to ice and I swore that if anything happened to her I would find Terletov before the night was over and make him pay.

Chapter Thirty

I turned and raced back down the hill, taking a staircase that I stumbled down three steps at a time. The battle was mostly finished by the time I reached the entrance where most of my teammates were cleaning up. I started counting heads before I even realized what I was doing. It looked like we had some injuries, but for the most part I found everyone we came with alive.

Except Amelia.

And Sebastian and Jericho, but I was less worried about them. They could take care of themselves.

"Where is she," I demanded when Xavier lifted his head at my approach. He was bent over Roxie who was kneeling over a traitor Immortal laying on the ground.

"She's over there," Xavier nodded his head to a square stone building. "Avalon, she's fine. She's with Jericho."

"You're sure?" I grunted, pinning him with my fiercest glare.

"I'm positive," he swore, holding up his hand in a gesture that asked me to stop and talk to him.

I slowed down to take some vitals of the situation. I was still concerned, but with the calm tone of Xavier's voice I could also relax and not bombard her with my concern.

"Did you get any prisoners?" I asked, noticing the man Roxie checked out was dead.

"No," Xavier ground out and then let loose a string of curse words. "We were in the middle of winning when they just started shooting each other. It was like they would wait until their magic was gone, then one of the other bastards would pull out a gun and shoot them. It was a blood bath, and I didn't even get to join in the fun."

"Shut up, Xavier," Roxie snapped, standing up to face me. "This isn't fun. Look at all these dead bodies.... this is anything but fun. Avalon do you have any idea what is going on? Why are they kidnapping humans now?"

"Humans?" I barked, my throat immediately feeling dry and scratchy.

Roxie's expression fell when she realized I didn't know this new piece of information. "Go talk to Jericho. He'll fill you in."

I paused for a few moments, gathering my courage. I really hoped I wasn't on the way to another pile of dead bodies. Those images were forever burned into my head. They were memories I would never be able to forget or forgive myself for.

"I think it's a contingency plan," I sounded distant and foreign even to my own ears as I tried to wrap my head around the horrific situation we were facing. "To answer your question, Rox, I think it's what they do when they realize they are losing. And I think they do it to protect their cause, or whatever secrets they are hiding."

"Who would do that? Whatever they are doing cannot be worth all of this," Roxie swept her arm toward the destruction of the battle.

"I agree," I muttered and then changed my mind. "Although there was a time when any of us would have done the same. How many did we lose against Lucan?"

Xavier and Roxie nodded somberly.

"And after what we found Siberia, we might want to rethink the whole suicide thing. I don't think I want to be taken prisoner just to end up like those Immortals we found." Xavier announced with sickening truth.

"We'll talk about that later," I acknowledged, hoping there would be a logical way to convince my people not to take such drastic measures. But as I thought about Siberia, or the two Immortals that had come to the Citadel, there wasn't much in the way of convincing me otherwise.

I followed the direction Xavier pointed and braced myself for whatever I was about to see. Upon rounding the corner to the back of the ancient building I saw Amelia first, wrapped in her brothers arms. She was shaking, her face buried in his chest.

She was crying, her body trembling from the racking sobs that shook her chest.

"What's going on?" I asked in my strongest voice, wanting an immediate read on the situation and an explanation for Amelia's emotions.

Really, I just wanted to pull her into my arms and assure her everything would be alright, but at this point those words would feel like a lie. And I couldn't lie to her.

Jericho turned at the sound of my voice, his face a mask of unfiltered anger. He gestured to the wall where bodies were slumped together in a pile of tortured misery. But they were alive.

Whatever I feared, everyone back here was alive.

I took a deep breath.

Maybe my first deep breath of the night.

I walked closer, using my magic to see through the heavy night and assessed the bodies lined up as if waiting for execution. They were mangled, beaten and abused. They looked up at me with distrustful eyes and bloodied faces. Their hair was matted and dirty, their clothes torn and frayed. They looked beaten and tormented. They were a sickeningly staggering sight.

“Human?” I gasped out, realizing that in the mixture of ten or so hostages there were at least five humans. If the realization and horror of the moment hadn’t sent me reeling I would have been able to make an accurate count. But I couldn’t even see straight, let alone do something as simple as count to ten. My vision was red, only red; a mixture of pure anger, fear and choking vengeance.

Amelia turned away from her brother and fled to me. I opened my arms just as she crashed into my chest. I pulled her close to me, letting her sob against my chest and taking her closeness as comfort. I kissed the top of her head that was covered in dust from the fight and whispered something soothing; although I wasn’t even sure I believed the mumbled words.

“Jericho?” I asked in a gruff voice.

“From what we’ve gathered, these are the victims of more *experiments*,” Jericho explained, his own voice was rough with emotion, tripping over the detestable word. “We think the…. the humans are being experimented on to see if there is a way to somehow inject magic into them…. Terletov is trying to make them Immortal.”

“What?” I bit out. I looked down at the shells of human beings intermixed with the tortured Immortals and gathered that whatever experiments they were trying were *not* going well. “Sebastian, get these people into the vans, now. But don’t leave them alone, I’ll send you help. Jericho with me.”

I turned away from the victims. They deserved my attention and sympathy but I had to get things moving. I had their safety to worry about now, plus the safety of my own men.

“First,” I kept Amelia tucked in beside me but walked with Jericho back toward the entrance where Gabriel and Silas were huddled together talking with the older Titans. “Why did we win? Was it planned, or were we better fighters?”

Jericho let out a rush of breath before he answered, “We were better, more skilled and practiced. They were weirdly strong, but they didn’t have any real experience. All of us have experience.” Jericho nodded around and I relaxed infinitesimally. It wasn’t enough that I could feel good about what was still before us, but at least they hadn’t thrown this fight in some bizarre master plan I didn’t understand.

I nodded in understanding before turning to my men. “Xander, Xavier, Titus and Roxie, go help Sebastian load those people into the vans. And someone find them water. Break into the gift shop if you need to.” Turning back to Jericho I lowered my voice and asked, “How many humans?”

"Five," Jericho bit out, drawing the attention of Gabriel, Silas and the four older Titans. "Three of them are Gabriel's nuns. One of those is badly injured, but she is alive. Then there are two other humans, American tourists. We're not sure yet how they came upon Terletov, but they are pretty severely damaged. It's two sisters who are still mostly in shock."

I exhaled another breath of relief. It wasn't good, but it helped that three of the humans were connected with Gabriel. I didn't know how to explain all of this to humans without some serious consequences, but having a smaller number made things appear easier.

I looked at the men standing around me and knew there were decisions that had to be made. We would have to split up from here.

"This is what I want to happen, Jericho I want you and Sebastian to escort the Immortals and the humans back to Romania. Get them on a plane and get them to the Witch. He will heal them, even the humans. Jericho, I want them on a plane and out of here tonight, do you understand?" Jericho nodded and so I moved on. "Silas do you have any vehicles nearby?"

"Yes," he agreed; his gray eyes were bloodshot and he looked disturbingly ancient in the darkness. "I have a garage that holds several vehicles not far from here."

"Alright, then I want you to take Christi and his men and go find your colony. Check in with them, make sure they're alright and then decide on a play to keep them safe. If you have to take them back to the Citadel do that. I don't want them exposed and unaware of what's going on anymore. In fact, I insist you get them back to the Citadel. After you've taken care of them I want you to start visiting every Shape-Shifter colony that we know about. I know some of them have started to assimilate back into society, but a lot of them chose to stay where they were. Make sure they all know the risks that they are facing and get them to safety. Gabriel you are going to come with me and my men. We're heading to Omaha where Kiran and Eden are. I'm going to hold a conference with all of the Regents. It's time we spread the word about Terletov and the threat he poses. The people need to know how dangerous he is. I cannot keep this a secret any longer. Does anyone happen to have a plane here? Most of us can travel commercial but I need the humans and Immortal prisoners to fly under the radar."

"There is an airstrip here that Lucan used." Christi offered. "I'm not sure what's in the hangar, but it's worth checking out.

"Alright, give Xavier and Jericho the location. Jericho you and Sebastian need to leave immediately. Go now and take whatever you need to out of the hangar. Call when you get there and let me know if there is a jet for us.

Otherwise the six of us will fly commercial. Hey, take Roxie with you. She can be the soothing female we all know she was born to be."

Several men around me snorted and I almost cracked a smile myself. I thought about the human women though, and knew they would need a face they could trust. And even if Roxie was tough as nails, she at least had a pretty face, a trustworthy face.

"Ok, Jericho and Sebastian will leave right away and the rest of us will stay to clean up this mess." I paused and looked down at the girl wrapped in my arms, fragile, traumatized and afraid. "Amelia, go say goodbye to your brother," I whispered in her ear. She still clung to me, although she wasn't crying anymore. "I want you to stay with me."

She didn't argue, but she did leave my side to find Sebastian. I watched her walk away and tried to figure out how I was going to keep her safe but also by my side at the same time. A few weeks ago I couldn't imagine hiding behind a throne and crown while I let other people fight my battles, but with Amelia in my life now I couldn't convince myself that this was worth it if I put her in danger.

And at the same time I could not let her out of my sight. The sound of her screaming tonight had stopped my heart from beating, stopped my lungs from breathing…. and I had decided in that moment I could never trust her with someone else again. Not even her brother. She was too precious to me and her life was too fragile. She was mine to protect, mine to fight for.

I just needed to ensure that she had the strongest magic she could. I needed to make sure she was as protected as Immortally possible.

Basically, I just needed to marry her.

I almost laughed out loud realizing I had just decided I would get married as easily as I barked orders for people to follow. And then the laughter died in my throat when I realized I didn't just want to marry Amelia to protect her, I wanted to marry her because I loved her.

I wanted her to be my wife.

I needed her to be *my life*.

Now I just had to tell Amelia all that.

"Do you want me to stay with the humans while they recover?" Jericho asked, pulling me out of my life-changing thoughts. The men around us moved to deal with the dead bodies and repair what they could of the ancient ruins that had become our battlefield.

"No, make sure they're set up. Make sure they won't leave until things are settled and then I want you to escort Talbott and Lilly to Omaha. I'm throwing them an engagement party and they should probably be there for it."

"Do you think this is the appropriate time for that?" Jericho asked, sounding very doubtful.

"No, it's not the right time for a party. But it is the right time to remind our people what we fought for, what we defeated Lucan for. This Kingdom is fragile, and the announcement of Terletov is going to shake us up. But I want them to remember that freedom is our top priority. Lilly and Talbott's wedding will do just that."

"Plus, they're your friends, right?" Jericho pressed and it felt good to joke a little after the traumatizing night.

"There's that too," I laughed low and deep.

Jericho sobered suddenly, "Avalon, is Eden.... I'm assuming she's alright?"

"She's fine," I assured him, hating the way his eyes flashed and deepened with emotion at the sound of my sister's name. "I just talked to her. We didn't have anything to worry about."

"That's good news," Jericho breathed a sigh of relief and then offered, "Good luck with the Regents. Say hello to my parents for me."

"Good luck with the humans," I echoed.

And with that we split up. I took my people and followed Silas to the path that would eventually lead us to his hidden garage. Jericho and Sebastian finished loading up the two eight-passenger vans and headed down the mountain to Lucan's, my, the Kingdom's airstrip.

Amelia was immediately in my arms after saying goodbye to her brother and I dipped my head to claim her mouth with mine.

"I have something to tell you later," I whispered against her soft lips.

"Is it good or bad?" she asked in her sweet accent.

"It's life changing. I hope you're ready for it," I teased, moving to pay her neck and jawline some much needed attention.

"Should I be afraid?" She asked in a breathy voice.

"Absolutely," I murmured. Even after the sweat and dirt of battle caked her skin, she still tasted irresistible. I pulled her body flush against me so that I could feel every part of her. I was suddenly very, very excited about what marriage would mean for our relationship. Even after the horror of what we were facing, Amelia was still the best and brightest thing in my life. I could not wait to make her mine completely.

Chapter Thirty-One

I woke up on our beach, a little disoriented. The first reaction I had was panic and action, but two seconds of well thought-out decision reminded me this was the place I created for Amelia on her birthday.

The night was comfortably warm, a gentle breeze floated over me and the moon overhead was impossibly bright. Stars twinkled above for miles and miles, stretching as far as this dream world would go. The sand felt like a plush cushion beneath the cotton blanket I lay on top of. The water lapped against the distant shore in harmony with nature, musical and soft.

I was a little out of it as I tried to remember where my human body was and how I got here. I rested my hands on my stomach, completely comfortable and willing to think it over for a minute when I turned my head and met the biggest golden brown eyes ever created.

Amelia.

"Hey," I whispered in the darkness.

"Hey," she whispered back. She was on her side, on top of the pale blue blanket of her own creation. I fell in love with the fact that she recreated our world, and that she was contented enough to add her own touches.

Her hair spilled over her shoulders and framed her delicate face. Her lips were pursed and the emotion behind her eyes worried me. I turned on my side so that I could look her properly in the eyes. I ran the back of my knuckles along her jawline in concern. She lifted her face into my touch and I couldn't stop the smile from spreading across my face if I wanted to. This was so close to my idea of perfection, it felt unreal.

"We're still on the plane to Omaha," she explained. She must have read the confusion on my face.

"I figured," I murmured. I was waking up, but taking my time coming back to myself. The battle in the Andes had taken it out of me, and the two day travel back to Lima and an international airport without sleep hadn't helped. There was only one jet in Lucan's old hanger and Jericho commandeered it in order to get the rescued prisoners back to Romania. Silas moved on with Christi Ludu and the other Titans to see if they could find his lost colony. And the rest of us were forced to fly commercial back to the States. I was fine; but it was just like somebody had slipped me a sedative the minute I finally sat down in first class. "Are you alright?" I asked Amelia, her pinched expression and furrowed brow had me nervous. She did not look alright.

Amelia shook her head, and then buried her face in the crook of her elbow. Her body shook once and her breath hitched into a sob. I scooted closer immediately, pulling her into my arms and wrapping her up inside my embrace.

"Hey, it's Ok," I whispered into her hair.

She nodded against me. She didn't cry again, but she stayed close to me, burrowing as close against my chest as she could get.

"What's the matter?" I pressed when I felt like she had gotten some control back.

She waited a full minute before answering. She took even breaths and kept her face flush against my chest. When I breathed, she moved with me. I loved the way she fit against me. "I was just.... I'm just trying to process everything that happened. Watching those men die was.... traumatizing. And then finding those nuns and the Immortals. Avalon.... I.... I just needed to feel safe."

She took a deep breath and cuddled closer, although there was hardly any space left between us. I tightened my grip around her, loving that she called me here. Pride and testosterone spread like rushing rapids inside of my veins as I realized Amelia pulled me into a Dream-Walk because *I* made her feel safe. On the outside I was the perfect picture of comforting boyfriend, keeping her close and comforting her as best as I could. On the inside I was more like Tarzan beating my chest in victory.

Avalon, King of the jungle.

I pushed those thoughts down, or tried to and nuzzled my face into the crook of her hair, breathing her in. She was intoxicating. And she trusted me. I had never felt like more of a man in my life.

We laid like that for the rest of the flight, ignoring the outside world, wrapped in our own, isolated cocoon. When the "fasten seatbelt" light finally came one, Amelia was settled down and relaxed again. We exited our dream world and reentered reality closer than we had ever been. And I was satisfied with the knowledge that our relationship was equally as secure.

"You look like hell," Eden mused when she picked us up at the Omaha Eppley Airfield.

"It's good to see you too, sis," I grumbled, throwing my backpack in the trunk of her Land Rover while Eden and Amelia hugged tightly. Amelia left her luggage in one of the vans in Peru when we split up with Jericho. I was lucky to have left quite a bit of clothing at Sylvia's house from when I lived with her, but Amelia was going to have to go shopping for a little bit of everything for now. The only thing she had managed to keep with her was her passport and ID to function in the human world. I appreciated her practicality.

I even found it sexy.

"I cannot believe my brother let you be a part of that," Eden sighed irritably, squeezing Amelia even tighter.

"Please," I grunted. "Amelia can take care of herself." I believed this, I wasn't ever going to let her take care of herself again, but I did believe she could. I had also noticed how Amelia bristled against Eden's words and I knew that she hated feeling like everyone babied her. I wouldn't baby her. I would protect her when she needed me, but I would never deny her the capable woman she was.

"That doesn't mean she should," Eden countered.

"Because you've always sat back and let others fight for you?" Amelia leveled her gaze with my sister's and I bit back my laughter.

"Touché," Eden huffed.

"She's got a point, E," I smiled. I put my hands on Amelia's shoulders, loving the delicate feel of them beneath my fingers and pulled her back against my chest. I dipped my head so that I could feel her soft hair against my cheek. "Told you, she can take care of herself."

"This is really happening, isn't it?" Eden stared at us in disbelief.

"This is really happening," I answered before Amelia could make up some excuse.

"Well, we're uh, we're just giving it a trial run," she explained anyway.

Eden looked us over with a tight squint to her eyes and then laughed softly. I knew she was keenly aware of my feelings so I knew her scrutiny had more to do with Amelia's emotions. I held my breath until Eden came back with something smart to say.

"Careful, Mimi, my brother does nothing half way," she winked at me and I relaxed.

It wasn't what Eden had teased Amelia with, it was the confidence in which she did it. Not only did Eden approve of us, she believed there was a mutual attraction between us.

These were all things I knew and could easily convince myself with. And if things were going slow and naturally between us I wouldn't have had to worry about them anyway, but since I planned to marry this girl and do it soon I had to hope she was tracking right along with me.

Gabriel, who had been a silent observer grunted something unintelligible and moved to sit in the front seat of Eden's car. Yes, even though I was not only King but the brother of the driver, Gabriel had surreptitiously called shotgun. Bastard.

It wouldn't have mattered at all, especially since I actually preferred to sit with Amelia in the backseat, but truth be told my legs were way too long for the backseat. Hell, I was way too big for the backseat.

Guess Amelia and I were going to have to cuddle.

The rest of us followed suit and climbed in Eden's banana colored SUV. Titus, Xander and Xavier had driven off already in Syl's convertible that Kiran drove down to the mid-sized airport.

The ride back to Sylvia's house was filled with a recap of the battle for Eden. Gabriel said his piece now since he would be bunking at Amory's old house with the rest of the guys.

Amelia gripped my hands tightly in hers while I retold Eden with excruciating detail what happened. Eden visibly paled when I talked about the human prisoners and the suicides and I worried about the health of her baby under this much stress.

She shook me off in our mental shared consciousness though, promising that even though her emotions were unavoidable the baby wouldn't suffer because of her despair. And even though I believed what she said, her health became another important reason to wrap this Terletov thing up.

"You're with child," Gabriel grunted with surprising tones of reverence in his voice when our conversation had died down. He had somehow known and I had to wonder for just four seconds if he read our minds, but then shook that notion off. He was incredibly perceptive.

And possibly he could read our minds too.

But probably not.

Eden looked stunned for just a moment before she was able to recover, "I am."

"Incredible," Gabriel murmured, looking at Eden like he had never seen anything like her before. "Avalon didn't say anything."

I wanted to defend myself, but Eden beat me to it, "We just found out. We're waiting to tell the Kingdom until the engagement party for Talbott and Lilly that Avalon's planning."

I hadn't known they were going to make the announcement that soon, nor did I know she realized the engagement party would be so soon. It shouldn't have surprised me, but for some reason Eden using her magic to use our connection for information did. Especially after her shocking bouts with morning sickness, I really believed my sister had to have Kiran remind her constantly to use her magic.

She was adorably oblivious.

"This means everything to your people," Gabriel all but whispered. "Your grandfather would have been…." Gabriel's voice broke just a fraction and while my jaw dropped in surprise from his show of emotions, Eden's instantly filled with huge tears that slipped from the corners of her eyes and trailed helplessly down her cheeks. She swiped at them with the back of her hands and the car swerved destructively across three lanes of interstate. "Amory would have been amazed."

I wanted to roll my eyes at my sister's dramatic emotions until Gabriel's last words. I expected him to say "proud" or "pleased" or anything but "amazed." His word choice filled the car with the same tone as his reverent awe and for the first time I sat back and admired what an incredible miracle Eden was carrying. After the sordid past of our people and the impossibility of the baby inside of her I had to agree. It was amazing. Eden was amazing.

If Eden and I carried a new kind of magic in our blood, what wonders did this tiny infant possess?

Beyond what this would mean for my people I had to admit the whole thing was exactly like Gabriel said, amazing.

Amelia's hands gripped mine tighter and I realized she was as emotional as my sister. That snapped me back to reality and I put a comforting arm around her and drew her close to me. A feeling stuttered and started inside my chest and then flamed out, growing rapidly through every pore and blood vessel inside of me.

Jealousy.

Not the kind that would keep me from being happy for my sister and her husband, but the soft kind that blossomed hope. For the first time in my entire life I thought about what it would be like for my wife to be pregnant with that same miracle. I wanted that. I wanted what Eden and Kiran had. And not because of what it would do for my people, for the first time in maybe forever, I wanted my wife and me to have a baby because of what it would do for me…. for my wife…. for us.

Yes, I definitely wanted that.

And I had the undeniable feeling that I was already holding part of that in my arms.

"Hey there," Sylvia called as she came into the kitchen from the living room. She was rumpled from sleep, her blonde hair sticking up wildly and her mascara smudged and black beneath her eyes.

"Hey there," I echoed in a huge smile. I stood up and swept her into a big hug. "It's been awhile."

"No kidding," she laughed when I set her back down. She immediately turned her back on me to give her undivided attention to the coffee pot that was gurgling with activity on the counter.

We were the only ones up so far. After a long night of talking things out with Kiran, planning an informational meeting and then the subsequent task of calling the Regents, most of the house was still asleep. I wasn't a very good sleeper to begin with, but since I had given my bedroom up to Amelia, the couch was in no way convincing for a late morning.

"When did you get in last night?" I asked Sylvia who had been at the hospital the majority of yesterday.

"I'm not sure," she grunted and then pulled the pot midstream to fill up her large cup. "Sometime after midnight but before now."

I laughed at her candidness. "You didn't want to sleep in?"

"I can't. I have to go back to the hospital in an hour," she explained and then took a sip of her coffee. I watched as the caffeine immediately went to work in her system and she relaxed against the counter. "It's good to have everyone back here," she mused suddenly.

"It's good to be back here," I agreed. While Omaha didn't feel like home necessarily, it was still comfortable and familiar. Part of me couldn't wait to hold a meeting at the club. After having been on the other side of the Monarchy the last time I was here, I was a little bit excited to take over the reins and test out my authority on this turf. "I'm glad I have you alone, Sylvia, I have a few things I need your help with."

"Mmm? What's that?" she asked, her eyes lighting up from behind her cup. She kept inhaling the aroma of the coffee like a serious addict. It was adorable.

"First, I'm sure you heard that Lilly and Talbott are engaged?" I asked.

"Yes, and how exciting!" she squealed. "Finally, right? You must be so excited for their wedding!"

"I am," I admitted in a more subdued tone. Even though Eden looked up to Sylvia like a mother, she was only in her late-thirties and I had a very hard time taking her seriously as an adult, even with her prestigious surgeon status. She was just too cute. "I'm so excited in fact that I've decided to throw them an engagement party."

I bit back laughter as I watched Sylvia's eyes narrow in suspicion. "*You* decided to throw them an engagement party? Like of your own free will?"

"Yes, why? Is it hard to believe?" I scoffed defensively.

"No, it's *impossible* to believe. You don't like parties first of all, and I have a really hard time believing that you would willingly throw one," she laughed.

"It wasn't my original idea," I conceded, "but it is important that I put my support behind their marriage. And not just in a business-standpoint kind of way. They are my friends. I do care about them. And I do want to celebrate this with them."

"Gabriel?" Syl asked and I shook my head negatively. "Angelica?"

"It wasn't one of my advisors," I grumbled, realizing the reason Sylvia was determined to get to the bottom of this.

"Your sister?" Sylvia all but squeaked, her smile growing wide over the lip of her cup.

I shook my head and bit back more laughter.

"Put me out of my misery Avalon, just tell me," she groaned sounding completely exasperated.

"What is the big deal?" I sighed, staring at the ceiling as if it was the most interesting thing in the room although I was kind of dying to tell Syl.

"The big deal is that I have never even seen you look twice at a girl since I've known you,"

"What? You make me sound like a celibate monk. I've looked at girls," I assured her. "Plenty of girls."

"That's not what I meant," Syl shook her head enthusiastically, sending her tussled blonde hair whipping around her. "Of course you've looked at girls, but you've never really *looked* at them. I'm not explaining myself well.... Um, let's see. You've always been duty and honor and destiny. I don't think you've ever considered a relationship seriously with anyone. So this, Avalon, is a very big deal!"

"Whatever, it's just a party," I sighed.

"Exactly."

I rolled my eyes and then gave in to girl talk. "Amelia.... it's Amelia."

Sylvia squealed in delight and set her cup down to give me a huge hug. And then she slowed down her enthusiasm, looked me in the eye with a pissed off expression and slapped my bicep angrily.

"What?" I grunted, rubbing the barely there sore spot on my arm.

"You're really serious about this girl," she accused, staring up at me with her big blue eyes.

I towered over her and she was tall for a girl, or er... woman. "I am."

"Like marriage serious?" she pressed and when I raised my eyebrows at her she explained. "I know how your kind works. You're like penguins when you fall in love."

"Penguins?" I laughed.

"Ugh," she grunted without explaining her animal metaphor further. "That's so annoying." She marched back over to her coffee cup and took a sip like it was a much needed hit.

"So… you're not happy for me?" I pretended to pout, finding her way more entertaining than offensive.

"No, I'm happy for you," she sighed sounding anything but. "Why wouldn't I be happy for you? You're only half my age and in love and going to get married and have lots of little royal babies and live happily ever after and blah blah blah…."

"Syl?" I whispered, concerned for the first time.

"Oh gosh, Avalon I'm sorry," Sylvia grumbled, her cheeks heating with embarrassment. "I swear I'm having a midlife crisis. Or like a uh, my-life-is-going-nowhere-I'm-so-alone kind of crisis."

"Oh, Syl," I sighed and pulled her back into a hug. I wrapped my arms around her and squished her to me, coffee cup and all. "You know you're seriously hot, right?" She giggled against my chest. "Not even lying. You say I never looked at girls, but I was half in love with you for like two full years of my life."

"You were *not* in love with me! Love and lust are two very different things," she screeched and then finally hugged me back. "Stop trying to make me feel better. Ok, I know I'm a catch. I just haven't found the right net yet."

"Net?" I barked out a laugh. "Is that what the kids are calling it these days?"

She laughed at me and then moved back to lean against the counter. "Ok, so you need my help planning this engagement party for kids that are way too young to be getting married?"

I smiled at her playful lack of enthusiasm. "Yes, please."

"You said a couple things, what else is there?"

Movement on the stairs alerted the fact that we were about to have company. I really did need her help and with both of our busy schedules I wasn't sure when I'd get her alone to ask her again. So I lifted my ring finger and pointed to the spot where a wedding band would one day be.

She mouthed her disbelief, her eyes growing big but this time they filled with utterly happy emotions.

I smiled and nodded proudly.

She quietly spun around in a crazy little happy dance and then leaned casually back against the counter just in time to greet Eden and Kiran.

We gave each other knowing looks over breakfast and I was so thrilled with our little conspiracy I was practically buzzing with excess energy.

Although that could have also had something to do with my plan finally being put into motion.

And I definitely ignored the part of my brain that rolled its eyes at my use of the word "finally" since I decided this all of three days ago.

Chapter Thirty-Two

"Kiran are you coming with us today?" Sylvia asked my brother in law over eggs and toast.

"Yes," Kiran answered decidedly.

"Ok, but then Amelia and I are going shopping," Eden warned Kiran. "My brother somehow managed to bring her into this country without any clothes of her own.

"Well played, Avalon," Kiran smirked at us from over his cup of coffee. Amelia blushed deep red beside me and I chuckled while silently wishing it were more like that. "Eden, Love, you're not going to get rid of me. I am desperate to know you're Ok and that our baby is as well." Kiran was so firm, so determined that the rest of us fell silent under the intensity blanketing the room.

"I'm fine," Eden all but whispered. She was already tearing up and I regretfully felt the press of her emotions against my own. "And our baby is fine."

"I want to see it," Kiran said softly but with the subtle command of a king.

"Ok," Eden whispered her consent, a lone tear drop slipping from the corner of her eye.

"Eden, I swear, if I cry because of your crazy pregnancy hormones I will never forgive you," I growled. I did my best to separate her emotions from my own, which was not easy with her so close and overwhelmingly sensitive.

She giggled through a sob and Kiran brought her against his chest, wrapping both arms around her back. She hiccupped another sob and buried her face against him, letting her unruly hair fall around her face to hide some of her embarrassment. Being connected to Eden right now was like the worst, most unsatisfying roller-coaster ride of my life. I was possibly the first man in the history of mankind that had to endure the terrifying and volatile journey that was pregnancy.

It was awful.

Women everywhere deserved medals just for being able to survive the hormones.

And I deserved the freaking Nobel Peace Prize.

Although enduring morning sickness and being constantly on the verge of tears were definitely not things I ever planned on bragging about.

Ever.

"Is everything Ok with the pregnancy?" Amelia asked from beside me, her own voice trembling slightly with nerves.

"Everything is fine," Sylvia explained with somewhat strained patience, which made me doubt her. I leveled my eyes with her and she raised her eyebrows defensively. "We are a little concerned with the strength of Eden's morning sickness, only because you all don't get sick. And from all of the other Immortal women we've talked to morning sickness is completely unheard of. So although that might be a bit concerning, it's not a bad sign. It is a symptom; therefore we are not looking at something like miscarriage since it seems to be fairly consistent. We also cannot do any blood tests, for obvious reasons. At least not here, in Omaha." Sylvia concluded sounding very much like the doctor she was.

"I didn't know you were still feeling nauseous," I accused Eden, turning my serious stare to her.

"I have been trying to keep it from you," she admitted sheepishly.

"Thank you," I returned, realizing I was happy I didn't' know about it.

"And you're sure there is nothing to worry about?" Amelia pressed, her face a bit whiter after the news.

"We're going to do our first ultrasound this morning. We were a bit early to hear the heartbeat last time, so I'm hoping the ultrasound will tell us more today," Syl finished up her breakfast and took her dishes to the sink.

"You'll call as soon as you find out anything? Or even nothing?" I asked Eden gently.

"Yes, I'll call," she confirmed from still inside Kiran's arms. "And then I'll pick you up to go shopping, yeah?" she turned her gaze to Amelia.

"Sounds great," Amelia replied. "Thanks again for the outfit Sylvia."

"Oh please," Eden answered for her. "I used to go shopping in there all the time. Aunt Syl doesn't keep very good inventory on the glorious stash she hoards."

"I don't hoard," Sylvia huffed.

"Oh really?" Eden laughed, snapping out of her crying funk. "Then what do you call a shopping addiction when you spend eighty percent of your time in scrubs?"

"Stockpiling with style?" Sylvia grinned smugly and we all burst out laughing.

"I'm calling an intervention," Eden announced light-heartedly.

"Speaking of scrubs, I better go get dressed so we can go," Sylvia moved to the doorway. "Avalon, I can take off for a couple hours this afternoon. Do you want to meet while the girls are off shopping this afternoon? We could check out some venues?" Sylvia's eyes twinkled when she said "venue" and I knew she was actually talking about ring shopping, but I was all on board with that agenda.

"Yes, that sounds like a great idea," I nodded and then sent her a look that told her to cool it with the enthusiasm. She didn't cool it, but winked at me before padding through the living room and up the stairs to her bedroom.

"Venues?" Kiran asked carefully as if he hadn't heard us right.

"Yeah, for Talbott's engagement party," I explained simply.

"You're not going to use the club?" he asked and I kind of wish I shared the stupid mind meld with him so I could tell him to *shut up.*

"I haven't decided yet," I replied cryptically. It was the truth; the Club was the obvious solution to our space problem. I mean with the number of Immortals we would have gathered in the same space our magic was bound to ripple through downtown Omaha and I wanted it contained and as underground as I could get it. But I also didn't want to give into something the Kendrick family set up and was still associated so strongly with their rule and monarchial ties.

Kiran didn't say anything after that but I could feel him assessing me from across the room. I shifted underneath the intensity of his stare. He might only be Amelia's cousin, but he was as fiercely protective as Sebastian and I really didn't want to get into it with my brother-in-law.

Especially before lunch.

But thinking about Kiran and his over-protectiveness, I realized there was more than one loose end I would have to tie up before I could ask Amelia to marry me. Besides convincing her that she was in love with me enough to marry me, I was also going to have to convince Kiran and Sebastian the same thing. And then I would need to make time to fly back to Paris to talk it over with Jean Cartier. Hopefully, he would be easier to convince. Having hated his brother-in-law, Lucan for almost his entire adult life, Jean was an easy supporter of mine once the Monarchy fell. Hopefully, it would be just as easy to convince him to let his only daughter marry me as it was to accept me as King.

But for some reason, defeating the Monarchy felt like cake compared to the campaign I was going to have to run for Amelia's hand in marriage.

Amelia and I cleaned up the kitchen while everyone else in the house got ready for Eden's doctor's appointment. She was unusually quiet next to me and I wondered how worried she was about Eden. I wanted to reassure her that Eden would be fine but I had my own concerns and so we worked silently next to each other.

We said goodbye to Eden, Kiran and Sylvia and then I took Amelia by the hand and led her into the living room. We sat down on one of Syl's overstuffed couches that swallowed you up as soon as your ass touched cushion. I maneuvered myself until I could face Amelia and took her hand in mine, moving my thumb slowly across the palm of her hand from the base of her thumb to the crook of her pinky and ring finger. Her skin was soft, perfect, pure cream against the rough pads of my own fingers.

"Are you alright?" I asked with as much softness I was capable of. In this moment it felt like she could shatter, like the wrong word or action would crumble her. I didn't want her to break.

"No," she answered in a sandpaper voice. "It's too much. I'm worried about so much and I feel like my insides are twisted so tight that.... I just.... I can't even breathe through this."

"Hey," I rushed to pull her close to me, cradling her in my arms and loving the way she fit against me, like we were created just for each other. "He's not going to win. You have to remember that. No matter what happens, you have to believe that justice... that goodness will triumph. You have to believe that what we do is right and because of that we will win."

"That sounds like a practiced speech," Amelia mused. Her fingers mimicked the movement my thumb had made on her palm and she trailed her thumb back and forth across my wrist. I cleared my throat as a deep haze of lust for this girl settled over me.

"It is. It's one I gave to myself about a thousand times during the whole Lucan thing," I admitted on a bitter laugh.

She lifted her head and cupped my jawline in her tiny hand. "You are an incredible man." Before I could respond she tilted her chin and kissed me so lightly on the lips I barely felt her touch. And in that moment something fierce and possessive swelled in my chest. With every passing moment I spent with Amelia my feelings for her grew. She proved over and over to me that she was the one for me.

Not able to respond to her compliment, I offered some advice, "Always remember the good things that we do. They have to outweigh the evil we fight against otherwise we lose. You have to visualize how this ends and how life goes on after we win; otherwise the present swallows you whole with despair."

"How will life go on after this is over, Avalon?" Amelia asked completely amused with my theory.

"Easy," I whispered. "It will go on easily. Talbott and Lilly will get married in the courtyard in the Citadel. They will beg for time off and I will be forced to give them an extended honeymoon although I will not be happy about it. In order to make them pay for their time off, I will force them to make public relations stops around the world, which will simultaneously enrich their honeymoon and serve my purpose of getting the word out about the importance of their marriage. Eden will gain seventy five pounds because her baby is obsessed with tater tots and she won't be able to stop eating them. She will give birth to a handsome baby boy which they will name Avalon the second as a thank you for everything I've done for them in the past. And since Angelica will no longer be forcing every eligible girl that comes to the castle into my path I will finally get some time off to go do some extended traveling, probably to an exotic beach where I can surf all day and drink a lot of rum."

Amelia was laughing at my explanation, her body shaking in mine and I fell in love with that feeling. Fell *in love* with it.

"Why will Angelica get off your case?" Amelia asked when she had subdued some of her laughter.

"Because I have you now," I murmured against her hair. "Because you'll be with me of course."

"On your island?" Amelia whispered.

But she sounded terrified.

"Yes, on my island," I replied confidently. This was the future after all.

"I cannot go with you to an island Avalon," Amelia sat up from me putting space between us.... space that I instantly hated.

"Why not? Don't you like rum?" I purposefully sounded obtuse.

Amelia burst into unexpected laughter and looked at me like she couldn't believe me. "Avalon, really? Who doesn't like rum?" she sighed and then snuggled back against me. I let out a breath I hadn't realized I was holding. And then so did she. "For a minute there I thought you were serious."

"About the island?" I clarified, my neck suddenly prickling with an unexpected crick. "I am serious, Amelia. After this is over, I want you all to myself. I want this to be.... I don't want this to end."

I didn't know how to say I wanted to be her future. I wanted her to picture me and only me when she visualized the end of this conflict without scaring her. Why was she so jumpy? I was ready to confess my undying love for her and claim her like a caveman and she wouldn't even consider rum and the beach with me.

She bristled in my arms. "Let's just get through this first, yeah?"

"Amelia, if you are not picturing me in your life when this is over, your view of the future is seriously messed up," I all but growled.

She jumped up from my chest and scooted back on the couch so that her cold feet were pressed up against the side of my thigh. She wrapped her arms around her knees and looked up at me from under thick eyelashes. I wanted to wrap my warm hands around her feet and run my finger down the perfect arch of her foot. I wanted to grab her ankles and yank her onto my lap so I could kiss her until she couldn't think straight. But I resisted, I forced myself to meet her where she was at and find out what craziness she was thinking.

"Avalon, daydreaming about a beach and rum is not taking this slow.... It's not really just seeing where this is headed either. That's a whole new kind of thing, that's setting up a destination and I'm not sure I'm ready for rum and an island," she admitted.

How did this go bad so quickly?

"I've known from the beginning where this was headed, Amelia," I admitted, hoping that if I shared my confidence with her it would somehow rub off. "I've always known we were headed for the beach and rum."

"You can't say that," Amelia shook her head as if what I was saying was completely ludicrous. And maybe it was. "Besides, even if there is a beach, which I'm not saying there is, but *if* there is then it's a long ways off. There is no way in hell my parents would let me run off to exotic locations with alcohol and my royal boyfriend. There would need to be a ring on this finger." She wiggled the finger in question at me.

I couldn't say for sure, but I was almost positive she was using marriage to scare me off. I almost laughed; she was in way over her head. I grabbed her ring finger and pulled it to my lips so I could kiss the place where my promise would be. Then I turned her hand over so I could kiss the inside of that same finger. She trembled against my lips and I took that as a good sign.

"Who said there wouldn't be a ring on your finger?" I asked casually. I took her whole hand back in mine and rubbed my finger and thumb over the same place, caressing it gently in my grip. I imagined what it would look like there, how it would feel to know that I could claim her as mine, that the ring would be a symbol of mutual ownership.... that the space on my same finger would bare her own representation of possession.

"Avalon," she gasped, snatching her finger away. "You cannot possibly feel that way. It's way too early."

"Amelia," I soothed meeting her terrified gaze and speaking with as much confidence as I felt. "I know three years ago I was a complete and utter jackass. I was oblivious to how amazing you were and I hurt you. Forever I will regret that. But since the day you came back into my life I have not once stopped thinking about you. You consume my thoughts. You consume everything about me. I was lost without you, floating.... drifting.... completely bored and without purpose. Which, by the way, it's really hard to get that way when *you're King.* And then there was you. You walked into my life and stole that part of me. You took whatever ugliness I had become and you reminded me of the man I could be, the man I was supposed to be. You are this beacon of light, this destination I will fight to get to. You are everything I need and want and want to become. I have fallen completely in love with you, Amelia. So yes, I do want a beach and rum, but most of all I want to give you a ring, because when I visualize my future, every scenario I come up with includes you. You are my life now and I will fight with everything I am to end this conflict and give you the life you deserve."

Amelia's eyes shimmered with unshed tears. A pit dropped in my hollow stomach and I suddenly worried that she didn't feel anything of what I felt. Maybe I was a complete idiot after all.

"How can you possibly feel those things for me?" she whispered, her throat thick with emotion.

"Because they make up who I am, Amelia," I smiled patiently at her.

"I don't think I can feel that way for you," she sighed sadly.

And the world stopped spinning. Officially, in that moment everything came to a screeching halt and I was sure I would explode. I *had to* explode, I *needed to* explode, because the possibility of living through this was a hell of a lot worse than internal combustion.

"What?" I coughed out, unblinking and dazed.

"I'm sorry, Avalon," Amelia whispered and then she got up from the couch and fled.

Well, Hell.

Chapter Thirty-Three

"They really don't make these things for comfort, do they?" I grumbled under my breath to Kiran. He snickered, trying to remain professional.

We sat on the two thrones that were set up in the downtown Omaha club. I shifted uncomfortably, knowing I would need a healthy dose of magic to get me through this meeting and not just because of the politicians sitting in front of me. Although to be fair, not all of the twelve regents were politicians, in fact, most of them were appointed by me and former Resistance team leaders or members of teams.

After Lucan's death and I was voted King, I spent a significant amount of time housekeeping the Kingdom's political system. Lucan had made some wise decisions when appointing certain regions and while they weren't all strictly loyal to them, many of them were career politicians that needed a healthy retirement and an exotic island exile.

Not a real exile of course, but it was my go-to incentive when trying to convince them they're community service was way up.

I adjusted the crooked crown on top of my head and gave my sister a smile. She wasn't seated with us in front of the Regents, opting for a quiet place to observe in the back. Even though, technically Kiran was only King by default of marriage, Eden was still uncomfortable sitting up here in front of everyone, so Kiran took over the public relations duties for her.

And recently for me too.

The club lights were on and bright, but because of the underground location and complete lack of natural light the large room felt gloomy. With only our small group gathered, the two-city-block size of the room felt incredibly cavernous, our voices echoing off the high walls and arched ceiling.

I eyed the polished bar in the back of the room with envy, wondering if I would be judged harshly for a midday scotch....

"Thank you for joining us," Kiran began in his most somber voice.

This was going to be an awful meeting. My stomach twisted with nerves. I didn't want to explain to these Immortals what we were up against, how I had failed them. They would want to know how to protect their regions, how to protect our people and I wasn't sure what to tell them. At this point not even humankind was safe and that was what terrified me the most: an enemy without standards or limitations.

Completely depraved.

Footsteps clicked down the tall, winding staircase in the center of the room caught my attention and I lifted my eyes to watch Amelia join our group. I had appointed Bianca Cartier as the Western European Regent, but her flight was delayed in Switzerland for bad weather. If she would have used her private jet like I suggested, she would have been able to make the meeting, but she was a little bit stubborn, which I was beginning to think was a family trait. She had insisted flying commercial was not only better for the environment, but the funds she saved could be used for some charity.

I don't know which one since I stopped paying attention at "better for the environment."

Amelia's golden brown hair floated off her shoulders as she hurried down the staircase, her tall high heels ticked against the staircase. She was dressed professional, since she was filling in for her parents and I couldn't take my eyes off her legs in her gray, knee length, tight skirt.

I swallowed against a building desire that was shaking me up inside, fragmenting my soul into broken pieces of confusion. Inside my head a voice was shouting to take my eyes off her, to look anywhere but her.... to stop torturing myself with something I couldn't have.

Or something that didn't want me in return.

But I couldn't.

I would rather punish my heart and torture my soul than look away from her gravitational pull.

My world had narrowed to her. To *only her*. And even if she didn't want me, I wouldn't be able to stop myself from wanting her.

From needing her.

We hadn't talked since I opened up to her two days ago. She had avoided me desperately. While I was still willing to play this game her way, with little expectations for our future, or at least letting her think there were little expectations for our future. She turned out to be smarter than me, explaining there was no way we could go back now. I had said it all, said too much and she was officially moved on.

Her words, not mine.

She broke up with me in one of those "it's not you, it's me" speeches.

She had wanted to move over to Amory's old house where Xander, Xavier, Titus and Gabriel were staying, but I convinced her to stay with Eden in Sylvia's house and I moved over. I hated it. I hated that she didn't think we could even stay in the same house together. It didn't make sense to me.

We hadn't been together for long, I knew that, but what we had was real and intense and undeniable.

Only she was denying everything. And it sucked.

She sat down in the back of the room with Eden and then pulled a tablet out of her purse to take notes on. She looked every bit the classy, studious citizen. She was incredible. And she was doing a fantastic job of looking everywhere but at me.

Because she was not mine anymore.

She didn't want to be mine.

I sucked in a breath against the black hole deepening the pit of my stomach. This sucked. This was awful.

And I hated that Jericho was a world away and not here for me to complain to. If anyone understood heartbreak, it was him. And damn it if I didn't need to capitalize on his experience and get over this hellish feeling.

I focused back on the other eleven Regents and forced myself to pay attention to the end of Kiran's welcome speech. We agreed he would take care of all the pleasantries and leave me with the meat of the meeting.

"You are all invited to stay in Omaha through the weekend and attend Lilly Mason and Talbott Angelo's engagement part Saturday evening. We can all agree that their union is quite significant and Avalon, Eden and I would appreciate your public support. Now I will hand over your attention to Avalon who will share with you the reason we are gathered today," Kiran finished and then gestured a hand towards me.

I stood up. Kiran was way better at conducting meetings from his sitting position on the throne, years of practice and what not. I had grown up standing in front of large groups of Immortals, planning strategically with group participation.

"There is a situation," I began not as confidently as I wanted to sound. I needed to be gentle, but not insecure. Damn it. I cleared my throat and began again. "A few weeks ago two Immortals arrived at the Citadel near death. We took them in immediately and gave them the best care that we could. Only hours after their arrival, they died." I paused, letting this sink in. I held their attention and now I would grab their curiosity. Reigning in their fear would be last on the agenda and what I handled with the most care. "It was not the King's Curse that killed them, nor was it old age since they were both young and could have been considered in good health once upon a time. They came to the Citadel, knowing they would die, but both of them wanted to die for a purpose. They were victims of some of the most grotesque and inhumane brutality I have ever seen, and with my experience.... that's saying a lot." I paused to mentally block out the months of imprisonment I had faced under Lucan's reign. I was mortal at the time and there were still nights I suffered from the haunting memories of my incarceration. I cleared my throat and continued in an utterly silent room, "Because of their bravery we learned that the evil we are now facing is a man named Dmitri Terletov."

"Impossible," Jack Smith, the Australian Regent scoffed. He was a big, burly man with an extremely awesome handlebar mustache that reached out to the middle of each of his cheeks and he was always wearing a straw cowboy hat lined with crocodile teeth. "Terletov is dead. This happened before Lucan fell."

"We were all under that impression," I agreed, bringing order back to the room. "The specifics of what happened or how he escaped are still uncertain. Eden herself drained him of his magic and we have been working with Titans that arrested him and personally put him in his cell. I want to give you every specific piece of information we have gathered so far, but I have to warn you that we are painfully, even dangerously under-informed. There is something at work that we do not fully understand yet. And as dangerous as ignorance can be, whatever Terletov is planning, scheming.... accomplishing, it is more dangerous than *anything* we have been up against yet."

I paused again to gather my thoughts while the Regents looked at each other nervously. They trusted me enough to know I would not exaggerate something like this. The mood in the room, even the current of electricity turned frightful and anxious. I was glad I wouldn't have to waste time convincing them of the danger we were in, but now I faced the task of catching them up to speed, which was a place I didn't want to be.

I swallowed against the bile that rose every time I had to think about Terletov and what he was doing to my people and then continued, "The Immortals that died were.... I don't know how to explain this to you properly, but they were changed. Their magic was not their own and whatever foreign force was injected into them was eventually what killed them. They gave us a lead to Siberia, where apparently Terletov had been conducting experiments in the old Titan training facility. By the time we got there, there was nobody left except a pile of dead bodies and left over equipment that still doesn't make sense to us. From there we followed him back to his old Latvian estate. We seemed to have interrupted his scheme there, where we intercepted a shipment of weapons and bullets. If you remember from when he kidnapped Eden, Terletov used guns with special ammunition to incapacitate his victims. These bullets are enough to completely shut down an Immortal. Although it doesn't kill you, it will put you into a very painful coma. But if you happen to be without magic, drained or otherwise incapacitated, they can absolutely kill. Eden and I seem to be somewhat immune to the bullet by way of her healing gifts, but everyone else needs to be aware of how dangerous just one hit, anywhere on your body can be. You will be unconscious within seconds. During this exchange we captured one of Terletov's men, only to have him assassinated by his own companion just moments later. From Latvia we followed Terletov to Peru, where we met more of his men in the mountains. We fought and won the battle, but without one living prisoner, we still do not have even a significant piece of information to explain Terletov's survival, his behavior or his motives. Other than the obvious, that being he is after the crown." I let the frustration seep into my tone, unable to stop the torrential downpour of helplessness that threatened to drown me. I forced my eyes up to meet my people, my people that trusted me and would follow me no matter what and I continued, "In Peru we found five more Immortals that had been held prisoner, badly beaten and abused. And more than that, we found five humans with them. They were as equally battered. They are all recovering in the Citadel as we speak."

"Humans?" Solomon Camera, the West African Regent gasped, standing to his feet. "What could he want with humans?"

"We think...." I paused to meet each of their eyes. "We think he was trying to infuse them with our magic. We think he was trying to make them Immortal."

The room erupted in nervous chatter, all of the Regents demanding more information than I could give them. I took a shaky step back, rubbing rough hands over my face. I ripped a rubber band off my wrist and pulled my unruly hair into a knot on the nape of my neck and let them talk out their fears with each other. This was a lot of information to take in and I couldn't blame them for needing to repeat my facts out loud so that they would sink in. When their fears started to take over the conversation completely, I stepped back in.

"Please," I called out respectfully and immediately the room was silent. "I am going to answer as many of your questions as I can, but I need you not to panic. This situation is frightening, I understand that, but unless we come up with a rational solution we will not get through this. Our first goal is to protect our people, I cannot.... we cannot lose any more Immortals to his sadistic experiments. That much is certain. We also need to start thinking of ways to protect humans, although it's not as though we can give them a public service announcement. In order to protect our Immortals and humans alike, we have to protect the crown first. I need unity, stability and I need you to project a united front for the world to see. I will now take questions, one at a time and if anyone has information or suggestions we will also take those. I have a team of Titans, led by Silas hunting Terletov now, but I am desperate for information. If any of you remember working with him, or speaking with him, even the most insignificant detail could help. What we do know is that he is highly secretive and incredibly meticulous. There are hardly any details we have been able to uncover and before we can interrogate his men, they either commit suicide or are taken out by a sniper. Alright, questions," I nodded my head toward Seiko Lee, the Asian Regent who had been in her position for three hundred years. She was surprisingly very disloyal to Lucan and even though her long, black hair was now peppered with gray I had come to enjoy her crass sense of humor.

The questions started then and went on for hours. I answered as best as I could but most were met with my own lack of information. The Regents were all tasked with taking the information back to their people and spreading the word. We worked out safety precautions and traveling restrictions, even a curfew, but I wouldn't enforce any of those. These were precautionary and suggestive. I wouldn't make my people do anything.

In the end I realized the most I could do was pray for their safety.

Terletov was beating us at this game and unless I figured out a way to stop him, my people would never be safe again.

Chapter Thirty-Four

"Are you glad you decided to have the engagement party at the club?" Sylvia asked me over lunch.

I met her on her break because she asked me to. There were some people in life just worth dropping everything for. She was one of them.

"Yeah, it makes it easy for Eden," I agreed.

"I thought you were the one planning this shindig?" Syl laughed at me.

"I am planning it. I plan, and then I delegate. I can't be expected to do everything," I winked at Sylvia. Although it was true, my decorating skills were not exactly what people jumped to when they thought of my strongest qualities. But I had a twin sister, that's what she was for. "Besides, ever since Eden got knocked up, she's been super lazy."

Sylvia gasped and then narrowed her meanest glare at me. I cracked my charming smile to let her know I was joking, but the daggers she was shooting at me did not disappear.

"Don't let me ever hear you say something like that again," she threatened and I held my hands up defensively.

"No promises," I smiled wider.

The waiter stopped by our table and we both ordered outrageous sized burgers, topped with jalapenos, grilled onions and fried eggs, and then I added sweet potato waffle fries and onion rings. There was no way Sylvia was going to be able to get through her pastrami burger, but she was definitely going to try. Stella's had the best burgers in Omaha, after all.

"You're coming tomorrow night, right?" I asked after the waiter refilled our sodas and walked away.

"Of course," Sylvia nodded. I nodded, I did know that. Lilly had one of those personalities that people rarely did anything with but love. "I adore Lilly, you know that. I'm also on airport duty with Eden tonight. Did you know Sebastian is escorting them over and not Jericho?"

"Yes, Jericho says they are having some issues with the humans that we rescued. One of the girls is not recovering well and he wants to oversee her treatment," I explained. "Besides the Cartiers are staying for the party so Sebastian should probably be here with his family anyway."

I swallowed against the lump in my throat at the mention of Amelia's family. She hadn't talked to me since she dumped me. Dumped me. I had been dumped.

I averted my eyes from Sylvia before she saw anything there. I didn't want to think about Amelia's rejection. I wanted to just move on, bury myself in work and finding Terletov. I had never wanted to fall in love to begin with. I knew this would be a risk and I was stupid enough to believe that after I found Amelia I would be untouched by heartbreak.

Ugh.... heartbreak.

It was more than a break. It was like my heart had shattered into miniscule pieces of pain and then splintered into every single working organ inside of me, slowly hemorrhaging me to death.

And the acute pain was so much more than being jilted.... It was imagining my life, my future, my very existence without her.

"I want you to come back to Romania with us," I blurted before she could see the dark path of my thoughts.

"What?" Sylvia nearly spit out her drink.

"At least during Eden's pregnancy. She wants to stay here for the full term, I know that. But it's not like she can give birth in your hospital. And with Terletov running around.... I want her safe. After the party, she needs to go back to the Citadel. She needs you, and I need to know she's well taken care of," I explained professionally.

"Avalon," Sylvia sighed and then met my gaze. "I understand your concerns for Eden and I agree. She does need to go back to your part of the world. But I can't just pack up my life and move to Romania for a few months. I have a job, a life, obligations.... everything is here for me."

"I would pay you, obviously," I explained, meeting the first of physical needs I knew she would complain about. And then I appealed to her emotional ones. "Sylvia, I need you. I don't think I can track Terletov efficiently if I am desperately concerned for my sister. I know you're worried about her too. Why not just take a short sabbatical from the hospital and put both of our fears to rest?"

"The money is not necessary," she rolled her eyes. "Avalon.... I.... let me think about it, alright?"

"The humans that are there," I pushed one last point her direction and hoped she would think seriously about my offer. "They need someone to talk to. Someone who knows what they are going through, someone who can help give them peace. And after the reports I've heard, your medical expertise wouldn't hurt either. The Witch involved with their care is the best we have besides Eden, but I'm not sure he understands completely what a human body needs in order to heal. You could help with their recovery."

"Now you're just playing dirty," she laughed at me, but I saw the wheels turning in her head.

Good.

The waiter returned with our food and for minute we were too completely involved with our own burgers to continue conversation. My southwest burger was heaping with toppings, and took two hands to hold. BBQ sauce, pepper jack cheese and egg dripped down my fingers onto the napkin used instead of a plate and I resisted the very real urge to lick my fingers before even one drop was wasted.

When our burgers were official devoured and the onion rings and fries had disappeared, Sylvia leaned back on her stool like she was in physical pain. I rubbed my stomach and contemplated a second burger.

"I brought something for you," Sylvia said quietly, pulling herself out of her self-induced food coma. She took a deep breath and let it out slowly before she continued. "Do you ever think that Amory knew he was going to die that night?"

The gravity of where the conversation was headed landed on the table like lead and I sucked in a sharp breath unprepared to answer her question. I sat silent for a minute, letting my thoughts collect, putting them in some kind of organized order and then I answered, "Yes, I do."

She returned my words with silence on her end as she seemed to think over my simple words. The bar/restaurant was noisy and uncomfortably crowded around us, the line of people waiting for burgers extended out the door, but with the conversation sitting idly between Syl and I, the room had narrowed to just our table, to just us as we contemplated the workings of my dead grandfather.

"Me too," she finally agreed. Emotion flooded her eyes, glossing them over with slick tears that threatened to spill over any second. I reached across the table and took her hand in mine, comforting her by running my thumb cross the back of her hand. She snatched her hand from my grasp and waved it at me as if I were making things worse for her. She shook her blonde hair out and pierced me with those same, tear-filled blue eyes. "I'm sorry; I didn't mean to get upset."

"It's alright," I told her in a gruff voice that betrayed my own emotion.

"Anyway," she shook her head again and started digging through her ginormous purse. "Before.... before everything happened, he and I had a talk. Your grandfather was an amazing man. I know you know that, but it just needs to be said. He was so worried about you and your sister, but at the same time he was *so* proud of you. I know that some of you can see things, like future things. And I really, truly believe Amory could. See things, that is. Anyway, he gave me this." She pulled a small, square black box from her purse and set it on the table between us.

I stared down at the ring box, afraid to even move. The velvet square sat in between our saturated napkins and empty baskets with fried crumbs left in them. It sat on the only piece of dry table between our condensation-dripping glasses of soda and the salt and pepper shakers. Questions, emotions, fears and hopes filled my head, but all I could do was stare at it. I didn't even really know what it was, let alone what I was supposed to do with it.

"I loved Amory," Sylvia admitted what all of us had suspected since the first time we saw her and Amory together. "He came into my life when I needed someone to take care of me, when I needed someone to love me. And he did both. He helped me get through med school and gave me pieces of this world that I wouldn't have known existed if it weren't for him. For a long time, he was my world. And I hoped that he would always be that way. Then you and your sister showed up." She gave me a sad smile and I suddenly realized when things had ended for her and Amory. He had given up everything for us, even things he should have been able to keep. Sylvia continued, "It was like he suddenly remembered what his purpose in life was, like he had forgotten or chose not to remember. But then there you were and I watched him come back to life. He had seemed happy and functioning before you two, but after I saw the change in him, I remember wondering to myself how I had never noticed how asleep he seemed before. Before you he was just surviving, even though he had good things in his life. After, there was purpose and hope and something so much deeper I don't think I'll ever fully understand what you two did for him. But I do know that he became fully himself again. We were over. And he ended things with such grace and love that I don't even think I complained. I didn't have time to complain because he somehow broke up with me at the same time he handed me a newborn baby and gave my life an entirely different purpose." Sylvia paused to laugh at the memories. "It was through that experience I realized he had never loved me. Well, not like I loved him. I can't say that he was using me, because he was a gentleman and considerate and everything a girl dreams about in a man. I know he cared about me, but he never loved me. Not like he loved her."

She paused and I took the opportunity to clarify, "Diana? My grandmother?"

She nodded meeting my eyes so I could see she didn't feel jilted. "Yes, Diana. Whatever they had must have been incredible, I mean the kind of stuff legends are written about because it wasn't too long after Eden came to live with me I realized everything he did, he was doing for her. Lucan, no not Lucan.... who was King before Lucan?"

"Cedric," I clarified knowing this part of history but I needed to let her finish.

"Yes, Cedric is the one that took her from him. And I really believe he spent every day after that just trying to get back to her. I can't even imagine what life was like for him after your mother disappeared. But by the time he found me, he was…. functioning. And then there were you two. And I swear it was like he had found Diana again. Everything in his life became about that, about vindicating his wife." She nudged the ring box toward me and I reluctantly picked it up and opened it. "Right before he died, he gave this to me. He asked me to hold on to it for you, Avalon. I think he knew Eden and Kiran would always end up together. Eden wouldn't need this, but one day he knew that you would. It's Diana's. It's the ring he gave to Diana."

I swallowed back a torrent of emotions and cleared my throat to keep it from closing completely. The ring, my grandmother's ring, was blinking back at me, but I could barely make it out through blurry, unseeing eyes.

This would not do.

I closed the ring box and set it down on the table. Then I stood up and circled around the high bar top table in one step, tugging Sylvia against me in one breath. I held her there while she sniffled against my chest and I clung to her, just needing someone close that felt the intense heartbreak of my grandfather's thoughtfulness.

We stood like that for a long time. The busy bar burst at the seams with people, hectic from a rushed lunch hour or trying to squeeze in anywhere to sit. And we stood in the middle of it all, lost in the tangled path of our own memories.

Finally I pulled myself together and came back to the present. I loosened my grip on Sylvia and took a step back so that I could look down into her eyes. She smiled up at me, confident and at peace. And it was then, when I saw the encouragement on Syl's face that I was able to sit back down and open the box again.

The ring was breathtaking; simple but elegant. The single pearl was raised up from the simple gold band. There was nothing spectacular about the ring, except that it was my grandmother's and that my grandfather had given it to her as a symbol of his love. I plucked the ring out of the box and turned it over in my hands. The setting was tiny and I had a feeling it would fit perfectly on Amelia's slender finger. On the back was an engraving that I had to extend my senses with magic in order to see clearly.

Eternity is only forever with your love.

I swallowed back a fresh wave of feeling and tore my eyes away from the engraving, away from one of the only men that would understand my future. She was looking at me with a mixture of hope and love and I was so thankful that she was the one I shared this moment with.

"I hope you didn't buy a ring for Amelia," Sylvia broke our silence from across the table, more like startled me back to the painful present. "I wanted to give this to you right away when you mentioned buying one, but I had to get it from my safety deposit box. It is absolutely perfect for her; she's going to love it."

Damn it. I knew Sylvia heard we broke up. I felt Eden telling her yesterday and had keenly shut off every single emotion and connection to Eden so I wouldn't have to suffer through it. I decided to take back my gratitude that it was Sylvia I shared this moment with.

"We're over, Sylvia," I choked out on a harsh voice just barely above a whisper.

"Avalon St. Andrew, since when do you just give up?" she scolded from across the table.

"Syl, she doesn't feel the same for me. She wouldn't look twice at this ring," I explained. The thought of Amelia rejecting not just me, but this invaluable ring made me regret eating so much for lunch. I was going to throw it all up. I wouldn't be able to handle her saying no to this ring.... this ring that single-handedly seemed to hold all of my real feelings and hopes and dreams.

"Trust me when I tell you that Amelia is a girl, and no girl walks away from a ring without at the very least looking at it twice." She smiled at me and I found myself smiling back. She would know more about girls than me. "Amelia was in love with you once, remember that."

"Not real love," I countered. "She had a crush on me, that's all. And I was a jackass."

"Avalon, don't minimalize a girl's feelings. We know our hearts better than you do and if she says she was in love with you once, then she was. Besides that, I was there. I was at the wedding, so I can confirm that she had it bad for you. You might have messed things up with her back then, but you don't have to do that now. Besides, since when have you ever given up a fight before?"

I thought carefully about Sylvia's words and wondered if there really was room to hope. "I guess, never." I answered her question, knowing without a doubt that I never had walked away from a fight in my life. And what better thing to fight for than Amelia?

"So why on earth would you walk away from someone you love?" Sylvia leveled her gaze with mine and I gulped. She was right.

In fact, in this moment I couldn't remember why I ever let Amelia walk away from me to begin with.

"Thanks, Syl," I met her gaze, confidently this time. She blushed and then waved me away, signaling the waiter for our check.

Amelia fell in love with me once for fighting for our people. My only hope was that she would have the same reaction while I fought for her heart.

Chapter Thirty-Five

A gasp, aggressive hands and a hard yank greeted me when I got back to Sylvia's house. Eden dragged me into the kitchen and shoved me against the kitchen counter. What the hell?

"Let me see it!" she squeaked in a not so hushed tone.

"You little eaves-dropper!" I accused but I couldn't hold back my smile.

"Shut up and let me see it!" she danced around in front of me, hopping back and forth on her feet and wiggling her greedy little fingers.

I sighed a long-suffering sigh but pulled the velvet box from my pocket. I held it out to her as if it was the most boring possession ever, but had to chuckle at the way her black eyes lit up like sparkling jewels at the sight of it.

She took it carefully out of my hands and opened it excruciatingly slow. I suffered through her theatrics and when she gasped another sharp inhale of breath it was worth it. Immediately she turned into a hysterical mess, tears streaming down her face, her nose running uncontrollably.

"Oh good grief, E, it's not like I'm proposing to *you*," I whispered, pulling her against my chest.

"But it's so beautiful," she whispered in a reverent tone. "And it's perfect for her." A sob hitched in her chest and she sniffled against me.

I sighed again, but this one was infinitely more patient. "We don't even know if she's going to say yes," I mumbled.

"She'll say yes," Kiran answered from the doorway. I turned around to face my brother in law who was looking at his wife with amused affection.

"Everybody is really confident of her saying yes, but she has pretty much already told me no," I reminded them. I let Eden go and she walked the ring over to show Kiran.

"She didn't say no to you, Avalon," Kiran explained. "She said no to her fears, to her own insecurity."

I thought about that for a moment. I thought about how I barely remembered her before she showed up at the castle for Eden and Kiran's return, how I had ignored her and mistreated her all those years before, how I had convinced her to see where our relationship would go without making her feel like there was a strong attachment and how I told her I loved her right after her very first near death experience in Peru. She was overwhelmed and overly emotional and I had dropped a bomb on her.

Maybe Kiran was right.

We had only been together for a very little time; of course she would be insecure about our feelings.

"I suppose you would know all about what to do when a woman says no," I laughed at the sight of Eden in Kiran's arms, her back to his chest while he looked at the ring over her shoulder.

"I would," he agreed seriously. Eden stiffened in his arms and shot me a nasty look. But then she went right back to admiring the ring. "I would also know a little something about fighting for the woman I love."

He had me there.

"Advice?" I asked, determining in that moment that I would fight just as hard, if not harder than Kiran ever did to convince Amelia she belonged with me.

"Get her to listen and when she's listening, tell her everything. Get it all out there. And then, after you've said everything you have to say, make sure she believes you," Kiran instructed.

Eden looked up at him and placed a kiss on his jawline. I averted my eyes before I was subjected to anymore of their grotesque public displays of affection. And when I looked back, Kiran had moved his hands to her stomach, holding it possessively.

My chest groaned in jealousy. No, not jealousy.... something stronger. Something like longing.

Make her believe you.

"Sounds like you know what you're talking about," I admitted.

"He does," Eden answered simply.

I walked back over to the happy couple and collected the ring from Eden. "Thank you," I said sincerely to both of them.

"I'm just happy you found her," Eden whispered.

"Me too," Kiran agreed and this time when he smiled at me it was like we shared something now.... like we were a part of the same fraternity or something. The "Why are our women so difficult?" fraternity.

I shoved the ring into my pocket, left the kitchen and bounded up the stairs to my old room. Amelia was sitting on the bed, talking on the phone to her mom. I stood in the doorway and made a show of knocking on the door gently.

She did a double take when she saw me and I watched her breathing accelerate with nerves. My magic immediately left me for hers and when ours tangled together in the confines of my old room I bit back a smug grin.

She started to tell her mom goodbye, while she avoided looking at me at all costs. That was fine with me. I stood in the door watching her. She was so beautiful. Her golden brown hair fell brushing her shoulders, making the urge to run my fingers through it impossible to ignore. Her smooth, exposed skin tempted me from across the room in her thin-strapped dress, revealing her shoulders, and delicate lines of her neck. Her fingers played idly with the hem of her patterned dress and without her knowing it she pulled it up her thigh driving me crazy.

There was something about having her in my space, about her sitting on my old bed that ignited feelings of possessiveness and pride deep in my stomach. I pressed against the ring box in my pocket, desperately needing her to wear it, to let me claim her as mine.

"Alright, have a safe flight," Amelia told her mom. "I'll see you in a few hours. Love you too mum, buh-bye."

She pushed end on her cellphone and then took a stabilizing breath before looking over to me. I waited patiently. Her magic was already deeply embedded in mine; I prayed this would be an easy battle.

But more than Lucan.... more than Terletov, this was the most important fight of my life.

"Avalon," she acknowledged in a surprised whisper.

Her gaze penetrated the very depths of my being; her eyes deep pools of emotion. And they were afraid.

I changed my approach. "I uh, I need to go pick up some things from Kingsley before the party tomorrow night. I need some help and everyone else is... uh.... busy." I didn't give her the choice to say no.

"Oh, um, sure, I can help you," she relaxed a little, a tiny bit of confidence returning to her expression.

"Alright, good. Are you ready now? I'd like to leave as soon as possible." I didn't even have to pretend I was impatient; I was absolutely in a hurry to get this girl alone and make her mine.

"Sure, let me just grab my sweater. I can meet you downstairs," she gave me a pleading look so I left her alone so she could get ready to leave.

Ten minutes later we piled into Eden's Land Rover and on our way to Kingsley. It was a Saturday so the school grounds were supposed to be empty. I had borrowed the key from Victoria Woodsen, the drama teacher, in order to pick up some things from her classroom.

"What do you need at Kingsley?" Amelia asked in a small voice.

"Eden suggested the party be Moroccan themed. One of the teachers at Kingsley spent some time there and has a generous collection of throws and oversized pillows. Eden says they will be perfect...." I trailed off. I didn't really have an opinion on the decorating, so at this point I was just following orders and trying to get Amelia alone.

"I've never been to Kingsley," Amelia commented in a voice just above a whisper.

"Really?" That was hard to believe. I thought everybody had been to Kingsley at one time or another. We had other schools around the world so that students could study close to wherever home was for them. But Kingsley was the coveted academy. Not to mention it had become somewhat of a tourist destination after Amory died and Eden and Kiran got married.

"Nope, never. Bastian and Kiran promised me they would let me join them once I was old enough, but by then everyone was confined to the castle and well... you know how that story ends. I ended up finishing school at Briar Rose because it was close to home," her tone was almost sad. I glanced over at her, silently asking for more of the story and she blushed a deep red. "Before he died, I always had to stay with Uncle Lucan," she finally whispered. "It was like he didn't even trust my own parents to keep me safe. He was never cruel to me.... never.... inappropriate or anything. But it was like he needed to.... possess me or control me. I was just another thing in his bag of tricks."

I was silent for a minute, thinking that over. In all honesty, I didn't know what to think. Maybe she cared about her uncle? Blamed me for his death? "I'm sorry Lucan had to die," I finally offered. And it was the truth. I hated the whole scenario and I would never rejoice in the necessity of an Immortal's death, not even Lucan's.

Well.... maybe I would rejoice a tiny bit if I could ever get my hands on Terletov.

"You don't have to do that," Amelia's head popped up and her eyes grew large with sincerity. "I didn't mean to make it sound like.... I'm glad he's dead; I mean I'm glad you're King. You are what our people need. You are the best thing for us. I mean... for them."

She looked away quickly, her eyes trained on Omaha flashing by as we drove toward Kingsley. I tried to keep the smile from tipping up my lips, but I was not successful. At least she was looking out the window.

"Thank you," I somehow managed to reply seriously without too much pride lacing my tone. I also had to force myself from fishing for compliments. Not that I didn't already know I was great, but there was something about hearing Amelia tell me how incredible I was that sent me buzzing with exaggerated confidence.

We were silent a few more beats and I eventually turned the Land Rover into the circular drive of Kingsley. I smiled as Amelia took in the red brick buildings with an expression of awe. The bell tower stood in the center of the cluster of buildings chiming the hour and the trees that lined and landscaped the property had turned to deep fall tones that blended nicely with the color of brick. Kingsley looked prestigious and well-kept. I was weirdly proud to get to be the one to show Amelia around.

"Well this is it," I gestured toward the Administration Building. My voice sounded loud in the quiet, confined space of the car.

"It's beautiful," Amelia whispered in admiration.

I pressed my hand against the ring box in my pocket and smiled to myself. This was as good of a place as any. I had to have courage. I had to lay it all out for her.

I looked back up and started when I realized Amelia was staring at me now instead of the school. I convinced myself not to gulp but I was pretty sure she caught on to my mental pep talk. Luckily, the ring was in the farthest pocket from her and I was very confident she couldn't see it with my palm pressed against it.

"Ready? The English and Arts Building is that one right over there," I pointed it out and hoped she followed my finger.

"Avalon, maybe we should talk first," she interrupted me, but her tone sounded regretful and careful. This was not the girl that was going to say yes to me, this was the girl that was going to try to explain away her feelings and convince me I did not want to be with her.

"Sure," I gave her a casual smile. "But later, I want to get in and out before anyone sees me."

"It doesn't look like anyone's here," she objected. "And what would you care if you're seen?'

"I uh, don't want to deal with fans," I bullshitted my way right through that one. Better to sound like an arrogant ass than have the "it's not you, it's me talk" again.

She snorted and I relaxed a little. That was the Amelia I loved, the one that didn't let me get away with any of that stuff. "You're worried about fans?"

"Always," I fed her some more half-truths. "I don't know if you've paid attention lately, but I'm a pretty good catch. The ladies are always trying to corner me.... you know, get me alone...." I trailed off and left her to her imagination.

Her eyes narrowed, flaring with heat. I didn't know if she was jealous or irritated with me, but either way I could safely say I got out of her talk. I opened the door and jumped down from the SUV before hurrying to her door so I could open it for her. She sat in the passenger's seat kind of stunned by my behavior and I couldn't help but take her hand and help her down from the cab.

"How about I give you a tour?" I suggested when she pulled her hand from mine.

"I thought we were worried about rabid, horny females?" she asked sarcastically.

"We'll just keep moving," I explained as gravely as I could manage. "They shouldn't be able to keep up with us if we don't stay in the same spot for too long."

"Right," she mumbled.

"Come on, Amelia," I dropped my voice an octave to appeal to her own rabid, horny, female pieces. "I promise this will be the best tour you've ever taken."

Chapter Thirty-six

We wandered through the empty Kingsley hallways. Our footsteps and voices echoed off the high ceilings and against ornate staircases. I pointed out the theater to Amelia and then made her laugh by telling her the story of Eden and the blown out windows in front of Sebastian. She hadn't known that Eden and Sebastian didn't get along at first. I explained how he was always bothering her and she was always overreacting. I also explained Eden's temper, something she hadn't been fortunate enough to witness yet.

Mrs. Woodsen, I couldn't think of her any other way. Even though I was now King and she was technically my subordinate, she would always be a frazzled teacher to me. I remembered her especially as Mrs. Woodsen when I stood in her chaotic classroom.

She had boxed up what Eden needed from her collection and placed it all by the door. We carried the boxes down to the Land Rover and loaded them in the trunk. Then I led Amelia over to the Administration Building for the official "tour" portion of our afternoon.

We walked through the lobby and Amelia stopped to look at the pictures of Immortal dignitaries and old Kings that still lined the walls just inside the door. Even though she wasn't here I avoided Mrs. Truance's desk. She scared me, plain and simple. I would always respect her attachment and loyalty to Amory, but the woman scared me.

We went upstairs and peeked in office doors, the teachers' lounge and then paused outside of Amory's old office. The office was completely different than I remembered it. I appointed Charles Lambert as principal as soon as I was King and he made the place his own. Lucan had made Seraphina's father head of the school after Amory's death. Even though Seraphina's alliance had shifted, her father's hadn't and he was on a watch list for Lucan supporters I thought could cause problems.

I was glad the office was different, glad that it no longer resembled Amory and his old world ways. Still, I stood outside the door, not even able to make myself go inside. I was reminded of chats and impromptu planning meetings while I attended school here, or even just stopping by to say hi. I could easily picture him behind his desk, reading old documents in extinct languages or doling out orders to me or Charles Lambert. For the first time in a really long time, I was hit by the injustice of his death and the loneliness of leadership without him.

I sucked in a breath and struggled to get my emotions in check. I wasn't in danger of breaking down and weeping or anything, but I was very close to forgetting my purpose for bringing Amelia here.

"Are you Ok, Avalon?" Amelia asked and I hated that my face betrayed any emotion.

Her soft, sweet voice pulled me out of my self-indulgent funk though and my head cleared. I looked down at her and let go of Amory. The ring weighed heavily in my pocket, the same ring he left for my inheritance.... for my future wife.

He hadn't left me alone, not really.

"I'm fine," I sighed. "This was Amory's old office." I cleared my throat and continued. "There are just a lot of memories here."

"I barely knew Amory," Amelia admitted solemnly. She peered in the office as if she would find him there and when she turned back to me she was thoughtful. "When he was around my family he spent most of his time with Kiran and Sebastian. Any my uncle obviously hated him."

"You would have liked him," I smiled pushing beyond the hurt of the past and into the promise of the present. "He was a bleeding heart too. You two could have saved the world together." I took her hand, slipping it into mine when she wasn't paying attention. Or maybe she was paying attention and was going to let me get away with it.

"I'm hardly a bleeding heart," she rolled her eyes at me.

"Oh so you attend conferences on AIDS research and summits about Human Trafficking out of the cruelness of your heart?" I teased.

"Showing up at meetings is hardly saving the world. It's more like a bunch of rich people throwing money at other people so they can save the world. I'm not doing anything personally to help those causes," she explained humbly. She shot me a look that told me I better agree with her.

"No, I completely agree with you," I announced. "Funding the cure for AIDS is probably the worst thing a person can do." She made a sound that was somewhere in between a long sigh and a grunt of frustration. I moved toward the back stairwell, deciding we could continue with our tour. "Why don't you wear diamonds Amelia?"

"Because they're ugly," she mumbled and I knew she was lying. She kept her hand in mine but I felt the way she became keenly aware of the connection. I wondered if she would pull away, but she didn't.

At least not yet.

"Amelia....?" I goaded.

We exited the Administration Building through the back exit and walked slowly along the octagonal path that connected the separate buildings. I guided her toward the bell tower, hoping we would be able to pause and enjoy the nice autumn afternoon.

And also hoping this would be an ideal spot to lay it out for her.

AKA propose.

"Fine, if you must know, I don't support blood diamonds," she sighed.

"But you can buy non-conflict diamonds," I argued even though I knew where this was going.

"That's not the point," she started to get fired up, her eyes flashing with passion and conviction. She was stunning. "It's the need, the consumerism that drives the market. If we stopped buying diamonds altogether, there wouldn't be diamond fields and slaves and children ripped from their homes to work for criminals. Diamonds wouldn't be in demand and blood-diamonds would cease to exist. Buying diamonds is essentially supporting a cause that murders innocent people for black-market riches."

I let that argument process with me and shushed the cynical part of my personality that argued if it wasn't diamonds it would be something else. There would always be crime, injustice, tyranny. Fighting for my own people had taught me that. Hell, Terletov had reinforced the point. She also had a point of course; maybe a naïve utopian point... but still she had a point. And mostly I just loved that sensitive, caring part of her too much to squash it.

"That's a good reason not to wear diamonds," I finally agreed after much thought. And it *was* a good reason. She was a good person. "See? You're a defender of the innocent, warrior for justice. You're a good person Amelia." My thoughts echoed out loud and I smiled down at her.

"Avalon you make me sound like something I'm not," she argued. "What you did.... what you do for our people.... that's.... you're incredible. I'm just trying to do my small part. It's nothing compared to what you do."

I opened my mouth to say something, but words failed me. We were standing under the bell tower in the middle of the Kingsley courtyard. All around us trees had turned brilliant yellow, deep orange or rustic red, and the colorful leaves floated and skittered across the ground around us. The sun was set just low enough in the sky that the unfiltered light lit up the space behind Amelia in a luminous glow that made her hair shine bright and gave her a halo. Her eyes filled with sincerity, her lips pursed in honesty. She was perfection.

This moment was perfection.

It was time to fight for her. But even if I lost her, I would always have this moment. I knew that to my very core. And I would remember her like this for the rest of eternity. I would remember how she made me feel, how she swallowed up my resolve and fears and hopes all at the same time and gave me something more to work for, something more to become. She moved my soul, the very depth of my being and I was helpless against her.

After all I was only a man.

And she was a force of nature.

"What?" she laughed after I stood staring at her for several moments.

"Amelia, I love you," I blurted out so much less eloquently than I had hoped.

There was a heavy silence that settled between us for several moments while I tried to collect my thoughts and she tried to politely get out of this situation. She glanced around frantically, at every single thing but me.

A lesser man would have panicked.

But I had been in a lot of fights. I knew how to read an opponent and I knew when an opponent was nervous.

I took her lack of eye contact as a good sign.

"And I know you love me," I declared. Slowly, painstakingly slowly, her wide eyes moved back to mine. Her cheeks blushed the deepest shade of red and her bottom lip trembled. "I was a jackass all those years ago, a complete tool. But my eyes are open now. I know what you are…. who you are…. and I know I'm never going to find this in any other person for the rest of my life. And Amelia, we both know how long that will be." She opened her mouth to respond, but I kept going. "I don't know what is stopping you from trusting me and trusting what's between us, but I do know this. I know that you were created for me. I know without a shadow of a doubt that you were brought to life to exist for me. And I for you. You make me the best version of myself. You make me want to be King and I didn't even think that was possible!" I laughed a little to try and bring a smile to her face. It only kind of worked. "You open my eyes and make me see pain and suffering and then you make me want to do something about it. You make me want the most out of life. Because of you I've stopped sitting on the sidelines watching it all pass me by. I can't stand the monotony that my life was, but with you it will never be boring again. I have never seen so much life, so much excitement in one person. You are more to me than all of that though, you're more to me than love. You are *everything* to me. Amelia, from the moment you walked back into my life I have wanted nothing more than to call you mine and to give you myself in return. Please let me love you," I finished on a whisper and then paused. When she said nothing I finished, "Please let yourself love me."

She sniffled and then a lone tear slipped from the corner of her eye and trailed down her cheek. "Avalon, I don't know what to say."

"Because you're so moved by my honesty?" I ventured, catching her tear with my thumb. I let my thumb move along her cheek, caressing her soft skin as it went. "Amelia, I love you."

"Call me, Mimi," she demanded, taking a step back.

I assessed her carefully. She was so afraid, so unsure of herself that my chest felt like it was split in two.

"Why?" I demanded as gently as I could manage.

"Because that's what all my friends call me, it's what I go by," she explained hastily.

I took a deep breath, wondering where her mind was. "I don't want to be your friend, Amelia. I don't think I ever wanted to be your friend."

"Avalon, that's just it. You don't want to be my friend now.... today.... But anything that happens with you is permanent. It's forever."

A sigh of relief whooshed out of my chest and I felt the constraints of panic release. "Is that what you're afraid of? The forever part?"

But then everything seemed to clamp down tighter when she sobbed, "No, it's not that."

"Amelia, explain it to me. I feel your magic wrapped up in mine, I feel how you want to be with me. What is keeping you from me, what is making you question what's between us?" I pleaded with her, so close to dropping to my knees and begging it was a physical ache in my legs.

She hiccupped another sob and inhaled a shaky breath. "Do you know that I didn't even know there was a problem with Lucan until after Eden took Sebastian's magic? He was my uncle and he spoiled me.... and I loved him and Aunt Analisa. My parents certainly never had political discussions with me and Sebastian was.... he is a good older brother. He tries to protect me from everything." She paused to collect her thoughts and I stayed quiet, refusing to interrupt the explanation I desperately needed. "After Sebastian became so sick, Lucan did nothing for him. He kept me close, always, but it was like he wished my brother would just.... die. And then Eden took him. I was terrified and I felt betrayed. I *loved* Eden immediately. The very first time I met her I think I worshipped her a little bit. But then, nobody had caught my cousin's eye like she had so I knew there was something special about her. Until she took my brother. And at the same time my cousin was *dying*. And I did nothing. Except maybe cry. Even then I didn't understand the extent of my Uncle's wickedness. It wasn't until Sebastian returned to London that I fully understood everything that was going on. But even then I didn't actively participate in your rebellion. I couldn't. Part me of me was frozen with fear of my Uncle's wrath and the other part desperately naïve. When you finally sieged the Citadel I did my part, but it was nothing compared to the bravery Eden showed, or.... you showed. I have been spoiled my entire life, raised completely above poverty and suffering. I have not wanted for anything."

"What are you saying Amelia?" I pressed gently.

"I'm not worthy to be your wife," she whispered, her accent thick through her emotion. "I'm not qualified to be Queen. I have lived a cushy, over-protected, indulgent life. The kind of existence you risked your life to save our Kingdom from. You say you love me, but you don't really know me," she shook her head frantically and sniffled against the sleeve of her sweater. "I like my toenails painted at all times. If one of them even chips I repaint the entire lot of them. And most of the time I pay someone else to do them for me. I, I own one hundred handbags. Nobody needs that many handbags. But.... I have an addiction. I can't stop myself, I *love* handbags. I get cranky when a taxi tries to overcharge me and sometimes, on very isolated occasions.... sometimes I have a cheeseburger."

"A cheeseburger?" I clarified trying my hardest not to laugh.

"Only when I'm in America," she whispered, her eyes filling with more tears as if she were truly ashamed.

"Have you had one since you've been here?" I asked in a solemn voice.

She shook her head negatively, her chin trembling with the effort not to spill her tears. "No, I've been trying to be good."

"So that's it? That's your entire list of faults?" I asked, finding it hard to raise my voice above a hoarse whisper.

She shook her head again and admitted, "It's just the tip of the iceberg."

"I see. Well here's the tip of my iceberg. I am a monster before my coffee in the morning, a complete monster. In fact I loathe mornings, but if I can sleep until six I usually consider that sleeping in. When things don't go my way my first instinct is to whine about it. Eventually I find a solution, but always I complain first. I am terrible with names, I think parties and social functions are a giant waste of my time and I have a really hard time listening to advice. I have been a horrible King up until about three weeks ago and before that I might have been the biggest idiot on the planet for not treating the future love of my life with the respect she deserved."

Amelia looked up at me, our eyes locking with a finality that relaxed my chest constraints. "Avalon, I am the exact kind of person you are trying to protect the Kingdom from. Why would you want me to be your Queen?"

"Amelia," I said her name reverently, worshipping the sound of it on my lips. "Honestly, I'm relieved you sneak cheeseburgers and whine about taxi prices. You may be those things but you are also so much more. You are generous and loving, you are compassionate and honest. I wanted to free the Kingdom from oppression, not from you, not from the most beautiful person I have ever met. You are not only worthy to be Queen, you leave me wanting as your husband. You are a far better person than I ever hope to be and I would not only be honored to be your husband, but eternally overjoyed. I love you, with all that I am, with all that I ever hope to be. You are the reason I want to be King, the reason I know that I can be King and without you in my life the Kingdom will lose out on the greatness I could be." I gave her a wicked smile, but hoped she knew how serious I was. "You will be a phenomenal Queen. Please trust me. Please, love me."

"Avalon," she sniffled. My heart paused in my chest, my blood frozen with anticipation. I needed

her to say yes to me more than I needed to breathe. "I think I was in love with you before I ever met you."

And then she threw herself into my arms and my soul sighed with relief and amazement. "You did?"

"I've only ever loved you," she whispered against my chest. "I fell in love with you in the Citadel, the night Lucan died. And even at Eden's wedding I only continued to fall. I tried to protect myself; I tried to keep my heart and feelings to myself. Never, in a million years did I think you would feel this way for me, that you would choose me to be your wife and your Queen. And it may be selfish, it's probably the worst thing for the Kingdom, but I can't help it... I love you, Avalon."

I looked down, into her sincere eyes and drank in this moment, committing it to my eternal memory. I brought my face to hers slowly, relishing every moment now that I was complete, now that I had the love of this woman I was finally the man I was supposed to be.

I kissed her gently, slowly, reveling in the feel of her soft lips against mine, worshipping the taste of her mouth, of her tongue. I pulled her as close to me as I could and wrapped her entirely in my magic. Our magics flashed around us in a spark of color, mine blue, hers the softest shade of gray. She was perfection and she was finally mine.

I paused our kiss before I could forget the most important part of our talk. She looked up at me with trust and love and all I could do was breathe. There was nothing else to do but breathe.

I took the box out of my pocket and fell to one knee. The position felt both vulnerable and natural at the same time. A new ripple of fear slithered down my spine, but I pushed forward with renewed determination.

"Amelia, will you marry me? Will you be my Queen?" I asked simply since it seemed everything else had been said.

She was surprised, probably shocked that I had come prepared with a ring and everything. I just smiled up at her, silently asking her to trust me again. She didn't say anything but nodded her agreement, more tears slipping from her eyes.

I had never felt this happy before, never this much of a man. I slid the ring onto her finger and was not surprised that it fit her perfectly. She looked down at it, seeming to literally shine with happiness, her inner light glowing brilliantly from within her.

I stood up and pulled her to me again. “It’s not a diamond,” she whispered in awe.

“No,” I chuckled. “It’s not a diamond.”

Chapter Thirty-Six

The room was full of every kind of Immortal. They were dancing, and eating and laughing and most of all drinking. The club was decorated in colorful tapestries that hung on the wall, with low benches covered in exotic patterned pillows. A dance floor had been placed in the center of the space, covered in tight red silk and sprinkled with orange flower petals. Hookah's had been placed around the room, the air filling with the spiced scent of tobacco.

This was a celebration.

Lilly and Talbott were the centerpiece of it all. They were glowing with happiness, never out of each other's reach. Talbott seemed thrilled to show off his bride to be, and with Talbott nearby constantly, Lilly even seemed comfortable as the center of attention.

The night was perfect, made only more so by my own bride-to-be who was currently dancing with her father. We announced our engagement to only our closest friends and family last night, Sylvia, Eden and Kiran, Lilly and Talbott, Sebastian and Gabriel. I called Jericho this morning to share the news with him but he was distracted by some problems the recovering humans were causing.

He sounded stressed out and pissy. And not two minutes after I told him I was engaged he hung up on me. Bastard.

We had also broken the news to Amelia's parents last night when we picked them up from the airport. I retroactively asked Jean for his daughter's hand in marriage. He consented but I suspected only because it was obvious Amelia wanted to marry me. The jury was still out on his exact feelings about our relationship.

I'm sure it didn't help that he didn't even know we were dating before we were engaged.

But none of that mattered because we *were* engaged.

Amelia *wanted* to be my wife.

"You look happy, brother," Kiran commented, sidling up next to me.

We stood on the throne platform overlooking the party. Our friends were gathered, dignitaries that needed to see a wedding like this and people I had never seen before were here to celebrate the first public marriage between a Titan and a Shape-Shifter since before Derrick was King. This was a momentous occasion.

"I am happy," I replied casually, but the truth of the words rang deep and loud inside my chest.

"When will you announce your engagement?" Kiran smiled at me like he knew a secret; probably he was thinking over what I was in for as a married man.

"Not for a while yet. I want to get through this Terletov thing and give Lilly as much attention as she deserves," I explained.

"She's probably hoping you'll take some of the spotlight away from her," Kiran laughed.

He was probably right.

"I'll never let her get away with that," I joked and then further answered his question. "We are thinking the All Saint's Festival, a year from now." Amelia and Eden started to make their way over to us and for some reason them together while Kiran and I waited for them felt like the most perfect moment, it felt like our family was complete. Eden and I had more than just each other.

"Will you be heading back to the Citadel with us on Monday?" I asked Kiran. "I need to make sure everything will be ready for the Festival."

"Yes, I think so. Sylvia has agreed to come back with us, which has put Eden at ease," Kiran answered. "Thank you for that by the way."

"It was just a suggestion," I replied humbly.

Eden and Amelia were sidetracked by a very pissed-off Seraphina. I tried to hold back a smile, but Seraphina had this way of making it look like her head could actually detach from her body and spin around in a complete circle when she got mad. Her long blonde hair flipped around her face and her hands held their deadly pose on her small waist.

Oh boy.

"Seraphina and Sebastian are no longer together," Kiran answered my unvoiced questions. "Seems, they were too different after all."

"She doesn't look happy," I mumbled.

"She is rarely happy," Kiran muttered back.

"Sebastian better watch out," I warned and Kiran nodded stoically beside me while we watched Seraphina dramatically flail in what could only be a reenactment of their breakup to her wide-eyed friends.

"Do you think-" Kiran started but Gabriel interrupted our thoughts, appearing out of nowhere.

His tanned, Hispanic skin was pale and ghostly, his orange eyes on fire with rage, burning brightly against the pallid color of his skin.

"What is it," I demanded, taking in his aggressive stance immediately and noticing a cellphone in his hand, gripped so firmly his knuckles had stretched tight across the black smart phone.

"Silas," Gabriel growled. "They were attacked near the colony. They took," his voice faltered and his eyes darted around the room desperately searching. "They took Silas. They took him alive."

Under other circumstances "alive" would have been a good report, or at least encouraging. But we all understood the dire consequences of being a prisoner of Terletov's. What it could mean for Terletov to capture Silas, one of the oldest and most prominent Shape-Shifters I could only guess. He was an advisor, a good friend and a mentor. My belly burned with anguish and the desperate need for retribution. I needed to find Silas alive and unharmed or my crown would mean nothing to me; I would take my revenge slowly and properly.

My hands clenched into fists at my side and I prepared to end this party now. We had to move. My mind started tying up every lose end here, who would be responsible to clear out the club, clean it up, see the more prominent dignitaries back to their hotels, get Amelia and Eden to safety. I assembled a team of the present Titans to go with me and handpicked my own men. This all happened in four point two seconds and then my magic flared with warning and the Titans surrounding the room for protection took a collective step forward.

Immediately I lost the sense of goodness and hope that had only seconds ago filled my blood. A deathly cold haze settled inside my veins instead. A startling snap of an ominous premonition flashed in my vision and before I could put the pieces together it was too late.

The upstairs door crashed open, the heavy wood splintering into miniscule slivers as it shattered in the door frame. Before I could even utter an order the stairs filled with dangerous Immortal men. They paired off down the long staircase and spread out into the suddenly quiet room.

There were initial screams and panic, but by the time Terletov's men filtered through the room my people were silent. Everyone in the room had, at best, just recently been informed of the unhinged psycho that is Dmitri Terletov; now they faced his men in the flesh while we wore our best party attire; they wore black fatigues and pointed those damned guns in our faces. We held champagne glasses and wore expensive jewelry.

Simmering rage and vengeance exploded into a hot boil just under my skin. My magic buzzed around me in feral aggression. I was no longer amused, this would end tonight.

I found Amelia immediately; she stood face to face with an Immortal wielding a gun. Eden was tucked protectively behind her and I wanted to growl in frustration. Amelia did not belong here with these men, nor should she be trying to protect my sister who was perfectly capable of defending herself.

But then there was the baby to think about.

I seethed in frustration. I shouldn't have to think about which scenario was better. I shouldn't have to weigh my options and decide if the blue smoke could heal an unborn baby if something was to go wrong. But Amelia could not be the one to protect Eden either. She could not.

This was just all around bad news.

I braced myself for the men to open fire, but when nothing happened I grew restless. I wanted to move to Amelia, to get her out of here as fast as I could. But I couldn't leave my people.... And the longer we stood in silence the worse the situation seemed to grow.

My bad feeling only intensified as the Immortal attackers stayed eerily still, watching their prisoners like hungry animals. Their eyes gleamed with a perverse pleasure that twisted the moral part of my soul and made me ill.

And then he entered the room.

I felt the magic first. *His magic*. Only I couldn't call it his, because it wasn't. Whatever surrounded him was unnatural and stolen, that much I was sure. He appeared at the top of the stairs, standing proud and confident. He slithered down the stairs as if he were floating, his abnormal magic detached around him, infecting the air with the repulsive disease he carried. I had only ever seen him through Eden's own memories, but I knew him at once.

He felt just like the Immortals that died at the castle. Except here he stood.... strong, tall, confident. Nothing made sense anymore when it came to him. How did he get that magic? And how was he functioning without his own magic?

"This is a private party," I stated with my entire air of authority. "You were not invited."

"And yet here I stand," he sneered at me once he reached the bottom step.

The entire room stood still under the watchful glares of his henchmen and their guns. But I had my own men. This room was filled with my army and we would fight to the death before innocent people were harmed.

"I'm going to have to ask you to leave, of course," I declared casually.

I found it a little strange that none of his men had come to cover the throne platform where I stood with Kiran. We were positioned in the back of the room, but still we were obviously in charge with our crowns positioned crookedly on our heads. Yet, none of the intruders made a move toward us.

I wanted, desperately wanted, to believe it was because they were afraid of us, but as my eyes darted around the room I realized how wrong I was.

"I can't do that of course," Terletov crooned in his thick Russian accent. He was standing in front of Lilly and Talbott and as he spoke he ran long, boney fingers down the length of Lilly's bare arm. I shuddered with Lilly and Talbott exploded in rage.

"Do not touch her!" he shouted before launching himself at Terletov.

The sound of Talbott shouting and then one lone shot rang loudly in room. More screams and Talbott dropped to the ground unconscious. A bullet to the head, clean and clear. A small trickle of blood ran down his temple and his magic beat faintly in the air. Not dead. He was not dead.

I took a breath to steady my nerves, to clear the red haze of pure, unfiltered rage that pumped in my heart frantically.

Lilly had her hands covering her mouth as if to smother a scream. When my vision cleared completely I saw the gun pointed at Lilly's forehead, the gun that kept everyone else planted firmly where they were. Lilly saw no gun. She only saw her fiancé lying in a puddle of his own blood.

He was not dead.

He was not dead.

Not yet.

"Terletov you will pay for that," I ground out, my voice trembled just the slightest. But it shook with fury and promised vengeance.

He ignored me on a long sigh and turned his beady eyes to my sister. "You have something of mine."

Eden shook her head firmly and pursed her lips. We opened our connection to each other simultaneously. She stood her ground; she wasn't scared, she wasn't afraid. We had been here before. Eden was trained and prepared.

He has Silas. I offered quickly.

She acknowledged me with an internal head nod and then to Terletov she said, "And you have something of mine. If you leave now and return Silas I will give you your magic back."

I felt more than anything else the powerful force Kiran was turning into while his wife addressed Terletov. I didn't blame him. I was ready to tear his sadistic head off just for standing near Amelia.

"That is a very generous bargain," Terletov smiled at Eden, his mouth twisting unnaturally and he looked more deranged than ever. "On my part." He finished.

Well, it was worth a shot.

"Here is what is generous," I called out, unwilling to let my sister talk to him any longer. I felt, almost like an audible sound, every eye in the room snap my direction. His goons stared me down with utter hatred and bitterness vibrating out of them and I wondered for half a second if this was what Lucan felt like when he stood against my men. "I will give you five seconds to leave this Club and return Silas and every other Immortal you've kidnapped for your sadistic experiments before I rain down my righteous judgment on you and your sheep."

"That is a nice offer as well," Terletov mocked me with a somber expression but a disdainful voice. "However, I must decline. I am conducting important medical research and need just a few more volunteers before my work is complete. Anyone here is welcome to join my cause. If you have the pure blood of the higher races you will be allowed to cross over this invisible line and help cure the disease that runs through our tarnished race. And if you are one of the animals that sees your purpose as something greater than a bottom feeder, we welcome you to offer your life for a greater cause." The glow of his face and excitement in his eyes was enough to make bile rise in my throat and my stomach to threaten, for the first time in my life, to empty itself all over my shoes. But these were *my* people and he was treating them like lab rats.

Or worse.

To their credit, nobody in the room made a sound.

"Terletov, you will not finish your *research*," I spat the word out, "because you will not leave this room alive."

Terletov kept speaking as though I hadn't said anything. "Or you can follow this traitor to your death, this replacement tyrant just as bent on the destruction of this race as the last King. But a warning, if you do decide to stay aligned with this corrupt Monarchy, know that you will not last long. Your time is up King Avalon. The Kingdom should belong to those who have the future in mind, who want to build up our race and rise to our potential."

I didn't want to think about what kind of potential we had if we killed Shape-Shifters and experimented on humans. I didn't want to talk about it anymore. This had to end.

Three things happened at once. I nodded to the Titus and Xander who had been standing close to Sebastian before we were invaded. They immediately turned on the gunmen closest to them. Titus shifted into a bear and attacked two of the gunmen by clawing their heads together in a resounding crack of bones.

I moved to Amelia at the same time, determined to get her and Eden to safety before this fight became a blood bath and they got caught up in the middle of it. I pushed and elbowed my way through the closely packed bodies.

And finally, Terletov grabbed Lilly by her styled red hair and turned her around so the gun was at her throat.

Chapter Thirty-Seven

Two of Terletov's henchmen grabbed for Eden but she was prepared for them. She shifted out of their way, dodging at least one bullet and if she got hit by the other her blue smoke healed her before it was obvious. With Eden pushing back from the gunmen, Amelia was snatched up in the struggle. Terletov fled with Lilly, using her as a body shield up the stairs, his men fighting off every Immortal that got close. They were relentless without restraint, shooting a bullet straight to the heads of those that tried to save her. The men who grabbed Amelia took off to the back corner of the club where a hidden door led to a staircase that would rise to street level.

Lilly.

Amelia.

My people.

Chaos ensued. The sounds of gunfire bounced loudly from the ceiling to the walls and drowned out the screams of innocents all around. Terletov had placed his men thick on the stairs so his escape was easy and met with little resistance. My men, the Titans that had been placed around the room, responded with their own gunfire, but they were ill-prepared against Terletov's shooters. They drew their swords, but unless they were close enough to strike they couldn't use them. And usually if they got close enough to use the sword a bullet had stopped them short of their goal.

And apparently our bullets did not hold the same kind of strength Terletov's did. Where his wounds resulted in unconsciousness immediately, our bullets seemed not to even phase Terletov's men. They fought on as though there was no weapon in the world capable of inflicting pain on them.

The whole thing felt stupid. I felt like I was trapped in a cartoon. My men looked ill prepared and elementary compared to the military-esque training and cool these bastards had. And weapons.... I might as well have armed my men with rocks and squirt guns for as much resistance as they were putting up.

I shoved my way through the crowd, desperate to get to Amelia. There were too many people I cared about in this room. I made my decision, I would get to Amelia first. I had to. I couldn't think straight with her being carted off by that kind of evil. Once she was with me I would be able to reassess. Once I knew she was safe with me I would be able to think clearly and get everything back under control. But even as I fought to get to her, I took stock of those I cared about most.

Gabriel had somehow managed to maneuver to Sylvia who was one of my prime concerns simply because she was mortal and I cared about her. Kiran and Eden had found each other in the crowd and were actively fighting together. Their joined magic, navy blue with their unprecedented strength and speed, was able to incapacitate the henchmen with a swift shot to the face or chest. They were working through the bad guys but not quickly enough. Lilly had disappeared with Terletov through the upstairs and Amelia was almost to the door, caught in the grasp of two goons.

I noticed that she was not the only hostage being forcefully removed. It seemed this was a cash and carry kind of event and if one of Terletov's Immortals could grab a victim and cart them away they were. The door to the street was open and bad guys and innocents were being herded through it one and the same.

There was no way to instruct the Immortals fleeing in pure terror that inside the room was safer, that on the other side of that door was a whole new kind of evil. The sound level was deafening in the underground club and they were so diluted with fear they most likely wouldn't have listened anyway.

A bullet sliced the air next to me, causing me to duck down and lose sight of Amelia. When I stood back up she was struggling fiercely in the arms. She tried her magic, zapping the men holding her but they ignored her efforts with surprisingly calm detachment. Finally, fed up with her lack of results, she bent forward and bit one of them on the hand that held her. I was encouraged by her ingenuity and pushed forward.

Another bullet my way, this time hitting the guy just in front of me. The silver metal pierced his skin and he dropped to the floor on impact. I ducked down again, trying to stay out of sight of the shooters.

A bullet might not knock me out, but it would slow me down and I had precious seconds to get to Amelia before she was out the door. I tripped over a fallen Titan that lay still while the battle raged on above him. His gun had clattered away from him and was being kicked around underfoot, but his sword stayed lodged in his hand.

Until Eden was kidnapped four years ago, the Immortal swords were the only real threat by way of weapon to an Immortal life. Titans were trained with them from the very beginning and every Immortal had grown up fearing them and the life they could take from you.

Guns were an entirely new weapon for our people. And the destruction these guns had the potential of carrying out was sobering. Still, the sword wasn't a terrible weapon to have in a fight. It could still get the job done if you knew how to use it.

My grandfather taught me how to use a sword the minute I turned seven years old. We were in Dubai. The air was dry and dusty, the sun deathly hot. Amory had taken me up to the rooftop of an apartment building, given me a sword and shown me how to kill an Immortal.

Just in case.

I was seven at the time.

I was twenty-two years old now.

And as I passed by the unconscious Titan I swooped down, picked up the sword, lunged three more feet and stabbed the first henchman I could reach.

His grip lightened on Amelia and as his sickly green colored magic poured from the flesh wound of the sword he slowly let go of her completely while his partner fumbled for his gun.

I ripped the sword from the first man's chest and plunged it into the thigh of the second man. He had started to move away from me while he loaded bullets back into his gun but I didn't have the time to play that game.

Where the sword sunk into the man's fleshy thigh, his identically acid green magic also flowed out from his body into the crushing space around us. He dropped Amelia's arm and pressed his hand down tightly around where the sword was sticking up from his thigh. The pressure of his hands did nothing to slow down the outflow of magic. Seven more seconds passed before he sank down to his good knee and then eventually fell over face first onto the ground dead.

These bastards turned out easy to kill if you got around their bullets.

I looked up from the dead man and into the eyes of my future bride. Relief swam in her deep golden brown pools and something so much better than relief, something like real, authentic, life-changing love.

I pulled her to me immediately and wrapped her in my arms. Our magics crashed into each other with silencing resolve. I shook against her, still so terrified of losing her. She clung to me, trembling in my arms, vibrating my heart with her petrified movements and there, in the middle of crushing bodies and frenzied violence we held onto each other as if these were our last breaths to be breathed.

Avalon, a bomb! Eden screamed in my head, leaving me with point eight seconds to react.

I threw my body over Amelia's and we hit the ground hard. My magic left my body of its own accord and met Eden's in the air only half a second before the bomb went off and everything slowed down to a crawl.

And then nothing but the whitest, most blinding light I had ever seen.

Ringing.

Loud and high pitched in my ear.

Slowly the fog cleared. Slowly. Painfully slowly.

The piercing tone in my ear drums lessened and the darkness lifted off of me like the heaviest blanket being pulled by the weakest limbs.

Unconsciousness is confusing and bleak, frustrating and muffled. The room came first. I was on the floor, over Amelia, debris and bodies were everywhere.

Memories came second. Amelia being taken by Terletov's men. The sword. The battle. The bomb.

Realization came last. I sprung to my feet and lifted Amelia into my arms. She was breathing and seemed to be relatively unharmed, but she moaned against me so I held her tight.

I was the only one standing in what was left of the club.

Bodies lay askew at my feet. The high beams of the ceiling were broken and splintered throughout the room. A large gaping hole had taken out a third of the ceiling and part of the wall that backed up to an alley. Wind whipped through the hole scattering loose napkins and strands of torn clothing. Dust and ash covered everything, every surface and person.

I breathed in through the choking, toxic air and forced myself to focus on the magical pulse of the room. Amelia's came first and most natural and then those that were stronger, Eden, Kiran.... Gabriel.

My eyes flew open and this time bodies were stirring. Most of the Immortals were simply unconscious from the close range of the blast and would come around soon. Eden and Kiran had sat up and Eden's blue smoke was already at work around the room. She sat huddled next to Kiran with her knees tucked to her chest. The amount of healing this room needed would take it out of her and I worried about the baby.

Don't. She whispered in our heads. *Avalon, let me do this. I know what I can handle. I know what's good for the baby.*

I nodded my acknowledgement. What could I have said to her? I wouldn't deny her this. I wouldn't stop her from helping what she could.

I searched for Gabriel knowing he was next to Syl. As if he knew I was searching for him, he stood up from behind the bar and brushed off the dirt and debris from his black priest's outfit. I locked eyes with him from across the room and he tipped his head in a positive way. I watched as he scooped up Sylvia into his arms and gave me a thumbs up from the hand that supported her back. There was a pulse. She was knocked out from the blast, but alive.

Amelia's parents moved in the back of the room, both alive. Titus, Xander and Xavier were on their feet helping others and checking the vitals of those still down. Sebastian was moving across the room to check on his sister who I had pressed as tightly to my chest as I could. Seraphina bent over Talbott as Eden's magic worked to remove the bullet that knocked him out.

They were alive.

I breathed.

Deeply.

And said a prayer of thanks.

Amelia's eyes fluttered open and she looked up at me grief stricken. Her sense had apparently come back quicker than mine. She pushed against me and I let her stand, but I held her close. I held her as close as I could and I had no intention of letting her go.

The bomb was enough to put us all on the ground and give Terletov time to escape, but it didn't seem capable of actually killing Immortals. In fact, the only two Immortals that seemed to have lost their lives were the ones that I put down myself.

I shouldn't have felt pride.

But then again, they shouldn't have tried to take her from me.

"Tell me it will be Ok, Avalon," Amelia whispered softly next to me.

I was silent. I couldn't tell her that. I couldn't tell her that everything would be Ok. And even while I felt relief that nobody of mine died tonight, it was short lived.

Talbott stood to his feet shakily. Seraphina helped him, supporting his weight with her shoulder. He asked her a question that I couldn't hear from here, that I *didn't want* to hear from here.

It was in his face then. Grief. Despair. Pain. Outrage.

He crumbled. I watched one of the strongest men I knew, crumble to the ground and come apart. He was a broken man, undone by grief.

It was utterly excruciating to watch, but I couldn't tear my eyes away from him. And as his wails and keening pierced through the leftover quiet my heart shattered with his.

Amelia gripped my shirt in her hands, clinging to me as if it were just as painful for her to listen to Talbott as it was for him to experience the night after it had already happened. Her fingernails dug into my skin, but I didn't feel any pain. I couldn't, not in comparison to Talbott. I had been left conscious to fight for the one I loved, to bring her back to me. And even though I didn't believe there was a single person here capable of getting to Lilly tonight, not after that carefully planned attack, it was disgustingly unfair that Talbott wasn't even given the chance.

"That will never be you," I felt myself say, my deep voice rumbled in my chest. But the sound felt far off and unattached. I tore my eyes away from Talbott to meet Amelia's eyes. "That will never be you." I said again in a harsh whisper, this time my voice felt at home in my lungs.

"I know," she answered back with perfect trust.

"Marry me," I demanded. She nodded, the fear in her eyes replaced with determination. I realized then that she might think I was still speaking about the future. "Tonight," I clarified. "I meant tonight."

"I know," she echoed.

Chapter Thirty-Eight

The sun was just waking up, filling the barren field with hazy, gray light. We had returned to the farm, another place that had been destroyed by battle. We stood over Amory's unmarked grave, over the hardened ground where my sister buried my grandfather.

Amelia's hand was clutched in mine and she stared up at me with wide, hopeful eyes. I pulled her closer to me, hating the distance, the small separation. Only a few more minutes until we were bonded as one, until she would be forever mine.

The gravesite was a completely abnormal place to have a wedding, I knew that. And the morning after one of the most traumatic nights of my life also probably terrible timing. But neither could be helped.

I could not become Talbott.

I refused that future.

And because I knew I was ultimately Terletov's goal, I had to protect everything that was dear to me. Amelia was most important, most crucial. I needed her to have my magic, to be protected by my bloodline. And there was only one way for her to have everything I had to offer.

So we gathered near Amory, mostly because the field was lined with huge maple trees that had turned yellow at the end of October and the harvested field made a beautiful backdrop. But also because we had moved to the farm until we could get out of Omaha and back to the Citadel. Most of the party left last night, as soon as they could gather themselves and their belongings they were gone. Until I could move our party we stayed at the farm where I felt the safest.

Which might be kind of ironic since it was the same place Lucan captured me and then dragged me away to jail.

Still, I wasn't going to argue with my gut. And my gut told me to come here.

Finally, and this point could not be argued even with myself, I wanted this to happen close to Amory. I wanted him to somehow be a part of this next step in my life. It wasn't easy getting married without him, or my parents, or even Angelica who had stayed back at the Citadel with Jericho. But I could do it if I was just near a part of him. And I felt like I was here. I felt like they were all here with me.

Gabriel, who had been staring down at Amory's grave for the past forty-five minutes, finally turned around. He was still in his priest's garb, even though it was dusty and the hem of his long black robe was shredded.

He had his rosary beads wrapped tightly around his fists and his orange eyes flickered brightly with emotion.

He would perform this ceremony and then he was off to find Silas. This was his last favor to me. I was releasing him of my service until he came home with Silas, found whatever vindication he needed or died trying.

His request and his words.

Eden and Kiran stood up with us, one on each side and the only other guests in attendance were Sylvia, Sebastian and Amelia's parents. Everyone else had left. Some to go home, some for the safety of the Citadel and those that worked with me had left with Talbott in search of Lilly. Gabriel would be joining them in twenty minutes.

"Let us begin," Gabriel announced. My eyes met Amelia's across the short distance and we listened to Gabriel as he said the marriage promises that we would keep until our last breaths. His heavy Spanish accent flowed over the words and even through his pain he made our ceremony sound respectable.

"Avalon and Amelia," he asked, holding our attention as we promised our vows to each other. "Have you come here freely and without reservation to give yourselves to each other in marriage? Will you honor each other as man and wife for the rest of your lives? Will you accept children lovingly from God, and bring them up according to the law of Christ and his Church?"

Amelia replied, "I will."

I echoed through the catch in my throat, "I will.

Gabriel went on to say more vows that we repeated. I looked with intensity, with everything I was as a man, as King and as her husband and promised her, "I, Avalon, take you, Amelia, to be my wife. I promise to be true to you in good times and in bad, in peace and in war. I will love you and honor you all the days of my life."

A tear slipped from her eye and fell to her still-dusty cheek. She smiled up at me the most dazzling smile I had ever seen. I leaned in to kiss her and earned a cough from Gabriel because it wasn't time yet.

There were no rings to exchange because Amelia was already wearing hers and refused to take it off and I didn't have one. Gabriel said a prayer and then announced to our small gathering, "In the name of the Father, the Son and the Holy Spirit I now pronounce you man and wife. You may kiss your bride."

I obeyed.

I leaned down and pulled her to me. I devoured her mouth in a hungry kiss that left me dizzy and wanting more. Our magics had been entwined together all night and all morning, but with the promise of forever firmly made they were free to meld completely together until they were almost one entity.

I would make sure the union was complete as soon as I could get this girl alone.

I felt the somber attitude of the morning cut through our happy moment and I reluctantly let go of my bride. I smiled down at her for one more perfect second while the light of the eastern rising sun lit up the wide open Nebraska sky in a rainbow of pinks, purples and oranges.

"I love you," I promised her.

"I love you too," she vowed back.

"Will you meet up with Talbott?" I turned to Gabriel, tugging Amelia against my side. She squeezed against me before slipping away to talk to her parents.

Gabriel and I turned to face Amelia and her family as they talked with Eden and Kiran in the frosted over field. Their breath puffed around them in small clouds. They laughed some, they cried some and they talked seriously most of all. This was a momentous occasion, and I was happy to be married, but not one of us would look back on this day with joy.

"Yes," Gabriel agreed. "We are going to track down Dmitri's brother, Alexi. Silas had decided to follow a lead that would have taken him to Columbia, so that is where we will go. I will meet them in Mexico City."

"I want you to end this," I instructed. "*End it.* Do whatever it takes." I glanced over at him with his eyes that flickered like flames and his robes. Damn it. "Am I asking too much of you?"

"No," Gabriel assured me. "I was created a warrior."

I grunted at that. "As was I."

"You will not fight anymore. You are finished. Now you will be King," Gabriel stated asking no questions only repeating answers he had decided on. "You have become the man you were meant to be."

I chewed on his words for several quiet moments before venturing into more personal, more dangerous territory. "And what about you? Are you the man you're supposed to be?"

A full minute of silence before he answered me, "I am the man I am supposed to be in this moment. And when I leave here I will hunt down a new destiny. It is not the wrong path, only a different path. The man I am supposed to be has yet to be decided."

"If you need me...." I offered, unable to respond to his cryptic riddles.

"I won't," He answered honestly. "And when I'm finished you won't need me either. I won't come back to the Citadel. Whatever happens, you no longer need me."

He was right, but I hated what his words really implied. I hated that he would give up our Immortal world again no matter what the outcome of his search was.

"Thank you," I said instead of all my objections.

"Avalon, thank you," he finished with finality.

And there it was. We had both given each other purpose in life; both helped each other find the right path. And now it was time to go our separate ways. His to rescue a friend, mine to my gorgeous wife.

Amelia looked at me from across the field and I tilted my head for her to come near while Gabriel left to say his goodbyes to Eden. She came willingly into my arms and stayed there this time.

"Will you go with him?" she asked, staring up at me, her chin resting on my chest.

"No," I shook my head. "I have decided to fight this war from my throne, from where I should have been all along." And that was the truth. If I hadn't been on the battlefield I could have been tracking Terletov better, more accurately. I could have suspected something like this would have happened, or done a better job of preventing it.

Or maybe I couldn't have.

But I knew now that my place was not on a battlefield where anything could happen to me. I had a call to rule this Kingdom and for the first time in my short history as King I needed to take that seriously.

And for the first time in my short history as King, that task didn't feel so bad. At least not when I had my Queen by my side.

"Let's go home," Amelia commanded. And I simply followed.

I ruled the Kingdom, but she ruled my heart.

Acknowledgements

This book was not planned or anticipated, but came out of a desperate need to write Avalon's story. For that, I want to thank my readers who have been so incredibly dedicated to The Star-Crossed Series. You fell in love with my characters as hard and fast as I did and because of your steady enthusiasm Avalon got to find love! Thank you for reading and thank you for supporting Indie!

And thank you to the bloggers that support not only me, but the entire Indie community. Every interview, cover reveal and author spotlight is the best kind of gift. You give your time and love generously and I am so grateful for that.

I want and need to thank God; this book is finished by only a miracle of His grace. Never in a million years did I really believe I could get to do what I love, and live this dream. Thank you God for Your unlimited patience, mercy and grace, those gifts I could not live without.

Thank you to Zach. You are the best kind of man. You are the inspiration for every love story I write, for every sarcastic comment and steamy make-out scene. I wouldn't be who I am today without you. Your vision is so much bigger than mine, you see things that I don't and we both know you bring the common sense to this marriage. I am so thankful for everything that you are and everything that you do for me and our kids. I love you.

Thank you to my family. Mom you are my biggest fan and I am so blessed to have your love and support. Thank you for kicking me out of the house for college, for encouraging me to travel and the hours of babysitting you put in to help make my dreams come true. I want to be the kind of mother you are one day. Thank you to Ron, Randy and Robbie. You are the kind of brothers that make me thankful I never had a sister, the kind that left me with hilarious and terrifying memories and the kind that showed me respect and what it felt like to know I was protected. And thank you to Stella, Scarlett, Stryker and Solo. I write for you. I write in between your hours of sleep, your activities, in between the owies and the crafts and the hugs and I wouldn't be writing if it weren't for all those blessings. I love you all so much.

A huge thank you to the girls that helped me put this book together! Sarah Hansen, who is quite possibly the greatest cover art designer in the entire world! You are absolutely brilliant. Thank you for putting up with my million questions, my neurotic visions and creating something that is simply incredible! Jenn Nunez, you are so much more than an editor! You are a friend, a therapist and a colleague. Thank you for enduring my long, nonsensical emails, my addiction to texting and finding all of those important holes! But most of all thank you for knowing the difference between discrete and discreet and Christi's real last name.

I need to thank Miriah, Brooke, Bridget, Diana and Lindsay! I am so grateful to have each of you in my life, not just as friends but as fans! You girls make this job fun; you accept the crazy, the scatter-brained and the chaos and support me through it all! Thank you for being the amazing support group you are. And most of all thank you for not letting me take myself seriously.

I giant thank you to Lila Felix, Jenn Sterling and Nancy Straight! I never imagined the support and friendship I would find in the Indie world. You are all amazing and I am so grateful for your friendship, your advice and your encouragement! I wish you all the best.

And finally, I want to thank the most amazing group of authors I know, my Hellcats! Amy Bartol, Shelly Crane, Michelle Leighton, Angeline Kace, Samantha Young, Quinn Loftis, and Georgia Cates! You have been an incredible support group! I am so grateful for your advice and opinions. You are not only some of the best writers out there, but by far you are some of the greatest women I know. I am blessed to know you and I cannot wait for the all the amazing things yet to come for you!

About the Author

Rachel Higginson was born and raised in Nebraska, but spent her college years traveling the world. She married her high school sweetheart and spends her days raising their growing family. She is obsessed with bad reality TV and any and all Young Adult Fiction.

The Reluctant King is the fifth book in The Star-Crossed Series.

Look for the Relentless Warrior, the sixth book in The Star-Crossed Series, coming early 2013

Other books coming in 2013 are Sunburst, the second book in the Starbright Series and The Rush, a new and more contemporary series.

Other Books by Rachel Higginson:
Reckless Magic (The Star-Crossed Series, Book 1)
Hopeless Magic (The Star-Crossed Series, Book 2)
Fearless Magic (The Star-Crossed Series, Book 3)
Endless Magic (The Star-Crossed Series, Book 4)
Starbright (The Starbright Series, Book 1)

Follow Rachel on her blog at:
www.rachelhigginson.blogspot.com

Or on Twitter:
@mywritesdntbite

Or on her Facebook pages:
Rachel Higginson
Or
Reckless Magic

Please enjoy an excerpt from Rachel Higginson's new book Starbright

Chapter One

The night had never been darker, the blackness surrounding the car, never so suffocating. Even the piles of snow pushed to the sides of the narrow road, did nothing to break up the oppressive darkness. The Stars above, shone brightly, I was sure of it, but they did so from behind a curtain of clouds that blocked the light from reaching the road. I felt swallowed up by emptiness.

I gripped the steering wheel tighter, my knuckles stretching until they gleamed white in the glow of the dashboard and my frozen fingers worked numbly against the cold plastic. The headlights of my old Jeep reached only a few feet in front of me and then stopped abruptly against a wall of darkness. I shivered violently, nestling my chin further into the down of my heavy winter coat and cursed the Nebraska winter for being equally as cold as it was desolate.

The farmland rolled away from the winding road, buried beneath several feet of iced over snow in every direction. Trees, planted for the privacy of farmers, lined the way home with empty branches and snowcapped tops. My breath puffed out in front of me, fogging up the frozen windshield and reminding me that the heater to my fifteen year old Jeep Cherokee remained unfixed.

"Tristan!" I growled furiously into the frigid air. "Why I let you talk me into another movie I will never know!"

There was no one there to hear my complaints, or sympathize with me against my best friend, but it felt comforting to make noise in an empty antique without a radio. Still, receiving not even a groan of empathy from the Jeep, I sat forward and peered into the impossible night ahead of me.

I knew these roads; I had each curve and turn memorized. The distance between Tristan Shields' house and my own was well traveled and practically sacred. Still, out in the country where street lights were for city-folk and the deer and the antelope tended to play, their familiar territory became a dangerous, never-ending expanse of nerves and tension.

Even in summer, unless the Stars and moon were bright and friendly, the country roads of the Nebraska farmland became shrouded in a heavy obscurity, the headlights of the best of cars mapping out the only visibility in the heavy cloak of night and beyond those flickering lights the world seemed to drop off the edge of a cliff into nothingness. But now, in the dead of winter, with temperatures well below zero, the night around my old Jeep seemed to have a life of its own, oppressive and angry.

I cleared my throat and mentally determined to conquer the creeping feeling of being afraid. I bit down on my lower lip and clutched the steering wheel tighter. My breath came out in shaky puffs of air, reminding me it was more than the roads and the night that curdled the most terrified places of my heart. It was more than the late hour and bitter cold that forced me to shiver and shift my eyes suspiciously in every direction.

It was the Darkness.

Not the country night, or the moonless sky. But the real Darkness. The Darkness that moved secretly through this world and threatened every living, breathing creature. The darkness that slithered in unseen places and survived on the death and rotten things. The darkness that I would fight until my dying breath.

But not tonight. Tonight I wasn't ready. Tonight, I was still only sixteen, and my parents were still off saving the galaxy while I stayed home to finish high school with an elderly woman as my keeper.

Something moved out of the corner of my eye. I could swear it. Swirling my head around, and keeping a steady hold on the steering wheel, I peered into the darkness, searching out the moving creature.

Nothing.

Nothing beyond the snow banks piled in the ditches and the swaying lifeless trees that were becoming sparser as I passed expansive fields blanketed under the white of winter.

I turned my attention to the road again and with a numb hand, brushed my platinum blonde hair under the brim of my stocking cap. My fingers snapped with electricity and for a moment the cab of my Jeep was lit with the sparks of static. Only a few more miles till home. I could make it. There was nothing to be afraid of.

But why did tonight feel so different?

So dark?

And then out of my peripheral vision I saw it move again. A swift shadow sliding effortlessly through the night, riding the whipping wind like a wave and dropping the frozen temperature several degrees lower. The pungent smell of rotting eggs drifted through the air.

I didn't have to turn my head this time to confirm. I knew it would be gone before my head could move in the right direction. Besides, they only existed in the peripheral, in the slight glances and far off places.

I had seen them before. Since before I could talk my parents would tell me about them, explain to me of their existence, warn me of their danger. I saw them everywhere, even during the day I could spot them, because they were everywhere.

Foot soldiers of a greater evil, sent to Earth, the last remaining inhabited planet, to prepare the way for their master. They were the evil in all things, the tyranny, the oppression, the hunger and violence. The Darkness. The force of wickedness that battled against the forces of good with one purpose in mind, to abolish the Light.

I was the light. And because I was the answer to their destruction I hunkered further into my winter coat and braved the bone-chilling cold.

It could be easy for me to warm up; even in a car with a broken heater it was the natural reaction of my body. I was born of the light, of the warmth. And to suffer against the natural elements was difficult enough, but the extra layer of malevolent chill became excruciatingly painful even in small doses.

Still, they couldn't know what I was. They couldn't discover me after all this time. At least not yet. So I breathed in the frosty air, feeling the burn in my lungs and forced myself to push forward a few more miles.

My parents had worked so hard to hide my existence and to blend in with normal humanity that no matter how easy it would be to ease my pain, I had to fight against the elements. I was brought to Earth as a baby, with the sole intention to one day take over as Earth's Protector. And so my parents had given up their positions as two of the greatest Warriors of their generation to raise an alien infant in the middle of farmland.

And it was here, in Western Nebraska, that I waited for the day the Earth would become my charge, my responsibility.

But that day wasn't today. I had years before I was supposed to deal with that kind of duty!

Years.... I promised myself.

And as soon as I decided these were regular Shadows, which had no idea I was anything special, another one flittered across my peripheral. I swallowed the lump that had taken up an annoying residence in my throat and felt the passenger's seat for my cell phone. I thought I laid it out before I started the car, but after blindly feeling around my worn upholstery decided it must still be hiding inside my over-sized bag.

I strengthened the grip of my left hand and thrust my right hand into the black hole of all my important possessions, hoping to come out victorious in three seconds or less. Defender of the last planet or not, I was hopelessly unorganized. My purse was a cluttered mess of unknown objects and somewhere, hidden in the melee was my cell phone.

I liked to believe I was brave. Or at least I would be one day. But tonight, all I wanted to do was call Annabelle, wake her up and forcefully let her know I would be home in ten minutes, just to hear her reassuring voice.

I thought about calling Tristan too and demanding to know why he thought we needed to watch an entire trilogy all in one night!

Lip gloss. Gum. Floss. Wallet. Candy bar.

Where was my cell phone?

The road was dangerously icy and my constant shivering did nothing to balance out my driving. I sucked in a frozen breath and then glanced down at my purse, hoping to be able to spot the phone right away.

Not there.

At least not right where I could see it in the one point five seconds I allowed myself to look. I heaved an irritated sigh and turned my eyes back to the road. Apparently that second and a half was way too long because standing in the middle of the road was a giant buck, poised and stilled only ten feet away.

I panicked. Somewhere in the rational-thinking part of my brain, I knew I was supposed to hit the animal; that it was safer to collide with the deer than slamming on my brakes in the middle of the night on an iced over country road. But my animal-loving instinct took over and my foot pressed furiously against the brake pedal while my hands jerked the steering wheel hurriedly to the right.

The next few seconds became a blur as my Jeep spun wildly out of control without even pretending to slow down. Belatedly I released my foot and tried to pump the brake but it was too late, the tail end flipped around to the front and then the front flipped around again and hit the snow bank at an alarming speed and bounced off.

As if in slow motion, my passenger's side rammed into the iced over snow bank and then flipped over what felt like several times until I smashed to the frozen field far beyond the road. My Jeep hit the ground with an ear splitting cry of metal crushed against a rock hard surface.

I exhaled violently, the seatbelt cutting into my awkwardly hanging neck and waist. I felt unconsciousness threatening to sweep me away as the broken bones in my right hand, where it had been crushed between my body and the armrest in the impact, screamed angrily at me.

If I were human I would already be unconscious.

If I were human, I would have a lot more to worry about than a broken wrist.

I wiggled my feet and tried moving my arms, just to make sure there were no other issues, before reaching over with my left hand and unbuckling the safety restraint. I fell gruffly against the impacted passenger side door and let out a fierce cry of pain.

I sat up and rubbed my shoulder that now felt displaced but not broken. Climbing into position I bent my knees and braced my hands, one strongly, the other gingerly, against the car around me and thrust my legs forward into the already cracked windshield.

The fractured glass moved against the force of my legs, but it took several more tries before I removed it completely. When I crawled carefully through the now gaping hole, the windshield remained intact, but definitely fissured and hung awkwardly across the sideways front hood, still attached near the driver's side.

I slid down the rusted green paint of my Jeep and landed softly in the snow. The night was still outside of the crash, silent and subdued. The snow that blanketed the landscape muffled the usual night sounds and the absence of animals, even winter ones, felt eerily dangerous.

Out of the corner of my eye I saw one move. A Shadow. The Darkness.

But it wasn't possible. They didn't know I existed, let alone that I lived here, in the middle of nowhere. I brushed my fear away and simultaneously readied myself for an altercation. I shouldn't be afraid. I couldn't be afraid.

These were mere minions besides. And even if I wasn't prepared to go into hand to hand combat with them, if they really knew who I was they would be more afraid of me than I was of them.

Or at least that's what I promised myself.

I lifted my head in search of the buck that caused all this trouble to begin with but he was nowhere in sight. Either he was frightened off by my car turning in wild circles just to avoid him, or he never existed in the first place, just an apparition that turned to the smoky wisps of evil.

But that would mean a purposeful attack. And that couldn't be. There was just no way they could know who I was.

Unless.... Unless, my parents had fallen.

I froze for a moment, my hands clenched at my sides, my chest a shallow cavity filled with a heart that refused to beat and lungs that refused to breathe and played through that possibility in my mind. They had been gone for several weeks, on a mission that specifically required their skill set. I hadn't heard from them since they left, and so it was entirely possible that they failed.

That they fell.

I gazed into the sky, willing the clouds to move out of my way so I could find them. If they were gone, I would be able to tell immediately, their bright lights would be blank in a sky full of their fellow soldiers. The sky was too overcast though, even with my powerful eyesight and ability to cut through darkness, the clouds were too heavy and clustered to see through.

I cursed uncharacteristically under my breath and then again when I realized my phone was still somewhere unknown in the dark abyss of my Jeep. As I wedged one of my booted feet into the space of my car, where the hood made room for my windshield wipers, I decided that even if my parents were gone, there was no amount of torture or distress that would have prompted them to give up my location. They worked their whole lives to keep me a secret, to prepare me for the day when I would remain here alone, and on top of that, they loved me. There was no way it was them.

I ignored the clustering Darkness as I pushed myself up and through the broken windshield, reaching for my spilled purse, whose contents littered the crushed passenger's side door. The Shadows weren't trying to hide anymore; they were coming for me, gathering around me as if waiting for the command to attack. I reached down hurriedly, ripping my coat against the rough edges of the broken windshield, but I managed to gather at least the important stuff into my purse before hauling it back with me and hopping down from the Jeep.

I tossed the purse that now only held my wallet and cellphone and a few random items that managed to survive the spill, onto the snowy ground and lifted my head to meet my enemy. They moved around me like a slow tornado of darkness. As separate entities they appeared like slender gusts of black wind, but united they became a solid wall of evil. Even my keen eye sight could not see through them, or my superheated blood feel anything beyond their oppressive iciness.

I had never seen so many Shadows in one place. I had never even heard of them organizing themselves into a unified attack. They worked separately and secretly; their purpose was to influence mankind, to spread the Darkness like a disease to every corner of this planet, not to outright attack it. The deer had to be them. And even in that instance, their work was not so much of a surprise. But surrounding me now was something so unheard of that I was more taken aback than actually frightened.

The wall of Darkness moved against me, tightening its spaces and obviously trying to be threatening. I remained frozen, unwilling to reveal my identity even in this frontal attack. I wished more than anything that my parents were here, on planet and nearby, but this was a battle I alone would have to fight or figure out how to outmaneuver.

One Shadow broke free from the wall and moved against me in an aggressive sweep. It sliced against my thigh before I could react, tearing my jeans where it made contact. My skin burned from the unreal cold that I could feel even in my bones. The slash spread out its icy tendrils across my leg and moved upward throughout my body in scary quickness. I felt my lungs tighten against the strain of the cold and my appendages go numb from contact. My first instinct was to cry out in pain, but I bit my cheek, willing myself quiet and for the first time thankful that my lungs held no air to expel.

I couldn't see beneath my layers of clothes, but I had been educated enough to know that my skin would be marked with the deathly blue lines that looked like raised, swollen veins from my skin and spread out in fingerlike vines until every inch of my body was covered in them. It was at that point, when the frozen effect of contact with the Darkness covered every inch of my body that a human would breathe their last painful, staggered breath and depart from this world. It would take less than thirty seconds, but in that time was more pain and suffering than should ever accompany a soul on their way to the afterlife.

The smell of sulfur burned my nostrils and made my ears ring from the pain of it. I wasn't human. And I wouldn't die from this contact. But I felt it more strongly than any human ever could. This touch, this evil, was in direct opposition to everything I was. As dark and evil as the Shadows were, I was light and goodness. As painful as their touch could be, mine was healing and soothing.

I made a split second decision, putting the pain aside; I decided, rationally, that I couldn't stay out of this fight. The wall of Darkness surrounding me was waiting for me to die. If I was human, as I had thus far tried to play off, I should be lying on the ground right now, writhing in pain, mere seconds from death. Even as I stood against the agony, I knew they already figured it out.

My parents hadn't even started with weapons training yet, beyond the casual swing of a sword and so I was left with only one option. Unfortunately it was also the option that would give this Darkness exactly what they were looking for: the answer to my identity.

I was a Star.

And not just any Star. The next Protector of Earth. I was a very important Star.

With swift movements, I unzipped my heavy coat and flung it from my arms. I moved into a battle ready stance and let the warmth, the warmth I had hidden deep inside me, bubble to the surface. My golden toned skin met my internal heat welcomingly and it spread across my body as quickly as a wildfire in a drought, healing my pain and warming me completely. I lifted my head heavenward, and let the light leave my skin and pour outward into the heavy obscurity around me.

I couldn't help but smile as my true essence found form in the night. I glowed, literally. Blinding, supernatural, burning light radiated around me until my human form was almost completely hidden. Heat and light left me in waves of self-protection, the Darkness desperately fled from my presence and my light that would cause them as much pain as their cold blackness caused me.

The smell of sulfur grew stronger for only a moment as my inner light singed some of the stragglers; they shrieked an ear-piercing sound that rang painfully in my ears. And then they took to the sky in an urgent escape from a battle they were hardly prepared for.

I smiled wider; calling back the blinding light into my body and reducing my essence to a slight outward shimmer. I reached down for my coat and slipped it back on, not bothering with the zipper. I didn't really need the warmth now; the warmth that lived inside of me was more than enough to keep me warm, but I also didn't want to attract anymore Shadows.

Even without the Darkness clouding the landscape, with the absence of my supernatural light the night felt extra dark. I couldn't wait to get home and to bed now that that was all over, but with my car upturned I needed to call Tristan to come get me. He wouldn't be happy about me dragging him out of bed, but his grandmother and my caretaker, Annabelle, couldn't drive at all, let alone come get me in the middle of the night. He would be even less happy when I offered him very little details about how I flipped my car over in the first place.

Just as I reached for my phone though, a single shot of light came careening through the atmosphere and stopped suddenly somewhere high above me, obscured by the thick cloud cover. I lifted my head, expecting my parents and when the light moved into two separate lights I grew even more hopeful. One light dimmed to nothing though, but stayed elevated, somewhere up in the dark sky. That couldn't be right. My parents wouldn't extinguish their light before they reached the ground.

They couldn't, it wasn't possible.

The sounds of crashing and metal slicing the air recalled my attention. I squinted my eyes and searched through the heavy gray for some sign of what was happening. The cloud above my head glowed in bursts of brighter light like a terrible and destructive lightning storm and when the sounds of terrified screeching and the horrid smell of sulfur reached my nose I recognized the light as a fellow Warrior.

But it was definitely not my parents.

The sounds of battle continued for several more minutes, as I remained rooted on the ground. I couldn't join the fight without a weapon and so I was left to assume who was winning by the sounds of weapons meeting targets and the high-pitched wailing of Shadows.

Eventually the battle died down in the heavens and the death toll slowed. I didn't know what to expect as the light darted in a fast line to my right and then shot from overhead to just a few feet in front of me.

A human would have needed to cover their sensitive eyes from the extraordinary brightness a fellow Star illuminated. But not being human, my eyes were made of the same light and so I just watched on with impatient anticipation to discover who had arrived to clean up my mess.

Out of the light, one figure walked forward, dim and obviously not a Star. When he was close enough that I could determine he was a man, an elderly man with snow white hair and leathered skin, I took a step back, unsure what to make of this gruff human looking person apparently with the ability to fly and see Shadows, making him decidedly not human. I shrunk into my coat, having the forbidding feeling I was about to be reprimanded.

"Stella Day?" He demanded, stepping directly in front of me. I nodded, unexplainably more afraid of him than the entire force of Darkness. "What in this great, dead Universe, do you think you're doing?"

"Who are you?" I deflected meekly. If he came to fight the Darkness, surely he saw me attacked only minutes ago.

"Does it matter who I am?" the elderly man huffed. "I could just as easily be Lucifer himself or an apparition of Darkness called here by your own stupidity! How could you just reveal yourself like that? You just gave yourself away! After all we've worked for, after all the sacrifices that have been made, you just throw it all away because you're a little inconvenienced one winter night...." He had stopped talking to me, or at least stopped looking at me, in favor of mumbling to himself in an angry, aggressive tone.

"I'm sorry," I tried again politely, "Who are you?"

"I'm the guy that just saved your life! That's who!" He turned his attention wholly back on me.

I took an intimidated step back.

"Well, not entirely on your own," a deep, amused voice behind the elderly man called. "You did have some help." The light had extinguished itself into its human form, and as the boy stepped around the angry man to smile disarmingly at me, I took another step back but this time more from surprise than anything else. The boy was perfect, physically perfect. He was my age, with disheveled dark hair that curled adorably at the ends. His eyes were a piercing shade of honey that would have glowed without his internal light, as it were though, they pierced through the night and found my eyes with a locking force that took my breath away. His jawline seemed chiseled out of stone and his broad chest still heaved with the exertion of battle.

There was no doubt about it, he was an Angel.

An actual Angel.

My Star Counterpart.

"No, not on my own, but we wouldn't even need to be here if it weren't for the naivety of youth," the elderly man continued to grumble.

I knew I should be offended after that comment, but I was so confused all I could do was look back and forth between the old man and the young man.

"Where are your parents, child?" the old man suddenly demanded.

"Uh, they're uh, they're on a mission," I stammered, wondering if they would ever tell me who they were. "They've been gone for a couple weeks."

"Of course…. Then this was a thought-out attack. They have been planning this…." He continued to mumble.

"Please tell me who you are," I dropped my voice to hide my desperation.

"Oh right, I suppose it's too late now to go back…." The elderly man turned his full attention on me and for the first time I noticed the color of his eyes were a dull red, as if they had shined like rubies at one time but were worn down with age or exhaustion, I wasn't sure. "I'm Jupiter, your weapons trainer, and this is Seth. He's your Counterpart. You obviously weren't supposed to meet for years yet, but tonight you decided to push up our schedule."

"I didn't mean to!" I gushed, suddenly feeling very guilty for saving my own life. "They attacked me. They came out of nowhere and they just…. ganged up on me as if they were waiting for me to do something! I honestly, I didn't have a choice."

"Then they must have known already," Jupiter sighed and then lifted his hands to massage his temples with surprisingly delicate fingers.

"That's what I thought," I agreed, finally feeling as though I had been heard. "But wait a second, why are you here? Where is the Protector? Why isn't she here to save me?" Realization flooded my thoughts with questions that I should have been asking from the beginning.

"You are the Protector, Stella," Seth answered gently.

I opened my mouth to argue but Jupiter cut in quickly, "Sidra is dead. We found her earlier this evening. She…. she was murdered."

"And her Counterpart?" I gasped, not able to completely comprehend the gravity of what they were saying.

"Nisroc was murdered right along with her," Jupiter replied in a barely audible voice.

"So that really does make me...." I couldn't finish my thought. I could barely hear them anymore as the world seemed to close in around me and my heart pounded out a deafening beat that heated my eardrums and seemed to shrink my lungs.

"The Protector of Earth," Jupiter finished gravely.

Made in the USA
San Bernardino, CA
19 July 2014